Acclaim for The Concre

"*The Concrete Sky* is the most engaging book I've read i
out being overly clever, the characters are among the 1
encounter, and the story's twists and turns are dangerously compelling. Marshall
Moore never proselytizes, but he does take a very sharp look at our society's methods of
marginalizing people it finds distasteful, inconvenient, or just plain weird. I can't find
enough good things to say about this book—please do yourself the favor of reading it."

—Poppy Z. Brite, Author,
Liquor, The Value of X, and *Exquisite Corpse*

"A wild, queer, and reckless ride into the flip side of the American dream."

—Neal Drinnan, Author,
Glove Puppet, Pussy's Bow, and *Quill*

"Marshall Moore has written something wonderful here. *The Concrete Sky* is a quickly
paced novel filled with lively characters and a wry sense of humor—a thrilling, sometimes shocking, read."

—Noël Alumit, Author,
Violet Quill Award-winning *Letters to Montgomery Clift*

"Marshall Moore is one of the freshest new voices to come along in many a year. *The
Concrete Sky* is reminiscent of Patricia Highsmith at her best with a dash of James Purdy
and James M. Cain. . . . The plot is like riding a roller coaster backward; you have no
idea what's coming next."

—Greg Herren, Author,
Murder in the Rue Dauphine and *Bourbon Street Blues*

"A combination whodunnit, who-will-do-what, and does-the-guy-get-the-guy? Moore
throws suspense, angst, and sexual tension into a fast-paced mix lacing it with lacerat-
ing comic dialogue and dancing on that dangerous fine line between reality and someplace else. A hot new voice in American fiction."

—Andy Quan, Author,
Calendar Boy and *Slant*

"A boy-meets-boy-in-a-madhouse-and-the-bodies-begin-to-pile-up-love-story like no
other. You can smell the flesh burning under the author's deliciously caustic pen. And,
reader dear, when you put this book down, you'll believe as I do in this simple truth: Revenge is a dish best served by Marshall Moore."

—Ian Philips, Author,
Lambda Literary Award-winning *See Dick Deconstruct:
Literotica for the Satirically Bent*

The Concrete Sky

HARRINGTON PARK PRESS
Southern Tier Editions
Gay Men's Fiction
Jay Quinn, Executive Editor

Love, the Magician by Brian Bouldrey

Distortion by Stephen Beachy

The City Kid by Paul Reidinger

Rebel Yell: Stories by Contemporary Southern Gay Authors
edited by Jay Quinn

Rebel Yell 2: More Stories of Contemporary Southern Gay Men
edited by Jay Quinn

Metes and Bounds by Jay Quinn

The Limits of Pleasure by Daniel M. Jaffe

The Big Book of Misunderstanding by Jim Gladstone

This Thing Called Courage: South Boston Stories by J. G. Hayes

Edge by Jeff Mann

Trio Sonata by Juliet Sarkessian

Bear Like Me by Jonathan Cohen

Goneaway Road by Dale Edgerton

The Concrete Sky by Marshall Moore

Through It Came Bright Colors by Trebor Healey

Elf Child by David M. Pierce

Huddle by Dan Boyle

The Man Pilot by James W. Ridout IV

Ambidextrous: The Secret Lives of Children by Felice Picano

Men Who Loved Me by Felice Picano

A House on the Ocean, A House on the Bay by Felice Picano

The Concrete Sky

Marshall Moore

Southern Tier Editions
Harrington Park Press®
An Imprint of The Haworth Press, Inc.
New York • London • Oxford

Published by

Southern Tier Editions, Harrington Park Press®, an imprint of The Haworth Press, Inc., 10 Alice Street, Binghamton, NY 13904-1580.

TR: 8.12.03

PUBLISHER'S NOTE
This is a work of fiction. Names, characters, places, and incidents either are the products of the author's imagination or are used fictitiously, and any resemblance to actual persons, living or dead, business establishments, events, or locales is entirely coincidental.

Front cover photo by Duane Cramer.

Cover design by Todd Hedgpeth.

Library of Congress Cataloging-in-Publication Data

Moore, Marshall.
     The concrete sky / Marshall Moore
          p. cm.
     ISBN 1-56023-435-0 (alk. paper)—ISBN 1-56023-436-9 (pbk. : alk. paper)
     1. Gay men—Fiction. 2. Psychiatric hospital patients—Fiction. 3. Murder victims' families—Fiction. 4. Washington. (D.C.)—Fiction. I. Title.

PS3613.O659 C66 2003
813'.6—dc21
                                                                                2002070699

To Jeff Teh and Bryan Jones:
Lights at the end of the tunnel while I was writing this.
To Brandon Brown: *In memoriam*.
And to Anthony Ly: Love love love.

Friday Night

Stranded at the sort of party where he'd have been happier investigating the titles on the bookshelves than talking to the other guests, Chad Sobran took another sip of wine and considered his options for escape. Conversations careened around him like bumper cars. He held himself in place on the sofa. He didn't know anybody in the room and wasn't sure he wanted to. There were about ten people left, now that Dalton and that guy he'd been talking to had vanished into thin air. Chad gave up trying to achieve oneness with the overstuffed cushions on the sofa. Next to him, a busty blonde girl named Reese had spent fifteen minutes babbling as soon as they were introduced. "You're gay. That's like so totally cool with me. So is my brother Julian, and like his boyfriend is this black guy named Dennis, and they're so cute together. Julian says Dennis is a total top. So what is this top thing, anyway? I just don't get that. I mean, is it like one of you is the woman and the other is the man? Dennis, you know, he must be really big. Whatever. Have you ever done it with a black guy?" Reese looked twenty and talked like a woman half her age. Braces fenced her lower row of teeth and she smelled like a strange cross between Juicy Fruit, cigarette smoke, and the red wine she was drinking. Irritated, Chad shocked Reese into a troubled silence by telling her he had just gotten out of jail the day before yesterday. He hadn't, but after three glasses of cheap Merlot he didn't care enough about truth, honor, and good social graces to listen to another word in that breathy helium voice of hers.

"I was only in for a week, but . . . you know. It was rough. The other inmates." Chad drew a deep sigh and visualized the shower-room gang rapes, hoping a shadow of residual trauma would cross his face. "Really rough." He lowered his voice to a whisper. "I dropped the soap."

Reese's lower lip trembled. She couldn't have looked much younger without splitting into an egg cell and a puddle of sperm. She slurped the wine left in her glass then wiped her lips with the back of her hand, never taking her eyes off him. Chad refilled her glass from the bottle on the coffee table, careful not to burn his sleeve on any of the votive candles, then refilled his own. He looked at her with what he hoped was a criminal glare. Someone turned up the volume on the stereo loud enough to make Chad's eardrums pulsate to the beat, and his annoyance enhanced what he hoped was a sinister aura.

"What were you in for?" Movie lingo from Reese. Cute. Next time she went to a party, she'd pin some hapless person's ears to the wall with endless talk about her brush with the underworld. She'd cast herself as the heroine and stage a dramatic escape. Just what Chad was trying to accomplish.

"I'd rather not say. You might get the wrong idea about me. I'm trying to put it behind me, you know? So anyway, my point is, all those things that supposedly happen to young, slim white guys in jail? They're all true." Chad fidgeted in his seat as if his ass hadn't quite recovered from the various uses to which it had been put.

Reese beeped. Chad couldn't think of another word to describe the sound she made. He looked down at his hands. Tonight he had put on three silver rings—middle finger and thumb of his left hand, index finger of the right. He twisted the thumb ring, then turned the hoop in his left ear. Left the right one alone. He stared off into space for a second, letting a nobody's-home look settle across his face like a layer of dust, and crossed his eyes. Would that make her think he was shiftier?

"Oh my God," Reese said, and inched away from him. Now and then she'd dart a nervous glance his way. She fumbled around in her Gucci purse, withdrew a crumpled pack of Virginia Slims, lit one with a pink Bic lighter to which she had affixed a glittery red heart-shaped sticker, and alternated between sips of wine and drags on her menthol cigarette. Her hands shook.

Chad basked in mild surprise. In the dim light of the party, he knew Reese couldn't see him blush. Strawberry blond himself, he was prone to turning deep scarlet at the slightest provocation. He excused himself to go to the bathroom and stayed in there for a few minutes, watching his reflection in the mirror. He met his own gaze, giggled at what he had just pulled off, looked away, looked back.

"Cheers." He raised his glass to his reflection. "You hardened criminal, you."

Dalton, not exactly a friend from work but the kind of guy you have a beer with now and then, had convinced Chad to come. "Just a few people, couple of bottles of wine, really mellow. You'll like the crowd." Everyone Chad knew had left Washington, DC, for the summer. Jerry Glint, his closest friend, had gone to visit his parents in Augusta, Maine. A novelty, the Glint clan. They liked one another. Chad couldn't imagine what that must be like. Teresa and Audrey, the lesbians down the street, had rented a villa in Montenegro, somewhere on the Adriatic coast. "It's the new Tuscany," Audrey had babbled. He had known her longer than he had known her girlfriend—since his abortive attempt at college, in fact. "It's hilly and gorgeous, and the tourists haven't discovered it yet. The war and the economic sanctions are still too recent. There's such energy there!" Energy, yes, but was there electricity? His friend Roger was on an internship in Atlanta and e-mailed ominous hints about transferring to Emory. Too much fun down there, he said. Roger's tall tales about beer, boys, and bacchanalia made DC seem like the hidebound conservative fishbowl it, now that Chad gave the matter some thought, was. And Greg, his only friend acquired outside of his brief interlude at George Washington University, before a drunk SUV driver had sent Chad's life on a strange detour, had moved to Missoula, Montana, on a trial basis. To see if he'd like it. Maybe he'd move. Or not. With Greg, you could never tell. All of which left Chad somewhat socially bereft. His roommate Rose was traveling—somewhere in the Mediterranean, last he'd heard. She was due home at some unspecified time. "Soon," she wrote in her last e-mail. That could be next week or next month. Dalton he liked well enough, cute in his earnest straight-boy-manqué all-my-friends-are-gay way, but this wasn't Chad's choice of Friday nights or even first runner-up.

Dalton drove them from the bookstore to this place in one of the apartment towers in Rosslyn, just across the Potomac River from Washington. Chad's car had enough gas to get to the Chevron station at the end of the block, but his wallet was running on fumes until payday, still a few days away. Dalton worked at Borders part-time to meet people. Chad worked there full-time in addition to working full-time as a temp, a professional juggler of administrivia from eight to five in various federal agencies and law firms downtown. He held down a second job to slow his financial hemorrhage, not to meet people.

And now Dalton had vanished, leaving Chad at this hopeless party full of people who were too young, too drunk, and too loud. He had been talking to some guy. Some hot, obviously interested, no doubt gay guy. (Damn him.) Dalton thought he was straight? He didn't have that femmy vibe some guys gave off, but he sort of lit up when you paid attention to him. He looked at men. Men looked back. Dalton was tall and rangy, rather well built, and had intriguing dark red hair. Handsome. The cute Latino he'd been talking to clearly thought so. Neither one was anywhere in sight, not for at least half an hour now. Chad had checked both bedrooms. He didn't need to read flashing electric headlines off the side of the Goodyear Blimp to guess what they were up to.

In the background, he overheard Reese. She must have been standing just outside the bathroom door. "That guy, Chad? The one who came with Dalton? Kind of blond hair, wearing the rings? Oh, come on, Jane, you know who I'm talking about. I think he's in the bathroom." A giggle. "You were talking to him when they arrived. He's wearing a denim shirt. Yeah, he's cute, I know. But listen: he's like a criminal or something. He said he was in jail." Another giggle. "I think he was, like, abused in there. And he might have liked it."

Another voice, a bit deeper: "I thought he was fucking weird. Guess I was right. He's a fag, isn't he?"

Chad tried to remember who Jane was. He remembered speaking to a brown-haired girl when he and Dalton had arrived. Twenty-five or so (his own age), with plain features, nothing especially memorable about her. This was her apartment.

The potpourri in the metal urn by the sink smelled fresh, floral. Rose petals, cloves, bits of citrus rind. The kind of thing drugstores sell next to the cash registers, in shrink-wrapped packets. Chad emptied the mixture into the toilet bowl, flushed, waited for the tank to refill, flushed again.

I am lost. How did I get here? Why am I still here? I am going to kick Dalton's ass tomorrow at work. I hope he shows up with a sore ass and a bitch of a hangover.

Chad opened the door and smiled at Reese and Jane, who both jumped. Startled, Reese stammered a greeting and took a step back. Jane regained her balance sooner.

"Your name is Chad, isn't it?" she asked. She spoke in the disinterested tone of a woman who has thrown too many parties.

He nodded.

"I was kidding about jail," Chad said. "The only place I've spent the last week was shuttling between home and my two jobs."

"I saw you in Borders on Wednesday night. You were working at the information counter. I asked you a question about a Barbara Kingsolver novel," Jane said.

"Did I answer it?" Chad wondered what she was implicitly accusing him of.

"After spending five minutes looking into your computer." She held her beer in front of her like a garlic bulb to ward off an advancing vampire. Through her T-shirt, Chad could see the sideways-8 bulge of a pierced nipple.

"It was broken, if I remember." Chad drained the rest of his Merlot. He already needed the bathroom again, but this exchange—he couldn't call it a conversation—had a weird, compelling appeal.

"You didn't have the book I was looking for."

"Popular book." Chad looked around. "Your bookcases are overflowing. Are you sure you don't already have a copy or two stashed away somewhere?"

"I'd know. So why did you tell Reese you went to jail?"

Chad shrugged. "The voices in my head commanded me to."

"Right," said Jane. "Next you're going to tell me the CIA beams microwaves into your brain, because you're part of a conspiracy. And everything on *The X-Files* is true."

"I sleep with a foil-wrapped colander over my head," Chad said. "Cross my heart." He twisted his thumb ring.

"You're nuts. Against my better judgment, I think I like you. Let's open another bottle of wine and go out on the balcony for a cigarette," Jane said. "Come on, Reese." To Chad, she continued: "So this guy Dalton you came with. Were you, like, *with* him? Or did you just come together?"

"We work at Borders together. I don't know him very well. Supposedly he's not gay. He says he's not, but I think that's because he hasn't clued into reality yet. I think he's hooking up with the Latin guy I saw him talking to. Who is that?"

"Nobody could accuse Dalton of having bad taste," Jane said. "Enrique is a friend of mine from work, and as we speak, they're up on the roof licking each other's tonsils."

Chad had a flashback: his own hand releasing citrus potpourri into the blue swirl of the toilet bowl. Would he get out of here without Jane knowing what he'd done? She struck him as the sort of woman who might appreciate his attempts at sabotage. Maybe the stuff had been a gift from an aunt she hated, and he had done her a favor.

"You're not seeing anybody, are you?" Jane, now solicitous, led him to the kitchen. She opened a cupboard and surveyed her diminishing stock of wine. "Rosemount Shiraz, a Cab-Merlot blend, or this bottle of Penfolds."

"Like Australian wine, do you?"

Jane nodded. "It's one of my cleverer affectations. French wine is so . . . I don't know. French. Let's go with the Shiraz. I've been hiding cheese in the fridge, and there's a box of pepper crackers from Fresh Fields in that cabinet. Look behind the boxes of cereal. Reese, would you get a couple of apples out of that bowl?"

Jane poured the wine.

"Do you still think I'm weird?" Chad asked.

"Oh, definitely. You work at Borders like ninety hours a week," Jane said. "I've seen you in there. You obviously hate it. I don't see why you don't quit. And you never did tell me if you're seeing any-body. All of that makes you a very weird boy."

Chad shook his head no. "I was seeing someone," he admitted. "For a few months, kind of casually. It fizzled out at the beginning of the summer."

"You like Dalton."

"Platonically. I don't want to get mixed up with some guy who's coming out and about to dive into the scene. I'm twenty-five. I went through that shit in college. I'm kind of past that. Dalton is going to do what Dalton is going to do, and if he wants to hang out, great."

"You like him," Jane persisted, motioning for him to follow her.

Chad shrugged. "I'd fuck him," he said. "More than once. But if he's not sure whether he's gay or not, it would have to end there."

"Maybe I should introduce you to Enrique," Jane said.

A degree of tension left Chad. For awhile there he had been want-ing to dislike these people, but the tide had turned.

"I have to go to the bathroom," Reese announced, waggling her empty wine glass. "Jane, want to come with me?"

"Yes, I really want to stand in the bathroom and listen to you pee," Jane said, rolling her eyes. "Don't go anywhere, Charles."

Before Chad could correct her, she pushed open the sliding glass door and stepped inside. Reese followed.

Chad leaned against the balcony. The view awed him as it always did. The nearby towers of Rosslyn lent a glow to the background, wash-ing out the sky a bit. The Washington Monument soared. The skyline twinkled. The Potomac shimmered black off to the southeast, Chad's right. Overhead, a plane roared toward National Airport, coming in for a landing. The flight path followed the Potomac, more or less.

"Chad!"

Hearing his name, Chad looked around. Nobody inside had turned in his direction. Nobody appeared to have shouted his name.

"Chad!"

Chad looked down.

A figure stood on the street below. Half in shadow, half not.

Chad leaned forward, to make out who it was. His blood ran like an ice floe, calving glaciers, when he realized who was standing there.

His brother Martin. The bastard, the asshole, the problem, the Prince of Darkness. *Shit.*

Martin bellowed, "Chad! What the fuck are you doing out this late?"

Chad inched forward to get a better look. There was no question whose voice it was. Three stories below, the parking lot to this building, a landscaped perimeter . . . but Chad couldn't see Martin's face.

The wine soaking his brain did something to his balance just then, because the next thing Chad heard was the door sliding open, followed by a loud gasp, and then he was airborne, head-first off the balcony. He had just enough time to observe his flight and react— *SHIT!*—and then he landed painfully in a hedge. Someone turned out all the lights.

– 2 –

Friday Night (Late)

The ambulance ride passed in a blur of light and sound. EMTs were clustered around Chad when, against the better judgment imposed by the crashing pain in his left arm and his head, he opened one eye. How many were there? Chad couldn't tell. Martin's face appeared between two of the EMTs for a second, a disembodied evil presence, Oz the Great and Terrible, then disappeared again. *Don't look behind that curtain.* Chad felt warmth flowing into him. The warmth chased the pain away, and it was good and clean and right. Chad rode the rest of the way to the hospital in a state of anesthetic bliss.

When they set the bone in his left wrist, the drugs weren't enough. He screamed.

Another shot, another bank of clouds rolled in, and Chad coasted for a while. He closed his eyes and the whole world went away again.

One member of the intake team leaned forward and looked over the frames of her little wireless glasses at Chad. He was barely awake. He'd tried, in his thick-tongued way, to get them to leave him alone. He wanted to call a cab and go home and get some sleep, but nobody would listen. Now this woman wouldn't give him a moment's peace. Her eyes were laser-beam blue. Despite the late hour—1:30 a.m.— she projected an air of competence and clarity. Chad thought her name was Susan, but it might have been Sarah.

"We know it's late and you've had a difficult day," she said. "But we'd like for you to talk just a little about why you're here. In your own words. We have to make just a few decisions before we let you go to bed."

9

Chad nodded. In the hospital, he had been given several shots. Antibiotics, he supposed, and drugs. Great drugs. His head was full of beautiful billowing cumulus clouds. They looked great and felt wonderful, but they got in the way when he tried to think. His eyelids banged together like cymbals sometimes, and like a xylophone other times, when he blinked. He blinked a couple of extra times, for the effect, and wondered if the Intake Team (they deserved capitals, he decided) could hear the musical noises coming from his face.

"Can you do that, Chad?" Sarah or Susan put her fingertips together in a templelike gesture that suggested both that she was listening intently and setting boundaries. Chad saw boundaries blinking in front of him like the reflective spots between the lanes of highways at night. When he squinted, the spots united to form lines. Like speeding.

Chad nodded again.

"I'm pumped full of drugs. You know that, don't you?" Of course they knew that. They had done the pumping. "Of course you know that. It's in my chart."

Another member of the Intake Team chimed in. Chad thought she might be a nurse. She didn't look like a psychiatrist, although he wasn't sure what psychiatrists were supposed to look like.

The clouds in his head shifted, dissolved, reformed. The psychiatrist had a brainy chic look. Even this late at night, Susan or Sarah didn't look bedraggled. Chad didn't know much about women's clothing, but he thought she shopped at the better stores. Would nurses and counselors have the salary to be as nicely turned out? His thoughts broke apart and scattered to the four winds.

"Chad?"

He had already forgotten someone had spoken. Not Susan or Sarah, but one of the other ones. He looked around at them and asked, "What?"

They looked at one another, then at him.

"Someone asked a question. I'm off in space. It's the drugs. I'm sorry. I'm not usually like this." Chad hoped they didn't think he was being rude. "Really, I'm not." That was polite enough, wasn't it? If he acted polite, then they'd let him go home. Or at least let him get some sleep. In the morning, when everything made more sense, then they could get everything squared away. When he had slept this off.

"We understand, Chad," said the woman who had to be a nurse. She had pens in her shirt pocket, and scissors, and a lot of other things. That seemed nurselike, having lots of things in your pocket, being ready for contingencies. Did nurses have extra pockets sewn onto their clothes? Contingency pockets? He should ask. He would ask. If he remembered. Which he probably wouldn't. "We know the basic reasons you're here, and we're sorry you found yourself in this situation. But if we could get a little more background information, then that will help us to know what medications to prescribe, what kind of treatment will work best for you, that kind of thing. We'll be able to make some calls tonight and get things lined up for the morning. If you're not up to it, we won't pressure you—you can go right to bed. But it would be very helpful if you can talk to us first."

Chad blinked at her and marveled at how loud his eyelids sounded. Waves of colorless disturbance rippled across the fabric of reality when he blinked. Everything around him looked like a special effect. And felt marvelous. If he didn't know better, he'd suspect this conference room was an image projected onto a body of water, and someone was throwing rocks in from somewhere just outside of his pool of vision.

Beyond the members of the Intake Team, Chad could see nothing but a white room with a framed print on one wall. He couldn't make out the name of the artist. Blotchy pastel colors might have been intended to represent a flower.

He tried to collect himself.

They wanted him to talk.

Now he felt a fraction less marvelous.

He looked down at the stitches on both of his arms, the cast around his left wrist and forearm. His face felt thick, as if his skin were a layer of stucco inexpertly plastered on. He had not inflicted as much damage as he could have. Fucked up or not, he could tell. Everything hurt, but could have been worse.

Five years ago, he had been in much worse shape. After a year as an exchange student in Spain, he came back to the States, spent an endless and miserable couple of months with his mother in North Carolina, then returned to DC to find an apartment and a job. The drunk guy in the SUV who knocked Chad's Matchbox-car Honda across two lanes of traffic and into a tree hadn't noticed the red light. He thought it was still yellow. Chad never saw him coming. He remembered sliding a tape into the stereo, wondering what that loud bang was, and that was it. Lights out. He woke up in intensive care.

Chad spent two weeks in the hospital—long enough to fall madly in hate with sterile rooms, all medical personnel, and their well-meaning, repeated invasions of his person. Broken arm. Dislocated shoulder. Three fractured ribs. Some torn ligaments. Whiplash. He was purple with bruises. He gave the docs plenty to do. And in the hospital, the food, the lack of sleep, the smell, the relentless pain—these things drove him crazier. Nobody would bring him anything decent to read. Discharged afterward, home to North Carolina, back to Mona's falling-apart-at-the-seams house, that pushed him right up to the edge. Mona was sick at the time, herself, always exhausted and short of breath, and the drive to DC wiped her out. She recruited a friend whom Chad had never met, a balding man named Gunther, to do most of the driving. Chad spent the endless trek down I-95 curled up in the backseat, praying to the malign nothingness that turned the wheels of the universe to please let him trade in his life on a new one. Gunther and Mona chain-smoked. Chad rolled down the windows and tried to sleep, but he hurt everywhere. How he'd be ready for school when the fall semester started, he had no idea.

Recovery took months. In some ways he had still not recovered. His academic career had been scuttled, as had his finances. And now here he was, back in the hospital again. Fucked up, busted up, out of luck. More poking and prodding, more needles.

When Chad hit the hedge three floors below Jane's balcony, he was conscious long enough to hear Martin pronouncing it a suicide attempt to Reese, Jane, and the other guests who ran downstairs screaming. Smug bastard. Chad had shut his eyes again.

"I'm sorry," Martin had told them. "He's like, unstable. You know? This isn't the first time."

When the ambulance arrived, Martin told the EMTs the same thing. They told the doctors who set the bone in the ER. Somebody in the ER called psych.

Chad, stuck without a visa in the border state between reality and anesthesia, just nodded. Martin stood there glaring. He issued an unspoken dare for Chad to disagree. What the hell, why not. He couldn't win. Broken wrist, drunk, kind of a loser to hear Martin tell it, why fucking argue?

Welcome to the psych ward.

Chad wasn't sure how he was going to talk his way out of this one. Life wasn't grand, and he had pounded at least a bottle of Merlot before going airborne, but it wasn't like he had broken the bottle and swallowed the shards.

Sooner or later he'd have to figure out where Martin had come from, how he'd found out about the party. What the fuck he was doing there.

"I was with a couple of friends at their apartment in Rosslyn. What hospital is this, by the way? George Washington? OK, thanks. We were partying. You know, candles and wine. Talking. Hanging out. These two girls and I went out on the balcony for some fresh air and when I saw my brother, I leaned too far and fell over the side."

Susan or Sarah gave a pert frown.

"If I wanted to kill myself I would have picked a higher floor."

Susan or Sarah made a face. Chad caught a slight hardening of her expression. Whatever medication they'd given him, it couldn't have been much of a dose, because of the alcohol already in his system. Pity.

"Your brother expressed some concerns about your safety. He said there have been previous attempts to harm yourself. Is this true, that you've tried to harm yourself?" she asked. "If your brother hadn't been there, you might not have made it to the hospital. It's just not something to be cavalier about."

"I don't think you have a clear picture of what happened. I was with a couple of friends. One of *them* called nine-one-one, not my brother. He shouldn't have been there in the first place. He was skulking around outside like a stalker. I think he was following me."

"Oh . . ." Susan or Sarah looked at the other members of the Intake Team. She blinked like a frog contemplating a fly. Any second now, she would lasso his head with her nine-foot tongue and drag him into her slimy red gullet.

Chad looked at the print on the wall. As his vision cleared, he could make out its design. One gigantic orange flower, like something Georgia O'Keeffe would paint. Had O'Keeffe ever painted a gigantic orange flower? She must have. She painted gigantic flowers.

Great drugs.

More please? Chad didn't dare ask.

"So what do you want to know?" he asked. "What else did my brother tell you?" The cloudy loveliness in Chad's head was dissipating fast. Before giving her a chance to answer, he added, "I broke my wrist. I'm kind of scratched up because of the shrubs I fell into. It's not like this is *that bad.*"

Someone else spoke up. "OK, I'll level with you. We know that you attempted suicide two years ago. According to your brother, apparently there's a lot of drug and alcohol use. Overall, it seems like there's a lot going on with you. That's what we were hoping you'd tell us." Chad didn't remember who this other person was. The counselor, probably. A balding but kind-faced fiftyish man in a tweed blazer, his voice twanging like a Texan's. He looked like the sort of community college professor who gives mostly A's and B's, and has given up trying to memorize his students' names. His belt and his shoes didn't match. What his name was, Chad had no idea.

Chad took a deep breath. Darkness was beginning to tinge the remaining head clouds around the edges. Dark colors were swirling into those fluffy white shapes. Inside, he had the same sensation he did when he was traveling and his plane began its descent toward the airport.

"OK. I admit that a couple of years ago I washed down a bottle of Sominex with a couple of bottles of wine. Seemed like a good idea at the time. I don't know if my brother gave you guys any information at all, but the gist of it all is this: I was at GWU on scholarship. After my sophomore year, I spent time overseas on exchange. Everything was going pretty well, and then I was involved in a car wreck right after I got back to the United States. Busted me up enough that I had to drop out of school. I tried to stay in, but my grades went to hell. I was fucked up on painkillers for weeks. The scholarship board was sympathetic up to a point, but they opted to stick by the rules. So I ended up losing my scholarship and am in major debt. I tried to go it alone, but tuition at GW is about as high as it gets. My student loans looked like the national debt. I couldn't repay them with the kind of work I was finding. I maxed out half a dozen credit cards trying to hold onto my car and my apartment, and lost all of it. I got a settlement from the other driver's insurance, but that didn't last long. My credit report looks like Bosnia when the Serbs went on the rampage. I couldn't handle the calls from collections agents. It felt like my future had been taken away from me, through no fault of my own. And I had some other things going on at the time. I'm not sure I want to talk about all of that right now. I'm too fucking exhausted. In retrospect it all seems incredibly dumb. Does that make any sense?"

They nodded again. The moment had a Terry Gilliam feel to it. The Intake Team looked like characters in a surrealist movie, nodding like wide-eyed, well-costumed automatons. They had already asked him questions from a yard-long standard form, checking off little boxes for yes or no, more or less in unison. In a minute they'd bark "next!" and push a big red button. His chair would tilt forward, and he'd plummet through a trapdoor in the floor into an oubliette, where howling lunatics would eat him.

The clouds in his head were gone. Chad felt like he was in a sports car commercial with the volume up too loud.

The professorish one looked through a chart. "If, as you say, falling off a balcony while drunk was not a suicidal jump, then it's questionable whether you should be here. I know you're exhausted, but if you could bear with us and speak to a couple of other issues, we can make the best decision in terms of what to do with you."

Chad took a deep breath. All traces of his comfy interior fuzziness had departed. This story wasn't going to have a happy ending, he could tell, so he resigned himself to whatever horrors lay in wait.

"My brother and I do not get along, no matter what he told you. I'd bet he told somebody I am mentally ill. Or that I have a drug problem, or I'm an alcoholic. Or that I'm a depraved promiscuous homosexual pervert condomlessly fucking his way through the male population of DC. My mother—our surviving parent, but not for long the way her lungs are going—has abandoned me because she's so appalled that I turned out queer. I have no meaningful friendships. I just hang out with shallow, unemployed club kids and we all shoot crystal meth, go to circuit parties, and have anal VD. He said the warts in my ass look like a plate of sautéed cauliflower. Is that a safe guess?"

Delayed reaction. Blinks. Heads turning. Susan or Sarah started to say something, then checked herself. The nurse—Lucy? Linda?—stood up, wobbling as if she were about to lose her balance. She kneaded her calves as she struggled to cross the room. "Asleep," she said, by way of explanation, to no one in particular. The door swung shut behind her.

"My brother is the one behind a lot of this. He's the one my mother has cut ties with, not me. For one thing, he's my half brother, if you want to get technical about it. He's the one who has the big problem with the fact that I'm gay. He's in the Air Force, stationed at Andrews, and he's got that stereotypically brain-dead military view on how men are supposed to be. The way I turned out is not OK," Chad said. "It's like he's fixated on me. He interferes in everything I do. He shows up at my house whenever he feels like it." He stopped to collect his thoughts. "To be honest with you, he'd have pushed me over that railing if he'd been there and nobody was looking."

By now Chad was trembling. He felt hot and cold at the same time. When he brushed his fingers across his cheek, his fingertips came away with a sheen of oil. He stared at his shiny fingertips and felt queasy again. If he could wash his face, he'd feel better. When had he last eaten? Lunch? Couple of late-afternoon slices of pizza at Pentagon City, after a masochistic trip in search of a new shirt to wear to work. He couldn't afford anything he liked. Consolation took the form of two giant slices with extra pepperoni and a large Coke.

"I don't feel so well," he said, clutching his abdomen. "If you have any meds that knock people out quickly, I'd like some. I don't think I can say anything else without losing it."

Looks of alarm.

"Are you safe?" asked Sarah or Susan quickly.

Chad's eyes widened. He was taking deep breaths and sitting as still as possible. He didn't want to start crying, because he didn't want to lose it in front of these people—however used to bawling patients they might be. His head pounded. He had passed beyond being exhausted into some new and uncharted territory: ashes. When people give up, they fade to an insipid shade of grey. He was a lifelike replica of himself, made of fine ash, like the cylinders ignored cigarettes turned into. One puff of wind, and he'd disperse into oblivion. Good night and good riddance.

Not such a bad idea, now that he thought about it.

"I really need to sleep. I can't . . ." Chad shook his head. "Can we finish this in the morning?"

"Sure," the professorish counselor spoke. "You've had a lot thrown at you, and we're certainly not going to make things worse by depriving you of sleep." His smile was so warm and genuine that Chad felt a tiny spark of—something deep within himself. "Your bed is ready. You have a roommate, Henri, but he's being discharged tomorrow. Going back to Montreal, I believe."

They showed him to his room and gave him pills to swallow. Martin put in a brief appearance, made concerned faces, gave Chad a hug that seemed more for the nurses' benefit than for Chad's, then left just as the pills were kicking in. Chad stripped to his underwear, crawled under the covers, and fell asleep in seconds.

Saturday Morning

Pain woke Chad from an uneasy, nightmare-riddled sleep. When he opened his eyes, he found a handsome green-eyed guy standing by the bed, staring down at him. Chad lay still, unsure what to do or say. He had a feeling the guy had been watching him sleep. Chad knuckled crusts of goop out of the corners of his eyes. He hurt too much to come up with a greeting ("Hi, nice to meet you. What are you in for?"), and if the kid was a full-blown lunatic, Chad didn't want to cross him. Chad's arms and head throbbed. Someone had battered him with a shillelagh in the night. There could be no other explanation for the skullquake he'd awakened with.

"I just came in here to see if you were awake yet," Green Eyes said in what might have been a British accent. What a great voice—husky, almost hoarse. He sounded much older than he looked. Chad wondered how many packs a day the guy smoked, or whether he was getting over a cold. And whether he had a driver's license yet. Wasn't this an adult ward? "Breakfast will be here in a few minutes. I thought I'd be a nicer way for you to wake up to than the nurses."

"They seem nice enough," Chad bluffed. He couldn't remember.

"They'll do. There's nothing wrong with them, if you overlook the fact that they're our jailors." Green Eyes offered a wan smile. Cute. He had not quite shoulder-length dark brown hair, almost black. He kept brushing has bangs out of his eyes. Clear porcelain skin. Hint of five o'clock shadow, but not dense enough to suggest he needed to shave every day. Compact and narrow hipped, the guy was take-a-second-look cute.

Great, I'm attracted to another patient. We can go out for coffee and talk about the side effects from our meds. We'll live happily ever after.

"I'm Jonathan," Green Eyes—Jonathan—said, fiddling with an earring. (He had two hoops in each ear; Chad wondered what else was pierced.) "And you are? I don't believe we've had the pleasure."

"Chad." His head was pulsating. He needed coffee, now. A cola at the very least. Was coffee permitted in the psych unit? God, to think that it might not be . . . Were they prepared for what an irritable fuck he'd turn into and the headaches he'd get? "If you really want to climb to the top of my list of favorite people, would you pull the blinds? The sunlight is way too goddamn bright."

Jonathan complied and Chad took advantage of the view. No way to tell what Jonathan's ass looked like in those baggy jeans, but then Chad supposed he ought not to be looking. Pedophilia didn't turn him on. This guy couldn't be old enough to have legal erections.

"I'm not Jon, by the way, or Johnny, or anything else with less than three syllables."

"I'm sure you're as complicated as your name. Look, Jonathan, I'll be honest—I think it's too early in the morning for me to have a conversation. Really. I'm a dick when I haven't had caffeine. And if we're going to be stuck in this place together for a few days, you don't want to be around me when I'm a dick."

Chad's head felt like someone had pulled off the top of his skull and replaced his brain with tumbleweeds of rusty concertina wire.

"Duly noted. The pleasure was mine." And—for the love of God—Jonathan bowed slightly, palms together like Gandhi or something, before leaving the room. He backed out the door, his eyes never leaving Chad. One more subtle bow, and Jonathan slipped out the door.

"Crazy people," Chad muttered. "Jesus Christ."

He closed his eyes again and dozed. Crazy, but cute and appealing nonetheless. Before Chad could drop off all the way, the click of the door opening brought him back. Footsteps approached. Chad opened one eye, saw a stout shape in the doorway, shut the eye again. He'd have kept it open for Jonathan.

"What's your name?" a woman asked, in accented English. This time the music behind the words sounded Spanish.

Chad mushed his pillow over his ears. The woman, whoever she was, walked over to the bed and shook him gently by the shoulder.

"What's your name?" she asked again.

Chad peeked over the edge of the pillow and saw a round, brown face. She had one eye focused on him, but the other one definitely had the door staked out for intruders.

"I'm Linda," she said.

She stared at him with one eye, saying nothing until a bubble of pressure burst within Chad. He introduced himself but did not offer to shake hands. He kept the pillow over most of his face, and his body beneath the blankets. The boner Jonathan's visit had inspired instantly wilted, like a salted slug. He hoped Linda hadn't noticed it tenting his blankets. Twenty-five is still young enough to remember the rules pertaining to beds and safety: the monsters won't get you if you keep everything covered up. You're allowed to peek, but not for long. If Chad continued to hide beneath the blankets, sooner or later a nurse would come along to save him. His head felt like a hundred car wrecks.

"You're a homosexual, aren't you?"

Chad woke up a fraction more.

"I heard them say you were a homosexual. That's OK. I've got death growing inside of me."

Chad couldn't quite see the connection, but he *was* in the psych ward. Who could say what would make sense to the other people here?

Linda went on, in a trembling voice: "It's black and purple, and it smells bad when I pee. Like asparagus, but darker."

Oh, Jesus. Chad forced himself to take a closer look at the self-proclaimed death garden. He wondered, *Does pee normally smell good, then? Can I look for it in shower gel and shampoo at The Body Shop?* Linda straddled the full-figured-gal borderline between zaftig and just plain chubby. Latina? Filipina? Chad couldn't tell where she was from, and he didn't want to ask. She wore red workout gear with white racing stripes down the arms and legs, and a red Stanford baseball cap. Chad closed his eyes and willed her to disappear in a puff of smoke. His arms throbbed. Linda did not vanish.

"Death," she whined. "There are lumps and clots of it growing in me. Inside my vagina. I could show you. There's a flashlight at the nurses' station."

"No, thank you," Chad said. His cranium pulsated. Could the hospital helicopter be dispatched to Starbucks? Would his HMO cover that?

"Linda, I don't think this gentleman wants to wake up to your 'I got death in my coochie' story. Why don't you go get yourself a chair in the meeting room? Group starts in a few minutes. Let him get up and get dressed." Chad's saving angel took the form of a petite black woman in a sunny yellow dress and a dark blue cardigan. She shooed Linda out of the room (Linda wrapped her arms around herself and rocked in place for a few seconds before shuffling out) and offered Chad a warm smile.

"You must be a nurse," Chad said, feeling transparent all of a sudden. All of the pigment in his body seemed to have leached into the sheets and mattress beneath him. He pictured stains formed by the red of his blood and his gashed arms, the crystallized ginger shade of his hair, the pinkish tan of his skin, a slippery sort of blue for his lungs.

"How can you tell?"

"You have pens and things in the pocket of your sweater. You look prepared for contingencies. I was thinking about that last night. Nurses and contingencies."

"Very good. How are you this morning?"

"Well, I'm in a psych ward after plummeting off someone's balcony into a hedge, and I've been falsely labeled a failed suicide. By now, my asshole brother has probably convinced the entire hospital I'm a risk to self and society so he can keep me here. I hurt everywhere. I'm dying for coffee. And the way people keep trickling into my room, I feel like the new llama at the petting zoo."

The nurse blinked a couple of times. The look on her face didn't change. Chad couldn't tell how old she was. "Just don't spit on anybody, OK? Those llamas can be pretty mean." She chuckled to herself. "Sounds like you've been better, but you still got your sense of humor, so things can't be all bad." She spoke with a terrific Southern accent: *can't* came out as *cain't*. Chad decided he liked her. "Don't let Linda get to you. She's a piece of work, no doubt about it, but she's harmless. Who else was in here?"

"Jonathan. Young guy, green eyes?" Chad wanted to add, *You know, the cute one,* but he managed to suppress it. "He woke me up. I think he was watching me sleep."

The nurse made an amused face. "Jonathan, huh? He's a trip." The nurse handed him a tray of breakfast. "Tomorrow, when you're up and around a little better, you can join everyone else for breakfast, but this morning we decided you could eat in bed. Those are your meds. You'll want to swallow them after you finish eating." She dusted her palms together. "Well, we could stand here and gossip about patients all morning if we wanted to, but I bet you really want your breakfast. The cafeteria here is OK, could be worse, could be better. You got eggs, bacon, a bagel, some fruit, and orange juice. Will that do?"

"If I don't get coffee, I will die," Chad said. "My head will crack open and my brains will leak out like tufts of stuffed-toy fiber."

"Then we should make sure you get a cup of coffee. You take yours black, or do you like cream and sugar?"

"Sugar, no cream. And tell me your name before you go? I didn't get it."

"Valerie. Why don't you get up and get dressed, maybe eat a little? I'll be right back with coffee."

Valerie turned to leave the room.

Off in the distance, Chad heard a television turned up, canned applause, a game show buzzer, a laugh track. Somebody won, somebody lost; Chad couldn't tell and didn't care.

A question surfaced. He stopped Valerie on her way out to ask about clothes. "I assume I'm going to be here a couple of days, at least. How do we arrange for me to get my clothes and toiletries here? My roommate, Rose, is out of town."

"Do you have a friend or relative in the area who wouldn't be embarrassed to go through your underwear drawer?" She smiled again.

"I'll have to think about that." Chad hoped one of his take-with-breakfast pills was a heavy-duty painkiller. With Rose and most of Chad's friends gone, Martin was the obvious choice, but Chad wanted not to involve him, if possible. Wanted not to see him, if possible. "It's a big request. I have to do laundry—I'm not sure what's clean. Not much. Jesus. And there's the issue of getting into my place. My roommate is God knows where in God knows what country doing God knows what, so that's going to be a challenge."

Martin has a key.

No. Chad would wear his dirty clothes for three days. He'd wear a hospital gown. He'd go naked before he would call Martin.

"Well, try to think about who you can call. Eat some breakfast. You'll want to get up and get dressed soon. Group doesn't start for about fifteen minutes, so you've got time."

Chad lay in bed another minute, shaking his head in amazement. *I've fallen through the looking glass.* He looked at the tray again to see if any of the food was labeled *Eat Me.*

"I saved you a seat," Jonathan said, the second Chad stepped into the group room.

Chairs—the kind with vinyl seats and wooden arms, the kind your ass sticks to after five minutes—formed a circle in the center of the room. Other chairs had been pushed into corners. Chad counted seven other people, besides himself: Jonathan (the easiest to look at); Linda (arms wrapped around herself, sucking her thumb like a toddler); a girl about his own age (white, with brown hair pulled straight back in a ponytail, in jeans and a sweater, pleasant on the surface); an older— fortysomething?—black man in neat corduroy trousers and a cardigan; a white man of about the same age (glasses, receding hairline, shabby clothes, waxy skin); a brittle-looking woman in her midthirties (white, dressed in black, wide-eyed and trembling); and another guy in his twenties, also white, kind of nondescript but smiling at everybody.

"You have bed head," Jonathan said.

Chad sat down. Other people trickled in.

Three days in here with no decent food, no stereo, no Internet access. No clothes, yet. No way to leave. Meetings in this bland room with its dreary inspirational quotes taped to the wall on squares of construction paper. Welcome to the gulag.

On second thought, this meant no phone calls from creditors. No mail to collect. No bills. There was a bright side.

"I just got up," Chad said. "Didn't have time to take a shower."

"You'll have time for that after group, unless they take you downstairs to the surgery center and remove your brain. But don't worry, they probably won't do that. Happens with only one patient in a thousand. You have to have the right tissue types and measurements. Did you ever read *Coma*? Robin Cook based that book on this very hospital."

Chad recoiled.

"I'm *kidding*, Chad. C'mon, it's not like you're in the loony bin surrounded by crazy people!" Jonathan punctuated this with a big wicked grin. Charmingly, he blushed.

"Oh, that's right. Of course. What was I thinking? I'm on one of those all-gay cruises to the Caribbean, and I'm surrounded by hunky men in Speedos. Want a piña colada?"

Jonathan looked thoughtful, but the blush lingered. "There are cruises like that? Maybe I should go on one. But I don't know about the hunky men in Speedos. I'm not really into muscles."

"I guess that answers that question," Chad said.

"The tousled look works. You should stick with it," Jonathan said.

"Well, I've got to get somebody to bring all my shit from home first. Before I leave on any cruises to Acapulco. I came in wearing the clothes on my back. The stitches are the only thing that's new. I could make a really bad pun about not having a stitch to wear, but I won't."

Jonathan smiled at him. Chad squinted to see if the green of Jonathan's eyes came from tinted contacts, but no abnormal circles of color gave the game away. Had to be natural. Very appealing.

"I believe you just made the pun you said you weren't going to make, you goofball," Jonathan said. "But you went in the back door. Very sly."

The circle of chairs had filled, their occupants comprising men and women, young and old, all races, the rest of them apparently straight, as far as Chad could discern. Nobody but Linda rocked in their seats, muttered to themselves, *looked* mentally infirm. But from the grizzled faces of one or two of them, they might have been living on the streets. Chad wondered where Valerie was with that cup of coffee. He gingerly touched his stitches. When his fingers came into contact with the ugly black thread and the puffy red flesh beneath, he felt light-headed.

"Do you really want to be dead?" Jonathan asked softly, after watching Chad stare at his wounds for a few seconds.

"I'm not sure what I want. My life back, maybe. Not to be lost. I don't know. Ask me again in a few days, after I've been psychologized."

The room had fallen silent. Jonathan's voice carried. Chad felt conspicuous.

"Good morning, everyone!" piped a woman's voice from the doorway.

A man in a wheelchair rolled into the room and took his place between two of the chairs. Rather dashing-looking guy, Chad thought. Kind of an updated Errol Flynn. Behind him was the blue-eyed woman from last night, Susan or Sarah.

"We're stuck in here for an hour," Jonathan whispered. "It's all this mushy, *How does that make you feel?* horseshit. If you're not sick to your stomach now, give yourself thirty minutes. I guarantee you'll blow chunks. I just learned that phrase, *blow chunks.* Isn't that hilarious?"

"Why are you in here, then?" Chad whispered back.

"Because I'm crazy, of course. Aren't you?"

"Umm . . . I guess that depends on how you define *crazy.*" Chad considered Jonathan for a moment. He had to be older than he looked. He had on jeans and a plain black T-shirt. For the first time, Chad noticed Jonathan had a small tattoo on the web of his left hand, between the thumb and forefinger. "What's that?"

"A tattoo," Jonathan replied. "Ink? Patterned into the skin?"

"I know that, dummy, but what's it a tattoo *of?*"

"Just a lightning bolt."

"Ladies and gentlemen, we'd like to get the group started now," said Errol Flynn. He had a movie star voice, too, manly and resonant. Chad suspected clients flocked to him just to listen to him speak. He probably made a fortune, if he had a private practice. "We also have a new person in the unit. And we're glad to say that Henri left this morning to go back home to Québec. He's doing much better, and he asked us to thank you all for your support."

Susan or Sarah beamed at all of them, a smile that stretched her features like Play-Doh. She turned her head to zap everyone in the room with the radiance from her face, and started a sporadic fit of applause. She applauded with the most enthusiasm, followed by Linda, who lolled to one side and made a sort of cooing noise as she clapped. Everyone else offered desultory golf claps.

"Introductions first, since we have someone new in our group this morning. Why don't we start with . . . Why don't we just start with you, Jonathan? Do you mind starting? Just say your name, and where you're from. Maybe a little bit about what brought you here and what issues you're working on, if you're comfortable sharing that. And finish up with one positive thing you're going to do for yourself today."

Chad looked at the unsigned cast on his left wrist again. His fingertips poked out of the plaster and looked as forlorn as he felt. By the light of day, plunging off the balcony after slurping up enough wine to drown a dolphin seemed intensely stupid. The tectonic plates in his skull crashed together and the lump in his throat hurt like a tracheotomy. Chad forced himself to take one little breath at a time, until he regained a measure of equilibrium. Hell if he'd fall apart in front of all these people.

". . . are you OK?" somebody was asking, when Chad's attention returned. It took him a moment to realize he was being addressed. "Chad, do you need a moment? You looked very pale just now."

Chad swallowed and wondered if he could speak. "Sorry," he said. "Zoned out for a minute there."

"Did you hear a thing I said?" Jonathan asked him, smiling. He looked sympathetic. "Can't have you wandering around here today without having a clue what my issues are and what positive things I'm going to do for myself."

"Me, too," said the woman on the other side of Jonathan, the wan chick dressed all in black. Her chin trembled. Stringy henna-tinted hair stuck to her face. Some got in her mouth and she left it there. She gave off a wounded-but-defiant image Chad found grating. "I really want to share my issues with the entire group. It's like so important that we all are here for each other." She had a cartoon quality: she tucked her lank bangs behind Dumbo ears. The hair fell back into place before her hands came to rest in her lap. She stared at Chad with Bambi eyes. Chad wanted an eraser.

"I'm fine," he said. "Just . . . dealing with it all. And jonesing for coffee. I thought Valerie was going to find me a cup of coffee, but I guess she got distracted." Once Chad started talking, the words became easier. He only had to force the first few out of his mouth. Then the lump in his throat dissolved, and his mouth began to work again.

"If you need to step out for a moment, it's fine—there's no pressure," Errol Flynn said, wheeling his chair around a few degrees, to stare straight at Chad. "Would you like for Jonathan and Gracie to reintroduce themselves?"

Chad nodded. He didn't care about Gracie but wanted to hear what Jonathan had to say.

"Jonathan?" Errol Flynn's look served as instructions to proceed.

Jonathan stood and offered another of those Gandhi-esque bows, endearing himself to Chad as he did so. Chad wanted to kiss him, and felt himself blushing. It felt schizophrenic to be quaking in pain one moment and thinking pornographic thoughts the next. "My name is Jonathan Fairbanks. Most of you know that already. My story's kind of complicated, and I don't feel like retelling it all right now—I'd put everyone to sleep, especially poor Chad here, because he hasn't had his morning coffee. Umm . . . it's enough to say that I'm in limbo right now while some decisions are being made about my life. And because I'm a homicidal maniac."

Two or three people gasped. Chad looked around. He heard a nervous note in the chuckles and titters that followed Jonathan's remark. In Chad's head, one or two red flags unfurled and started flapping in a fresh breeze. Jonathan continued. "The positive thing I'm going to do for myself today is . . . I don't know. I haven't decided yet. Maybe I'll spend some time online looking at college Web sites, and try to get a clue where I want to go, once I'm out of here."

Errol Flynn—Chad made a mental note to ask the man his name once he got the chance—looked pointedly at Jonathan for a beat, then nodded. "Very good, Jonathan. Thank you. Gracie?"

Chad tuned her out. He leaned toward Jonathan and whispered as quietly as possible, "Homicidal maniac?"

Jonathan winked dangerously and nodded. "That's for the future," he whispered.

"Sidebar conversations should be taken out into the hall," chirped Susan or Sarah. "It's important that all members of the group respect the person who is speaking. It's just really important that we show each person that level of respect. Is everyone in agreement on that?"

"Absolutely!" said Jonathan, a little too loud. Everyone looked at him.

"You are the devil," Chad whispered as Marcus, the black man in the corduroy trousers, began to introduce himself.

Jonathan nodded, looking grave.

– 4 –

Saturday Morning

No one brought a cup of coffee to keep Chad's head from exploding. The members of the group spent half of their allotted hour introducing themselves. The range of issues to be worked on astounded Chad in its narrowness and lack of variety. The words *self-esteem* came out of every other mouth.

"I'm really focusing on myself and my self-esteem, and doing what's best for me, you know? Like, I've allowed myself to get into a really negative space, and I'm surrounded by all this bad energy, present company excepted, and it's because I have really low self-esteem. When I get out, I'm going to do a lot of reading . . . you know, books and articles, on self-esteem, because it's just really important to build yourself up. You know. In terms of self-esteem." Chad writhed as Louise, a heavyset young woman who had straggled in just after Errol Flynn (whose real name was Lawrence) and Susan (not Sarah), shared that sentiment.

Another issue to be worked on was self-centeredness. This from Thomas, the other twentysomething guy, whom Chad decided could have been handsome with a shower, a haircut, and clothes that fit: "I'm realizing that it's not always all about me, you know? It's important to keep yourself as your focal point, but when you do all this work it's also important not to lose sight of other people. I wouldn't have lost my job and gotten so deep into drugs if I had given some thought to how it would impact all the other people in my life. You know, like my girlfriend and my family."

"It's just really important that you consider that maybe low self-esteem is behind your self-centeredness," Susan said. She could not seem to utter a sentence without inserting the word *just* at least once. She just couldn't seem to. Chad wanted to race home and hide under his bed. He'd vacuum out the dust bunnies first. Then he'd stay under there until this all blew over. Until Martin and his high school dropout wife and snot-factory kids dropped off the face of the earth. Until Experian, TransUnion, and Equifax forgot the name Chad Sobran. Years, if need be. And he wouldn't stay in the same room with anyone who couldn't speak in complete sentences.

"Chad? Would you like to introduce yourself now?"

He gave the group a vague Mona Lisa smile and tried to think of what to say other than, "Have a nice life, everyone. I'm out of here."

"I'm Chad Sobran," he said. "I'm in here because I had a few drinks too many, fell off a third-floor balcony, and landed in shrubbery. Got knocked out cold when I hit the ground. Really lucky I didn't fuck myself up worse than I did. When my brother Martin found out what had happened, he convinced the ER docs I was trying to kill myself, so here I am."

Murmurs of, *I'm sorry, ouch, poor guy,* drifted toward him. Chad couldn't identify who was saying what, but he found the words unexpectedly comforting.

Don't be nice to me, he thought. *I want to leave. Don't make me want to stay.*

"As for my issues, I don't even begin to have a clue what I'm supposed to be working on. Getting through all this, I guess. Getting out of here. Maybe figuring out what to do about my brother. I call him the Prince of Darkness. I want him to leave me alone. He doesn't have to like my life." Chad shrugged. His throat was constricting again, and his face burned.

"Thank you, Chad," Lawrence said, nodding.

"Just one more thing," added Susan. She offered him a rictus. How could she do that to her mouth without causing her cheeks to split like water balloons left on the end of the garden hose too long? "What's one positive thing you'll do for yourself today?" She dazzled him, blue eyes incandescent behind her little glasses, blinding glare reflecting off her perfect white teeth from the lights overhead.

Lobotomize you with a rectal thermometer, Chad thought. He smiled in spite of himself. "I'll just get through the day, I think."

"You're not going to do anything special? Like . . . just . . . write a poem?" She pronounced it *po-wum.* Chad just stared at her. "Or really explore with your counselor what kind of strategies you can use to help with your issues? Or . . . I don't know, maybe try to get some exercise? All of those would be very positive things you could do. Very impactful. It's just really important that you work on moving forward." She took a deep breath. Her eyes seemed to move closer together, and she made a cup of her palms like a peasant woman begging in Bombay. "Healing."

Impactful?

"I for one think it's just *really important* that Chad get through his day," Jonathan said, standing up before Chad could open his mouth. "Don't you think so? He's obviously got a lot going on right now. Perhaps he just doesn't want to be the center of all this attention?"

Jonathan's delivery was so subtle, Susan couldn't tell she was being mocked. She blinked at Jonathan, then gave Chad more of her too-wide smile. How could anyone continue to *beam* like that for so long without spontaneously combusting? If Susan had ever been pregnant, no doubt the fetus had been burnt to a crisp in the kiln of her womb. He surveyed the group. A few other faces held smirks and grins. One woman giggled, then faked a cough, blushing scarlet. Chad noticed Lawrence noticing—and opting not to intervene. Something about the tautness of skin between his cheekbones and his eyes conveyed mirth. Lawrence looked down at his sweater—too heavy to wear outside but just right for the permafrost conditions of the hospital—and picked at tufts of wool. *Go Jonathan,* Chad thought. He slumped back in his seat, relieved to be off Susan's tender hook. Jonathan sat down again and leaned toward Chad until their shoulders touched. Lawrence looked up from his sweater and saw how they were sitting. Again, Chad got the impression that Lawrence was taking in every detail.

"Not bad for a homicidal maniac," Chad whispered out of the side of his mouth.

"I do what I can," Jonathan murmured.

Nobody came up to talk to Chad when the session ended. He sat next to Jonathan as everyone trickled away, alone or in pairs. Gracie, the nervous, fluttery one whose mother had to be a parakeet, stared the longest. She turned around, took a step in their direction, then shook her head as if answering no to a question only she could hear and hurried out of the room. Lawrence wheeled himself out last, following in Susan's contrail of aggressive smiles.

"Do the other patients think you have the plague?" Chad asked.

"I make them nervous," Jonathan said. "It's my age. I remind them of their miserable childhoods, I guess."

"Whatever it is, tell me the secret. If I had to listen to one more person talk about low self-esteem, I was going to blow chunks."

Jonathan smiled at that.

"If you stay long enough, which I hope you don't, you'll notice an alarming habit among the inmates," he said. "They start to define themselves in terms of their problems. Like Gracie. She doesn't talk about herself as a middle-school social studies teacher, which she is. She doesn't talk about the Siamese cats she breeds, or her oil painting hobby. Not anymore. All you hear out of her is depression. Medication. Self-esteem issues. Poor self-image because she doesn't have big enough breasts."

"There's always silicone," Chad said.

A thought hovered in the back of his mind as they left the room together: *The other patients are afraid of him.*

"Think I'll be able to order Chinese food?" Chad asked Valerie when the morning group ended. He caught her at the nurses' station and accepted her apologies for forgetting his coffee. A new patient had been admitted, and Valerie had been the only nurse available at the time. She rushed into the staff lounge to pour him a cup, and when she placed it in his hand, his entire body smiled. "If lunch is like breakfast . . . umm . . . I don't mean to be rude, but I could really go for some kung pao chicken."

"Once in awhile, a patient asks about that. Really, we can't go down that road. It would be a logistical mess, all that food coming in. We're swamped already. And there's a security issue."

Chad blew on the surface of his coffee and took a sip. Valerie had done the impossible, and gotten it sweet enough.

"You've got a session with Lawrence right now, don't you?" Valerie flipped through Chad's chart.

"Do I?" Chad sipped more coffee. His head throbbed less. "He didn't mention anything. But then, I all but sprinted out of the room after the group session ended."

Valerie smiled. "Not your favorite way to spend the morning?"

"Is it anyone's?"

"Some people get more out of it than others. Now and then somebody accuses us of having those groups just to get the patients out of their rooms."

Chad considered. "I guess it's better than lying in bed brooding."

Out of the corner of his eye, Chad noticed Jonathan standing nearby, close enough to be within earshot.

"Have you figured out who you can get to bring you some clothes?" Valerie asked. "If you'll give me the number, I'll make the call myself. I believe you've got to get in there for your appointment with Lawrence next." Someone began to wail, punctuating Valerie's sentence with a bizarre keening noise. "Linda," Valerie explained. "She probably just used the ladies' room. She flips out when she pees. Sometimes she holds it all day and ends up in terrible pain. It's not a nice thing to have to tell you, but you're going to be here for a few days, so you might as well know."

"Thanks, I think," Chad said. "Look, where my clothes are concerned, I'm at a loss. My roommate is away. So are my close friends. That knocks out everyone I could ask. I'd rather not see my brother."

Another nurse—a compact white woman in a beige dress and a maroon cardigan, who made Chad think *soccer mom*—excused herself and interrupted them to ask what time Valerie's shift ended. Chad surveyed the nurses' station. There were three people behind it: Valerie and the soccer mom, plus a dapper thirtysomething black man Chad had noticed earlier, dark skin in sharp contrast with his white shirt, hair in neat shoulder-length dreadlocks. Model-handsome, very regal. Chad wasn't sure whether he was a nurse, one of the psychologists, or what. He didn't have pockets full of pens and adhesive tape. Must be a doctor. He smiled and nodded at Chad, then returned to the notes he was writing in a chart.

"Well, the best I can do is tell you to think about it. If your brother lives near you and has access to your apartment, maybe get him to bring some things and drop them off. We can make sure you don't see him. Just bear in mind we can't send hospital staff around to collect things for you. But as soon as you let us know, we'll make sure the person gets called, if you're too busy to make the call yourself." Valerie smiled at him. "Why don't you check with Lawrence and see if he's ready for you?"

Because I'd rather go back to bed. Drained, Chad forced himself to smile. Two patients from the just-finished morning group session wandered up and stared blankly at Chad and the nurses.

"Come with me," Jonathan said, inserting himself between Chad and the gawkers. "I'll walk with you down to Lawrence's office."

Heads turned as they walked away. Overhead, one of the fluorescent lights flickered a strange yellow, lending the corridor a creepy funhouse quality. Jonathan's skin took on a jaundiced amber hue.

"Where did you get so much presence of mind?" Chad was speaking from the bottom of a well. He kept plunging back into the dark. "I'm so confused by all of this. It makes no sense whatsoever. One minute I'm fine and then BOOM! I'm like, where am I? What's my name? You're a lot better at being in here than I am."

An odd look crossed Jonathan's face.

"That's a strange thing to say," he said. "I don't think I want to be good at being a mental patient." He shrugged. "It's really not so different from high school."

5

Saturday Morning

Lawrence, the updated Errol Flynn, was sipping tea (Earl Grey, according to the paper tag dangling over the side of his cup) in an office that looked as if it belonged to someone else. Posters of flowers and children hung on the walls, their corners ragged from age. An avalanche of file folders on the desk partially concealed a school bus-yellow Lunchables box. More books on a low bookcase by the door: memoirs from a veritable playground of battered children, . self-help titles, self-esteem manuals, and a Dilbert comic book whose humor had probably been leached away by the volumes on the shelf next to it. Dead carnations in a plastic drinking glass. One opaque window filled the room with a queer bluish light. For a second, Chad thought he had fallen into an early Picasso painting.

"This office. It's very you," he remarked, eyeing the clutter.

"I'm only here a few hours a day, depending on the number of patients I have here," Lawrence explained, offering a dry smile. "My own office is over in Clarendon. And I make it a policy to be able to see the surface of my desk at all times."

"That's good to know."

"Why don't you have a seat? I removed the chair that's usually behind this desk. Obviously I don't need it, so this is your lucky day. Think how much more comfortable you are, for having lucked into a psychologist who uses a wheelchair." That dry smile continued.

I smell like unwashed armpits, Chad thought, tinged with embarrassment. *So much for the deodorant that works overtime.* He sat in the proffered chair, stared down at his jeans, thought for a second, then admitted he was at a loss for words.

"My disability is something I just get out of the way, right up front, as a housekeeping item. It's true we're not here to talk about

me, but I wanted to make sure you're not uncomfortable with me being in a wheelchair. You never quite know how people are going to react."

He was going somewhere with this, or using it as a way to gauge
Chad's reaction, or to gauge something.

"You're an educated guy, Chad, or at least the notes I've read say
so. And based on what I've observed, you have a pretty good head on
your shoulders—except where beer and balconies are concerned."

This brought a reluctant smile to Chad's face. *Merlot, not beer,* he
thought. *But there's nothing to gain from correcting him.* By the light of
day, it was hard to feel anything but foolish for slurping glass after
glass of the stuff and leaning so far over Jane's balcony—on Martin's
account. The moment had a stupid sort of reverse Romeo and Juliet,
Wherefore art thou quality, in retrospect.

Like a half-dozen moths taking flight, an iota of tension left Chad.

"Back to housekeeping for one second. Your curiosity about me is
normal and appropriate. And if you haven't been around people with
disabilities before, you may even feel a little embarrassed that your
legs work and mine don't. Also normal and appropriate. I'm just saying this—I'm *saying* this—to reassure you, so it won't get in the way
of the other work we have to do."

Chad smiled with just a little less reservation.

"So you just think it's really important that I—just—work on my
feelings in that area. How I really feel."

Out in the hallway on the other side of the door, someone ran by,
crashed into something, and screamed. Sounded like a car alarm going off. Same pattern of shrieks and whoops. Linda? Who else on the
ward made that much noise? More running footsteps as, Chad guessed,
staff rushed to the screamer's aid. Chad's grin melted away. *How the
hell did I end up in this place? But the more important question is, how the hell
do I get myself out?* The screams stopped as abruptly as they had started.

Lawrence nodded. The little wrinkles at the corners of his eyes
seemed to deepen, but that could have been a trick of the light. He
wheeled his chair to the left, to get a straight-on view of Chad. "Something like that," he said.

"Well, then, as long as we're getting housekeeping items out of our way, let me get something off my own chest. My deodorant has quit working. My hair feels like mucilage. Some of my more personal parts itch. I'd gladly lop off a finger or two to take a shower right now. So if I seem abnormally squirmy, it's because I'm self-conscious on my own account."

"Thank you," Lawrence said. "I'll have to admit, I can tell you were on a bender last night. I know things have been rushed for you this morning, so I'm not inclined to hold it against you. It won't go down in your permanent record."

"I'm just so relieved to hear that. I think it's just really important that details about my recent hygiene oversights not go down in my permanent record. I'd hate to be denied credit or employment because I neglected to wash my pits this morning before group."

Lawrence's smile continued, but he looked a bit harder around the eyes.

"For the sake of maintaining a positive attitude and good relations on the unit, may I suggest you be careful toward people whose grasp of English isn't quite as impressive as yours? Without naming names, certain people around here, both patients and staff, can become quite touchy if they feel they're being mocked." His gaze remained level with Chad's. "Even if they do need a few lessons in public speaking."

Chad nodded. "I believe I get your point."

"I believe you do. Now let's move on. You were unconscious last night when you were brought to the ER. Fractured wrist, some cuts and scrapes, possible concussion. And somewhat intoxicated. Your brother Martin told the EMTs and the admitting staff that you have been highly depressed and suicidal, that you have substance abuse issues, and that you might be HIV positive. That last night was an attempt to take your own life. On the basis of his statements, you were admitted for seventy-two-hour observation. We can keep you that long, but not a minute longer."

"I'm with you so far."

"And from the things you've said so far, there is a deep rift between you and Martin. He has a pattern of interfering in your life, despite the fact that you're an adult. He may be behind some of your prob-

lems. You attribute this to his discomfort with your sexual orienta-
tion. Yes?"

"I'm still tracking with you."

"Good. What we need to determine, then, is whether your own issues are severe enough to warrant commitment. This morning he filed
a motion to have you committed . . ."

"*What?*" Chad was out of his chair and on his feet instantly. His cast
collided with the arm of the chair. He slumped back in his chair,
grinding his teeth. Reality rippled around him like curtains in a breeze
as he cradled his injured wrist. "Ohfuckmywrist," he hissed. "Jesus
Fucking Christ, that hurts."

"That can't have felt good."

Chad shook his head no, still wincing. He forced himself to take a
deep breath.

"Do you need a moment?"

Chad nodded.

"Do you need a doctor?"

Chad took deep breaths and looked down at his wrist, expecting to
see pain glowing in a flame-red aura around it, melting the plaster
like candle wax. He shook his head no again.

When he'd got his breath back, he asked Lawrence to continue.

"Now, to be perfectly honest with you, Chad, we'll need to conduct
some evaluations to be sure what we're—you're—dealing with. I
won't do you a disservice by overlooking the possibility that you
aren't functioning as well as you seem. Don't get me wrong. But I've
talked to Martin on the phone, and his approach is too aggressive. So
take that as comfort. Unless there's some really deep stuff going on
with you, not readily apparent, commitment is not your primary concern right now. Getting well is."

"What on earth did I do to deserve this?" Chad's blood roared in his
ears, the same noise as a freeway at rush hour.

"Probably nothing. We will find out soon enough."

"No, I need to find out now. That psycho bastard fucker wants me
locked up to make his life less challenging—I need to know what
the hell is going on!" Chad's wrist throbbed less. His head throbbed
more. He wished he came with an on/off switch. Frustrated to the

point of apoplexy, at that moment he'd have gladly shut off the lights and ceased to exist.

"Then let's explore that. What do you think is going on?" Lawrence's face was as impassive as before.

"I can take a guess," Chad said.

"Then enlighten me. Tell me why you think he wants you committed. Are you suicidal? Does he think you are? Would he benefit from having you institutionalized?" Lawrence scratched his chin. "Not to get all touchy-feely on you, but I want to know how you're reacting to this. What you're thinking."

Chad considered the options. "Thinking? It's all I can do to think in a straight line," he admitted. Pain oscillated from his wrist, but not as fiercely as before. "If I weren't in a muddle already, now I have this to contend with. Jesus Christ, what a mess." Cradling his head in his hands, he stared at his feet and tried to think of the next logical step.

"I have to be direct with you," Lawrence said. "And I can speak for both myself and the rest of the staff. We are on your side, in the sense that you are our patient and we're going to figure out what your issues are, what kind of treatment options are best. Medication, we've started. You'll follow up with Dr. Perkins later today. Counseling, too. Which is why you're here with me, now. Commitment if it turns out you're not capable of functioning in the outside world. But that's for us to determine together. We will not support your brother's efforts if they are unjustified."

"I suppose that's good to know." Chad remained focused on breathing.

"Now what do you think is motivating Martin to file papers?"

"He has a very rigid, very limited view of who I am. You remember part of my story, I think—car wreck, lost my scholarship, had to drop out, got into partying and painkillers, tried to off myself a couple of years ago. I was also in a relationship he had a problem with, and he sabotaged it. Got the other guy in a lot of trouble, and what happened to me afterward . . ." Chad shuddered. This part could wait. "He sees me as this fucked-up little party boy with this self-destructive lifestyle, but I'm also a threat . . ."

"That could be interpreted to mean he cares about your welfare," Lawrence observed, taking advantage of a pause.

Chad shook his head. "No, there's more to it than that. When he found out about me being gay he went off the deep end. He's a macho asshole, very military, very conservative. Card-carrying member of the God 'n' Country club. He refuses to get a clue.

"Since the relationship he busted up, I haven't dated anyone seriously. I'm kind of scared to. Earlier this year I met this guy, and it was going pretty well. But I think I set it up to fail because I couldn't get free from Martin. Every now and then he asks why I'm, you know, still into the homosexual lifestyle, if I'm not getting tired of it yet. He talks about introducing me to these women he meets in bars when he goes out with his friends. And get this—he asks how my bowel movements are, because he's convinced all this passive anal sex I must be having is wearing out my sphincter. If he had access to my laundry he'd check my underwear for skidmarks. I'm not kidding.

"When I try to tell him this is just how I am—there's no lifestyle I'm trying out for the sake of being rebellious—he sort of shuts down. He doesn't want to hear it."

"Why do you suppose he's so threatened by your sexual identity?"

"I don't think he's gay, if that's what you're wondering." Chad's intestines tied themselves in knots. *Keep breathing.* "But he's my brother. It's too gross to think about." Chad shuddered at the thought.

"Has anything ever happened to suggest he might be closeted? Has he ever touched you, or have you ever seen evidence to suggest he has had relations with men?"

Chad shook his head, skin crawling as if he'd just discovered a maggot at the bottom of his cup of coffee. "Nothing at all," he lied. Or was it a lie? Chad wondered. Sometimes the difference between a lie and the truth is only a matter of perspective. *They can keep me here seventy-two hours,* he told himself. *Not a minute more.*

"What do you suppose he's up to, then?"

"For whatever reason, that I'm gay and not ashamed to show my face in public disturbs him. Profoundly. I threaten his worldview or something. I make his paradigms hurt. And then his wife is this beaten-down wreck of a woman. I know he slaps his kids around if they so much as look at him funny. He used to do it with me too, but it hasn't happened in years. I'm not that intimidated by him anymore." *Or am I?* "In any case, if he has me out of the way, then he doesn't have to change the way he thinks. Of himself, of his own sexuality perhaps, of me, of politics, of what it means to be a conservative white male in postmodern American society. I don't know. Does that make sense?"

Lawrence nodded. "It's a possible explanation. It all makes sense, based on the limited information I have."

A sharp knock on the door derailed Chad's train of thought.

"Chad? *Chad?* I know you're in there! I've got to talk to you right now!"

Martin.

Chad's heart missed two or three beats. Like finding a state trooper in one's rearview mirror when one has been cruising at ninety: the worst kind of rush.

"How the *fuck* did he get in here?" Chad hissed at Lawrence.

Lawrence, wide-eyed, shrugged and seemed unsure whether to answer the door. Chad sat quietly, trying to breathe normally, as his muscles clenched and his stomach grew heavy. He would need the rest room in a few minutes. Lawrence picked up the phone and dialed a number.

"Ann, this is Lawrence. I'm in session. OK, good. Yes, I had noticed there's someone banging on the door, thank you." He rolled his eyes at Chad. "I want you to call security and have them escort this man out of the building."

He hung up.

"Whatever Martin's purpose in coming here, interrupting our session is unacceptable."

The symptoms of a panic attack include a rapidly accelerating heartbeat, dizziness, shallow breathing, and a flushed face. One breaks into a sweat and has difficulty standing upright. Sometimes one experiences acute pangs of nausea. Vomiting is not unknown.

"Are you OK?" Lawrence asked.

Chad shook his head no.

"I want you to lean forward slowly and put your head between your knees," Lawrence instructed him in a quiet voice. "Take deep breaths. You'll be OK."

"Chad, I brought some clothes!" Martin shouted through the door. "I know you don't have any." Another sharp rap followed.

"Chad, I know you're in there and I know you don't want to talk to me, so here's the deal: I'm dropping off your duffel bag and going home. Call me when you can, bro. We need to talk. Soon."

This was followed by the sound of something dropping to the floor, landing against the door. Chad heard footsteps retreating.

"If we can hear his steps through the door, then he's practically stomping away," he remarked. "He must want to make sure we know he's leaving."

"Do you want me to open the door to see if he's gone?" Lawrence asked.

Chad nodded.

Lawrence opened the door.

No Martin. Just the overnight bag, a dark blue canvas thing embroidered with the Fahrenheit cologne logo. Martin had given it to him years ago. Chad liked the bag, although he would not have chosen it for himself. He checked it to see what Martin had packed for him. He was surprised to see things he actually wanted to wear. It would have been just like Martin to pick out nothing but the oxford shirts and preppy khakis Chad wore to work, a none-too-subtle exhortation to be normal! *Be normal!*

"Is everything in order?" Lawrence asked. "Does it look like you have everything you need?"

Chad laughed to himself.

"Underwear. Looks like he remembered everything else. Even did laundry, because I know this shirt was dirty. But he didn't include underwear. Deliberately or not. With him, you never know." He checked his bathroom kit, found everything there: toothbrush, toothpaste, deodorant, shampoo. Dental floss, even. "I'm kind of surprised he didn't jack off into the bag after he packed it," Chad remarked. *Oh shit, no. I didn't just say that.* "But then, I guess he's too smart to do anything that obviously twisted when he's delivering this stuff to a psych ward. Eyebrows would rise."

"No telltale sperm traces, then? We could probably get an ultra-violet light, if you want to be one hundred percent sure," Lawrence said.

"No sperm. But no underwear, either."

"Maybe he found skidmarks," Lawrence said.

Chad barked laughter. "I like you," he said.

6

Saturday

Chad and Jonathan sat at opposite ends of a wooden-armed pastel sofa in the TV lounge, next door to the group room with its chairs in a circle and its quotes on the wall in faded pink, orange, and green construction paper. The fabric of the sofa felt pebbly and worn, like it had been found on the sidewalk before it was brought here. Chad thought it would be a good idea to wash his hands when he stood up. The lounge smelled as if someone who didn't drink enough water had urinated in the corner. The decorating scheme suggested a gone-to-seed beach resort: pastels, framed Impressionist posters, vases of fake flowers here and there. Chad tried to open the windows, but they were fastened shut. "Can't have us lunatics climbing out and running loose among the sane, well-adjusted citizenry of our nation's capital," Jonathan had remarked. "Crazy folks on the loose—never a good thing."

"Why does this place remind you of high school?" Chad took a cautionary sniff of his left armpit. He had showered, borrowed a pair of Jonathan's underwear, which was mortifying but vaguely erotic at the same time. Jonathan wore boxers, and Chad was used to boxer briefs. Chad tried to convince himself that he looked normal but was distracted by his equipment swinging free inside his jeans. "I didn't have this much structure in high school. And we got to go home at the end of the day—lucky us."

"I grew up in boarding schools in Europe. After I came back to the United States last year, I was enrolled at one of those military schools where you have to wear a uniform and salute the upperclassmen and get tortured a lot."

"I'm trying to picture you in uniform, with buzzed hair."

"It's not a pretty picture."

"Don't sell yourself short," Chad surprised himself by saying.

"I like my hair long like this. It's going to be even longer before I'm done with it."

Chad's mouth had developed a mind of its own. "I wasn't just talking about your hair."

Jonathan's gaze became unfocused for a second. Then he offered Chad a small, sideways grin. "I'm supposed to be the bold one, here."

"I fell off the edge of the world yesterday," Chad said, showing off his plaster-encased and stitched-up arms to emphasize his point. He pointed at his cast. "This morning, Lawrence told me I have to begin writing myself new rules."

"And is it working?" Jonathan asked, the barest hint of a challenge in his voice.

"It seems to be, so far. I'm taking my progress incrementally."

"Incremental is good. One step at a time. One inch at a time, to put it another way."

Pressure mounted behind Chad's eyeballs. They wanted to shoot out of his head and dangle like wet yo-yos.

"But what you really want to hear about is my military school. Freshmen in bondage, and all that," Jonathan said. "Don't try to deny it."

Chad shrugged, helpless. *I will never be that sharp,* he thought. As a kid, he had been somewhat sharper of tongue, but Mona tended to slap him when he talked back. Martin, too, only he used his fists instead of the back of his hand. Chad's tongue dulled fast. "OK. I won't try to deny it. Tell me how the upperclassmen used the big flag that flew over the quad to tie you up, gagged you with a jockstrap, and gang-raped you for forty-eight hours straight."

"You have a bright future in the gay porn industry," Jonathan said.

"And you were about to explain why designated free time reminds you of high school." Chad dropped an unsubtle hint by checking the time. Which credit card company owned his watch (a Skagen)? Chase Manhattan, he thought. He wondered if they'd like it back next month, in lieu of a check. "We've only got an hour. Then we're off to art therapy, or whatever. Very exciting."

Jonathan made a jacking-off gesture with his right hand. "Yeah, art therapy is next. Maybe we should masturbate, save our come, and use it for paint." For an instant he looked older than Chad felt. "That would be kind of erotic, wouldn't it?"

Chad could only nod.

"You'd probably rather talk about your brother than hear about military school," Jonathan said.

"I'm still too pissed off. If I were to start talking, I'd just get angrier and go off on this incoherent rant, and you'd decide I was insane or something."

"You're in a psych unit. Sanity is not the common denominator here," Jonathan said. "But I'll talk about school. Here—and there—you have a very rigid structure imposed upon you, ostensibly for your own good. At school, all the students were given breaks throughout the day, but never for very long. I'm talking about the military school, not the boarding schools where we ran amok. Since most of us were there because we were troublemakers, we weren't left alone for more than a few minutes at a time. Some guys weren't even allowed to go to the restroom without supervision."

"Sounds charming. There you'd sit, trying to take a dump in peace, knowing some goon is outside the door, listening." Chad grimaced. In that environment, he'd swell up and die. Sludge would leak from his pores. "I don't know about you, but some things I'd rather take care of without an audience."

"Reminds me of that awful woman Linda. The one who goes around moaning about her twat full of death. Every time she uses the toilet she starts wailing. She tries to hold it and ends up bent over in pain. She wets herself, then starts screaming her lungs out and has to be sedated. Other times, she gets a muscle spasm down there and can't go. The nurses have to catheterize her. It's shocking." Jonathan stopped himself, made a face, then asked to change the subject.

"To what?"

"Like maybe to the fact that I really want to kiss you? And since there's no way of knowing how long we'll be in here—you know, when we're getting out—there's no time like the present?"

Chad stopped breathing.

Jonathan didn't wait for permission. He lunged across the sofa. Chad had a half-second to process what was about to happen, then

Jonathan's lips were pressed softly against his own. At first Chad couldn't move—he was too shocked—but after the initial surge of ohmygodness, his entire body responded. Jonathan tasted and smelled as good as he looked. The electric jolt of Jonathan's tongue in his mouth nearly caused Chad to come, then and there.

Jonathan moved so that his body was above Chad's.

"Careful with my stitches," Chad whispered, feeling helpless but sort of liking it.

I could get into being a bottom if this is what it's like, flashed through his short-circuiting mind.

"You are a hardened criminal, aren't you?" Chad asked, when their mouths separated.

Jonathan nodded, eyes still closed.

"We should quit before somebody barges in and starts screaming," Jonathan said.

Chad reluctantly let go of him. Jonathan sighed again and squirmed to get his erection pointing in a more comfortable direction.

"Suddenly I feel like a virgin," Chad said. "Maybe it's just that I've never fooled around in a psycho ward before."

"Mmmm. Losing your psycho ward virginity. We'll have to take care of that one before we get discharged."

"Absolutely." Chad wanted to rip off Jonathan's clothes, then and there, and lick every square inch of him. But the image of molesting Jonathan on this sofa softened him up. They'd get sticky for all the wrong reasons.

"Neither of us is nuts," Jonathan said. "We should break out of here, run away to South America together, and live in a hut on the beach."

"Beautiful image," Chad said. "But I don't think they're too crazy about gay boys down there. I keep reading about death squads and disappearances in Brazil."

"Venezuela, then. Ecuador. I don't care. Anywhere but here."

Chad looked out the window.

He jumped when screams emanated from the hallway, directly behind his back.

"Case in point," Jonathan said. "How is anyone supposed to get sane when they're locked up with people like that fucking psychotic cunt Linda? I'd like to toss her ass down an elevator shaft."

"I'd stand guard," Chad grinned. "I'm already sick of hearing her. She woke me up this morning. Did you see her in my room? She wanted to get a flashlight and show me her parts."

"Just what you checked in here to see, you know? Like when you're filling out your forms or talking about your goals in group. *And today I just want to take a good long look up inside Linda's pussy to see these clots of death she keeps talking about. I'll make great progress if I can just do that. I feel sure!*" Jonathan punctuated this with retching noises.

"Yeah, and if you take a good long sniff while you're down there . . ."

"Don't!" Jonathan screamed.

They settled down, looked at each other expectantly.

"How did you get in here?" Chad asked. "Does it bother you that I want to know?"

"I'll show you mine if you show me yours," Jonathan answered. "Your question is a version of that game little kids play with their privates." He winked. "I don't mind showing you. Or telling. Whatever."

"Well, I want to see those, too. But tell me why you're here first."

"We'll run out of designated free time before I'd get three paragraphs into the story," Jonathan said. He pointed to his wristwatch. A Rolex, for the love of God. Less than ten minutes left, then it would be time to go to art therapy and draw pretty pictures for the professionals. Use a black crayon and you're fixated on death. Red symbolizes blood and violence. Blue is the healing color of the sky and the ocean, unless you use dark blue, which means you're depressed. What color means you want to abscond with the underage patient and fuck for a week? Royal purple? "But I'll give you the basics if you want them."

"Fire when ready." Chad retreated to his end of the sofa, wedged a cushion behind him, sat with his back to the armrest. He crossed his legs, and, once seated in a yoga pretzel position, added, "But if you really did go out and chop somebody up, be prepared in case I scream and run."

"I'd just tackle you," Jonathan said. "I used to run track. I bet I'm faster."

This was a moment for a sofa with clean upholstery, candles on the coffee table, incense, soft ambient music pulsating in the background. Edera, Delirium, Deep Forest, one of those groups. Linda's yowls had subsided, but a low-grade hospital babble persisted. An ambulance whooped past. Chad guessed someone was being express-delivered to the ER like a bloody deep-dish pizza. Phones rang. Through the intercom came periodic announcements and pages Chad couldn't decipher.

"You know what PTSD is. Post-traumatic stress disorder." When Chad nodded, Jonathan continued. "That's basically what happened to me, but it's a little more complicated than that. I'm from Connecticut. My parents live—used to live—" his face clouded, "—outside of Hartford, about halfway to New Haven, and I was there until a couple of weeks ago."

"What happened?"

"They died," said Jonathan.

"Oh Christ, that's awful—at the same time?"

Jonathan nodded. "More or less. Not quite. But close enough. My father murdered my mother, and I saw it happen. He meant to kill me, but I got out of the house just in time. He shot at me while I was running out the door. Missed, obviously. Then shot himself."

"I don't know what to say," Chad stammered. "That's horrible. I want to say something, and I can't."

He didn't have to.

Jonathan closed the distance between them with the speed and grace of a leopard, and kissed him again. No sooner had Chad slipped his tongue into Jonathan's mouth, leaning into the kiss, himself on top of Jonathan this time, when a door opened and more screaming commenced.

They bounced off each other and flew to opposite ends of the sofa in less than a second.

Jonathan's knee connected with Chad's groin, sending red fire engines of pain blazing through him. Chad curled into a ball and moaned, eyes squeezed shut.

Gracie stood in the doorway, face dead white, hands at her cheeks like the figure in the famous Edvard Munch painting, screaming her lungs out.

She remained there for a few seconds, then turned and fled.

"Oh shit, oh fuck, oh shit, oh fuck," Chad panted, nausea a corrosive force dissolving him from the inside out.

"After we throw Linda down the elevator shaft, can we kill Gracie next?" Jonathan asked, rubbing Chad's knee.

"Absolutely." Chad fought for air. "You give her a shove while I stand guard."

Within seconds of Gracie's noisy departure, a nurse whose name Chad didn't know stalked in.

"What on earth happened?"

"That's what we'd like to know," Jonathan said. "We were sitting here on the couch talking, and she came in and started shrieking like a banshee. Are you people out of Thorazine and straitjackets, or what?"

"Jonathan, you're needed at the nurses' station. I believe someone's here to see you. Chad, how are you doing this morning?"

Chad gave her a thumbs-up sign and tried to look chipper. Conflagrations of pain still blazed in his scrotum.

The view of Jonathan walking away somewhat made up for the fact that Chad still couldn't breathe right. Chad knew that Jonathan knew he was looking at his ass as he walked out of the room. He had barely cleared the door when Gracie skittered in, crablike, and took a seat on the other end of the sofa.

"I'm a lesbian," she said. She glanced at him then turned to look the other way. Her movements were jerky. She sort of twitched when she moved, as if her joints needed oil.

"How nice for you," Chad said.

"You're in love with Jonathan." Gracie refused to meet his stare.

"I think that's overstating the case," Chad said, trying to roll with the punches. "He's smart and cute and fun to hang out with. Based on an acquaintance of less than twenty-four hours. I'm not ready to shop for a china pattern with him."

"I've been talking about this with some of the other folks around here. You know, on the unit. Patients. Look. There are some things about Jonathan you ought to know, before you get yourself too mixed up with him, because it might not be safe." Gracie still wouldn't look at him. She looked down at the floor, hair concealing her face. She sat with her toes turned inward, like a young girl waiting outside the principal's office.

Chad didn't speak.

Neither did Gracie.

They stayed there, neither one moving—him looking at her, her not looking at him—for a few moments.

Finally, Gracie cracked: "Some of us think he murdered his parents, and that's why he's really here."

"Gracie, I don't mean to be rude, but there are people on this unit who think John F. Kennedy is still the president. Can you be more specific?"

"There's more. The police have been here talking to Jonathan—a lot. The staff are doing their best to keep them away, but there's not much they can do. Like today. He's talking to the police now, because of the murders."

Chad shook his head. "That's to be expected. They *were* murdered, and he's the only survivor."

"I know, I know! But they found a gun in his bedroom!"

"So what do you recommend I do?"

"Get away from him."

"I appreciate your concern, but I don't think you have any reason to worry. The story sounds a little farfetched . . . If there was a gun, it could have been in his room for any number of reasons. Maybe one of his parents put it there. I don't know. Besides, I can't exactly hop in my car and drive off to some safer destination."

"If you still don't believe me, ask him who killed Joseph last week."

"First, you'll have to tell me who Joseph is."

"He was in the hall across from Jonathan, until he killed himself. People think Jonathan made him do it."

"You want me to believe Jonathan did? Jesus, Gracie, what do you think he is, a teenage gay Hannibal Lecter? That he can talk people into killing themselves if it suits his demented purposes?"

"No, no, nothing like that. That's not it at all. You know. It's just that Joseph was hanged by a noose made from his bedsheets. His room was across the hall from Jonathan's. We all think Jonathan did it somehow."

"Gracie, I think we need to stop talking about this. Next thing you're going to tell me is that he used telekinetic powers to levitate this Joseph person's body into the air, to slip his head through the noose."

Tears were streaming out of Gracie's eyes, yet she made no effort to wipe them away.

"You should believe me! You're in love with him, and you're going to be sorry! Don't say I didn't warn you!"

Her wailing, shrill enough to create an unpleasant pressure against Chad's eardrums, was attracting attention. Several other patients clustered in the doorway to see what was going on in the room. Again, Chad felt like a zoo animal.

"He's probably a murderer," Gracie sobbed.

"I'm glad you care, but I'm kind of mystified," Chad said. "Maybe we shouldn't talk about this anymore. I'll go get one of the nurses." Anything to get out of this room.

7

Saturday (Later)

Gracie was right about one thing, Chad noticed: a pair of plain-clothes cops (both brown-skinned, perhaps Latin—a woman in a plain beige pantsuit, and a darker man, handsome, in a blue light-weight sweater and khakis—he wore a badge clipped to his belt; hers hung on a chain around her neck) were talking to Jonathan by the bank of elevators.

With a chime, one elevator opened. The freckled security ape at the desk by the elevators nodded at them, then glared at Chad. The ape breathed through his mouth, Chad observed. Mona would have told him he'd draw flies if he didn't shut his mouth. The cops stepped into the elevator. The politely helpful expression on Jonathan's face gave way to a look of bland annoyance.

"We should talk," Jonathan said, brushing his hair out of his eyes. He stuck his hands in his pockets, and Chad fell in love with the square inch of skin visible through the tear in the left knee of Jonathan's jeans. He wanted to hold Jonathan down and kiss him through the torn denim. The broken wrist might pose certain challenges, but Chad was up for trying.

"I think you're right. I just had an interesting talk with one of the patients," Chad replied.

"And whoever it was warned you that I've been talking to cops and detectives as long as I've been here, and that I'm probably a murderer." Jonathan's voice dripped with bitterness. It streamed out of his mouth like stomach acid after one has thrown up several times and has nothing else left in one's system. "Depending on who got to you, I shot both of my parents myself, and strung up that fat fuck across the hall because he kept trying to get me to suck his cock and I didn't want to."

"Oh." Chad didn't know what else to say.

They looked at each other. Jonathan's eyes were a fierce shade of green and bloodshot red, the colors of a Christmas where nobody gets presents.

Chad could feel eyes on them. Two or three of the staff huggybears were watching. So were the patients milling around in the corridors. Out of reflex, he checked to make sure his fly was zipped. "Look, we've both got to be other places," he said, finally. "I didn't say I believed what I heard. The source didn't strike me as being the most reliable person on the unit, you know? As in, a few electroshock treatments this side of catatonia. Let's find someplace quiet after the next group, and we'll talk about this stuff."

"Sure." Jonathan looked ill.

If he's faking, Chad thought, *he's fucking good.*
Nobody is that good.

"Excuse me, Chad, may I have a word with you?" Valerie's smile hadn't wavered since Chad's arrival, but this time he noticed something in her expression or body language that suggested she didn't like what she had to tell him. More bad news waiting in the wings.

"Will I wish I had gone to my next group after I've heard this?"

"Maybe. But let's have a seat in the staff lounge and talk about it in private."

Chad followed her around the corner. Valerie unlocked the door to the lounge, checked to make sure the room was empty, then invited him in. One huge table had been formed by pushing together two wood-veneered rectangular workbenches. A coffee-stained white tablecloth almost covered the surface of the table. Mismatched chairs surrounded it. Bookshelves overflowed. Two old telephones—the kind whose earpiece holes Chad expected to find clogged with wax— on one shelf were not plugged into jacks. Chad saw a tiny rest room with a folding door.

"Normally we use an empty room for this kind of thing. But today we're pretty much stuck. The unit's full. You're getting a roommate any time now, by the way. So it's either this or the broom closet."

Chad wanted to scream *Will you get to the point?* but restrained himself.

"Things are already happening pretty fast for you, Chad. And they're about to start happening faster."

"I know this isn't going to be good news."

Valerie's smile was gone.

"It's not. I hate having to tell you this. Your brother Martin initiated commitment proceedings this morning. I believe Lawrence told you that. But there's more. And we have to discuss how you're going to deal with it."

"Don't leave me hanging," Chad said, putting his head in his hands. The broken bone in his wrist and his gashed forearms throbbed. He had swallowed enough Percoset to numb a giraffe but his arms still hurt . . . very mysterious. Had to be a bad sign. What else had he done to himself?

"Your brother filed papers this morning to do several things. He wants to have you declared incompetent, and have himself appointed as your guardian. The rationale he gave was your alleged drug abuse and suicidal behavior. I'm getting ahead of myself a little bit so just bear with me. He also wants to have you committed for at least six months. It's unlikely your insurance will cover a private placement, even if there were space available, which there isn't—not here, and not in any of the other hospitals I know of. More than likely, he's going to try to have you transferred to St. Elizabeth's."

"Holy fucking shit," said Chad.

"Normally I'm not one to swear, but in this case I have to say I'm right there with you. Now do you want the good news?"

Chad nodded.

"Couple of things. First of all, Dr. Perkins and I have had a long talk about your case. You've probably figured that out already. Based on the reports we've already shared with him, he is leaning toward giving testimony in opposition to the idea of having you committed. If things even get that far. They don't always. You should keep that in mind. Now, Dr. P is with patients all morning, but he left instructions that you call in—"she checked her watch—"twenty-five minutes. As for guardianship—well, you can talk about this more when you've got him on the phone. But the bottom line is that he also thinks it's inadvisable and unnecessary at this point."

"I think I'm relieved."

"That's good. Because there's one other thing you need to know. The time frame."

Chad's stomach did a roller-coaster plunge toward the floor.

"In most cases, the process typically takes a few weeks. That's just for one petition. A judge can usually dispose of that without much difficulty. In your case, there are three: commitment, incompetence, and guardianship. If you were a Virginia or Maryland resident, you could probably be through with it sooner, but the DC courts . . . you know." She smiled. "Multiple requests. Overcrowded dockets. There's no telling. Dr. Perkins will tell you more when he talks to you." Valerie handed Chad a folded slip of paper with a phone number in the 703 area code scribbled in purple ink. "All I can add is that you shouldn't panic. We've already seen your brother's behavior. He has been calling repeatedly. He stops just short of making threats—what he'll do if we don't pass his messages on to you, who he'll call if we don't keep him apprised of your progress, and so on. I've even taken a couple of those calls myself. He's badgering us. He's oppositional. He's inappropriate. Somebody up front made the mistake of telling him you had been assigned to Dr. Perkins. Martin started calling him too. Dr. P was not impressed. He also told me he didn't think much of the shotgun approach your brother's taking. It's just too ambitious to be convincing. You may have a whole bunch of issues of your own, but it's hard to make a case for letting your brother be your guardian. Not if this is how he behaves."

"I actually feel better, hearing that," Chad said. "Slightly."

"Well, look," Valerie said, putting a hand on his arm. "It's almost lunchtime. Join the art therapy class, since there's enough time left . . ."

Chad cut her off. "I think I need a lawyer. I'd rather not try my luck with the yellow pages. Got any suggestions?"

"Maybe that's a question you can ask Dr. Perkins when you call him."

"That's a good idea. Look, nothing against the art therapy program, but I'd rather go back to my room and spend some time alone. I have to figure out what to do about this."

Chad thought about Jonathan's military school comments. No privacy. Someone stationed by the restroom door. Structure.

Valerie nodded. "Sure," she said. "Absolutely. If there's anything we can do, you be sure to let us know."

Chad found it impossible to find anything of comfort in his room. Where the patients' lounge was spartan, the individual rooms were just stark. Institutional fake-wood furniture, narrow single beds, one big window with blinds that needed dusting. A single framed print— pastel pink desert flowers of some sort, with a pastel orange sunset in the background, another Georgia O'Keeffe knock-off—made the room look even more austere than blank walls would have. He crawled under the blankets and allowed himself to brood.

Rose never got like this. Chad admired the cold-blooded way his housemate would do whatever had to be done, whether she enjoyed it or not. She was in grad school part-time at American University, worked for a law firm on the Hill, and liked to snuffle cocaine off her girlfriends' breasts. She'd be a comfort right now, even if rooming with her had its shitty moments. She could be shrill. *Shut the fuck up and think about your situation,* she'd say while jabbing a cigarette at him like Bette Davis. *It's probably not half as bad as you're letting yourself think. There is no reason to wallow like this. It's nauseating. I feel ill. Cut it out.*

But Rose was away. Rose was in—where? Some Mediterranean country. Chad suspected she was in Greece, but her knack for finding cheap ways to get to new and more obscure (albeit photogenic and fabulous) places never ceased to amaze him. She had mentioned spending a week on Corfu with some woman she had met via the Internet. Chad thought she was going to Istanbul somewhere along the way. A quarter Turkish, Rose visited her grandmother's home country whenever she could. "Wouldn't want to live there," she claimed, "but everything's the right price. Dirt cheap." For now, Chad had the house to himself.

Jonathan would be comforting. Chad could lie with his head in Jonathan's lap. Jonathan could stroke his hair. He'd probably do it if Chad asked.

Committed. He had never seen St. Elizabeth's but imagined the place was a dungeon. Kind of like the facility in *One Flew Over the Cuckoo's Nest,* only less cheerful. Not as well-decorated. And with grumpier staff. At least here he was in a private facility with more or less functional people. Some of them were openly nuts, but the place didn't stink of piss and shit, and the only person given to random abject screaming was Linda. The idea of being locked up in St. E's made Chad's guts writhe.

Could he break out of here? St. E's, if it came to that? People had busted out of places with much more stringent security measures. Alcatraz came to mind.

Where the hell would he go? His mother wouldn't be in any position to help. Poor to begin with (white trash probably came closer to the truth, but he wasn't in the mood to be uncharitable), she had smoked for years and her lungs were on the brink of giving out. All Mona did during the day, he suspected, was watch TV and smoke. Morbid as she was, she probably kept a calendar with big black Xes to mark the days she'd lived through. Her house down in North Carolina reeked like an old ashtray. (When Chad was a little boy, Mona would vacuum the rugs and kick up at least as much ash as she exhaled.) Her hacking could be heard from the front yard. Chad supposed he could go there. But if anyone were to look, that's where they'd check first. Not that he'd be able to stand Mona for long.

He started nagging her to quit when he was ten. He brought home brochures from the American Lung Association and scattered them around the house. Since Mona couldn't be bothered to dust, Chad often had to blow a fine layer of ash off tabletops and bookshelves before he set the pamphlets down for her to find. The largest stack he left on her bedside table, under the ashtray.

"Chad, honey," Mona said one afternoon when she decided she'd had enough of his good intentions. She was getting ready for work— night shift at a diner off the highway to Morehead City. Lots of college kids from East Carolina University and North Carolina State stopped there on the way to the beach. "I want you to go gather up all those goddamn antismoking pamphlets you brung home from school, OK?"

Chad went from room to room picking up brochures. He began to doubt he wanted to do the science project he'd been planning—the one where you put the cigarette in the detergent bottle you've packed with cotton. Since beginning his antismoking campaign, Mona's nicotine intake had, if anything, doubled. Just to spite him, he suspected. She was like that.

"Now honey. I want you to listen to Mona very carefully. You are going to tear up those brochures one at a time, right here, right now, as I finish doing my hair. You are going to tear them into such little teeny pieces that they're impossible to read. If you finish before it's time for me to leave for work, I'll cook you some dinner. If not, you'll have to figure it out for yourself. OK?" She exhaled a long, slow stream of smoke in his face. Chad swallowed a sneeze. His eyes watered and stung, but he stood perfectly still. Mona didn't have Martin's temper, but she could be just as mean when you pushed her. "Because I do not want to quit smoking. It feels good. It tastes good. And I do not for a *fucking minute* believe any of that *shit* about lung cancer."

She flapped a hand at him. The ember of the cigarette between two fingers missed his nose by an inch. Chad saw streaks in the air: shocking pink fingernail polish, orange tobacco ember.

"Start shredding if you don't want peanut butter and crackers for dinner." With that, Mona applied a crimping iron to her fried yellow hair.

Outside the psych ward, the wail of a siren brought Chad back to the present. Another ambulance bringing some poor bastard to the emergency room.

"You look like you could use some company."

Chad almost jumped out of his skin.

Jonathan crept into the room and shut the door behind him. He moved quickly and quietly, catlike. Chad found Jonathan's stealth arousing. Less room in the front of his jeans, all of a sudden.

"You startled me," he said, shifting sideways to conceal the bulge.

"I was watching you for at least thirty seconds," Jonathan said. "I'm surprised you didn't notice me standing there."

"My mind's on other things. You could have taken off your clothes, stuck a bouquet of tulips up your butt, and done a cartwheel into the room—I'd never have noticed."

"Nice image. I'll keep it in mind for future reference." Jonathan took a seat next to Chad. "Do you prefer purple tulips or the white ones? Pink? No—wait—don't answer. I'll use my imagination and surprise you one of these days."

Jonathan smelled like he'd just taken a shower. Chad recognized the shower gel he used, some blue stuff that was supposed to smell like kiwifruit.

"I was eavesdropping at the nurses' station," Jonathan said. "You didn't say your brother was so ambitious—incompetence, guardianship, wanting to have you committed. That'll keep him busy. Unless you're really nuts and need that level of care. Which I doubt."

"You stuck your tongue down my throat before I got the chance to tell you what was going on," Chad responded. He smiled. "Not that I minded. Given the choice between licking your tonsils and talking about how my asshole half brother wants me put away, I'll take the tonsils."

"How bad is it?" Jonathan asked. Before Chad could open his mouth, Jonathan added, "No, wait. That didn't come out right. I mean, what are his chances? Do you think he'll succeed?"

"I don't know what to think. To be honest with you, I don't have much information yet. Valerie just told me a few minutes ago, and I've been in here trying to figure out what my options are—if I have any. She didn't think Martin's prospects were good, but I don't know if her opinion counts for much. I'm supposed to call my psychiatrist at lunchtime, to get the rest of the story."

"Jesus." Jonathan took Chad's hand.

"There's more. Martin doesn't just want to have me committed. I assume he's talking about putting me in St. E's, although I guess it's possible I could end up somewhere private. It depends on my insurance, which is a cheap HMO. I'm not even going to pretend to understand how the whole thing works. I think the system is designed to confuse people."

"Jesus," Jonathan said again, giving Chad's hand a squeeze.

"But wait," Chad said. "I'm on a roll. There's more."

"How can there be?" Jonathan asked, massaging Chad's hand. "What, do you have cancer or something?"

"No, that would be my mother. She's down in North Carolina. She's been chain-smoking pretty much all her life. Her lungs are— how do I put this?—in about the same shape as the ozone layer over Antarctica. They're like a few shreds of spongy black tissue in her rib cage. Her doctors don't give her much time."

"So am I guessing Martin wants you out of the way, so whatever you inherit, he'll get control of?"

Chad nodded. "That thought crossed my mind. But Mona barely has two cents to rub together. I don't know why Martin would bother. Besides, she and Martin are not in touch. If we were from a rich family, you know, it would be a different story. But Mom lives in this shitty little bungalow near New Bern, with a dirty cat, dirtier furniture, and a lot of overflowing ashtrays. She quit her job a few months ago and went on disability. When I said she didn't have much time, I meant it. The doctors don't know why she's still alive. As far as her house is concerned, it may be worth a little bit, but we're not talking about Bill Gates money."

Chad hated the idea of going back to New Bern for any length of time to dispose of her belongings. He could picture escalator shafts of sunlight slanting through his mother's smoke-yellowed windows, making golden rectangles on her unvacuumed carpet, while her cat yowled in the kitchen. He'd have to go down there. It would have to be done. The idea left him more depressed than ever.

"They're not in touch?"

"Case of mutual contempt."

"That seems odd." Jonathan stretched out on the bed next to Chad. "You'd expect the gay one to be the black sheep, not the dumb jock who enlisted straight out of high school."

Chad nodded. The thing was, Mona (he couldn't make himself think of their mother as Mom) never got over the fact that Martin joined the Air Force, went to Germany, and didn't stay in touch. She imagined herself to be fascinating in a hard-bitten, blue-collar way. She thought she was an outstanding mother, never mind her inability to keep the utilities on and groceries in the kitchen. Her vanity knew no limits. Martin offended her on some basic level, and she never forgave him. Explaining this to Jonathan, Chad felt presumptuous for hurting. His confusion felt like a luxury. Jonathan was an orphan. His father had killed his wife, Jonathan's mother, then committed messy suicide. Jonathan had witnessed most of it. Had nearly been killed himself. If his father had been a better shot, Jonathan wouldn't be here. His only inheritance would have been a little real estate: a few square meters of the family plot.

"But it's not like that," Jonathan said. "I hated them, and I hated going back to Connecticut between terms at school. That's the point everyone here keeps overlooking. No matter how many times I try to explain. My mother was one of those society drunks who sucks down a liter of gin at the country club, shags the tennis pro, and wrecks the car driving home afterward. I can't tell you how many mailboxes they had to replace because she kept running into them. She went through a lot of bumpers, too. Carmencita, the maid, told me that. My father was a lawyer in this huge Manhattan firm, and he left to catch the train every morning at six. When he opted to come home at night, which wasn't often, it was always after ten. He kept an apartment on the Upper East Side so he wouldn't have to travel as far. He had two or three mistresses. He never tried too hard to conceal them. As for me, you know, I barely existed. I was like one of the cars, or the taxes—something they paid other people to take care of. Killing myself has never appealed to me. Nor has running away. There's too much money involved and, anyway, when I was in England and they were here, it didn't seem as urgent that I get away from them. Across the Atlantic was far enough. I know that makes me sound like a whore, but that's the truth. I know how much they're worth. Were worth. They were horrible people, completely selfish and deranged. I even put some thought into killing them myself, or arranging for it to be done, when they brought me back here from England. I was that desperate to get away from them, but it would have been too obvious. Anyway, my father lost his mind and saved me the trouble."

"Would you think I was full of shit if I said I understand completely?" Chad asked.

"I'd wait until you were finished speaking," Jonathan said. He pinched Chad's nipple. "It could go either way."

"Well, in my case, I just got here, so I don't know if any of the staff expect me to be all wrecked with grief over Mona—I never really call her my mother; she's like this harridan who gave birth to me—but I'm not. It bothers me, and I'm sad, but you can't cry too hard for a woman who told you she got pregnant with you because a rubber broke, and gave birth to you only because she lost her abortion money gambling up in Atlantic City." Chad pinched Jonathan's nipple back. "I won't say I hated her. Hate her. She's not dead yet. That I know of. Maybe she is and nobody has called to tell the crazy boy he's an orphan."

"There's a lovely thought," Jonathan said. "Why didn't you hate her? I would have, after that."

"Maybe I did," Chad said. "Half of me hated her. And the other half of me felt sorry for her because she had to scramble so hard for· what little we had. Then another half of me resented her for giving birth to me in the first place, into my horror show of a life, and for acting pissed off that I wasn't bowing and scraping in gratitude at the favor she had done. I spent most of my childhood believing I'd have been happier as wads of nonspecific fetal tissue splattered around inside an abortionist's suction device. Having Martin for an older brother . . ." Chad shook his head, thinking back. "Proof that karma is a powerful force and I was a mass murderer in my past life."

"Maybe you were meant to be a mass murderer in this one, and you haven't found the right circumstances yet," Jonathan said.

"Could be. I'm not going to pretend I understand my life. Why do we end up with lives like this?" Chad asked, stretching out carefully and curling up next to Jonathan. The cast around his wrist made him clumsy. He didn't know how to move. They lay next to each other, shoulders and sides touching. "How did this happen? It's like it crept up on us when we weren't looking. At least when you get crabs you can think back to the people you slept with and the public toilets you sat on."

"Life is what happens while you're busy making other plans," Jonathan quoted. "You were about to finish telling me about your brother. I got off on that tangent about my parents. Sorry." Jonathan nestled against Chad.

He doesn't seem to mind the obvious tent pole in the front of my jeans, Chad thought. *I think he's doing this to me on purpose. Think? Hell, of course he's doing this on purpose. He knows I'm into him.*

There wasn't much more to tell. Martin put on a uniform and went to Germany. Wasn't heard from for a few years. Wasn't missed. It was the only break from him Chad had ever had.

"I did well in school and got the scholarship to GW. I left, too, but I at least called and visited and made an effort," Chad said. "I didn't particularly enjoy it. My mother is not a happy woman. She's hard to like. As her health has gotten worse, so has her temperament—not that you can fault her for that, but it doesn't make her easy to take. I don't have any other relatives, and neither does she."

"So what about this thing Martin is trying to do?" Jonathan asked. When Chad went rigid, he apologized for hitting a nerve.

"I'm waiting to find out. Valerie took me aside to drop the bombshell, and for now I'm in limbo. I've already decided that if I get sent to St. E's, I'm going to run off on foot. Probably won't get far, but it's worth a try. Maybe I can make it across the state line into Maryland. It's not far. It's something to shoot for."

Jonathan pulled away to turn over and look Chad in the eye. "You're being serious. Your brother wants you put away. I wasn't one hundred percent sure you were being serious."

"Yes." Chad nodded. "I am dead serious. The hearing is supposed to be in a couple of weeks. I don't know what the hell to do, other than call my psychiatrist and hope he can nuke Martin in front of the judge." A thought struck him. "Maybe he'll do something wacko in court and the judge will see which Sobran ought to be shot full of Thorazine and left in a soft-padded room. It's a straw. But I'm going to grasp it."

"Mmm. There's something else you should grasp," Jonathan said, moving closer, raising up slightly. "I can tell you want to change the subject." Then his tongue was in Chad's mouth.

Again, that electric shock, the short-circuiting feeling in his head, the *we shouldn't be doing this* thrill of necking like teenagers (well, Jonathan still was a teenager) in the hospital. The thrill and danger of getting caught.

"We've got enough time," Jonathan said. "You've still got fifteen minutes before anyone's going to start looking for you."

"I wish we didn't have to rush through this." Chad looked into Jonathan's eyes.

"When we're both out of here," Jonathan said, "we can do whatever the fuck we want, any time we feel like doing it."

"You have a point." Chad pulled Jonathan toward him as aggressively as his cast and stitched-up forearms would allow.

After a few minutes:

"Let's lose the clothes."

A nod.

"You've got a pierced navel—cool, I like it. How long have you had it?" Chad asked.

"About a year," Jonathan said. "Glad you like it. Funny—my parents never knew I'd had it done."

"I bet they hated the tattoo, though."

"I've got another one. Bet you can't guess where. Want to see it?"

Rustling. Faint squeak of the bed.

Voices out in the hallway. Gust of wind against the window. A siren.

"Oh. Fuck this cast. Ow."

Jonathan's underwear had to come off before the small Celtic knot tattooed just above the line of his pubic hair could be seen.

"I got that one in Scotland," he said.

"You've got a great dick," Chad said.

"So do you. Let's see what it tastes like."

Thoughts like out-of-focus subtitles passed through the back of Chad's mind. *Does time stand still at moments like this, or does it surge forward with an unstoppable tidal force? Does it exist at all, or do we exist in some realm outside of time, where the passage of seconds and minutes has no relevance? I want him to come in my mouth.* FIFTEEN MINUTES glowed in the same darkness, a slide-projector image in an empty classroom.

Then it was over, and Chad remembered himself and where he was and why he was here. He and Jonathan lay jammed together on the narrow bed, covered in sweat.

"We've got time to spare, I think," Chad said, when he could speak again. He smiled when he heard the gravelly edge now present in his voice. Rose called it blow job laryngitis.

He could feel Jonathan nod.

"We smell like sex, though," Jonathan said. As Chad sniffed, he couldn't disagree. He was smeared with Jonathan's sweat and spit and come. "I like it, myself, but if that brainless bitch Gracie catches a whiff, it'll send her off the edge."

"She's already off the edge," Chad said. "Should we take a shower?"

"There isn't time," Jonathan said. "It would be too obvious, after emerging from your room like this. Somebody's bound to see me. But I'd like to."

Kissing Chad's ear, Jonathan stood up and gathered the clothes they'd dropped on the floor. The silver hoop in his navel glinted. Chad curled himself across the bed just so, to kiss the wispy trail of hair connecting Jonathan's navel with his crotch.

"Say I don't get locked up, just for the sake of argument," Chad said. "Is it nuts to want to know where you're going once you get out of here?"

"Assuming I do get out of here," Jonathan said. "There's nobody trying to keep me behind locked doors, but I'm not eighteen yet."

Chad's blood cooled.

"I saw that," Jonathan said, with an obscure sideways smile.

"Sorry," Chad said. "I sort of suspected you weren't eighteen but was trying not to think about it. Why here? Why this unit?"

"The others were full. Just as well. Could you imagine me on a teenagers' ward? I'd eat them alive. Look, don't freak out. Three weeks and I'm legal. My lawyer's going for a court order to have me emancipated immediately, so I can handle my parents' estate. Or at least get access to it."

"Messy," Chad said.

"No matter how you look at it, it's a mess," Jonathan replied. "Especially with the cops involved. But to answer your question, I don't know where the fuck I'm going when I get out of here. I was going to take off a year before dealing with college. Sooner or later I have to get my GED. With everything that happened, finishing high school wasn't possible. So I had thought I might do that, and take time to travel. But I have nothing planned. Can't say whether all that freedom is a good thing." He shrugged, then stepped into his underwear and jeans, hopping on one foot when he got off-balance. With baggy pants on, his waist and hips seemed even narrower than when he was nude.

"You should get out of here," Chad told him. "I'm going to look like Quasimodo trying to get dressed while I'm all busted up. Might be scary. Besides, we shouldn't leave the room at the same time."

"And you have to make a phone call."

Chad nodded yes. "It's going to be interesting."

"The more things change, the more things stay the same." Jonathan slipped on his T-shirt and left the room, closing the door behind him. Chad wondered what the hell he meant.

He's seventeen, Chad thought. *What the fuck am I doing?*

Homosexual statutory rape, replied a more educated version of Martin's voice. *You just committed homosexual statutory rape in the psych ward of GW Hospital, and you better believe I'm going to use it against you.*

But it wasn't rape. I didn't rape him. He instigated it. Fresh nausea bloomed in Chad's belly. Keeping this from Martin probably wouldn't be too difficult. Would it?

Tell that to the judge, fagboy.

8

Saturday Afternoon Through Sunday Night

"Tell me you're going to nuke my brother in court," Chad said, once he and Dr. Perkins had gotten past the preliminaries.

I sound like a desperate asshole, he thought. Then: *He's a shrink. He's used to people sounding like desperate assholes, under circumstances like these.*

"I can tell you're anxious, and you have good reason for concern," said the psychiatrist. Chad tried to recall where he had heard this voice. The richness of tone, a twinge of a Southern accent—these struck a familiar chord. Chad thought Dr. Perkins was black, but he couldn't be sure. Was he the gorgeous dreadlocked man Chad had seen in the hospital? That would make sense. "Valerie telling you you're facing this competency hearing, that's enough to ruin anybody's day. I haven't met you in person yet, so I can't say with certainty whether I think commitment is appropriate. But your brother's actions are enough to make me question what *is* appropriate. And I will tell the judge that. It's clear there's something going on. I don't think *nuke* is the right word for what I'm going to do to your brother, but I do have questions for him. I don't think you should give yourself an ulcer."

Chad felt a milliliter of tension ebb away. He scratched at the skin beneath the rim of his cast.

"Worrying is what I do best," he said. "I make a pretty wicked mushroom omelet, but that's nothing compared to the talent I have for worrying."

"Then deprive me of the pleasure," said Dr. Perkins. "And save the mushroom omelet for a special occasion. For now, we know we're going to have a run-of-the-mill court proceeding in a few weeks. Want my professional opinion? Try not to worry. Your brother is trying too hard, and I'd bet my MD the judge will see through it."

"Have you actually talked to Martin?"

"Briefly. Just long enough to say I'm not authorized to share information about you in the absence of a signed release form. That may be the reason he has taken this approach, to force the issue. I've talked to you less than five minutes and I don't have to ask whether you'd even consider . . ."

"I'm not going to sign a release form," Chad interrupted.

"Sounds like you've made up your mind." They laughed. "I can't say much about your brother, not having met and evaluated him, but he did seem eager to bypass some important procedures that exist to protect people in your situation. That is not a good sign. That's about it for my perception of him."

"You knew I wanted to hear that," Chad said. "Thank you."

"Quite welcome. Now, here is what will happen at this hearing. At this point, you're only in the hospital for seventy-two hours. You haven't displayed suicidal ideation. You are clear on what's real and what isn't, so we've been able to rule out psychosis, schizophrenia, the more debilitating disorders. Now, there's going to be testimony involved. Is there anyone who can testify that you are basically of sound mind? That you hold down a job, pay your bills, and aren't going to take a shotgun to the mall when you're having a bad day?"

"Probably my counselor here would be able to say something," Chad stammered. "Lawrence. Whatever my friends said probably wouldn't count for much, right?"

"Unfortunately, you're right. The judge wants to hear professional adults from the health care industry say that you're fairly well adjusted, given the circumstances, and that you're capable of making rational decisions. I doubt your friends know the lingo, no disrespect meant."

Chad shook his head as if Dr. Perkins were looking at him instead of listening on the phone. He remembered to say, "None taken," after an awkward few seconds had elapsed.

I have to get out of here, he thought. Picture of himself on a plane. He had never given much thought to the inherent consolation of liftoff in years. Not since leaving for his year in Spain. The phrase had popped into his mind on the Atlanta-to-Madrid leg of the flight. *The inherent consolation of liftoff.*

Dr. Perkins had said something. Chad became aware of the psychiatrist's voice through mental movies of himself on a lounge chair with a glass of wine, staring out over the Mediterranean. Sunset, the sky pink and saffron, idle clouds, crisp breeze off the sea raising goose bumps faster than the wine could dispatch them. In the background, Dr. Perkins sounded like Charlie Brown's teacher. "Bwa bwa bwa, bwabwa, bwa."

"I'm sorry? Somebody walked by and distracted me for a minute," Chad lied. "What were you just saying?"

"I was just summing up what you should expect. One final point: if we release you at the end of the seventy-two-hour observation period, it'll be very hard for your brother to make a case for commitment. If the professionals here don't think you need that level of care, he's not likely to convince a judge just by pointing out that you've gone through some rough patches. I know it'll be tough to keep from worrying. As full as the court dockets tend to be, the hearing won't come around for at least two and a half weeks. Your brother's attorney will try to make you sound like John Hinckley Jr., with a different obsession. But I'm digressing. I'll be making rounds this afternoon, and I'll want to see you around five. Think you can be there?"

"Let me check my schedule. Damn. I'm really swamped, you know, but I'll do my best to work you in," Chad said, thinking, *Easier said than done.*

"You'll be fine," Dr. Perkins assured him.

Of course Chad wasn't fine. He wanted to go home. Home was a nebulous concept. The increasingly rare times Chad talked to Mona, she had a disturbing propensity to refer to her own house, and by extension the entire state of North Carolina, as home. Chad disagreed with her but didn't care enough about the issue to argue the point. For now, home was the townhouse in the Eastern Market section of DC, which Rose had bought via a first-time homebuyer's program. Chad had a comfortable bedroom and bathroom to himself. They were never clean, but they were his. Both doors locked.

The afternoon dragged by. Chad had trouble deciding which he liked less—the interviews or the activities. The interviews were the mental equivalent of a body cavity search. If he had to be penetrated, he'd have preferred a well-oiled cock to all these questions. Repeating his entire history for an army of shrinks meant remembering the whole mess. It left him feeling worse than he had at the outset. Did he suspect growing up fatherless, with a single mother who could barely make ends meet, had made things difficult? Had he come to terms with his mother's impending death? Had Martin? Were they close, growing up? *Only while he was beating the crap out of me. You can't get much closer than that.*

As for the activities, they recalled the parts of grade school Chad could have done without—the ones that involved playing well with others. All he wanted was to go sit alone under a tree with a book. The presence of so many helpful, concerned people made Chad want to take up habits like smoking unfiltered cigarettes, driving at night without his headlights on, and setting small children on fire.

"We're going to work on positive visualizations. OK?" Susan chirped to one group.

Jonathan kept this activity from being too deathsome: "Like picturing myself at a brown café in Amsterdam smoking a bowl and drinking coffee with my boyfriend, for example?"

Susan's smile appeared strained around the edges. If her cheeks cracked like the floor of Death Valley, would Linda start screaming? Gracie?

"I'm not sure we need to be picturing ourselves doing drugs," Susan warbled. Her eyes really were close together. Very Cubist. "It's just not the healthiest option."

"*You* don't have to picture yourself doing drugs," Chad said. "I think Jonathan just meant that he himself saw it as a positive image."

Susan frowned, prettily. Low giggles and snorts erupted from other members of the group. Gracie's face had gone very red. Linda was nowhere to be seen. Perhaps she had used the bathroom this morning and was in bed recovering from the shock.

"I . . ." Susan's mouth opened and closed. Chad spied a chip of pink lipstick on a front tooth. "I think we need to focus on more positive images than the drug dens of Amsterdam, Jonathan. The purpose of this technique is to put yourself into a safe space. Now really. Can you tell me where you feel safe?"

"Tiffany's," Jonathan said. "Nothing bad can ever happen to you when you're at Tiffany's."

"I'm afraid this is all going to go down in my permanent record," Chad said, six hours later, wrapped around Jonathan.

Dr. Perkins did, in fact, turn out to be the handsome black doctor with the long braided hair. A magnetic field surrounded him. When you sat across the room from him, you couldn't help turning your head to look. A pornographic fantasy or two flitted through Chad's mind during their session, and he suspected Dr. Perkins knew what effect he was having and used it to his advantage.

Chad spent much of the day being interviewed, coughing up secrets like bits of lung. Positive imagery was supposed to make him feel all warm, fuzzy, and safe. The interviews would reveal details the various shrinks, busybodies, and huggybears could use to turn him back into a normal person with a normal life. Chad could almost see the house in the suburbs. His stomach clenched. What crap. Having Jonathan curled up in bed with him, naked, sticky—this made him feel warmer and fuzzier than anything else had recently. Safe? Like home, *safe* was a slippery term. With Martin running loose and Mona ten minutes from expiring, the idea of safety seemed abstract and irrelevant.

"Dr. Perkins didn't think much of our tag-team approach to group this afternoon. I assume one of the nurses told him."

Jonathan smelled faintly of antiseptic hand soap. Chad wondered what he had washed with it. Outside, the roar of an arriving helicopter.

"My doctor didn't, either," Jonathan said. "I wouldn't be surprised if they tell us we're not good for each other. You know, like, not good influences or something."

Chad considered. "I'd be surprised if they go that far. It's not like we're not adults, you know."

"Speak for yourself. I'm seventeen, remember?"

"Don't remind me."

"That you just committed statutory rape again?" Jonathan gripped Chad's cock for effect.

"No. That I'm enjoying it so much."

Before dinner, one of the evening-shift nurses took Chad aside to tell him who his new roommate was: Jonathan.

"How the hell did you pull that off?" Chad asked Jonathan a bit later, as they ate slabs of mystery meat, gravelly rice, and a flaccid salad. No red wine, though. That would have made the meal almost tolerable. Red wine, consumed in sufficient amounts, can make anything almost tolerable.

"I asked nicely. I said you're one of the only patients close to my own age, and nobody would benefit if they assigned either of us some flaming homophobe. And I was careful to ask somebody too new here to be threatened by me yet."

"You are the devil," Chad said.

Jonathan nodded. "I know."

Visiting hours on the psycho ward were something like Halloween in reverse, Chad thought. Well-dressed normal people came and knocked on doors, and the scary creatures answered, hoping for handouts. Chad expected Martin to show up sooner or later, but not his wife, Cindy.

Chad and Jonathan were finishing dinner.

"The rice has a fine consistency, don't you think?" Jonathan asked Gracie. He chewed another spoonful with the exaggerated jaw action of a cow.

Gracie's chin trembled.

"I'd call it al dente," Chad offered. "It's not quite crunchy, but there's a solid heft to it when you bite down. You know you're not eating jook."

"I don't know what jook is," the young guy with low self-esteem said. Chad couldn't remember his name. "I'm not afraid to admit that."

"I think you're both being snobs," Gracie said. "You think you're better than everyone else here."

"Leave the boys alone, Gracie," Marcus spoke up.

Chad and Jonathan exchanged a surprised look and stopped eating.

Marcus continued. "If making fun of the food helps them pass the time here, let them do it. I think they're funny. Chad is right—the food's shit; we all know it's shit—so why pretend otherwise?"

"I still don't know what jook is," Low Self-Esteem Boy said. "I want someone to tell me what it is."

"Rice mush," Chad said. "Boil rice long enough and it sort of disintegrates. Asians eat it for breakfast." He inspected a spoonful of the stuff, put it down again.

"Ew," Gracie said.

"How about this?" Jonathan speared the slab of breaded meat.

"I think it's supposed to be a chicken cutlet," Marcus said, getting in on the fun.

"I know what a cutlet is," said Low Self-Esteem Boy.

"Tastiest vinyl I've ever eaten," Chad said. "Whoever engineered the juices ought to win the Nobel Prize for chemistry."

"Maybe it used to be a patient," Marcus said.

"Really does taste lifelike, doesn't it?" Jonathan asked, cutting the meat into tiny cubes. "Anyone want to bet I'll find veins when I cut it?"

"You are like so gross!" Gracie pushed her chair away from the table.

Marcus and Low Self-Esteem Boy watched her walk away. Chad and Jonathan looked into each other's eyes. Chad's heart skipped a beat.

But I don't want to enjoy myself here!

"You've got a visitor, Chad," the evening-shift nurse—a chipper girl just out of school, not as pert as Susan but too fresh and apple-cheeked for Chad's nerves—announced.

"Do I want to know who it is?" he asked nobody in particular.

"Knowing what I do of your family," Jonathan said, "I doubt it. I'm going out for coffee. Call me on my mobile when you're done. You can join me there, and we'll go out for some real dinner and maybe a late movie."

"Translated," Chad said, standing up, "that means you're going back to the room to read."

"I love how perceptive you are," Jonathan said.

Chad expected Martin and got Cindy. He wanted to like Cindy but couldn't. Failing that, he wanted to dislike her. Couldn't do that, either.

When Martin met her, she epitomized Chad's image of the rural Southern military girlfriend: bottle-blonde hair sprayed up into windswept wings too solid to be mussed by any movement of air weaker than a hurricane, narrow face dwarfed by her coiffure, midi tops, and tight jeans. She drove a black Trans Am. The one time Chad rode in it, he wouldn't look too closely at the backseat. Dried come is easy to spot on dirty vinyl. If Chad was sitting on crusts of his brother's semen he didn't want to know.

Martin married Cindy when she told him she was pregnant. Out went the sprayed-on jeans. She let her hair go back to its natural brown and surprised Chad by looking rather nice after the transformation. He still thought Cindy wasn't the sharpest knife in the drawer, but the sight of her didn't hurt his eyes like fingernails shrieking across a blackboard hurt his ears.

Brittany, their oldest child, was on Ritalin almost from the moment she left the womb. Alexander, their second, showed signs of being a bright, well-behaved boy. Martin would beat that out of him soon enough.

Cindy, over time, had grown into more matronly proportions. She wore black slacks and jeans because she thought they made her ass look slimmer (he had overheard her saying so on the phone once), and she liked sweatshirts and T-shirts with sequins. Red and green at Christmas. Orange jack-o'-lanterns at Halloween. The overall effect was something like an ice cream cone: wide hips, big chest, narrow tapering little legs that came to a point in, today, confectionary pink shoes.

What she and Martin talked about, Chad couldn't begin to guess. Martin was into beer with his buddies, football games, and stalking Chad. Cindy liked Bible school, card games with the other preschool moms, and the Dixie Chicks. She had traded in her Trans Am for a used minivan and affixed a "Mom's Taxi" sticker to the rear window. All of which was fine, but Chad couldn't get his mind around the idea of his satanic bastard brother driving kids to Little League and changing shitty diapers.

Cindy thought you couldn't be gay if you didn't call everyone girlfriend, work as a hairdresser, own a poodle, and die of AIDS or a bashing before the age of forty. Chad perplexed her almost as much as he perplexed Martin. Now and then she'd cock her head to one side, squinch her eyebrows together, and ask why he didn't have a girlfriend yet. "Why not? I mean, you're not really gay like those other guys you see on the talk shows. You're plenty cute, and lots of girls would . . ."

"Nice of you to drop by," Chad told her, accepting a bouquet of white and dyed-blue carnations, shaking her hand instead of hugging her.

In the back of his mind: *You left Martin alone with the kids?*

"Your brother told me you had . . . you know. That you were here. I thought I should stop by. See how you're doing."

"Here I am." Chad made a sweeping gesture. "Normally when I fall off balconies I recover someplace a little nicer, like the Ritz-Carlton. But they were full, and I couldn't get a room at the Mayflower either." Cindy giggled. "Shall I show you to my suite?"

Chad sensed an ulterior motive. Spying for Martin? He led her to his room, asked Jonathan if he'd excuse them for a minute, and hoped Cindy wouldn't notice their body language. Jonathan said he'd be in the lounge watching FOX programming with the rest of the inmates. But he took his book (Sartre's *Nausea*, untranslated), Chad noticed.

"Hell is other people," Jonathan quoted, closing the door behind him.

"He seems real nice," Cindy said. "Look, Chad. Your brother and I are just real concerned about you." Cindy seated herself in the armchair by Chad's bed. She crossed her legs and looked prim.

"My brother has filed papers to have me declared incompetent, Cindy. He's trying to have me committed, with himself appointed as my guardian. If those aren't acts of genuine, heartfelt concern for my welfare, I can't imagine what is." Chad didn't want to be spiteful—he did believe Cindy meant well in her own way, unlike Martin—but he wanted to know what the hell she was up to. Martin's marriage baffled him. Cindy baffled him. Chad assumed Martin hit her. From the way the kids cowered, Chad assumed Martin hit them, too. Especially Alexander, who would never grow up to be a big dumb stud like his dad. On the other hand, Cindy always presented a united front where Martin was concerned. Chad had never caught so much as an exasperated sidelong glare directed at his brother. Best to proceed with care. "Do you think it's too much to ask for him to leave me the hell alone? If he spent less time interfering in my life, he'd have more time for you and the family. And I'd have fewer problems."

The look on Cindy's face cooled Chad's blood: a frigid second of unblinking eye contact, the suggestion of more intelligence than he'd ever credited her with having. Then Cindy's usual bovine smile returned. Her eyes went unfocused. She looked around the room, smiled at the ersatz O'Keeffe print on the wall, smiled wider at Chad.

He twisted the ring on his thumb, shocked himself by breaking into a sweat.

Maybe Cindy supports Martin's interference because it keeps him out of her hair and away from the kids. Maybe she's here spying not on his account, but for herself.

Which scenario was worse?

"Oh, I definitely think Martin has your best interests at heart," Cindy said. "I mean, your finances are in such bad shape, you know, and just last night we were talking about you filing for bankruptcy. Ever since that car wreck, you just haven't been able to get it together, and, you know, we have our doubts. Don't you think you'd be better off with somebody looking out for you? Making the hard decisions?"

"It was so nice of you to stop by," Chad said. He feared what else might come out of his mouth. The fewer words, the better. He tried to look bleary. "I think I had better get some sleep. The new meds I'm taking really knock me out."

"Oh!" Cindy stood, and laughed in a self-deprecating way Chad knew she used when she wanted to one-up someone. "I wouldn't want to wear out my welcome!"

She pulled him toward her in an awkward, unreciprocated hug, gave him a smeary kiss on the cheek, and flounced out of the room. *Cindy isn't finished with me any more than Martin is,* Chad thought.

Jonathan crept out of Chad's bed to keep from being discovered when the nurses made their late-night check. Chad hated for him to leave, even though he was only eight feet away.

The nurses made rounds in the morning, waking everyone up, dispensing those meds meant to be taken on an empty stomach.

At breakfast, Gracie stared at Chad without blinking for longer than he would have thought possible. Jonathan discreetly put a chunk of banana down the back of her dress and, again, got away with it. Gracie squirmed and fidgeted as the mushy hunk of fruit slid farther and farther down. Chad imagined it being sucked into her butt with a milky yellow slurp. He could not finish his cornflakes.

Group.

Long talk with Dr. Perkins, followed by another one with Lawrence. Chad fixed on the idea of his release throwing a wrench into Martin's legal machinations, but Dr. Perkins and Lawrence wouldn't give away anything concrete. They made positive, encouraging noises, but they wouldn't say whether they were inclined to let him go when his seventy-two hours were up. Chad wanted to hope for the best but had forgotten how.

The torpor of the routine in the hospital made Chad crave a nap. He had a terrible sense of time in the outside world spinning by dangerously fast. His mother's health was not going to get any better, but if she died he didn't want to be in the loony bin when it happened. Martin wasn't going to oblige him by diving in front of a Metro train and grabbing the electrified third rail. Chad felt he'd have at least a twinge of control anywhere other than here.

"Look at this as a vacation," Susan said. "Not everyone gets to just check out for a few days."

"Then bring me a margarita," Chad snapped.

"I'm starting to bite people's heads off," Chad told Lawrence. "I haven't been like this before."

"It's going down on your permanent record," Lawrence responded. He sipped from his omnipresent cup of Earl Grey. "Crap, it's still too hot to drink." He looked annoyed. The moment passed. "If anything, you're progressing. I don't think you'd have the urge if you didn't feel safe. Don't worry about it. If somebody's working your last nerve, say so. It's healthy."

"I'll try to keep that in mind."

Night had fallen.

Cindy called but did not show up. "Just wanted to check in on you, honey. Me and Martin are just so concerned." Not a word from Martin. Ominous.

Chad and Jonathan sat next to each other at the back of the room during the least cloying group activity they'd had yet: a video. And not even a too-smarmy-for-words one. Someone with a few brain cells firing had rented an Albert Brooks movie, *The Muse*. Jonathan said he had seen it on a plane from somewhere to somewhere, but he had taken several long trips around the same time and tended to get his in-flight movies mixed up. Chad had meant to see it before its theatrical run ended, but time slipped away.

"Is it an accomplishment to be able to say I got through the day and nothing happened?"

"I'd say that's an accomplishment. You have more to be happy about than I do. The cops want to talk to me again tomorrow, and my lawyer said that the judge is waffling on whether to emancipate me. What a stupid fuck. I mean, my parents are dead, they have no close family, and I'm going to turn eighteen in a few weeks. The only reason I'm in here is because there were no beds in any of the local adolescent facilities. And it's just as well. I fucking hate my peer group." He rubbed the tattoo on the web between his thumb and forefinger with the other thumb. "What on earth does that asshole think he would accomplish by denying me emancipation? I'd write him a letter pointing that out, as politely as possible, but Harry, my lawyer, thinks that's inadvisable."

"Could the judge interfere with you handling the estate?"

Gracie was watching them. Linda, quiet for once, was enthralled in the movie. She was rocking and muttering in some language or other, but no screams about her vaginal death issues had been heard all afternoon. The other people in the group seemed rapt, as well, at least as much as a group of highly medicated mental patients in uncomfortable chairs could be.

"I don't think so. There are trusts and things, but for some bizarre reason it looks like once I'm out of there it won't be a problem getting my hands on them."

"At least you don't have to worry about looking for a job and making ends meet, you know?"

"That's true. But having too many options is just as bad. I mean, there's no motivation to do anything. I can design Web pages. I'm good with graphics. I can write nice clean code. So there's no problem finding work, not that I need to. It's more like I want to get out of here and take a long hot shower, to wash the smell of this place off myself. I want to go as far away from here as planes can fly me. And the fucking cops. Do not even get me started on the fucking cops."

"OK. I won't get you started on the fucking cops. Why don't we hold Gracie down and gouge her eyes out with plastic spoons from our next meal, though? She keeps staring."

Jonathan nestled closer to Chad. "I love the way you think."

Gracie seemed to sense she was being talked about. Her eyes, already bulbous, grew wider. Goldfishlike. She sprang up and yelled, while pointing a trembly finger: "I really have issues with the fact that you two are not respecting others with your public displays of affection! I have issues with that! I am not comfortable seeing you all over each other! You're practically fisting each other back there!"

Chad's testicles shriveled instantly.

Even Jonathan gasped.

"How on earth does she know what fisting is?" Chad whispered in Jonathan's ear.

"I'm not even sure I do, but from the sound of it I don't think I want to."

Staff swooped in like the Luftwaffe.

Linda emitted a series of air-raid whoops. She tore at the sides of her hair, leapt out of her seat, and ran smack into the nearest wall, where she commenced to beat her head against it.

Marcus, Chad's favorite person on the unit (other than Jonathan), laughed quietly to himself. His face betrayed an equal mixture of disgust and amusement. *At least there's one other sane one,* Chad thought. *He has to be the only other one here besides us who isn't totally fucked in the head. On the other hand, he's probably an ax murderer.*

There was a second of perfect crystal lucidity, and then four staff baboons were in the room. Assertively, calmly, firmly, they spouted directions. They took over. Silence fell like a truckload of fish.

Chad and Jonathan exchanged a look.

"Nobody will notice if we slip out," Chad whispered.

Jonathan nodded.

Taking advantage of their place at the back of the room, they moved quietly around the edges of the mêlée and crept out the door.

In the hall, just when Chad thought they were safe—

"Them!" Gracie screamed, pointing a finger.

"Us?" Jonathan asked, wondering how she had gotten free.

"Public display of affection! It's against the rules on the unit!"

A nurse whose name Chad didn't know made a face like she was about to cluck her tongue. "Have you two boys been getting overly friendly?"

"We were sitting next to each other," Jonathan said. "This is not a big deal."

"I don't understand what the problem is," Chad added. He needed to say something, however lame he felt. "I think this has been blown out of proportion. You'd think we had all our clothes off back there, from the way she started screaming."

"You might as well have!" Gracie wailed.

She had this very direct way of staring, Chad noticed. Almost as if she were hungry.

His broken places hurt.

"Gracie, let's go back to your room. You need some time to cool out before you escalate. Is it time for your meds?"

Gracie permitted herself to be led away, but she did not take her eyes off Chad.

"What the fuck was *that?*" Chad asked once he and Jonathan were alone.

"Jealousy. She has a crush on you."

"Ugh!" The idea chilled him. "She told me she's a lesbian. Whatever gave you that idea?"

"Chad, I may be seventeen, but I've been around. OK? The woman has a crush on you. She wants you to tongue her dewy folds."

"I think that image is going to give me nightmares for the rest of my life."

"What do you think the odds are we won't be disturbed for the rest of the night?" Jonathan asked. "I want to take off all your clothes and lick you everywhere."

"I don't know what the odds are." Chad leaned back against the pillows, with a shrug. "Whatever they are, I guess we'll have to play them."

– 9 –

Sunday Night Through Monday Evening

Chad woke up sometime in the middle of the night, rolled over, and found a warm empty place next to him instead of Jonathan. He sat up, knuckled his eyes to get them working, and looked around. He saw the outline of Jonathan standing very still by the window, dark against dark.

"Come back to bed," Chad croaked, his throat sore. He had gone down on Jonathan with a bit too much enthusiasm.

"I can't sleep," Jonathan said, also raspy—for the same reason, Chad noted with a twinge of boorish pride.

"Come back to bed anyway."

"In a minute. Go back to sleep. Don't worry—I'm not going anywhere."

Later, Chad woke up again, somehow aware Jonathan had departed once more. The bed was still warm in the area where Jonathan had lain until . . . when? How many minutes ago? Chad reached out with a palm and stroked the rumpled sheets. He breathed deeply, trying to smell traces of Jonathan, but succeeded in bringing up wafts from his own armpits. He still smelled like their exertions.

Must have gone to the bathroom.

He fell asleep again.

Valerie woke Chad up with a smile, a glass of orange juice, and a little paper cup of pills.

"Good morning, sunshine!" she beamed, a few megawatts below Susan's supernova output but brighter than Chad could handle without immediate coffee in large doses.

Chad started to ask where Jonathan was, but he caught himself before he got the question out. The staff had to know they were an item, had to have seen this kind of thing before, but Chad didn't want to be conspicuous. Dazed, he accepted the juice and the pills. At breakfast, he would have access to coffee. He could picture it, the cup of coffee steaming when he poured it from its thermos. Too hot to drink, but Chad would know it was there. The smell alone would give him a burst of energy.

"This isn't fresh-squeezed," he said when he washed the medication down with treacly orange juice.

"Use your positive imagery and make yourself believe it is," Valerie replied, watching him to be sure he had swallowed the pills. Procedure.

"I'd rather make myself believe I'm drinking it in Barcelona."

"Honey, if it gets you through the day, you visualize yourself flying through space like Superman," Valerie ribbed him.

"Now there's an image," Chad said, sitting up, uncomfortably aware he was naked under the sheets. Valerie must have seen any number of naked patients, but he didn't want to add his name to the list. "Fresh-squeezed OJ and strong coffee first thing in the morning. At one of the cafés along the Rambla."

"The sooner you get up, the sooner you can have that cup of coffee," Valerie prompted him. "It's better than usual today."

"Honest? Cross your heart, hope to die, stick a rectal thermometer in your eye?"

"Ew!" Valerie crossed her heart with an index finger. "You have a nasty mind."

"It's worse when I haven't had coffee."

"I'll keep that in mind." Valerie waved at him and left the room. "Now put your clothes on and go get some breakfast, before you drive us all up the wall."

Morning group began with a disaster.

Susan looked uncharacteristically somber. Lawrence's skin was waxy white, as if he had not slept in two or three days.

Once everyone had filtered in, Susan announced she had bad news.

"I just need to let you all know that there has been another death on the unit. We're doing everything we can right now to get through this together. I just don't know how it could have happened, or what was going on . . ."

She went on in circles a few more sentences before Jonathan interrupted her to ask who had died.

"Just cut to the chase," he said.

"Linda," Lawrence said. "She fell down the elevator shaft sometime during the night. We're trying to find out how it happened."

"Jonathan pushed her!" Gracie screamed, lurching forward, breaking the stunned silence in the room.

"I wish I really were clever enough to have pulled *that* off," Jonathan said. "Because if I were, then I'd have already plotted your death, too, and I'd get rid of you next." He smiled at her with all the parts of his face except his eyes.

Chad wanted to applaud.

Gracie drew up in her seat, turned sideways, and pulled her legs up toward her chest. She wrapped her arms around her knees in an upright fetal position. The two women sitting next to her made reassuring noises and stroked her hair.

"You seem to have some kind of fixation on Jonathan and me," Chad said. "And this would be a good time to get over it. I am not interested in you. I'm gay. Deal with it."

Group members watched this interchange with the dumbstruck expression of cattle whose rectums have just been zapped by electric prods.

Gracie began to snuffle.

Two or three others chuckled. Someone was crying. Nobody had liked Linda much—her ongoing, inarticulate rendition of the *Vagina Monologues* had been driving everyone crazier, or so it seemed to Chad— but a death was a death, and this one came close on the heels of another death. As Chad scanned the room, he noticed an unusual number of stares in his and Jonathan's direction. Suspicion and dark thoughts lingered at the back of fuzzy minds. Eyes were quickly averted when caught looking.

Christ, they think he did it. Or we both did.

But then, how do I know he didn't?

He looked at Jonathan, who was playing with his cuticles. There was something inexplicably charming about the tattoo on the web between his thumb and forefinger. It should have looked trashy (growing up in eastern North Carolina, Chad knew from trailer trash) but didn't.

I hope he didn't do it, Chad thought. *I don't think I like the idea of him throwing Linda into the elevator shaft while his dick was still wet with my saliva.*

Martin called three times that morning, always while Chad was in sessions the staff wouldn't pull him out of. Martin never left messages more detailed than, *Call me back,* which Chad refused to do. Throwing away the slips of paper staff handed him turned into an odd ritual for Chad. He and the nurses would exchange knowing smiles. He'd crumple the note. Into the trash it would go. Chad's aim improved after the first dozen.

"He sounds really concerned," Greta, the nurse who handed over the second message, said.

"Stalkers always do."

"You think I did it?" Jonathan asked Chad at lunch.

Chad swallowed a spoonful of watered-down wonton soup and wished for cilantro, pepper, and a dollop of soy sauce. And, as long as he was making wishes, a new life, a better wardrobe, no debt, no troublesome relatives, and a Maserati.

"It crossed my mind."

"It has crossed the mind of everyone else here, I think. They're all looking at me like I was Jeffrey Dahmer with a shred of some boy's foreskin between my two front teeth."

Chad eyed his detumescent spring roll. "Hospital cafeterias should not attempt to prepare Asian food."

"You do think I did it."

"Actually, I hadn't even thought about it yet. I suppose it's possible, but then it's also possible the pope will come to his senses and start performing gay marriages in St. Peter's. While he's at it, he can e-mail Sinéad O'Connor and ask her to rewrite all the hymns for the Catholic Church. Did you toss Linda down the elevator shaft?"

"I adore you." Jonathan sipped from his glass of water and peered over the upper rim like a character in one of the old movies he said he loved.

"I should hope so. The alternative would be that you are using me for sex."

Jonathan leaned forward.

"No, I didn't throw her down the elevator shaft. But I'll give you something to think about: Peter Piper picked a peck of pickled pep-. pers. But where did he put the peppers after he picked them?"

"The police want to talk to me?"

Chad was on his way down the hall to meet with Dr. Perkins. Last obligation of the day. Valerie, whose shift was about to end, flagged Chad down to drop this bomb.

"This isn't how psych units are usually supposed to be, is it? I somehow missed the part about the police interrogating people who are supposed to be here to deal with their issues. What if the questioning makes me lose it?" He adopted whiny tones to needle her, mostly in jest: "What if they scare me and make me get worse instead of better? What if I lapse into catatonia and they beat me to a pulp with their batons? Or, like, shoot me or something? Is there medication for that? Will I have to have shock treatment? Will Dr. Perkins be able to glue my shattered psyche back together?"

Valerie giggled. "You're a trip, Chad. Your issues have got nothing to do with these cops and their business."

"But this isn't normal, is it?"

"Honey, nothing about the last two weeks has been normal. Ever since . . ." Valerie stopped herself.

"Ever since what?"

"Nothing." Chad admired her ability to recover. "I started to jump to a conclusion I shouldn't have. Dr. Perkins has agreed to wait fifteen minutes for the police. It shouldn't take any longer than that."

Same pair Chad had seen earlier. They emanated the same beige aura of competence. However style-free they might be, they'd see through any clouds of bullshit that wafted their way. Their smiles had points.

Detective Gonzalez asked, "How well do you know Jonathan Fairbanks?"

"We're getting to be friends."

"Would you say you're close?" Detective Gonzalez, Beige Woman, had on blue eye shadow. She stared so intently into Chad's eyes, he couldn't help but notice the thick sky-blue smudges beneath her Brooke Shields monobrow.

"I'd say I spend more time with him than anybody else on the unit. Is this the sort of question-and-answer session where we'd all be a lot happier if I had an attorney?"

Beige Man, Detective Vargas, flinched. He moved his chair half an inch to the left, and light from the fluorescent bars buzzing overhead glinted off his glasses. Deliberate? Caught off guard, Chad blinked.

"It would really help us a lot if you'd just answer a few questions. We're investigating the deaths here in the hospital, and Jonathan seems to be at the center of them. If you know anything that could help us—if he has told you anything—it would be a good thing."

Ah, Beige Woman secretly wants to be Martha Stewart. Don't we all.

Chad lost the thread of the conversation. Images of Beige Woman thatching her patrol car for the holidays danced in his head.

Beige Man prompted him. "Chad?"

Why not shoot for the moon?

"Just today, at lunch, Jonathan was saying how everyone here is acting like he did it. When he really didn't. I think he's getting frustrated."

The Beige Ones exchanged laden glances.

"He said that?" Beige Woman seemed dubious.

"Why would I lie?"

"Because you're fucking him?" Beige Man asked in a mild tone of voice.

Chad's mouth opened all by itself.

"Umm . . ."

"You are, aren't you?"

Chad scrutinized Beige Woman's face to see whether she had anticipated this line of questioning. They couldn't be working from a script. If she was surprised she did a good job of concealing it.

"Not in the strictest sense of the term. I haven't actually entered him, although I think it's a great idea, now that you've brought it up. Perhaps we'll have to do that, later, unless you cart him off to jail." Chad stared straight into Beige Man's unblinking brown eyes and ordered himself not to throw up.

"But you are covering up for him. He must have said something. Like what kind of condition the body was in. Whether anything special had been . . . done to it, let's say."

The flaccid spring roll and garbage stir-fry Chad's stomach was still laboring to digest nearly re-emerged. *Pickled peppers? What had Jonathan said? Peter Piper's pickled posterior, or something?* At first, Chad couldn't speak. Maybe Jonathan had been involved somehow. *Martin will find out about this somehow,* an interior voice gibbered. *This will come out in court.*

"I'm a psychiatric patient," Chad said. "And you're in a locked unit in a hospital questioning me without an attorney." Jonathan would be pleased. "Why don't I just confess, myself? I was having kinky sex with her. She was so overcome with pleasure she ran screaming down the hall and jumped into the elevator shaft because she couldn't imagine any experience surpassing the pleasure I had given her."

This time, Beige Woman could not maintain her poker face. She looked like she smelled a fart.

"But then, I could be lying," Chad said. "I may have no grasp of reality whatsoever. You should check my charts. See which meds I'm on."

"I think that will be all. Chad, thank you for your time." Beige Woman glared alternately at him, then at her colleague, as Chad stood to leave the room.

"What's this about something being wrong with Linda's body?" Chad demanded of Dr. Perkins, once the door swung shut behind them.

"Other than the fact that it's dead?" Dr. Perkins tucked a stray braid behind his ear. He had full lips and rich skin that brought to mind some kind of dessert. No apparent razor stubble on his face. Chad could imagine what that skin would feel like if he were to reach out and stroke his psychiatrist's jaw. Chad felt sure Dr. Perkins was also gay, but he'd been through the mental health mill enough times to know which questions not to ask. The nice professional head-shrinkers would just reflect the question back on him, and turn it into a learning moment, while giving away nothing of themselves. *How would you feel if I were gay?* Chad also felt sure his psychiatrist had a taut chest, abs like cobblestones, and a body like sculpted obsidian. He wasn't likely to find out for himself.

Put a lid on it, Chad. He is not available for that.

"Right. Other than that. I thought that was kind of a given. Was it defiled somehow? Had she been assaulted?"

"I can see you're feeling a sense of urgency around this." Dr. Perkins crossed his legs, then uncrossed them again.

"The cops think Jonathan did something to her, and that I'm somehow colluding with him."

"Then I'll tell you. There was a great deal of chili powder in Linda's underwear. When we went through her clothes drawer, we found that someone had sprinkled hot pepper into Linda's panties."

"As much as she went on about having death in her vagina, that's kind of blackly perfect, isn't it?"

"Perfect?"

"Ugh. That didn't come out right. Whoever killed her had a definite sense of humor."

"You find it amusing?" Dr. Perkins frowned, crossed his legs again, and kept them crossed this time.

"Only in the way I find Beltway politics amusing. Once you get past the bleakness, senselessness, stupidity, and horror, it's quite entertaining."

"You put a peck of pickled peppers in her pussy?" Chad asked Jonathan later.

The session with Dr. Perkins had gone well because it concerned the particulars of Chad's imminent release. Tests had been given. Meds had been administered and seemed to be working rather well. Interviews had been held. Specialists had been consulted. The verdict: Chad didn't seem dangerous to himself or anyone else. At the end of his seventy-two-hour stint, Chad would be free to leave. And when the hospital doors closed behind him, much of Martin's ability to argue for commitment would cease to exist. Which didn't mean he was out of the woods yet, but . . .

Jonathan smiled.

"The police won't say they think I did this or that, but they've asked from so many angles I had to remind them I'm a minor child whose parents just died violently, and that my lawyer is a pit bull with a JD from Columbia." He reflected. "The longer I stay here, the more I feel like an extra in *One Flew Over the Cuckoo's Nest*. This place is surreal. I think I'll be out in a few days. The docs all seem to think I'm out of the woods, in terms of the posttraumatic stress shit that brought me here in the first place, and the cops don't really have a case or even evidence . . ."

"Will you go back home to Connecticut?" Chad asked.

"Home?" Jonathan mused. "I don't think it has ever felt like home. I only visited, never lived there. Home is a funny concept for me, because it suggests attachment. I don't feel attached to anything."

"I see," Chad said.

"I'm not sure you do, to be honest, but it's OK. Your heart's in the right place."

Chad put his hand over it to make sure.

"How soon 'til you get out?" Jonathan asked.

"Matter of hours."

"Then we should make good use of our time."

Naturally some idiot called Martin to come pick Chad up.

As soon as Martin arrived, he launched into the All-American routine that never failed to piss Chad off. Bad enough to be leaving Jonathan here. Martin's macho routine was the last thing Chad needed. With Valerie and two other nurses present, Martin asked why Chad hadn't returned his calls.

"Because I didn't want to talk to you." Chad stuffed the last of his clothes into his duffel bag and zipped it shut.

"I'm not so sure they should be letting you out of here, man. You're so fucking hateful."

Chad wanted a few quiet minutes alone with Jonathan, but Martin hovered like a wasp.

They didn't have time to say goodbye. Chad had written down Jonathan's address and phone number in Connecticut. Jonathan asked him to keep it simple, because so much was up in the air.

"I promise we'll reconnect," he said, again leaving Chad amazed at his seventeen-going-on-thirty-five sophistication. "I'll call you when I'm out of here, and the dust settles up in Connecticut."

Martin stood by the bank of elevators (one of the four had been taken out of service in the aftermath of Linda's death, and was cordoned off with yellow tape), tapping a foot. The look on his face combined disbelief, impatience, some disgust, and a little amusement.

"Please don't say anything," Chad told Martin as soon as the elevator doors clunked shut in front of them. Whatever influence Jonathan had on Chad's mouth got pinched off like an umbilicus once the elevator began its descent. Even with a pair of Jonathan's Calvin Kleins hugging Chad's ass and the salt taste of Jonathan's dick on Chad's tongue, he could not work up the nerve to speak freely. He managed, "Just drive me home, drop me off, and leave well enough alone."

"Do you have a problem?" Martin glared.

Chad stared at the worn-away numerals on the elevator buttons. *Were all the elevators in the DC metro area made by Otis? Did any other company manufacture them?*

"You want to have me committed." No sense in giving Martin ammunition by mentioning the uphill battle Dr. Perkins said he'd face in court, where commitment was concerned. Let it come as a surprise. "You want to be appointed my guardian. You want to have me declared incompetent. No, there's no problem whatsoever. I think those are wonderful ideas. Why don't we drive straight to St. E's from here, and save us all some time? I'll bang on the front gates until they let me in."

He won't hit me in the hospital, Chad reassured himself.

"I'm only doing this for your own good," Martin said. "You're so fucked up you don't know how to take care of yourself."

"I just want to go home," Chad said.

"Do I look like a motherfucking taxi service? Do you know how much effort it takes for me to keep an eye on you, with you out there doing all this crazy shit to yourself? Like I haven't got a wife and kids at home?"

Then you should be home with them.

"I just want to go home," Chad repeated himself. The asphalt under his feet shimmered in the heat as they walked down the street to the spiral parking garage where Martin said his truck was. This early in the summer, and already the air glimmered as hot city pavement scorched it. Things would only get more brutal from here. "The sooner you take me there, the sooner you can get home to your wife and kids."

"Fuck you, man. I didn't drive in all the way from Andrews for you to give me shit."

Chad hefted his overnight bag. It wasn't that heavy.

"I can take the Metro," he said. "It's right down the block."

Chad walked away before Martin could answer and didn't turn back to see his face.

The sky looked grim as Chad walked down the block toward the Foggy Bottom Metro station. The humidity, a silver shroud suffocating Washington, felt dense enough to swim in. It pressed down like an immense concrete slab. His shirt and jeans adhered to his skin the second he had stepped out the sliding glass doors of the hospital. Still, better to smother under Venusian atmospheric conditions than endure a twenty-minute ride across town with Martin. Beads of sweat trickled from Chad's armpits and shoulder blades toward his waist. He asked himself why he didn't live somewhere with less oppressive weather, like San Diego. A flash of lightning in the wall of clouds that loomed blackly overhead caught his eye; he quickened his pace and hoped he wouldn't have to wait long for a train. Rush hour hadn't technically started yet. The sooner he could get home, the happier he'd be. The sky portended a flood. And the sooner he could put the hospital out of his mind.

A muscle below his left eye started to twitch. The man at the farecard machine next to him was scratching the side of his nose with the same rhythmic intensity he'd seen in Linda and a couple of the other less functional patients. Flakes of something white (boogers? nose skin? dead lice?) littered his mustache and the front of his dark blue shirt. Huge wet patches darkened his armpits. Splotches of a red rash formed a pestilent garden around his receding hairline and above his ears. Way too much reality for this time of day. Chad averted his gaze and hurried toward the platform, where lights flashed to indicate an approaching train.

Maybe I would have been better off if I'd gotten brain damage in that car wreck. I wouldn't have to worry about towering student loans, the cost of living in Washington, character assassination by credit report, and all the other crap that goes along with being a debt-ridden young adult.

As Chad boarded the train, he recognized that he was getting himself all worked up. Payday still wasn't here yet, and he knew the check from the temp agency would amount to about two hundred dollars less than the amount he needed to send to various creditors and utility companies. This figure didn't allow for groceries and what bare-bones entertainment he allowed himself. (Rose often paid for things like that.) Although the train was air-conditioned, a couple of drops of sweat leaked down Chad's back and sides, and one rivulet flowed itchily down his forehead. By the time he got home, the storm front would have moved closer, and if he squinted just right he knew he'd be able to see the air itself. Grey haze swirling around like a cotillion of wet ghosts. Why the hell did people live in this fever swamp voluntarily?

The scintillating job market. All those high-tech companies in Northern Virginia. All those staff jobs on Capitol Hill, where you get to blow the country's power elite after power lunches in power restaurants. All those jobs at Washington's nonprofit agencies, where you can do meaningful work and earn

less than entry-level retail. Of course. There's no limit to your opportunities.
Just bring your own oxygen.

Chad estimated it would take another half-hour to forty-five minutes for the storms to begin. Just enough time for him to get home,
light a few candles, unplug his computer (which MBNA owned more
of than he did), maybe fix a drink and a snack, and stretch out on the
sofa with the new Dean Koontz paperback potboiler. There was
enough time left in the day to stop by the temp agency and talk about
another assignment. On the other hand, what a loathsome idea. An
hour and a half of paperwork, probably a lecture on taking care of
himself and being more responsible, followed by a dash through a
monsoon. He'd get both bored and drenched. Home, then.

In his fantasy, he told Marina, his broad-bottomed bitch of a supervisor at the temp agency, to go fuck a cactus.

Chad regretted checking the mail. Rose had her usual stack of bills,
a postcard from someone in Lithuania, and a thick envelope from
Housing and Urban Development—he vaguely recalled something
about her applying for a job there, although he couldn't imagine the
public sector would pay more than her evil law firm did. She had gotten several similar items from the government in the last few months.
He made a mental note to ask her what kind of job she was looking for
but forgot when he paid closer attention to his own mail. A fresh
batch of nastygrams from creditors is never a boost to the spirits. Two
Visa cards were a month late, and he had sent the minimum payment
not quite just in time for the other two. The MasterCard was just disaster. Chad had cut the thing up last month, after drinking four
glasses of wine for moral support. He owed the company a healthy
four-figure sum (down from the low fives, which was at least some
progress), and had no idea when he'd get it paid off. The year 2100,
maybe. Then there were the gas cards (two), the department store
cards (three), the late fees on four Blockbuster videos, and student
loans on a degree he had never completed.

Then there was the IRS. He hadn't filed taxes for the last few years.
Someone had noticed. He owed them about $5,000.

A pyrotechnic daydream followed: spray can of Lysol plus cigarette lighter equaled homemade flamethrower. Chad would crisp those bills and let the wind scatter the ashes to the four corners of the earth, or at least the four corners of the District.

Rose and Chad lived in a shabby-chic row house on Capitol Hill, in the southeast quadrant of the city: broad avenues, green parks (except during the most scorching weeks of late summer), and elegant old homes with exposed brick walls and stained glass transoms above front doors. The neighborhood had its run-down blocks (the crack whores and gang wars were in a different part of the quadrant) but retained a comfortable atmosphere without being too expensive. They lived a few blocks from great little restaurants, shops, and a couple of Metro stations. Chad loved the place. The house itself felt homey and fun. Chad was never embarrassed to have guests over. The furniture mostly belonged to Rose. She had an eclectic mix of the unpredictable and bizarre: clean modern stuff from Scandinavia (well, IKEA, which wasn't necessarily the same thing), temple tchotchkes from South Asia, dusty junk from consignment shops in Baltimore. The goddess Kali glared from a shelf at posters from the last two John Waters movies. Lacquered wooden elephants from one hemisphere marched across a blonde wood coffee table from the other. There was enough variety to keep the eye busy but not so much as to cause sensory overload.

Rose wasn't home yet. As long as Chad had the house to himself, he decided to enjoy the peace and quiet. He put on a Tori Amos CD and was just opening a bottle of Heineken when the phone rang. Reflexively he switched off the stereo, killing the opening strains of "Spark," and looked out the window to see if a squadron of white vans was inching its way down the street to take him away. Martin would have had enough time to organize something like that.

Chad's blood froze.

The phone rang again.

His pulse and blood pressure rocketed up the way they do after a near-miss car wreck. His eardrums throbbed.

Rose and Chad had an understanding. They had caller ID units attached to every phone in the house. Chad, who couldn't afford his own line, never answered unless he recognized either the name or number of the incoming call. Rose burned up money but at least had the income to stay ahead of her bills. Nobody likes talking to collections people, and Rose got annoyed when cornered by some asshole from Schenectady or Dubuque who threatened the direst consequences imaginable if Chad didn't pay this bill in full yesterday and Rose didn't tell him so at once. "I'm only his roommate, you bitch," she'd been forced to say, more than once. When the caller ID box showed "NOT AVAILABLE" or "ANONYMOUS CALL," Chad and Rose did not answer the phone.

When it showed "SOBRAN, MARTIN," they also did not pick up.

Chad darted to the nearest box. The grey LCD window read "NOT AVAILABLE." His heart slowed a bit, and he felt oddly relieved, as if by not grabbing the phone he had avoided disaster by a hair. He didn't owe any less money as a result, and the quality of his life wasn't markedly improved by missing today's dose of venom—still, he felt better. Did collections agents not realize their prey might just have caller ID?

"Fuck you," Chad said to the phone.

He stuck out his tongue and wagged it, returned to his sofa, contemplated its ragged upholstery and the drifts and dunes of cat hair clinging and shifting thereon, and decided to opt for his own bed. Rose's cat was forbidden to enter the bedroom, on pain of shaving or immolation. Chad liked the beast but didn't want fur coating every available surface.

The phone rang again as he was climbing the stairs.

"Suck my ass," Chad said to thin air. "Bite me! Eat my fuck!" He danced a precarious jig as he ascended the rest of the staircase, waggling his ass at the telephone as he went, trying not to notice the cramps still snaking through the center of his gut. That hospital food. Late nights with Jonathan. It was catching up with him.

Jonathan.

What if Jonathan was trying to call?

Chad had explained how he screened incoming calls. Jonathan knew to leave a message.

It couldn't be Jonathan.

Could it?

In Chad's bedroom (the door creaked open ominously, like something from a Lovecraft tale), he switched on the window a/c unit, turned off the ringer on his extension of the phone, and stretched out on the bed. With the bottom of the beer bottle he pushed aside the books (*Oliver Twist,* which he used as a soporific, and last year's *Let's Go* travel guides to both Spain and Italy, not that he could afford to go farther away than down the block to the corner store) on the bedside table, the first of three alarm clocks he used to ensure he got to work on time (or close), a dog-eared IKEA catalog, and an empty glass with a sticky ring of dried cranberry-raspberry juice at the bottom. He switched on his lava lamp and started reading.

The sound of the front door slamming downstairs woke Chad up. He didn't know he had been asleep.

10

Monday Night

"Chad!" Rose called. "Are you home?"

"No, it's Blake, Chad's evil twin! Run if you value your life!" Chad screamed. Then, as he heard her heels clicking on the stairs: "What the fuck are you doing here? You're supposed to be in Turkey or something, aren't you? Corfu? Crete? *Lesbos?*"

"Oh no, it's Blake, Chad's evil twin! Help me! I just peed in my pants from sheer terror!" Rose screamed back.

She strolled into the room and stood hip-shot like a model showing off her tan. She was wearing a blue linen dress thing Chad hadn't seen before, and chic sunglasses that couldn't have been purchased anywhere but some European island with an unpronounceable name. Her body language said, *Am I fabulous or what?*

"Hey, fag," she said. She saw his cast and stopped midstride, but didn't ask him what had happened.

"Hey, dyke." Feeling very fuzzy between the ears, Chad blinked at her and tried to focus. If he had obvious eye boogers, Rose politely did not point them out. The light filtering through the blinds seemed dim, but night hadn't fallen. Behind the mechanical roar of his air conditioner, Chad could hear rain. Rose looked more composed and fresh than anyone had a right to be after strolling late on a rainy summer afternoon in Washington. As far as Chad could tell, Rose had no stray frizzy hairs; God only knew how much varnish she had applied to achieve that effect. Her makeup was flawless, not at all goopy from the rain, heat, and humidity. The blue thing she was wearing didn't appear too wrinkled, and it wasn't wet. How did she do it? If Chad had been a woman he would have been a rumpled horror after a day like this. Even as a man he was afraid to look too closely when he passed mirrors under typical DC weather conditions at this time of year. "What are you doing home?"

"Civil unrest," Rose said. "The Cypriot Greeks and the Turks were at each other's throats again, so I jumped on a plane and got the hell out." She paused. "I'm lying. It was because I missed the weather here. It's so *moist*." She sat down next to him and lowered her tone a notch. "So when they make a movie about me, do you think we can get Parker Posey to play . . . me? As long as we're in Fantasyland, how about this: I can hang out on the set and serve as a consultant, and do her between sets." Rose inspected a fingernail, then stole another glance at the cast. "I wonder if she likes girls."

Chad shrugged.

"What's not to like?" Rose asked.

"Vaginas," Chad said. "Breasts. Curvy smoothness. Shall I continue?"

"Lick my box," Rose said.

"Thanks for the offer, but I think I'd rather die."

She hoisted a beautifully manicured middle finger at him.

"Guess where I've been the last few days?" Chad asked her.

"The loony bin."

She never failed to shock him. "How did you know?" Chad stammered.

Rose looked slapped. "I was joking. You're being serious. You're also wearing a cast. What the fuck happened? I can't leave you alone for more than twenty minutes, can I?"

Chad nodded. "Martin."

"Jesus." Rose let out a low whistle. "Then we need to have a talk, and that will require ample quantities of wine and food. You're not going out tonight, are you?"

Chad shook his head. "I feel like a freshly exhumed zombie. To be honest, it's nice to be home. There are worse hospitals out there—I ended up at GW—but it wasn't exactly the Ritz-Carlton."

"Then we must eat like piggies, and take large loud vulgar gulps of wine. Is there anything decent in the house?"

"Not us, that's for sure. I think there were some vegetables in the crisper before my unplanned vacation to Loonyland, but they're probably fermented or evolved or something. They weren't fresh to begin with. As for wine, I doubt it, unless you want to open that bottle of Grgich Hills I'm not supposed to know you have."

"I don't. Tell you what. If you'll start chopping anything still edible, I'll trudge through this downpour down to the corner store," Rose said. (Usually Chad made the trek to the store, since Rose was the better cook, and she had developed a habit of asking if he needed cash for the store. Chad always needed cash for the store. At any given moment, his checking account was the financial equivalent of Sarajevo. Checks he mailed out to pay bills blew gaping holes in it like mortar fire.) "I have a twenty and some ones on me. That should get a drinkable bottle of wine and a few veggies."

"My wish is your command."

"Don't hold me to that. I might make you get a sex change and become a lesbian, just for the vindictive thrill of literally making you lick my box."

"Watch your mouth, woman, or I'll put moldy peppers in your pasta sauce."

For the first time Chad felt thankful he had pitched over the balcony and gotten busted up. Had he made the customary walk down the block, and had Rose not crossed his palm with silver, then he'd have done something with his credit cards akin to Russian roulette. He kept them in the back of a little plastic box otherwise used to organize business cards. A few still worked. Others did not. At least two more of them should have been cut up already, but Chad didn't have the heart so soon after the last plastic-chopping session. To buy even a few simple things at the grocery store, he'd have been forced to review his statements, comparing account numbers and balances, and select the cards with enough room left not to embarrass him at the checkout counter.

Chad changed into jeans and a T-shirt, stepped into a pair of Birkenstocks, and made his way down to the kitchen. Most of the vegetables he found in the fridge had devolved too far toward a state of oozing mushiness to be smelled without gagging, much less eaten.

He salvaged a solitary bell pepper from the crisper and minced it into such tiny pieces that it was practically sauce itself.

Chad learned to cook because Mona usually couldn't be bothered. He would stand in the kitchen throwing together a rudimentary meal as she smoked, drank glass after glass of iced tea or gin, and talked at him. Now and then she reminded Chad that he was alive because a rubber had broken.

"I know, I know," he'd tell her, feeling bored and hollow inside that she would say such a thing. "You gambled away your abortion money. Lucky you. Lucky me. Can I finish my homework now?"

"You shouldn't get smart with me. I gave you life. I put this roof over your head." Mona made this her mantra. By high school, Chad had grown bored with the dance. "I'm so fortunate. Every night before I go to bed, I get down on my knees and say thanks to God for this wonderful life I have. He even answered one time. He sent me a fax. It said, 'I could have made you a starving child in one of those Feed the African Babies infomercials with Sally Struthers. There but for the grace of Me go you.' "

Eventually Mona found other things to kvetch about. She kept most of her dire mutterings to herself, in an increasingly sotto voce, as she smoked cigarette after cigarette.

On the subject of Chad's father, she refused to budge. Once she let it slip that he was an irresponsible bastard asshole. She then changed the subject. "I have to go take a poop," she announced. "Where's my lighter?" Chad left the house.

Chad suspected his father, whoever he was, still worked and lived in New Bern, or nearby. He suspected Mona even saw him from time to time, at a distance. Which would help to explain her ill humor. Perhaps Chad had even bumped into him or seen him somewhere: the trucker taking a piss beside him at the rest-stop urinal, the balding cook at the grocery store deli, the mailman who wore a prosthesis below the knee. He couldn't come up with a scenario he liked. Was it perversity to keep wondering? It wasn't like there would ever be a touching moment of rapprochement. He wouldn't turn out to be anyone Chad would want to know; odds were he was a beer-swilling fag basher with a bowling-ball belly, stained shirts, psoriasis, and three yellow teeth.

Where the hell was Rose, anyway? Had the rain washed her away? Had she drowned in the gutter?

Chad wondered how someone could stage an escape with no cash to speak of, no ID, no idea where to get fake papers, nothing. Maybe that's what his father had done. He might also have been a glamorous stranger, just passing through. The concept of exiting his life tantalized him. Not via a bottle of pills or a razor blade, but on a plane bound for someplace where the sky was usually blue and the natives didn't speak English. Not that he could actually do it.

Half an hour later the sauce was simmering fragrantly on the stove. Bottles of basil, oregano, thyme, and marjoram sat clustered on the countertop, along with a few cloves of garlic. Chad approved of the wine (two bottles of a Chilean Merlot, tasty but budget-minded; Rose and he were both South America fans in a number of ways), especially now that he had two glasses of it in him. He started scrubbing peppers and mushrooms for a salad, as Rose chopped lettuce.

"Pour a slug of wine into the sauce, would you?"

"Only after I pour another slug into me." Chad nearly sliced his hand on the corkscrew when it slipped from his grasp. He gulped with exaggerated loud vulgarity (Rose looked pleased), then splashed wine into the sauce, making it smell even more rich and delightful.

"Lush," Rose said, wagging a finger.

"Do you blame me?"

"No, if I had your life I'd drink twice as much as I already do," she said. "Be a saint and refill my glass."

Chad refilled his own, then poured more for her.

"Nice to know that chivalry never died out," Rose said as Chad sipped wine and peered over the top of his glass at her. "You're such a gentleman."

"So are you, Butch," Chad said. "I'm sure your girlfriends would agree with me."

"You cunt!" Rose giggled and hurled vegetables. Chad was glad they weren't stir-frying tonight. She had a strong throwing arm and he didn't want to dodge heavier missiles like jicamas or heads of cauliflower.

"Hey!" Chad yelled, ducking into the pantry for cover. "Are we going to cook dinner or reenact 9 ½ *Weeks* right here on the kitchen floor?"

The sauce saved him by boiling over. Rose subsided. Chad emerged from the pantry but kept a safe distance even as she gathered the now-bruised vegetables she had hurled.

"You're a very sick woman," Chad told her. "I have concerns about you."

"You, my therapist, my psychiatrist, my parents, both girlfriends, most of my co-workers, and just about everyone else in the Western world," Rose said, rinsing the vegetables and beginning to chop. "It hardly makes you unique."

"I always thought I was unique," Chad whined, cowering in the doorway lest she start tossing food again.

"Illusions, by their nature, are always sweet." Rose quoted a line from *Dangerous Liaisons,* her favorite film.

"Oh, fuck you. Cook my supper, bitch."

"What on earth made you think you were a man?" Rose batted her lashes at him.

"My dick." Chad grabbed it through his trousers like a homeboy (thanking God it wasn't small).

"I don't know; I could strap one on and be better hung, I'm sure." She tossed more vegetation into the sauce, stood back from the stove, and looked content with herself. "Shall we retire to the verandah for mint juleps?" She waggled the bottle of wine. "You can tell me what the fuck has been going on."

"Let's."

She followed Chad outside to the tiny covered patio around back; they sat on the bench and watched the rain. A fine mist of water droplets bouncing off the side of the house or blown in on the breeze coated Chad as he told Rose about his three days in the hospital. Parts of his story cracked her up. Others elicited streams of profanity that would have impressed a career Navy man. Still others made her say she was frightened for him.

"Hate to interrupt you, babe, but I'm getting drenched out here, and it's not because Sharon Stone is sitting on my face. Time for dinner."

Chad continued the story inside. Bits of sauce sailed past his lips when he spoke, and stained the tablecloth. "It's like, other than Martin, all I can think of these days is knowing I'm six figures in debt. Six figures in debt. Lions and tigers and bears, oh my." Talking about this made Chad crave more wine. Somewhere along the way, Dr. Perkins must have said something about interaction between alcohol and his meds, but Chad couldn't remember and didn't care. "Add to it the fact I can't get Jonathan out of my head, and Martin wants to have me put away, permanently, and I'm not sure how I'm supposed to deal with all of this. The hospital people seemed to think I should keep a positive outlook and treat it like a challenge. They did let me out, after all. But still. A challenge? What the fuck is that supposed to mean? Gee, I'll do my best to rise above this obstacle, and shucks, if I do happen to get locked up with my psychotic brother as my keeper, what a personal growth experience that will be!"

"I owe more money than you do," Rose said, cutting him off. "And Martin can be dealt with. You're having a pity party."

"In the form of a mortgage, which you're not behind on," Chad reminded her. "You have a decent job. It pays well."

Rose studied him. "Well, my credit's still good, but I have expensive tastes, and haven't learned how to say no when I get a new card in the mail. Sometimes I get tired of myself, too." Rose allowed this much, then finished the last of the wine she had bought. "I should have bought another bottle."

"Just say no!" Chad tried his best Nancy Reagan face, but doubted Rose recognized it, even when he provided a clue. He pulled on his forehead as hard as he could to imitate a facelift. Rose didn't laugh. "Look," he continued. "I'm tired of thinking about credit. Especially the negative kind, which I have so much of. And God knows I'm tired of having no other thoughts in my head but how to get myself out of this predicament." Chad drank the last of his wine and relaxed as a benign, rosy calmness eased its way through his system. "I want to cover new ground. Martin seems determined not to let that happen."

"Well, until now, you haven't really done anything about your money problems, short of trying to pay your bills on time. Don't even get me started on Martin. All paying the minimum accomplishes is making interest add up. There's the credit counseling service," Rose suggested. Chad wanted to gag. He had tried that already, without telling her. The counselor, a stick-thin, fiftyish balding queen in a bright pink oxford shirt and a red necktie with kittens on it, who had frosted the remnants of his hair then dyed his mustache to match, had told Chad to cut up all his credit cards, return as many items purchased with plastic as possible, sell his car for whatever it would fetch, take the Metro to work (he usually did, anyway), and take out a debt consolidation loan for the rest. He'd have the whole thing paid off by the year 2023. And his eyes had never left Chad's crotch the whole time. "And you could try for a consolidation loan," Rose added.

"Right," Chad said. "With my credit, I'm really going to get approved for one of those." He shook his head. "I couldn't even finance a pack of gum, Rose. You know that. When people with credit like mine leave banks after applying for loans, the tellers laugh and throw spitballs at the door."

He quit talking. This was a variation on a conversation they had been having off and on for at least a year. As the bills piled up, the tone and form varied slightly, but the gist was the same: when will this shit end? The answer had not changed: there was no end.

"There's always the bankruptcy option."

Chad shook his head. "You can't make student loans go away by declaring bankruptcy. I've already looked into it. It's easier said than done."

"With your credit, you don't have a lot left to lose," Rose said.

"So I go bankrupt. Then what happens? I'm still in debt. I've wiped out my credit, I won't be able to rent another place or buy a car for years, and I'm still stuck with the same shitty dead-end jobs. Bankruptcy won't make my life any less horrific. Just different. I don't see the point."

"One of the attorneys at work was talking about bankruptcy, but he put an interesting spin on it. He was saying that you can buy one of those HUD houses for zero down, then get a few new credit cards and max out the cash advances. Get one of those one hundred twenty-five percent home-equity loans from some shady bank, then hide all the money. Couple of hundred thousand, give or take. Then declare bankruptcy. Say you lost the money gambling in Atlantic City or Vegas. I guess Atlantic City makes more sense for us. You can drive there and not have to show a plane ticket. You're six figures richer, and a couple of years later you're back in the game."

Rose had a certain gleam in her eye. Chad looked at her through the maroon-tinged bubble of his wine glass, then peered over the rim. After a bottle of wine and the dregs of his afternoon dose of painkillers, he felt magnificent and expansive.

"You're considering it."

Rose nodded.

"It's something to think about," Rose said.

"Beats buying lottery tickets," Chad said.

"That's a low hurdle to jump," she sniffed. "Just about anything beats buying lottery tickets. Want more pasta?"

"If there's any left. More wine, too, but I think we're out." There were two Powerball tickets folded neatly in his wallet, as well as a Maryland Lotto. Chad didn't mention this. He felt sure Rose knew he bought them, or suspected. "So are you thinking about doing this, or are you actually planning it?"

"Well, I don't know that I should take the credit, and I'd have major qualms about implementing it." She munched and mused. "Hard to say. I don't like owing so much money, but let's be brutally honest, here. Who actually wants to buy one of those HUD houses? Look where most of them are located. I'm mortgaged to the hilt on this place, but it's appreciating, and I can do a consolidation loan to package my own consumer debt. It could be a lot worse, and I have it a lot better than most people."

"Me, for instance."

Rose shrugged. "That thought is holding me back, more than anything else. Your situation reminds me that I don't have it too bad.

And in addition, why go to all that trouble when you'll just find your-self back in the same stupid fix in a few years?"

Chad shook his head, bereft of answers.

"Are there other ways out? Is that the only approach you've found, so far?"

"No, unless you want to talk about me becoming an escort on the side," Rose answered. "And that would require boffing men."

"Eeewwww! Boffing men! Fate worse than death!"

"Don't be such a side effect," Rose said. "Enough of this gloomy shit. Tell me more about this guy Jonathan. No talking about money and no talking about Martin. Not allowed. We need something more en-joyable to discuss, or we'll ruin our digestion."

The phone startled them by ringing again. Chad checked his watch. The rule of thumb for collections Nazis was 7:30 in the eve-ning. They were close, but not over the wall yet. The phone continued to ring. Rose and Chad looked at each other.

"Do we answer it?" she asked.

Chad shook his head no and scrabbled over to check caller ID: NOT AVAILABLE.

Another ring. The pasta in Chad's stomach turned into aquarium gravel.

"Maybe it's Jonathan," Rose said. "Why don't you answer it? If there's a long pause when you pick up the phone, hang up."

Chad pressed the talk button on the cordless handset.

"I was wondering when you'd finally answer the goddamn phone." Jonathan sounded irate. "I was beginning to think I'd have to throw someone else down the elevator shaft to get your attention."

"Isn't that a little extreme?" Chad asked. He wondered if Rose could see him glowing. Hearing Jonathan's voice, cheesy as he felt ad-mitting it to himself, attaching words to it in his head, lit him up from the inside. He felt better already.

"The extreme always seems to make an impression." Jonathan quoted from the movie *Heathers;* on the spot, Chad decided he wanted to marry him.

Chad stomped on the floor and hissed *shhh* at Rose, who had turned around and—like a schoolgirl—with her back facing Chad, had wrapped her arms around herself and begun to make loud smoochy noises.

"My roommate is being an obtrusive cunt," Chad said. "You should come throw her down the elevator shaft."

"You know I didn't do anything to Linda, don't you?" Jonathan asked. "Well, anything much. I certainly didn't toss her fat butt down that shaft. About the pepper, I'm going to plead the Fifth. But I didn't kill anyone."

"Isn't this a strange conversation? I think this is a strange conversation. You're supposed to tell me how much you miss me, and how horrible the psycho ward is without me, and how you can't wait to get out."

"You already know those things, don't you? I'm getting out of here tomorrow or the next day, I think. There are signs and portents."

"And harbingers?" Chad filled a glass with water from the cooler (DC tap water had been determined by the EPA to have about the same level of purity as a Calcutta sewer), gulped it down, returned to his chair.

Rose gave up on him and started to put their dirty dishes into the dishwasher, now and then turning around to give long-suffering glances that said, *You expect me to do this all alone?*

"Yes, of course, the harbingers. We can't forget those. My lawyer thinks another judge will hear our case tomorrow. Someone he plays golf with. I don't know how it works, but as long as I get my emancipation and get out of here, I don't care."

"Going back to Connecticut?" he asked.

"Not for more than a few minutes. I don't give a fuck about my parents' personal effects. As far as I'm concerned, we can have a bonfire. Harry wants me to come back and sign paperwork. He says it's best we don't delay. I don't want to stay in the house, though. Maybe you could come with me."

"Like I could afford a ticket. I wish I could. Tomorrow I have to go see if I still have a job."

"That bites. But wait. Dude,"—the word sounded funny in Jonathan's intermittent British accent—"I have just inherited more money

than I can count. Obscene amounts of money. If you want to go to
Connecticut with me, you're on the train. It's not a problem."

Chad turned inside out.

"I shouldn't . . . I mean, you know . . ."

"I'll call you back tomorrow when I know more. This evil bitch is
hanging around, waiting to use the phone, so I should get off. I miss
you, OK?"

"I miss you too . . ." Jonathan hung up just as Chad got the final
word out.

So he hadn't done anything *much* to Linda? Chad wondered what
that meant. The pepper he knew about. But was there anything else?

When Chad switched off the phone, he found Rose staring at him.
"Someone has been shot in the ass with Cupid's arrow," she said.

Chad shrugged, and tried to get the goofy-happy look off his face.
"I like the guy," he said, returning to his chair. "What can I say?"

"Does he have pubic hair yet?" Rose asked. "Have his testes de-
scended?"

"Yes on both counts," Chad answered. "I've checked."

"I don't have to tell you how much trouble you're courting here,
do I? If Martin gets wind of that guy's age, he'll rat you out to the
cops as soon as he can get one on the phone. You do know this?"

"What am I supposed to do, Rose? Call him back and say, *Sorry, we
can't go on seeing each other, because you're three weeks shy of being a legal
adult. And oh, while we're at it, would you mind not telling anyone we've had
sex?* Be real. I like the guy. He's way beyond his chronological age."

"Just . . . oh Christ. I'm about to utter a platitude. Just be careful. I
would hate to see this have an unhappy ending for you. I'm sure he's a
nice kid—I mean, a nice guy . . ."

Chad interrupted her. "No, you meant, *A nice kid.* Admit it."

"OK, you're right, I did mean that. Nice guy, nice kid, whatever.
He's good for you, or he's giving you something you need right now,
attention, affection, love, I don't know. Or maybe he gives a good
blow job and that's all there is to it, and you just haven't come to that
conclusion yet. Whatever. Damn, I should have bought more wine.

Anyway, my point is, you have got to keep him as far away from Martin as you can."

"I think we've established that. We've got to keep *me* as far away from Martin as we can." Chad rocked back in his chair. "Cindy, too, while we're on the subject. She's up to something."

"Beaten-down slag," Rose said, glaring at her empty wine glass as if she could refill it via sheer force of will.

"I wouldn't be so quick to underestimate her. When she stopped by to see me, I got a hint that there might be more wheels turning under that mop of hair than any of us suspected," Chad said.

"I can't begin to imagine."

"Be that as it may."

"Just take care of yourself, Chad. This shit with Martin is scaring· me. I love you a lot, and I don't want to see you get hurt or get hospitalized when that's the last goddamn thing in the world you need, or worse." Rose pushed her chair away from the table, and stood. She wobbled a little. Too much wine. "I'm going to call it a night. I'm still kind of jet-lagged."

She blew him a kiss and went upstairs.

Chad sat alone at the table, wishing he could stand the taste and smell of tobacco so he could justify a cigarette. This would be the perfect moment for one, but he couldn't tolerate that eye-stinging, nose-hair singeing stench.

A minute later, Rose walked back into the dining room.

"Two things," she said.

"Shoot."

"I'm going to look into the age-of-consent laws tomorrow. You may or may not have anything to worry about. I'm half-remembering something, and I want to be sure I'm right. Martin may not have anything he can use against you, even if he gets you two shagging on videotape."

"Do that," Chad said.

"Second thing. Have you told him about Barry?" she asked.

Chad's blood went cold. He shook his head no.

"You might want to," she said.

11

Tuesday and Wednesday

"I can't believe you're back so soon after an injury like that," trilled Marina. She had on glitter eye shadow, gold flecks among the earth-toned smudges under her pencilled-on eyebrows. When she leaned back in her chair and crossed her legs, embarrassing white commas of flesh showed between the buttons of her stretched-to-its-limits blouse. If one of those buttons were to pop loose, it might fly through the air and blind him.

Go fuck a cactus, Chad told her in his head. He visualized her trying to engulf a saguaro, offered his sunniest smile, and projected his best imitation of put-upon, tattered charm. He wondered what novel tortures he and Jonathan might dream up for her, if she tried to thwart him. Ground glass in her glitter makeup? Superglue in her Preparation H? Or maybe they could clip and twist the underwires in all of her brassieres?

Dr. Perkins would not approve. He'd politely call Chad a raving misogynist, suggest that these fantasies indicated an antisocial ideation, and encourage Chad to work on strategies for reducing his pent-up hostility. Exercise, probably, and buckets of Paxil.

I don't dislike women. I just don't like people much right now. Women are people. Quod erat demonstrandum.

"I'm sorry I didn't call you from the hospital," Chad said. He revisited the third grade and crossed his fingers behind his back to make it not a lie, or not as much of one.

"Well, your brother Martin did, so there's no problem at all. He's such a polite young man. Air Force, isn't he? We all have our ups and downs." Marina looked so maternal that Chad's bowels cramped. To Chad, a maternal vibe meant she was about to pull out a battered pack of Winstons, mix herself an all-gin martini, hawk up bits of lung tissue, and describe the venereal diseases she'd caught from men with names like Tater and Lucky Sam while pregnant with him.

"What did Martin tell you exactly?"

Marina blushed. She returned to a more normal sitting posture. Her blouse hid the flesh commas once again. "That you . . . umm . . . well, I think maybe we should have a conversation about your . . ." She put effort into it, twisted up her face, and made herself spit out the words she clearly found distasteful. "About the substance abuse issue." She paused to take a breath. Was she panting? Had it been that difficult? "As you know, Capital Staffing Services has a strict no-drugs policy . . ."

Chad could see where this was going and as an alternative wanted to brain her with the marble paperweight on her desk. Made of pink stone, easily a foot long, it spelled out her name in big block capital letters and had polyester (Chad doubted Marina would spring for silk) flowers woven through the holes. She said she had ordered it after seeing an infomercial on cable late at night. He believed her.

"What did Martin tell you, though? How did he put it?" Chad leaned forward, all pretenses of sunny, beleaguered charm abandoned. If he looked like a viper he'd call it success. Syringe fangs would have been nice.

Marina tried the drugs n' alcohol line again, and he interrupted her. "I don't mean to be a jerk about this, Marina, but did he tell you I got fucked up and tried to kill myself by jumping over the balcony?"

She turned the same shade of red as the rising mercury line in the thermometer between Chad's ears.

Marina never failed to have that effect on him.

"You have authority issues," she pointed out after a week on his first assignment, an administrative assistant position at the Department of Energy. *No shit.* Chad had been hired to sit at a front desk unde a flickering fluorescent light, juggle an octopus tangle of incoming phone lines, take messages for a dozen federal GS-whatevers who never seemed to be in their offices, and, inexplicably, take notes in several meetings whose purpose he could not begin to fathom. Everyone involved spoke in strange acronyms. They carried themselves with a mixture of boredom and self-importance. When Chad asked what the meetings were for, the explanations he got made less sense than the bureaucratic babble they expected him to record. He gave up, called Marina at the end of the day, and asked for an assignment where people spoke English. Or Spanish. He was bilingual. Spanish would be great. Bring on the Spanish speakers. Did any of the embassies need administrative support?

"I can already tell I'm going to have to keep a close eye on you. I think you have a streak of insubordination a mile wide," Marina pointed out, as if Chad hadn't already noticed that for himself.

"Well, if you have a glossary of government babble, then I promise I'll study it before I go back. I really do want to know what the people around me are saying."

"The people at the DOE would like to keep you two more weeks. Think you can stick it out, without giving anyone a hard time?" When Marina had obtained a promise that Chad would not feed anyone's mail to the shredder, she added, "I'm going to keep checking in on you. You have a lot of potential. I'll make sure your next assignment is something you like better. But you have to remember who's the boss here."

She placed him in the Embassy of Honduras after that, which delighted him, then she sent him back to the feds after three days. They wanted him back because the woman he was replacing while she was out on maternity leave had experienced complications delivering her baby. Wouldn't be back for at least a month. And Marina had a temporary worker from San Pedro Sula to send to the embassy. All the *hondureños* were delighted. The Department of Energy drones buzzed with joy. Marina beamed, next time she saw Chad. She twisted her jowly face into a fake pout of sympathy, then handed over his paycheck.

"If you don't like it, there are a hundred other temp agencies out there."

And she wondered why he had authority issues?

"For what it's worth, Marina, I had a few glasses of wine that night and fell over the railing. I didn't jump, and I wasn't on drugs. Martin told the same thing to the doctors in the emergency room and won me a three-day vacation in the psych ward. I'd really appreciate it if, in the future, you don't even take calls from him. And if he says it's an emergency, go back behind him and do some fact-checking."

"I understand you're angry," Marina said. She pursed her lips.

"I just want to go back to work," Chad said.

"But our no-drugs policy . . ." Marina blushed. Her skin turned blotchy and red. "I really have to insist. I can't afford for our clients to have doubts or reservations about a placement. I have to be able to know I'm not sending someone with a problem."

"Jesus Christ, Marina. I am not an alcoholic. I do not have a drug problem. I am not suicidal. My brother is the one who ought to be in that hospital, not me." Chad wondered if there was any point in continuing this discussion. Marina kept fidgeting in her seat, in obvious discomfort with the subject of Chad's supposed addictions and suicidal tendencies. But he could tell she had made up her mind and could not be induced to budge from her position.

"I think I'm going to have to ask that you get a . . . you know—" she blushed a deeper shade of scarlet, uniting most of the blotches on her face and neck into a solid crimson mask, "—a urination test before we'll be able to place you on another assignment. I can't just ignore something like this. You understand." She fanned herself with a manila folder.

"Only too well," Chad said.

His authority issues surfaced.

Maybe he'd get a good reference out of her. Maybe not. In the grand scheme of things, it didn't matter. He hurt his unbroken wrist slamming the door behind him on the way out.

In the Metro station, Chad sat on a bench and fumed. He seethed and boiled, and his underwear chafed his butt. He felt too self-conscious to scratch. This made him even more pissed off. Around him, commuters stirred and shifted. A black woman standing beside him, wearing a pantsuit and sneakers, sang along with her Walkman music. A white boy in immense baggy jeans, who looked thirteen or so (*not that much younger than Jonathan,* a voice at the back of Chad's mind gibbered), stood with a skateboard under one foot. Sooner or later a train would come, he supposed. The Washington Metro system had signs on each platform to indicate when the next train would arrive, but the sign overhead wasn't working. Like his future. He had no job—well, the bookstore, but for what they paid him he'd have to work ninety hours a week to make ends meet—and only a very small paycheck on its way. His Borders check was spoken for before he even had it in hand (two days and counting). Why did facing facts have to suck, more often than not? Either he'd have to submit to Marina's urination test or sign on with another temp agency.

Maybe Martin would fall in front of an oncoming Metro train.

Maybe Martin would get botulism and die. Or flesh-eating bacteria. That would be fun. The doctors would quarantine and then dismember him, with the best of intentions. He'd be reduced to a series of red plastic bags with biohazard labels. How fitting.

Maybe Martin would come to his senses, realize he lacked any redeeming qualities at all, and leap off the Ellington Bridge.

Chad thought, *I should be so lucky.*

Rose pounced on Chad the second he closed the front door behind him.

"Have some wine. I've opened the Grgich." She poured him a glass.

Alarm bells rang. Chad accepted the stem and said, "Something has happened. It probably isn't something I'm going to like."

"I'd love to ask how your day has gone so far, but there's only so much to hope for where that twat Marina is concerned. She's a viper. But you don't want to hear about her. There have been two phone calls."

"I should invest in a pager," Chad fretted, sipping. The Chardonnay filled his mouth with cool greenness. He took another sip and cautiously set his knapsack on the floor.

"No, you should try taking your cell phone with you and actually turning it on. You know the joke about the definition of mixed emotions?" Rose gestured for him to follow her to the sofa.

She smelled like a lily of the valley. Chad had given up his attempts at keeping track of her perfumes.

"I've heard several versions of it."

"It's seeing your mother-in-law drive your new Mercedes off a cliff," Rose said. She pointed. "Your glass is half-empty."

"As opposed to half-full," Chad observed. "Very apt. Pour me some more, will you? And then tell me what the fuck you're about to tell me."

"There have been two phone calls." Clearly Rose had had a day. Like Chad's glass, the bottle of Chardonnay was also half-empty, as opposed to half-full. "One was from your mother. About your mother. A nurse made the call. Mona's in the hospital again and it looks really bad this time. She's on a respirator. She wants you to go to North Carolina right away. Nobody thinks she's going to make it."

"Fuck." Chad swallowed the contents of his glass in one gulp, idly wondered again if the alcohol would interact with his meds, and decided he still didn't give a shit. Couldn't make things worse, just different, and maybe more interesting. If his liver failed and he required a transplant, his HMO would be sure to find a way to sleaze its corporate way out of paying for the procedure. Chad would then be left with a new lease on life and maybe a quarter-million dollars more debt to go along with the one hundred dollars-and-something grand he already owed. Delightful! He asked Rose for another refill. As she poured, he asked, "What did the nurse say?"

"She didn't go into much detail. She told me to have you call as soon as you got home. Here's the number." Rose offered a yellow sticky-note with a phone number in the 252 area code written in purple ink.

"Christ. I hope this isn't another Chicken Little 'The sky is falling' thing," Chad said. "She's a drama queen."

He felt sick inside. It wasn't from the alcohol. Mona was probably on her way out this time. He pictured her with the cigarette she claimed she couldn't breathe without, tying back her hair in a ponytail to hide the black roots she hadn't had time to bleach before running out the door for work. She'd zoom out of the driveway, leaving behind clouds of scorched-oil exhaust.

Mona had never been pretty, as far as Chad knew. She had never been the sort of woman who could walk down the street and turn heads, unless someone wanted a gasp of air that wouldn't char their lungs black from her secondhand smoke. Workmen at building sites didn't whistle. Mona knew this, and Chad suspected she had always been pissed off about it. It wasn't the sort of thing he could ask her about.

All of that, finished. Mona was never going to have her redemption if that's what she was looking for, her white knight, her lucky lotto ticket. All her life had been a hardscrabble series of failed, cynical romances and long nights waiting tables in diners. She always managed to find the money to keep a nice TV set in front of her armchair and good gin in the cabinet, but from Chad's standpoint his mother had a miserable life. Now it was going to come to a shitty end. They weren't close and he couldn't deal with her company for more than a few minutes at a time, but still. The whole dirty picture depressed him beyond words.

"Do you think it's for real this time?" he asked Rose. "I mean, did the nurse say?"

"I guess you're about to find out. And on to call number two. Jonathan wanted to let you know he'll be discharged this afternoon, and he said he hoped to see you once he could wrap things up in Connecticut."

Chad took a deep breath. He reached for the damp bottle and filled his glass. He could already feel the buzz setting in. Reality felt fuzzy around the edges, sprung like an old sofa covered with pillows and blankets. "Mixed emotions," he said. "I'd call that the understatement of the decade."

"I actually talked to Jonathan for about ten minutes. If he's as cute as he sounds, you should keep him around. It's about goddamn time you hooked up with somebody who doesn't have the kind of face you forget five seconds after you've seen it."

"I'm not going near that."

"He said don't bother to call because by the time you get home there's a good chance he'll have already left."

"Jesus."

Rose nodded.

"So is he going to stop by here, or call, or what?"

Rose frowned. "He wasn't too clear what he meant to do once he was discharged. He said something about needing to talk to his lawyers and arrange for some funds to be transferred to his bank account, or some babble like that. He also said he didn't have much to wear, and he wanted to take care of that before he goes to Connecticut. I told him to go to Pentagon City for his mall fix." She shrugged. "I expect you'll hear from him."

"But the question is, will I be here if he shows up on the doorstep? Jesus. Mona could not have chosen a worse time to keel over."

"Fucking cancer," Rose agreed. "Kind of makes me want a cigarette."

"Or a joint," Chad said. "Those don't have filters."

"I have a bag upstairs."

"You evil slut!" Rose never failed to impress him. If Chad's left wrist hadn't been in a cast he'd have applauded.

The phone rang again as Chad exhaled a lungful of bittersweet, intoxicating smoke. So much for Marina's urination test. He coughed. The world shimmered. He remembered the cymbal clouds from his first night on the psych ward and reflexively cradled his broken wrist.

Jonathan hadn't gotten around to signing the cast, and Chad wouldn't let anyone else near it.

The cordless phone handset in Rose's bedroom included caller ID. When Chad recognized the 252 area code Mona had left, he answered.

Not without trepidation, and some trembling.

Dread simmered behind the sparkling layer of splendidness the joint had imparted.

"Chad, it's your ma, and I'm in the fucking hospital this time. I made them take the fucking tube out so I could call you myself. The docs say I need to make some plans." She launched right into it, gasping and quacking. Even high, Chad recognized a thick quality to Mona's voice. Morphine.

"What kind of plans?"

"You know. Don't be dense. Final ones."

"Christ." Chad covered his face with his free hand. Across the bed from him, Rose mushed out the joint and looked worried.

"I'm so doped up on morphine I don't know up from down, and I can still feel my goddamn lungs rotting away."

Chad instantly felt sober. The back of his throat burned from the smoke, and he pictured tiny cancer cells appearing in the painful spot and growing out of control like fatal kudzu.

"I need you to get yourself down here as soon as you can, OK? I can't talk much longer—it fucking hurts too much. Can you come tomorrow?" She hacked, then sniffled loudly.

"I . . . uh . . . I suppose so."

Rose's eyes were wide like dinner plates.

Go, she mouthed.

"Yeah, I can," Chad said.

"Good. Leave as early as you can. I don't want you to miss me."

"Don't worry. I won't."

First thing in the morning Chad left DC, his stomach gurgling from a combination of hangover and dread. Rose lent him $200 against his Borders paycheck. He wouldn't have been able to afford the gas otherwise. He had a travel mug full of coffee, a bottle of Evian, a Ziploc bag full of Captain Crunch, and an apple to eat on his way. He supposed he could drive through a fast-food place somewhere near the Virginia–North Carolina state line and would reach New Bern around four.

Rose had promised to do her best to put Jonathan in touch, whether that involved passing phone numbers to him or tying him to a chair until Chad returned.

"You should really take your cell phone," Rose told him.

"I tried turning it on this morning. They've cut it off. I got behind on the bills."

"Jesus Christ, Chad."

"Don't remind me, Rose."

Depending on the traffic, the drive between DC and New Bern can go quickly because after the Northern Virginia suburbs I-95 passes through a very few outposts of civilization: farmland, the occasional small town, Richmond. Chad listened to one CD after another and let his mind wander. He kept his speed around 75 miles per hour and avoided unpleasant encounters with the Virginia Highway Patrol, once by the skin of his teeth, rounding a curve on the freeway that cut through the middle of Virginia's soporific capital city.

Chad thought it odd he had heard so little from Martin since the outburst at the hospital. While refreshing, Chad knew these silences often meant trouble. Possibly Cindy and the kids needed, and were actually getting, attention, but more than likely the bastard was up to something. Martin tended to mix pouting and plotting. When Chad rebuffed him at the hospital and took the Metro home alone, Martin had probably burst a few blood vessels, experienced further personality disintegration, and put together the first steps in a revenge plot. Chad sighed.

Chad also thought about Jonathan. The time in the hospital had been enclosed in a sort of psychic bubble. And now, from outside the bubble, Chad's perspective on his time in the psych ward had changed: it felt more like something he had heard about, not experienced directly. It had happened, no question, because he still had a hickey or two, but where could it go from here?

Better to think back.

Jonathan resembled someone much older and more experienced, both in the sack and out. Chad meant to ask him why. He didn't object at all, but Jonathan's sophistication threw his own perceptions into question. Were all seventeen-year-olds like that these days? Chad didn't know any. Was it realistic to imagine Jonathan would stay in DC to see what happened since there seemed to be nothing to keep him in Connecticut, once he had dealt with his parents' estate?

What if he thinks all I want out of him is his money? That thought chilled Chad's insides. Worse was the thought that followed: *What if he did kill those people?*

Neither scenario seemed likely. Chad didn't believe Jonathan had murdered anybody, but knew it would be naive to ignore the idea altogether. *I'm not going to know one way or the other until I know him better. Which I know I want to do. It's really that simple. As for the money? If he jumps to that conclusion, it's something he did on his own, with no help from me.*

Neither question had an easy answer. Chad decided to focus on driving. His subconscious could do the heavy lifting.

And how the hell did Jonathan learn to give head like that, when he couldn't have been out of the closet more than a few years? The boarding school in Britain surely hadn't offered classes in advanced fellatio technique.

Those zany Brits.

Chad stopped for lunch in one of the little towns that barely existed beyond exit ramps and a couple of stoplights, stopped to take a piss in another, stopped for gas in a third. Emporia, Roanoke Rapids, Rocky Mount, Wilson: the kind of places young people with any sense leave, he concluded, after a Carter-era Buick full of big-haired trailer trash speeding out of a nearby Wal-Mart parking lot nearly took the side off his car.

As expected, he rolled into his mother's driveway at four.

Her car was there. She was not.

A sense of *It's for real this time* hung overhead like Mona's cigarette smoke. Mona, the perpetual attention seeker, had finally been upstaged. By the Grim Reaper.

Martini, Mona's yowling horror of a cat, screeched when he saw Chad coming, puffed up, and scratched at the screen door. The grass, a shaggy jungle on the verge of going to seed, clearly hadn't been mown for a couple of weeks, and a disintegrating stack of newspapers lay in a yellow clump around her front steps. Insects whirred as Chad walked up the driveway to let himself in. In the trees, birds screamed. In the gaps between these sounds, the silence seemed huge, overwhelming, after the urban roar of Washington. No sirens could be heard, no car horns, no rhythmic thunder from homeboys cruising around with the windows down and the bass up.

I should have gone straight to the hospital, he chastised himself, unlocking the door. Martini streaked outside and squatted on the lawn. From the smell in the house, the litter box had overflowed again. The air felt brown and hot and rancid, and Chad got the horrors imagining the layer of cat dung and cigarette smoke forming in his nostrils and sinus cavity. Chad knew how to find the hospital—that wasn't the problem. He supposed he wanted to see the house for himself, to see how far his mother had slipped since he'd been away, before going to see her in person. But the decision had not been a conscious one; now aware of his reasoning, he regretted it. He couldn't stay here. He'd choke. *If she dies I'll have to hire people to come in and clean. There's no way it'll sell in this condition. Nobody in their right mind would live here.*

Martini finished taking a dump and was now twining around Chad's legs, meowing, leaving variegated tabby hairs all over the cuffs of Chad's jeans. Chad pulled his shirt over his nose and mouth to obscure the stench (his deodorant smelled better than the air) and rummaged through the cabinets until he found a box of dry cat food. Martini tried to eat the dry brown pellets in midair, before they landed in the bowl. How long had Mona been in the hospital before starting to call?

"Don't let anyone break in, beastie," Chad told the cat.

He opted not to leave his overnight bag in the house. It would take on that smell. He'd have to burn his clothes, which would then have to be replaced, which was not a thing he could afford to do.

"This, of course, begs the question of where to sleep tonight," Chad said aloud. "Sleeping here is not an option."

He opened all the windows in the house before leaving. Mona had shut them. Then, from the smell, she had painted the walls with fresh turds from Martini's box while smoking an entire carton of cigarettes. Chad gagged in the bathroom where Mona kept the cat box. The volume of shit had surpassed the volume of cat litter, and Martini had taken to using the linoleum. Chad had to step around clumps of dung to reach the tiny window, and nearly lost his balance trying to open it without stamping on a large brown smeary object. In the back of Chad's mind a voice suggested he'd have no choice where to stay because he couldn't afford a hotel room; it was here or his car.

"Fuck."

On the way out, he could smell the house on himself. He blew his nose with a crumpled Burger King napkin from his glove box—that mitigated the stench somewhat—and made a mental note to stop by Wal-Mart on the way back from the hospital to buy incense, Lysol, plug-in perfume bombs, and baking soda. With more money at his disposal he would have liked a HEPA air purifier in every room, but then, by the same line of reasoning, with more money he'd also have driven a paid-for BMW 3 series coupe down from DC instead of a shitty little Toyota upon which he'd be making payments at 18 percent interest until, roughly, Armageddon.

Chad wondered if Mona's homeowner's insurance had lapsed. If it hadn't, maybe he'd just torch the place. Where could one rent a flamethrower?

After stops at McDonald's for a large Coke and a couple of boxes of McJunk to eat, Chevron to top off his only-half-empty tank and scrape bug corpses off his windshield, and a flower shop for some tulips he doubted he could afford, Chad recognized what lay behind his procrastination. It wasn't just that he dreaded seeing Mona weakened and on the brink of death. He couldn't stand the thought of entering another hospital so soon after being discharged from the last one.

Chad sat under the yellow glare of a sodium light in the hospital parking lot, looking down at the ghostly pink spray of tulips wrapped in white paper, on an anthracite vinyl seat that looked black now that the sun had started to set.

I could leave.

But he couldn't.

She may not even still be alive.

But she probably was. Mona would find a way to attach a cigarette to her respirator before she'd go hacking into that good night, raging, *Doesn't someone have a light?*

Chad turned off his portable CD player, grabbed the bouquet of tulips, and strode up to the front entrance without allowing himself time for a second thought.

Mona lay in a tangle of tubes and sharp things and things that dripped and things that beeped. Her sky-blue gown had bunched up under her left armpit. A white robe Chad didn't recognize lay draped across her lower body like a blanket. Her hair had thinned. Her scalp shone sallow beige-pink under the glare of the fluorescent hospital light. The buzzing tube lights behind their opaque panels made everything look yellow and ugly. Mona already looked yellow from years of nicotine. Now she looked like the rough draft of a wax museum replica of herself.

She didn't seem to realize he was there.

A nurse approached him with an apologetic look on her face.

"She's on a very high dose of morphine," the nurse—DINAH, according to her name badge—said. Dinah had affixed several smiley-face stickers to the badge.

"How coherent is she?"

"She just dosed herself before you got here. I think she wanted to mask the pain so it wouldn't be too obvious when you arrived, but she forgot that she's always zonked out right after she does it."

"How long until it wears off enough for her to be coherent, then?"

The nurse looked at her Swatch. Chad could see that all the numbers on it were jumbled up, and in different typefaces.

"Couple of hours, but at this time of night, she might just fall asleep. If you want to check back at around nine, that's one option. Or call. Otherwise, come first thing in the morning after rounds and she should be a little more together."

Chad shuddered.

Several emotions competed. The nurse left him to check on other patients. He took a seat next to Mona's bed, to sort out what was going on inside his head:

Horror at Mona's condition. She looked shrink-wrapped. Her sallow skin, her sunken face, her oily and stringy hair, an IV drip, and the various monitors she was attached to did not suggest a happy ending—just a slow death in a sterilized room.

Annoyance and a gibbering layer of panic that he had driven down here from DC on borrowed money to find her too out of it to tell him why he had come. What did she want him to do? Take her out of

here? Take her home? Take her back to DC with him? Was that possible? What if she died in the passenger seat next to him? Would she
make a smell in the car? Would he have to put the body in the trunk?

Fear of what would happen if he had to stay here more than a day or
so. He just didn't have the fucking money, and he doubted that Mona
did. What if she *didn't* become coherent again? There was a very real
chance of him becoming stranded here, waiting. The $200 from Rose
would last only so long. It would get him back to DC, and she would
lend him more if it came to that, but he was sick of feeling like Rose's
charity case.

Concern that Mona would continue to linger like this, alternating
between states of mindless intoxication and terrible pain. Should she be
moved to a hospice? Were there any with space available? He doubted
the informational recordings listed in the front of the phonebook had
advice on making final arrangements for your indigent, dying mother.

"Excuse me?" A man's voice knocked Chad out of his ruminations.
"Are you Chad?"

When Chad nodded, the nurse (short, a little chubby, with round
baby-fat cheeks but in his midthirties) handed him an envelope. The
wide-eyed way—name tag, Dwayne—the nurse stared at Chad suggested attraction.

"She tried to hold out until you came, but by this afternoon the
pain had gotten to be too much. She decided to write you a letter instead."

"Thank you for delivering it," Chad said. He wanted to open it, but
he had more questions. "I had no idea she was in the hospital. I mean,
I knew she had cancer, but I didn't know she was this far gone. Can
you tell me what happened?"

"Sure." Dwayne the nurse sat in a second chair. He took a breath.
"That's cancer for you. You can never predict it."

"Right," Chad said. "She's been going through this for a few years."
He shook his head. "We knew it was in a part of her lung that
couldn't be operated on, so the only question left was how long she
had. Not what could be done about it."

"I'm glad you're that clear on things. Are you prepared for this?"

"Can anyone be?" Chad shrugged. "Like I said, this has been going on for a couple of years. I guess the end has to come sooner or later. It's just that she didn't tell me things had gone this far." He had to stop talking; the lump in his throat made it hard to speak.

"I'll give you the quick-and-dirty, if you want. You don't seem to be up for a long technical description." When Chad nodded, Dwayne continued. "In the last few months, the cancer has spread rather fast. Now it's not just her lungs, but numerous other organs. She has talked about going into a hospice—she knows she doesn't have much time left—but she was also talking a lot about just going home."

"I don't think going home is the best idea," Chad forced himself to say. "I stopped by there before I came here. It's in terrible shape. I'm guessing she's been too sick to take care of it. The catbox smell alone is enough to fry the hair in your nose."

"I'm so sorry," said the nurse. He crossed his legs.

"Hospice, then?" Chad asked.

"I guess you'll have to talk about that with her—if she wakes up and gets clear-headed enough. I'm so sorry to have to put it like that."

"I think I need some fresh air." Chad felt claustrophobic and ill. Something inside him lurched. "Would you excuse me?"

He ran out of the room, folding the envelope and stuffing it into a pocket. On his way out, he heard Dwayne offer to help if there was anything he could do.

"I'll be back in the morning, or later tonight, or . . ." Chad barely made it to a rest room before throwing up.

12

Wednesday Afternoon and Night

Chad sat in the half-empty (as opposed to half-full) parking lot of one of the new hotels along New Bern's riverfront, staring straight ahead, numb, mind blown black like an old fuse melted in its glass shell. He had rolled down the windows of his car to let in the breeze. Around him, people came and went, sometimes stopping to look in at him. New Bern, located at the confluence of the Neuse and Trent Rivers, forty-five minutes from the clean white beaches of the Outer Banks, had come to life in the past few years. These days, every other car had Maryland or Pennsylvania plates. Condo developments were sprouting like dandelions. The downtown historic district had acquired enough cafés and interesting shops to keep the northern expats coming back: Savannah Lite. When he got out of his car to walk around, the increased number of pedestrians didn't make him feel safe, for once. He imagined they could all see Mona's note burning a hole in his pocket, radioactive and lethal now that he knew what it said.

Chad, this is painful to write but its nothing compared to what I have lived thru for the last few years. Now the docs say I'm at the end. Not much time left. Few weeks. Few days. Who can say? Do you know how scary that is and how sad? I DON'T WANT TO LAY THERE AND ROT FOR WEEKS BEFORE I GO. IT HURTS TOO DAMN MUCH. And on the fucking Morphine, I'm out of my mind anyway. No point in living any more, but you can't tell the docs that, they just give you that smile and don't want to help.

You have got to help me, Chad. I don't want to go to the Hospice. Just make them let me go home. And then you can help me. You can make it quick. I changed my Will to leave the house and what little insurance I have in your name, but there's more. Money you and Martin never knew about. Hidden. You help me out, I'll help you out. Everybody wins.

Think about it, kiddo.

Love, Yer Ma. Mona.

Chad ordered an espresso at a coffee shop, took a seat outside, and read the note again, a hand gripping each side of the sheet of hospital stationery to keep the wind from ripping it out of his grasp. He read and reread the note until the sun set and the buzz from the sodium light overhead started to annoy him. The breeze off the two rivers stung his face—he knew he had gotten a touch of windburn from sitting there in a daze, and maybe a touch of late-in-the-day sunburn on top of that. His cheeks felt tight, his lips chapped. It hurt to blink but that could have been tears. His stomach growled: he wanted to eat a horse, an elephant, any large creature would do.

He kept hearing Mona's voice in his head: "Help me die, Chad, and I'll make it worth your while." Even though she had never spoken those words aloud to him, it was the sort of thing she would say.

Chad wished he were on a vaporetto chugging down a canal in Venice. Back in Spain where nothing bad could possibly happen to him, and even if it did, it would still be in Spain: better there than here. Anywhere but here. (Hadn't he always felt this way about North Carolina? *Anywhere but here?*)

With Jonathan.

He thought of Jonathan to give him a break from thinking about his mother. How had this thing with Jonathan happened, anyway? How had it attained speed, momentum, weight, relevance? Jonathan was a seventeen-year-old kid. True, he seemed like he was a thirty-five-year-old in a late-teenage body, but the numbers on his driver's license didn't lie. They added up to something scary. Why the allure? Was it just that they had bumped into each other, right place right time, when neither had anywhere else to go? Or would they have hit it off outside the halls of the GW psych ward?

Would he think Chad was a gold digger?

But I'm not—I'm not! A voice in the back of Chad's mind protested. *I am not a gold-digging ho, and I don't need a urination test, and I don't need to be locked up! Things suck!*

Most of these questions couldn't be answered. Impossible to imagine what would have happened if they had met somewhere else because, well, they hadn't.

"Help me die, Chad." Mona's voice again. Quacking like the cancer-riddled duck she was. "Fix me a martini and put me out of my fucking misery. I'd do it myself, but I'm too goddamn weak. Help me out, here, and I'll make it worth your while. Just don't be stupid with the money, and for God's sakes don't let Martin anywhere near it."

Chad felt hollow. What would it have been like to have a mother who didn't reduce their relationship to a transaction every chance she got?

I've got to be crazy, he thought. *I am really, honestly, truly hearing voices in my head. One, at least.* He had a follow-up appointment with Dr. Perkins in a week. He wondered whether telling his psychiatrist about Mona's note would win him another visit to the psych ward.

On the way back to Mona's house Chad stopped at Wal-Mart for cleaning supplies. He felt like a photonegative of himself. He felt like he was on Jupiter, where the atmosphere is toxic gas and gravity renders your shopping cart too heavy to push.

After he had recovered from his wreck-related injuries, Mona encouraged him to buy another car as soon as possible. The insurance settlement from the drunk driver could give him a down payment. Buy something small and economical, finance the rest, and put the rest of the insurance money toward tuition. Chad, still reeling from the shock of losing his scholarship, thought Mona's idea made sense. Hence, the Toyota. Hence, the sky-high interest rate. Drug-fucked after two months on painkillers, he had bought the first car he saw—a green two-door Tercel. It had the personality of a toaster but could be trusted not to break down too often. Negotiation? Chad couldn't be bothered. The salesman, a coffee-skinned African, had grinned a big fluorescent grin and asked if Chad would like undercoating and a rust-proofing treatment. *An additional two grand? Sure. Where do I sign?* Even at the time, he knew Mona wanted him out of her hair and out of her house as soon as he could walk without falling down. Chad bought the Toyota, signed on all the dotted lines, drove back to DC two days later to find places to live and work.

Hindsight tortured him as he pushed his shopping cart down claustrophobia-inducing aisles:

I should have transferred to a cheaper school. I could have moved back here and gone to Carolina, maybe. NC State. One of the other UNC schools—Charlotte, Greensboro, Asheville. Charlotte resembles a real city these days. That might have been OK.

I shouldn't have bought the car. DC has a subway.

I shouldn't have listened to Mona. Mona is the only person Mona has ever cared about.

I shouldn't have chosen a cart with a wobbly left front wheel.

But here I am. Fuck it.

Chad hefted a gallon bottle of Clorox. Bleach as metaphor for empty checking account? Mona probably had Clorox under her kitchen sink. *Everybody has a bottle of Clorox under their kitchen sink. If they don't, they ought to.* Chad put the bottle of bleach back on the shelf and regretted not surveying Mona's cleaning paraphernalia before this shopping trip. He knew he ought to go easy on himself—dying mothers and putrescent finances do not contribute to lucid, rational thinking—but he figured he had nothing but $50 of room left on one credit card beyond Rose's mercy loan of $200. Beyond that? *Behold, the void.* He couldn't afford to waste five bucks on a scrub brush if Mona had a perfectly good one on a hook in her pantry. He couldn't afford the gas for an extra across-town trip to return the shit he bought and didn't need. Even the hamburger and fries he meant to buy at a drive-thru on the way back to Mona's house required a certain level of thought before he spent the money.

He moved on to a bottle of Drāno and wondered what suicide by self-dissolution would be like. Wasn't he doing something like that anyway, financially? If he were to open the bottle, chug the contents right here in the store, how much of his insides would be left when the ambulance came? It sounded too painful to contemplate. The thought made him queasy. But he'd heard of people opting out by swallowing the stuff before. The movie *Heathers* had used the idea of death by Drāno to good effect. Fascinating idea, to do oneself in by dissolving one's internal organs.

Would people gather around in a circle to watch him scream, writhe, and dissolve in a fizzy blue puddle on the floor, like the Wicked Witch of the West? If enough people came to watch, maybe someone would think to bring popcorn and Cokes from the deli.

What had really been in Dorothy's bucket, anyway? Chad had his theories.

That espresso he'd sipped by the river felt enough like a slug of Drāno in his stomach to put him off the idea. Chad shuddered.

He threw a pair of yellow rubber gloves into the shopping cart, eschewing the Playtex version because those cost forty-three more cents than the generic Wal-Mart offering. No way was he going to scrub Mona's shit-encrusted floors with his bare hands.

He moved on to the Glade Plug-Ins. Price be damned, he threw a dozen into the cart. Every spare outlet in Mona's house was going to get one of these babies. He'd make the place an olfactory jigsaw puzzle of cinnamon, vanilla, and honeysuckle if it was the last goddamn thing he did. It was either that or torch the place.

A bottle of pine-scented multipurpose cleaner seemed like a safe investment. He could mop with it, clean countertops, and swab toilets. Genocide for germs.

Shopping had never humiliated him before. Not like this. He ran up his cards in the years following the wreck: the clothes, the Skagen wristwatch, a couple of trips to Europe, good shoes, books by the dozen. Working at a bookstore, you couldn't get away from the books. In the life Chad grew up believing he would have, there was no room for questions of making it from one paycheck to the next. Sometimes he bought things in spite of the bills, knowing perfectly well he couldn't really afford them, just because he knew he'd lose his fucking mind if he went on scrimping and scrabbling and making do with ramen noodles and thrift-shop shirts. One time Chad prepared a budget on his computer and threw up on his bedspread when all the numbers at the bottoms of the columns came up red.

How would Jonathan react to all of this? Would he be revolted? Chad thought not.

Were there Wal-Mart stores in Geneva or Zürich or Bern, or wherever Jonathan's boarding school was?

Chad had been to Geneva and Lausanne. Loved them. That lake. Those mountains. The pristine Switzerlandness of it all. He shook his head. A life of mediocrity spun itself out like spider silk. Maybe he'd abandon DC, move back here, and get a job selling real estate or something. He could do the insipid fag thing and style fat Baptist women's hair. Why not? He was never going to go back to Switzerland at this rate.

Or was he? Mona's note had put a different slant on things. Waiting in line at the checkout counter, he tried to see the world through clearer eyes. Mostly all he could see was an Alpine case of acne on the checkout girl's face, but he was trying.

How much money was there and where did Mona get it? Chad wondered whether he would ever find out. Whether she would wake up to tell him. Whether, in the end, it would matter. He wondered how she had managed to hide the cash so well. People living (barely) on disability and Social Security had to be careful to hide their windfalls. Uncle Sam made the credit bureaux look generous when it came to slashing the amount of the monthly check and expecting thousands in back pay, right now. Chad had accompanied Mona to the Social Security office a few times and eavesdropped on other people's problems. He had overheard people who clearly didn't have enough money to buy clothes be told that the government had mistakenly been overpaying them for a few years and, now that the error had been identified, would cut their monthly pittance in half. How they were supposed to pay the rent, keep the lights on, and buy food for their kids was *their* goddamn problem.

Fuck Uncle Sam, Chad remembered thinking. *Why not sell drugs?*

So how much money was there?

Probably a few thousand, not much more, he decided. *There couldn't be.*

Was a few thousand enough to make it worth Chad's while to help Mona kill herself—or to do the job for her, if she couldn't manage it alone? The thought made his stomach clench. A ribbon of espresso-flavored stomach acid burned the back of his throat. With Mona, there always had to be a bottom line. So he was risking imprisonment and scandal—so what? In jail, someone else would handle the bills. His only sources of concern would be the struggles to keep his asshole roughly the same size and elasticity, and his HIV status negative, after all those unsupervised group showers with big burly inmates.

Chad decided to stop by the hospital once more before driving back to Mona's house. He didn't know if there was a protocol for dying mothers, but a constant bedside vigil was out of the question. Frequent visits would have to suffice.

The phone next to Mona's bed started to ring the second Chad stepped into the room. Mona stirred. Chad had enough time to see that she hadn't come to, before picking up.

"Hello?"

"Hey, you." Jonathan. Finally some indication of things going right. "How are you?"

"I've been better." Chad looked back at Mona. Her mouth hung open. At least she wasn't drooling in her sleep. He supposed the morphine had dried up her saliva. "Things down here are pretty grim. How about you?"

Jonathan said he was fine. Out of the hospital, at last. He had taken the train up to Connecticut, met with his attorney, signed a lot of papers, done one or two things the IRS wouldn't like. Things seemed to be getting sorted out.

"The judge decided to go with the emancipation. It's official: I'm a grown-up."

"We'll have to drink a glass of champagne, then."

"My mother loved Veuve Clicquot. I'll pack a couple of bottles when I leave. There's nothing else here I want, not really."

"How are you holding up?"

Mona grunted in her sleep, stirred, then lay still again.

"As well as can be expected. I hate paperwork, but I'm glad to be out from under them. My parents. I don't know. I'm managing. I don't like being in this house. I have to admit that much. I keep seeing my father's face. When he was pointing the gun at me he looked like he hated me, and he wanted to splatter my fucking brains across the wall. I want to get his face out of my head." A long pause followed. "But I'm being dreary. I should be celebrating instead. I'm emancipated, in several ways. So now I can rent an apartment or buy a car all by myself. Lucky me."

Chad asked, "Didn't you already have a car?"

"Never needed one. The story has a sort of sick happy ending, though. My parents' cars are now mine. So I have a Mercedes-Benz and a Range Rover at my disposal."

Chad felt an ungracious stab of envy.

"I know what you just thought," Jonathan said. "It was something like, *Fuck you,* because I've got these cars and you have a piece-of-shit Toyota, right?"

"Well, I wouldn't say it was that strong," Chad admitted. "But let me tell you: my own mother's house is as different from your parents' place as it could get and still be inside this country. It isn't quite an Appalachian hillside shanty, but it's pretty disgusting. She's been too sick to take care of it for I guess the last few weeks. She hasn't changed the cat box. The cat has been crapping everywhere but in the box. There are cigarette butts everywhere. Dirty dishes. I didn't see bugs, but I didn't stay long enough to get a good look, just a good whiff."

"Christ, Chad, I'm sorry. What can I do?"

Chad fell silent for a few seconds. "Nothing, I suppose. It's good you called, though. You're in Connecticut now?"

"Yeah. I called your place in DC, and Rose gave me the number at the hospital and also your mom's number. She told me I sounded cute as hell, and that if I didn't call you right away she'd track me down and kick my ass into orbit around Saturn."

"You're at your parents' place?"

"Yeah, believe it or not. One thing Harry did was to hire a cleaning team. It must have cost a fortune, but they did a good job. You can't tell the place was an abattoir only a few weeks ago."

"What do you say after that?" Chad asked. "Congratulations? Jesus."

"Yeah, no bloodstains. How cool. You don't sound good, Chad."

"I'm not. I'm kind of in a dilemma. Mona's right here, out cold on a morphine drip. I feel funny talking about her with her lying three feet away from me. But her house, oh my God, it's beyond belief. I'm going back there with some cleaning supplies I bought, and a hundred of those Glade Plug-Ins things and about a gallon of Lysol spray. The nurses keep coming in, too."

"Is there a public phone? Find one and make a collect call. Got a pen?"

Chad found one, copied down the number, and hurried out of the room.

"I miss you."

"I miss you too."

"Is it OK if I come down?"

"You shouldn't see the place like this. It's a fucking horror show."

"Chad, I don't have any reason to stay in Connecticut."

"Why don't you meet me in DC when I'm back? It shouldn't be long."

"You don't know how long you're going to be in North Carolina, Chad. You're counting time until your mother dies. I'd like to be there with you. If that's OK. I don't want to be a pain in the ass . . ."

"You're not. I promise. I'm just too fucking embarrassed for you to see me like this. To see this side of my life. It's not a boarding school in Switzerland."

"That's not all I am, Chad. I'm not Sloane Ranger Biff, the rugby-playing Polo model. You know that."

"Fuck. You're right. I'm not being fair."

"Don't worry about it. You're dealing with some intense shit right now. Look, I may need to be here another day or two, but I'll call you again tomorrow sometime."

"Promise?"

"Cross my heart, hope to die, stick a needle in somebody's eye."

Jonathan didn't sound shocked at Mona's request, but then a guy who has seen his father shoot his mother then commit suicide is not going to be shocked by much.

"That's nasty," Jonathan had said. "Are you going to do it?" After a couple of seconds, Chad had said he didn't know. Rooting for Dr. Kevorkian was one thing. If mortally ill people wanted to die and couldn't do the job without help, then why shouldn't help be available? Whose body was it, anyway, and whose life? God's? The government's? As if. "But now I'm the one facing this decision, and she's turned it into a straightforward, old-fashioned bribe. She's not just saying, *Help me die;* she's saying, *Help me die and I'll pay you.* I'm not entirely OK with the idea to begin with, but this is just—well, to use your word, nasty."

To mitigate the cat-box stench, Chad wore a nose-and-mouth carpenter's mask. He had applied a layer of his Speed Stick to the outside of the mask. Every breath smelled like armpits and excrement. With Mona's old broom he swept up cat turds. He cleared a path from the bathroom door to the cat box. Martini wound around his ankles, yowling affectionately.

"Do you want me to come down there?" Jonathan had asked.

Clots of feline fecal matter were stuck to the floor and wouldn't come up just with the broom. Chad would have to spray something on them. His gorge rose, an acid tsunami.

"I don't know what's best," Chad had said. "My mind is totally blown. Mona could go at any time. I'm not just going to cave in and do what she wants without thinking about it first. Maybe I'll head back to DC for a day or two. I don't fucking know. I can't afford to stay down here, and if she's got money I could get my hands on to make this all easier, she's in no position to tell me where it is. Dumb bitch. Bless her heart. I've got to think about this. I know I'm not making any sense."

"It's OK. Think out loud if it helps you sort everything out."

Chad still hadn't gotten anywhere. There were too many variables. When they said their goodbyes, he didn't think he had accomplished anything other than sounding like the psycho he obviously was, given where he'd spent the last few days.

He had been trying to pry one of Martini's foul offerings up from the floor; when it came loose, Chad was caught off balance. Bits of shit flipped up and sprayed his face and clothes. He fell down and landed in more.

Chad yelled and began to vomit before he could even get the mask away from his mouth. It filled with hot chunky fluids that leaked down his chin. He caught a whiff of Speed Stick on top of the other smells in the room and gagged again.

He sat in the hall, pounding his fists on the floor, assaulted by disgusting smells, sick, crying, overwhelmed. Flashbacks of himself at age five bawling in his bedroom under threadbare covers, curled up with his big purple teddy bear—beaten up by Martin for some imaginary offense while Mona snored in her armchair on one of her rare nights off, an empty bottle of gin, a martini glass, and a jar of olives on the floor beside her. Chad's skin crawled. He pulled off the yellow rubber glove and with the back of his latex-scented hand, he wiped puke off his chin. Just for this alone he supposed he could let Mona suffer a few days longer while he made up his mind whether he'd help kill her.

After laboring well into the night, Hercules in the stables, Chad took a cool shower in a tub now safe to touch with bare skin, and put on a pair of boxers and a T-shirt. Mona's washer and dryer passed the sniff test, so he threw his dirty clothes into the machine and added extra bleach. So what if everything came out lighter? It was a sanitation issue. Satisfied he'd get the shit out of his clothes, he decided the next step needed to be fixing a tall, cold soothing gin and tonic. He went rummaging in Mona's liquor cabinet and found Tanqueray. *Hmm.* He poured, stirred, sipped. The tonic water hadn't gone flat yet, but it had only a couple of usable days left. *Interesting.* Expensive stuff for a woman on a fixed income. Even if she was a lush. *Maybe there's something to this money thing after all.*

Chad decided he would sleep on Mona's screened back porch. He set up an electric fan by a lounge chair folded flat to make a cot and filled a pitcher with ice water in case the night got hot. Over the hum of the fan, he could hear the screech of crickets and cicadas. Pine trees creaked in the breeze. Sometimes a car would pass, but the constant dull roar of DC traffic was conspicuously absent. He stretched out on the chaise, pulled a sheet over himself, and felt more relaxed than he'd have expected.

Exhaustion will do that, he imagined Jonathan saying.

Chad sipped his drink.

If Jonathan were here, he'd be appalled by the mess. As would anyone. But then, he didn't seem to care about pedigree. He claimed he didn't, at least. Chad had to take his word for it.

If Jonathan were here, they'd be stuck sleeping together on this folding lounge chair. Could be fun.

No, Jonathan would get them a room at some hotel.

Chad thought instead of what they could get up to in a hotel room. Those clean sheets, just waiting to be despoiled. Nice white towels to soak up quarts of come. A mammoth TV upon which they could watch the soft-core smut channel and imitate positions. A pillow fight whose loser must forfeit his clothes.

Where did Mona keep her towels?

Dick poking through the fly of his boxers, Chad went back inside to find one, slightly surprised that he would need it. Those plug-in air fresheners had drowned out the cat-box smell enough that Chad's jutting dick didn't deflate from colliding with a solid brown wall of stench. Mona kept dishtowels in a drawer by the sink. Jacking off into one struck Chad as sort of icky and blasphemous, but he did it anyway. And liked it.

13

Thursday Morning

"Is there any other family?" asked the nurse, a new one, a zaftig red-haired woman named Sue. Rather pretty in spite of her rouged wedding-cake chins, Sue occupied herself with checking Mona's vitals and noting them in the chart as Chad looked on. Mona's chart was as thick and grim as a Tolstoy novel.

Chad and this nurse stood next to Mona, looking down at her rather than at each other. Was there such a thing as nurse burnout? To be sure, nurses got fried after years of their own grueling work, but had anyone ever observed and documented the condition of becoming burnt out on *them?* Chad thought nurses, as a whole, were vital to the survival of humanity, but he had seen too many of them in the past week.

"None that matter," Chad answered. "I have a brother, but we try to pretend he doesn't exist."

He had Mona's note folded in his back pocket. It burned his left buttock like a brand. His right buttock, when he paid attention to it, felt just like it usually did: the ever-present, if rather empty, Coach wallet back there, still owned by Chase Manhattan and accruing the wrong kind of interest at 23.66 percent, if you wanted to get technical about it. Chad studied Mona's face. As before, her mouth hung open, and her skin looked even worse with the sun shining on it—a ghastly paraffin greyish-white color, the deterioration obvious.

"She's not going to wake up, is she?" Chad couldn't look at Mona for long without feeling sick.

"The odds aren't great, but with morphine, you can never tell. Her doctor might consider reducing the dose, to see if she comes around. Just consider how much pain she's in, as you think things through."

"It's never far from my mind," Chad said. "I don't know what the procedure is, but I want one last chance to talk to her before the end comes. She left me some instructions in a letter, but she's not clear on that part. I've still got questions. Do I just tell you I want her to get less morphine, or do I have to tell a doctor?"

Sue nodded. "I'll put a note in her chart."

"While we're being existential," Chad said, "I need coffee. Where's the cafeteria?"

"Down on the first floor. It's not the best coffee you'll ever drink, but it'll wake you up."

"I could use a couple of gallons. I'm not a morning person," Chad said. He twisted his thumb ring.

"I can see that," Sue said, walking toward the doorway. "Go get· yourself a cup and think about what to do. We'll keep an eye on your mama for you."

Coffee sloshed down the sides of Chad's cup, scalding his fingers, as he fiddled with the pay phone in the cafeteria, trying to coax a dial tone out of it. No matter how many times he flicked the hang-up lever thing, he got nowhere. *Naturally, the fucking telephone is dead.* Dry clicks in dead air. He raised his hand to lick the coffee off his fingers but stopped when he realized that would coat his tongue with hospital pay phone germs. *Hepatitis, anyone? Cholera?* He took a closer look at the phone. Some imbecile had folded a drinking straw and then wedged the wad of plastic into the coin slot. *Brilliant.*

Chad blew across the surface of the coffee, into which he had dumped several packets of sugar, a dollop of honey, some half-and-half, and an ice cube. Seemed cool enough to drink. He licked tan off his fingers, then took a cautious sip: the stuff tasted like asphalt lightened with several packets of sugar, a dollop of honey, some half-and-half, and an ice cube. He forced down a swallow, and then another.

Overhead, the light flickered, went out, came back on. Chad shook his head in disbelief.

The checkout counter lady in grubby white tie-on things told him he'd find another pay phone down that hallway (she pointed) and to the right, next to the rest rooms, outside of the radiology department.

Chad wondered whether locating radiology and the cafeteria so close made sense, and what kind of tumors he'd get from his bagel (plain, toasted, cream cheese) and creosote coffee. The checkout counter lady wasn't wearing a dosimeter. Probably a good sign.

Rose was actually home. She answered as Chad took his second bite of the bagel. When she asked who was speaking, his answer sounded like *womfle-pomfy-shomf*.

"Chad," he said, after swallowing a fist-sized bolus of bagel. It had expanded in his mouth. No other explanation made sense.

"You sounded like you were choking."

"I nearly was. I think this bagel I'm trying to eat is made of concrete. I thought it would go right down. It didn't." He took a sip of his sweetened battery acid. "I need a sanity moment."

"And you called me," Rose giggled. She hadn't been awake long; Chad could tell from her voice. "What a novel idea."

"It's all relative," Chad said. "Look, I'm at a total, utter, and complete loss on what to do, and I want to hear your take on the situation."

"Wow," Rose said. "A total, utter, and complete loss? As opposed to just a total and utter loss? Or an utter and complete loss? That's intense. Start talking. I'm going to crawl downstairs and start a pot of coffee."

"I bet it's going to be better than the shit I'm drinking now." Chad waited for Rose to grind beans, then outlined the fix he was in: Mona zonked on morphine and unable to communicate; her grisly final directive, delivered as a note by a nurse; the emotional blackmail of a payoff in exchange for bumping her off. The filth in her house. Chad's inability to leave and his inability to stay.

"I have to go back to work. I'm so fucking broke, it's scary. But on the other hand, if there's money around I kind of have to be a whore and hope I find it." Chad sipped his loose approximation of coffee.

"Think about what you said. If you were to leave, you know she'd die about the time you hit Fredericksburg. You'd get here a couple of hours later, only to find out you had to turn around and drive straight back. Now, how much sense does that make?"

"Don't even go there." Chad shuddered. "I'd stay at home to get some sleep before driving back, anyway. Why not? It's not like I could bring her back from the dead by schlepping down I-ninety-five again."

Grinding roar of Rose pulverizing more coffee beans.

"Jamaica Blue Mountain this morning, or Kona?" Chad asked. "I thought you were finished."

"Both. With a dollop of Irish Cream. I'm feeling bold. So what are you going to do?"

"Stay here. Couple of reasons. If all I'm going back to, in terms of employment in DC, is another round of temp agency crapwork plus twentysomething hours a week at Borders, I can just as easily do that here. New Bern's a backwater, but it has a bookstore or two. I'll subsist."

"Will you use Marina as a reference? Won't she tell anyone who calls to—how did she put it?—make sure you get a urination test?"

"Christ. Don't remind me." Chad had somehow drunk half his cup of battery acid, and he still had his insides. "I guess I'll . . . fuck, I don't know what I'm going to do about that."

"List my cell phone number instead of the real one at Staff-o-Rama, or whatever it's called, and fax me a copy of your resume. Or tell me where to find it," Rose said.

"You're a lying scheming bitch and I love you," Chad said.

"I know you do. You have no choice. It was preordained. Jesus, this coffee is good."

"I hate you. The crap I'm drinking barely qualifies as coffee."

"Then close your eyes and think of Kenya. Look, you know the other thing you haven't brought up," Rose said. "There's supposedly this stash of money somewhere, right? Wouldn't it be convenient if you could find it? You wouldn't have to worry so much about work, and it wouldn't matter so much whether your mother comes to."

"I wasn't planning on saying so that bluntly, but you . . ." Chad's words trailed off. "That pretty much sums it up. If I had a clue where to start looking, that would make my life a lot easier."

"Think about it," Rose said. "She isn't a gullible old lady who'd sign over her house to the first handsome encyclopedia salesman that knocks on her door. She was pretty incapacitated before she went to the hospital, right?"

Chad sipped the last of his coffee. His lower back had begun to ache from standing hunched over and from tension.

"I'm not sure where you're going with this, but keep going," he said.

"There can't be too many places to hide it. You don't think she'd bury it in a jar in the garden, do you? How could she dig the hole, and what would happen to it in a heavy rain? Eliminate the places someone in terrible pain couldn't reach. She'd want to get her hands on it quickly, if she needed it."

"Is your last name Marple or Poirot? Are you holding out on me?" Chad asked. "I can't believe I didn't think of that already."

"Umm, hello! Your mother's dying. You're not supposed to be able to think clearly. If you were, whoever's writing your lines ought to be fired."

"Right. OK, that gives me some pointers. I should go back to her house and start looking."

"Sounds like a great way to spend the day. I know I've always been a sucker for a stash of money of dubious origin," Rose smiled. Chad could hear her smiling. "You'll be fine." Why did people keep telling him he'd be fine? "Go see if Mona's awake yet."

"I'll just do that."

"Oh, Chad. Last thing?" This didn't sound good. "You might want to know Martin has been calling. I stupidly picked up the phone without checking caller ID last night."

"What did you tell him?" Chad imagined Martin showing up at the hospital or, worse, at Mona's house. That wouldn't be the worst thing in the world, but it would come damn close. "Please say I've run off to Siberia to raise reindeer and live in a yurt."

"You'll love this. Your lying scheming bitch dyke of a roommate— you left out the dyke part earlier, and I'll thank you not to do it again—told one of her bigger lies this year. I got fed up with hearing his voice on the phone, so I said you were traumatized by your stay in the loony bin and were, thanks to my credit card and a last-minute Internet airfare special, on a plane to Boston for the weekend."

"Boston?"

"I was going to say Pittsburgh, but there's nothing to do there that I know of, except for the Warhol Museum, which takes half an hour. Boston seemed more plausible. It's more fag oriented. This is your cue to sound grateful and appreciative and in awe of my conniving brilliance."

"I'm grateful and appreciative and in awe of your conniving brilliance. Do you think Martin bought it?"

"He asked for the name of your hotel. I told him you were staying with friends whose names I couldn't remember. If you opt to call him, press star whatever on the phone so the number won't show up on his caller ID."

"You rock. You are a conniving, lying, scheming, cunning dyke bitch and I adore you."

"If you were a girl, we'd have to get married."

"If I were a girl, I'd still like dick."

"Those can be strapped on. Now get out of that fucking hospital. Go do something useful and find your mother's money. You'll feel much better when you're solvent."

"Doesn't everyone?"

Before returning to Mona's room, Chad tried to call Jonathan in Connecticut. The phone rang and rang. No answer, no machine, no voice mail. After a couple of minutes, Chad felt forlorn and gave up. He listened to crackling coming through the earpiece, the absence of dial tone, then hung up.

"I'm at a loss," Chad explained to Dr. Collins, Mona's oncologist, a clear-eyed, clear-skinned Barbie doll in her early thirties. Without the white coat and the stethoscope around her neck, Chad would have pictured her as a marketing junior executive, or perhaps an aspiring soap opera actress without the big hair. He outlined his situation. "She could wake up or she could stay in this state for weeks, right?"

"Most likely," Dr. Collins said. "I think we're looking at keeping her a couple more days, until she stabilizes. She's going downhill—her vital signs are deteriorating and there's evidence that the cancer is spreading more rapidly—but this isn't quite the end. We're close, but we're not there yet."

"Think she'll wake up if we reduce the morphine? I was told she might."

"If you had asked me that yesterday, I'd have told you something different." She shook her head. "I'm sorry to have to tell you this, but that's not something I'd recommend doing. Legal questions aside, she'd be in horrible pain. Cutting the dose would be both cruel and pointless. There's a very good chance it's too late to have a coherent talk with her. I know that must be difficult to hear."

"It's OK. We've done everything there is to do," Chad said. Except find the money. "Will she be moved to a hospice?"

"Not quite yet, but very soon, at this rate. As the next of kin, you have to decide where she goes. I think hospice is a good idea, but it's your decision."

"She wants to go home," Chad heard himself saying. "She doesn't want life support. Or at least I'm pretty sure she doesn't. I don't think she likes the idea of going into a hospice. She doesn't want to linger, if it can be avoided."

Doctor Barbie looked at him shrewdly. "I'd be very careful if I were you. This is a big decision with far-reaching consequences. Be sure this is something you've thought through. Here's my card. If you need anything, you can reach me at this number."

They shook hands. Dr. Collins left.

Mona stirred.

Chad was shaken.

Mona had admitted she'd first coughed up blood during the year Chad spent in Spain. She kept the matter to herself. She and Chad never talked about health problems in the first place. Mona wanted attention like she wanted air, but she stopped at bleaching her hair white and wearing shocking pink miniskirts to work in cold weather because she knew her tips would double. "Exhibit Your Symptom" was not a game she liked to play, unlike other Southern women of Chad's acquaintance.

She cut back on the Winstons and the sharp, pinching pain seemed to subside for a bit. The bloody hacking stopped. Must have been her throat, she told herself. Maybe a touch of emphysema.

When she wrote to Chad her sporadic letters contained mindless descriptions of the weather in New Bern, her nights out line dancing in Greenville and sometimes Raleigh, the little cowboy boots she had bought. Mona talked about herself and her surroundings. What had gone wrong with the house. How much her utility bills were. The color she had dyed her hair last week and the color she wanted to try when this shade grew out. She would end with endearments like, *I guess you're enjoying being a jet setter so much you're gonna forget about us regular folks back here in America. It must be nice.* Chad could never quite convince her that he hadn't gone to Spain just to party, and quit trying. The fringe benefits of living in the late-night capital of the planet could not be ignored.

She wrote to Chad in DC once a month, give or take a week, and the extra effort of a trip to the post office cut the frequency in half. Chad stopped reading her letters after three months in Madrid. She had nothing to say. He considered severing ties with her altogether, but he didn't want to be like Martin. That was the only thing stopping him.

In Madrid, Chad could pretend he was an orphan. The seediness of his childhood in North Carolina might as well never have happened. He didn't have to cultivate an air of mystery because the other students who became his friends found his illegitimate small-town American roots fascinating. Iñaki, a Basque from Bilbao, once said he was like a character from a Robert Altman movie: half tragic, half comic, and making things up as he went along. Lionel, a German from Munich, agreed with him and argued the point one night when they were all drunk. Henri, an Alsatian from Strasbourg, thought they were both pretentious assholes. "He's not the usual stupid American tourist, and that's the important thing. He's our Chad. Now will you two please hold him down while I pull off his pants? I have lust. I am having an attack of lust."

When you're lying curled up on the floor with lots of blankets and pillows and your three favorite wine-soaked Europeans, and you're in an apartment whose balcony overlooks the Retiro, you can't help but believe it doesn't get any better than this. Lionel's head is in the crook of your shoulder, and you have some of his hair in your mouth because you like the way his shampoo tastes, especially after all that cheap Bordeaux. Iñaki and Henri indulge in an extended, mouth-open kiss that soon engulfs Lionel, then you. Of course you are an orphan, and there is nothing but this, and this is as good as it gets, world without end, amen. North Carolina? Where's that?

Later, when he stopped to think about it, Chad supposed he had Mona to thank for some of this, but he couldn't bring himself to write her a letter and say so. Most of his correspondence with her during that time was an extended remix on the theme of, *It's warm there, you bleached your hair again, and your cat has diarrhea? That's nice.* He would then get back to whatever and whoever he was doing.

Chad looked at Mona again and decided not to die if he could avoid it. Best to put it off as long as possible and, when the time came, to go quickly and quietly. Lingering—bad idea. Looked painful. The purple-yellow pouch of flesh where the IV needle dove in. *Yikes.* He could see the discoloration through the brownish blood-spotted strip of tape securing the line. The tube in her mouth and the chaps on her lips reminding him of *National Geographic* photo spreads of Death Valley in high summer. The bedpan reek beneath the scrubbed-clean Lysol smells everywhere, and the carrion her flesh was turning into. Definitely best to avoid dying.

Chad could talk. The driver who hit him was a nineteen-year-old undergraduate fuck in a big SUV. The guy had shot a fifth of Cuervo with his drinking buddies back at his fraternity house, then decided to make a run to Safeway for more salt and limes when supplies ran out.

Chad's car collapsed, affording him about as much protection as a refrigerator box. The doctors' pronouncements all started with things like, "If he had been going just five miles an hour faster when he hit you," and "If you hadn't been wearing your seatbelt." Chad survived, but barely. The road to recovery hadn't been paved and there were times when he wanted a permanent detour, if not a nice commuter train with upholstered seats. He came within a hair of dying, then moved back into Mona's house to watch her start the process herself.

Mona's illness overlapping with Chad's injury forced them into a closeness that neither of them liked, but neither could avoid. He convalesced; she coughed. When he could finally move around, he fixed tea and sandwiches to feed her when she returned pallid and trembling after her trips to the hospital. "It's cancer," she said the day they told her. "But they think they can get it." Her vanity took the form of chasing him out of her house. She didn't want him to see her frightened and sick. He went back to DC; the doctors irradiated the thing in Mona's lung until they were convinced they had killed it; remission was declared.

Neither of them spoke a word to Martin.

Mona started coughing again within a year.

By that time Chad was dating Barry, and Mona never mentioned her health, except to send a letter to say she had stopped smoking and then started again. The letter arrived in a stack of nastygrams from collection agencies. Chad had set them all on fire and driven to Barry's apartment in the middle of the night, wondering how this could possibly be his life.

– 14 –

Thursday Morning (Later)

Nobody else had sent Mona flowers. Chad's bouquet of pink tulips looked lonely. The room, like every other hospital room he had seen, seemed designed to drive people away. Only those who enjoyed discomfort and didn't want visitors would stand a chance of recuperating here, Chad concluded after five fidgety minutes in a chair too low and hard for him: masochists and misanthropes. And the patients themselves? Chad felt he had hit on something. Maybe the furniture had been designed to encourage the patients to stage a quick turnaround time. The medical equivalent of McDonald's. Get in, do it, and get out. Recover or die, but don't *stay* here, for God's sake.

Mona stirred. He wiggled her, tapped her shoulder, said her name, said it again louder. He took the oxygen monitor off her big toe. The skin felt cold, and her toenail had an unpleasant yellow hue. He had intended to wiggle her toe, but this was like touching a corpse. As if to spite him, Mona would not respond or open her eyes.

"What do you want me to fucking *do?*" He flopped back into the torture-rack chair, crossed his legs, uncrossed them. The skin under his cast itched. Worse, his wrist itched on the inside, where he couldn't do anything about it. Meant the bone was healing. Good, but the sensation was making him nuts.

A passing nurse stuck her head in and glared at him, making *shush* noises and shooting lightning bolts out of her eyes.

Chad supposed he'd have to ask someone about the procedures for transferring unconscious patients. Did he need a power of attorney? Was just being her son authority enough? Would the hospital officials let her leave?

He paced.

Too little time passed.

Someone had oiled the hands of the clock with molasses.

Every time he tried turning the TV off, a nurse came in to turn it on again. Talk shows blared. Jerry Springer first. The nurse changed the channel, and tuned in to Oprah. Oprah was leading chants. Men in green robes seemed to be levitating a foot above the floor. Ommmmm. Chad turned off the TV again, and the next nurse turned it on, turned up the volume, looked at him in a puzzled way. *You don't want to watch TV?* After twenty minutes of this on/off struggle, Chad unplugged the television set and bent the metal prongs. He wanted to snap one off but his fingers lacked the strength, and one hand was mostly useless.

I can't leave. I can't stay. I can't leave. I can't stay.

Chad stared out Mona's window. Time crept. He often looked up from the book he couldn't get into, a dreary Manhattan-in-the-eighties cocaine epic by a writer barely old enough to drink in the clubs he wrote about. Neither Mona nor the book improved. He left it in a vacant lounge and went to look for better reading material. The hospital gift shop offered a junk food diet of Lay's potato chips, Jackie Collins novels, pretzels, and room-temperature Diet Coke. Hopeless. Sometimes he would walk down the hall and say hi to the nurses, who were concerned because the TV in Mona's room no longer worked.

I can't leave. I can't stay.

Lions and tigers and bears, oh my.

Chad decided to call Rose from a pay phone again to alleviate his boredom.

"I'm going fucking nuts down here," he told her.

"Well, your brother came banging on the door this morning. I was getting ready for work. Running late, of course. He refuses to believe you're in Boston. Wanted me to give him flight numbers so he could call the airline. I told him to suck my left tit."

"Ew!"

"Figure of speech," Rose said. "I doubt he'll think to look down there—he's cunning but not that bright—but just keep in mind, when you get back, he's going to be all over you, wanting to know where you went and what you did."

"Jesus Fucking Christ, how did I get born in the same family he did?" Chad wondered whether the call had been wise. He didn't feel bored any longer, but he wasn't sure dread and vague nausea were the best replacements for the boredom.

"How's it going down there?"

"Vile. I can't leave and I can't stay. What the fuck am I supposed to do? Just follow the instructions she left in that note and smother her with a pillow?"

"If you can't do anything for her, then do something for yourself. What about this money she claimed to have?" Rose asked.

Chad shrugged, then realized Rose couldn't hear him shrug over the phone.

"I have no idea. It may not even exist. I didn't look for it last night because I'd have gotten covered with cat shit."

"That's beautiful, Chad. Look, you could get a temp job down there, couldn't you?" Rose, as ever, made sense in times of crisis. "There's no good reason for you to return to DC. In fact—and don't interpret this to mean I'm trying to get rid of you, because you know I love you to little bits and pieces—but with Martin here, maybe you should consider living someplace else."

"Lovely," Chad said. His head spun. Leave DC? The thought had occurred to him, but he had never taken it seriously. His friends were there. "Remember the war in Croatia, after it seceded from Yugoslavia? We'd read in the *Post* about how you could sit at sidewalk cafés in Zagreb and watch the shelling off in the distance? Martin's like that. Now and then a mortar will hit a building nearby, but most of the time . . ."

"Great metaphor, babe, but you're so full of shit sometimes I don't know what to do with you. Go ransack Mona's house. Look for the money. If you find it, you'll be able to think clearly. If not, look in the yellow pages for temp agencies. I'm doing pretty well right now—I'll hook you up. You won't get stuck down there with no money for gas, or whatever."

Chad's throat closed up.

"I hate . . . being so pathetic," he said, with effort. His eyes stung, and if there had been a mirror nearby he would have broken it without a superstitious second thought to avoid the sight of himself.

"You're not pathetic, just stuck. There's a world of difference. Look, there are a couple of other things. Martin's wife called me here. How the fuck she got my number, I have no idea. She started asking me these questions about you. She was so obviously snooping I couldn't believe it for a minute. Like, I didn't think she was that dumb."

"What the fuck?"

"*What the fuck* is right. She wanted to know if I thought you were a risk to yourself, among other things. And did you have some kind of hostility issue, because she was *just so concerned*. I was like, *Bitch, have you lost what feeble shreds of a mind you have?*"

"Oh, this makes me sick." The nausea rolled back in like the tide. Chad put a protective hand over his stomach. "What the fuck is she up to?"

"Well, it gets even more bizarre. First she launched into that line of inquiry, then she dropped the subject when she saw it wasn't getting her anywhere and started asking me questions about Martin. It made no goddamn sense at all. Had I seen him? Did I find him threatening? How often was he at the house? Did he have a problem with you? I let her go on a little longer, just to find out where she was going with it."

"Well, what the hell did you tell her?" Chad sat down. The metal-wrapped phone cord stretched to its maximum length, refused to budge another inch, forced him to stand again. He compromised by slumping against the wall.

"As little as possible. I work for a law firm, you know, so I know how to use lots of words without saying much."

"She has to be leaving him," Chad said. "Jonathan thought of that when we were in the hospital. Nothing else makes even a feeble shred of sense."

"Unless she's just nuts and operating with no rational motivation at all," Rose offered.

"No, she has an agenda. She might even be smarter than she lets on. What a horror show. So what else has gone on?"

"Couple of other people called for you. I'm drawing a blank on the names. Your friend who went to Atlanta? He left a message. He's back in town and wants to get together. Sorry, I'm blonding out on the name. Robert or something. I know you want to know. No word from Jonathan, though."

"Probably busy with his lawyers," Chad said, disappointed. Partly. Roger had called; that was good news. Chad stared at the back of his right hand. Then the left. The web between the thumb and the fore-finger, where Jonathan had that lightning bolt tattoo. Delicious and just slightly déclassé. Chad made a fist. Maybe he should get a tattoo somewhere. Not on the back of his hand, though.

"You'll hear from him," Rose said. She had a telepathic knack for sensing when he needed reassurance. "The last thing is a question you may not want to hear, but which needs to be asked. It's a law firm thing. Does Mona have a will?"

"Yes, and I've been so wrapped up in . . ." Chad's voice ran out of steam. "I can't think straight. I hadn't thought about the will, and she even said she had one, in her note."

"Go back to her house and *find* it, Chad. Do it now."

"You're so right, and I'm so out of here," Chad said.

"One other thing, speaking of being busy with lawyers. I haven't forgotten about that age-of-consent thing. I'm totally swamped after that trip. OK? But I will look into it, I promise. If it's the last thing I do."

"You're the bestest."

"I know. Now get your ass back to that house and look for that money."

The stench had abated, but after several hours in a hospital where the air burned his nose with the smell of disinfectant, and after driving across New Bern with his windows down, Chad felt woozy when he got his first whiff of Mona's house. He left the front door open but locked the screen door to let air circulate. He opened all the windows again, lit every candle he could find (Mona had a number of vanilla-scented ones), and burned incense cones on upturned coffee cups. Then he retreated to the back porch to gulp oxygen and think.

Chad stretched out on his chaise-lounge cot, shirt off, and tried to imagine where Mona would stash money.

Where had she spent most of her time? In front of the TV. But would she put her cash in a room she rarely used, or somewhere she could get to it fast, even in her weakened state?

She's my mother. I ought to know her well enough to predict her behavior.

The pine trees surrounding Mona's house creaked in the breeze. The Washington area didn't have pines like this, tall trunks with no branches near the ground and only a few up top. Chad felt a small pang at the thought he'd grown up here and soon would have no reason at all to come back.

Mona meant it this time: her body had failed her and she wanted out. Chad wondered if he could stomach saying no to her request any more than he could stomach saying yes.

She hadn't mentioned final arrangements beyond her basic message of, *Get me dead as soon as you can.* Chad assumed she'd want to be cremated, since, desiccated by the cancer, her body wasn't in any condition for mourners to look at. She wasn't presentable.

Could she be revived long enough to . . .

No, she can't, Chad told himself, putting a firm stop to that asinine line of thought. *She's not going to wake up, and it's all up to you from here, so grow a dick and stop thinking like that.*

There had to be a will. Note or no note, there had better be a will, because Martin would slime his way into a chunk of the estate, such as it was, if he could. Chad didn't like the thought of reducing all this to a series of financial transactions, but none of them were close. Hell, they didn't even like one another. He couldn't avoid being motivated by green dollars when he was worth so many red ones.

Thoughts of Martin pissed Chad off enough to get him off his ass, to start looking for Mona's money. He felt nauseated at the prospect of Martin showing up at the hospital, to bluster his way into the center of things, a silver-tongued Prince of Darkness making the nurses feel warm and moist and gooey inside. Chad recognized how much easier his own life would be had his brother at least been born ugly.

The crunch of tires on gravel outside stopped Chad's treasure hunt before it started.

"Oh Christ! It's Martin," Chad muttered, hurrying to the front room to take a look outside.

The engine sounded big enough to be Martin's truck. Ominously, it stopped.

Queasy with dread, Chad hesitated a second before he climbed across the sofa to look. He brushed the curtain aside with his cast.

Who the fuck drove a blue Range Rover and had business here? *Connecticut plates.*

Someone knocked on the door just as Chad made the connection.

He flung the door open and knobbed a dent in the 1970s-era wood paneling Mona had painted off-white.

"Jonathan!"

They kissed hello, then kissed again, longer this time, stopping every now and then to look at each other up close. Jonathan stood a bit shorter than Chad remembered. This made him smile. He tasted mint from Jonathan's mouth. Such soft lips.

"*What the fuck are you doing here?* is the question I know you're dying to ask," Jonathan said when they had seated themselves on a sofa that passed Chad's sniff test.

"Well, that, but it comes second after *How the fuck did you find this place?* and ahead of *How long did it take you to drive down here?*" Chad caught his breath. The rush of fear-inspired adrenaline hadn't quite abated. "It's so good to see you. I've been going crazy down here."

"Careful, you don't want another vacation at Club Meds."

"I do. I really am crazy, remember? I can't believe you're here. So how the fuck did you find this place? How long did it take you to drive down here?"

"Rose told me your mother lived in New Bern, and I had her name and number already. I called information and asked if the address was listed along with the phone number. After that, it was as simple as printing out a map off the Internet." Jonathan shrugged. "How long did it take?"

"Do I want to know?" Chad asked.

"Eleven hours. I'd have made better time in the Mercedes, but I thought the Range Rover might be more useful." Chad wondered what this meant as Jonathan continued. "I got the idea last night around midnight. Couldn't sleep. I wanted to see you. So I took a shower, packed my gear in the truck, and left."

"I can't believe you're here. I know how stupid that sounds, but I mean it. You can't imagine how . . ." Chad stopped himself before he finished his sentence. *How horrible it's been.* Of course Jonathan could imagine that. Very few people out there could imagine it with Jonathan's clarity. "OK, rewind. Let me try again before you decide I'm an unredeemable asshole and leave screaming. I hate being here. The house smells like a cat box and is still barely habitable. Mona is basically dead but still breathing, and the doctors tell me there's a microscopic chance she's going to wake up and tell us what she wants. I'm broke. Things suck."

"Can you just leave?" Jonathan asked, snuggling closer.

If the smells of the house offended him, he was doing a great job of hiding it. In fact, if the house itself offended him, he wasn't letting it show. Chad felt a stab of embarrassment. He had grown up in this place, which had looked like a Dumpster and smelled like a kennel until last night. Jonathan had grown up in exurban luxury and European boarding schools.

Chad filled him in. "It's not even the money, although I've been trying to figure out where it is. She's trying to bribe me into killing her. We weren't close, even though I came down to visit regularly and made sure she was taken care of. If she had just said she wasn't strong enough to end it all, and would I please help her, that would be one thing. But she reduced it to a financial quid pro quo, and now she's too far gone to keep up her end of the deal."

"You've decided to do it, then?"

Chad flinched.

"From the look on your face, I'd say you haven't."

"Well, no, that's the problem. If I were in her hospital slippers and too wasted to pull the plug by myself, I'd want help. So I'm trying to work up the courage to figure out how. But I don't want it to be because she paid me. If I get caught, think how it would look."

Jonathan's eyes widened. He let out a low whistle.

"I'm impressed," he said. "You've got more balls than you realize. Did you know that?"

"Even you pointed out I'm pretty well hung," Chad reminded him. "Why is it such a surprise?"

"So what are you going to do?"

"I figured I'd spend the day searching the house and stop by the hospital later this afternoon. There's nothing to be gained by staying there. Hell, I couldn't even buy a Coke without wondering how I was going to afford the gas to drive back to DC." Chad stopped himself. "Look, I'm sorry to be dumping all this shit on you. You didn't drive for hours to hear about this . . ."

Jonathan interrupted him. "Don't be stupid. That's exactly why I drove hours to get here. Because you're in bad shape and I wanted to see you and be here for you. We helped each other get through our time in that stupid fucking hospital, and now that we're out, why can't we keep doing the same thing?"

Chad couldn't answer him.

Jonathan continued. "Don't worry about the money, either. To be blunt, you're about to inherit this house. It may not be a penthouse on Park Avenue, but if I lend you a couple of grand, I know you'll be good for it."

"You're going to make me cry, you asshole," Chad said, choked up. "Is that what you're trying to do?"

"No, I'm just being real." Jonathan kissed him again. "I couldn't stop thinking about you while I was in Connecticut. I like you a lot—more than a lot—and I want to keep getting to know you. The usual rules don't apply to us anymore. That one-step-at-a-time dating bullshit. So I've got money and am in a position to share it with you—big deal. We'll come out even in the end."

Chad lost it. He cried on Jonathan's shoulder, really cried for the first time since he could remember, as if a pipe or duct inside him had broken. Jonathan held him and stroked his hair. After a few minutes, Chad began to get himself under control.

"I look like shit now, don't I?" he asked, with a sniffle.

"You're cute when you cry," Jonathan said, kissing his wet cheeks.

"So do you want the grand tour before we tear this house apart?"

"Sure." Jonathan stood, then offered a hand to Chad.

In Mona's bedroom, Jonathan casually asked if Chad had thought to look under the mattress. That was where people always stashed money in books and movies. Under the mattress.

Jonathan lifted one corner and, with trepidation, Chad slid his castless hand underneath to feel around.

"There's something in here," he said, heart racing again.

"Why don't you pull it out?" Jonathan said. He was grinning. Chad could hear it in his voice.

Chad withdrew a large manila envelope, opened it, and looked inside.

"Jesus H. Christ."

Money.

"That wasn't difficult," Jonathan said.

Chad's knees got weak, and he sat down hard in the middle of the floor. Feeling stupid, he dumped the cash in his lap. It made an impressive pile. These dollars, unlike his own, were green.

"It was under the mattress," he said. "Probably the last place I'd have looked."

Jonathan winked at him and said, "I know."

Thursday

"There's almost thirty-eight thousand dollars in this stack," Chad said, awed. He had never handled a stack of bills larger than the till in his cash register at Borders. Would Jonathan think him tacky if he held the money to his nose and sniffed? If so, Jonathan would get over it. The bills smelled dusty. He sneezed.

"Twenty-three in mine," Jonathan said. Then he sniffed his own money. "It doesn't smell very good, does it?"

"No." Chad fanned the bills out like cards in a poker game. Enviable hand: all hundreds. "I guess I don't have to worry about having enough gas to get back to DC."

"I guess you don't." Jonathan smiled as he handed over the money. "We should eat someplace good for dinner. Your mom's house is cute, but I doubt there's much here we'll want to eat, and the atmosphere's a little off."

"You're a demented genius. Don't you need to take a shower or anything?"

"Mmm. Well, sure. Actually, yes. Let me get my backpack out of the car, and then show me where the bathroom is."

Chad hadn't felt this comfortable with anyone since Barry. It scared him. He had no idea where Barry was now. The abrupt end hadn't left room for them to exchange promises or talk things over. He'd called once to say he had decided to get out of the Air Force, either with a discharge, if one could be arranged, or by not reenlisting when he had the option several months later. His injuries weren't enough to warrant an overnight hospitalization—nothing had been broken except his nose and his spirit—and Chad suspected Barry would move as far from suburban Maryland as possible, geography permitting. He'd probably gone home to Seattle to lick his wounds. Aside from a certain amount of sneaking, the thing with Barry would have worked. Just like that—gone.

Water under the bridge now. Chad hoped he'd hear from Barry again, but he had no idea how to find him or what he'd say. "Oh, by the way, Barry, I tried to kill myself after what happened. Fucked up the attempt and lived. One of the few times in my life everything was going really well, and it all got taken away from me overnight." He knew the questions Barry would ask. The hardest ones would be about Martin, and those Chad couldn't possibly answer.

He blinked and knuckled his eyes, to clear away his final image of Barry lying on the floor of Chad's apartment, blood caking his blond hair, nose broken, eyes blackened. He lay curled in the fetal position, pants down, coughing and crying, on the edge of going into shock. They had been ambushed.

Did Jonathan have any idea what he was getting into? And after Chad told him everything, because of course he would have to, would he give a damn? Chad thought not.

With the sound of water running in the background, Chad called the hospital to check Mona's status.

"She's out like a light," a female nurse with an iced tea and magnolia accent answered. "Same as when you were here this morning. Vitals are weak and getting weaker. She could rally, but honey, none of us are holding our breath, not now. The doctor's already talking about advance directives, and whether we should go ahead and turn that respirator off. Next time you stop by, you two are gonna have to have a little talk, and I'm afraid it won't be too easy."

"I'll stop by this afternoon, a little later," Chad said, feeling lame. After a second's hesitation, he added, "If anything happens, I'm at the house, trying to figure out what she wanted done. She didn't exactly leave clues. I can be reached here."

A respirator. How miserable.

Turning it off. Even worse.

Chad, morose, considered pulling off his clothes and joining Jonathan in the shower. As much as Chad craved the contact, he decided

the time could be more usefully spent investigating the remnants of
Mona's office. She had a desk and filing cabinet, both overflowing
with envelopes, notices, and bits of paper, in the tiny room that had
once been his bedroom. The stale air pressed against his sinuses and
temples. He opened the window wider and wondered again whether
he'd be better off to take a torch to the house and be done with the
whole thing once and for all. He could drop the match here, in the middle of all this paper. There'd be that fire-taking-off sound, FOOMP,
then a conflagration.

If she kept a will anywhere, it's in here, buried under all this shit.

Old photos on the wall in gold drugstore frames looked blandly
down at him as he searched: one picture of Martin and Chad, both in
little-boy jackets and neckties Chad remembered Mona buying one
afternoon at Sears, the two of them posing at some far-distant cousin's
wedding over in Kinston. Twenty minutes before they had left for the
wedding, Martin had snipped the lower button off Chad's jacket with
a pair of kitchen shears, blamed the damage on Chad, and gotten
Chad spanked with a long wooden spoon. Chad took the photo off the
wall, carefully removed the picture from its frame, and ripped it in
half. The half containing more of Martin, Chad tore to small shreds
and sprinkled over the mound of trash in the garbage can by Mona's
desk. He looked at his own side of the picture for another second, then
tore it in half as well. To say goodbye to the past, he supposed.

Another picture of Martin glared down at him. *Why had Mona kept it?*
"Asshole."

Chad pulled the frame off the wall and dropped the whole thing in
the trash. Felt like removing stains from the collars of his white shirts
or following the instructions for prescription medicine. *Repeat as necessary. Take as needed.* Chad dropped a third framed photo into the trash,
then a fourth, and continued until Jonathan emerged from the bathroom shirtless, wearing jeans sagging low over narrow hips, Calvin
Klein's name embroidered on the black elastic of his underwear, navel
ring glinting and lickable.

"You don't look so great," Jonathan said after a second or two of
surveillance.

"I tried looking through the office but made the mistake of looking at the pictures on the walls. Had to do something about them. They were looking at me."

"The ones of Martin?"

"Yeah, the Martin ones." Chad nodded. "What a perceptive beastie you are. I could fall head over heels for you."

"Falling in love with me? Yikes! My sinister plan has been discovered!" He idly scratched his left armpit. "What happened in there?"

"Too much reality. I overdosed on it and had to get some fresh air. It's like, wake up and smell the cat turds, Chad."

"Want me to go in there with you?"

Chad nodded. "I have to find the will. Without that, things could get kind of sticky for us." He realized what pronoun he'd chosen only after it had left his mouth. *Us?* Jonathan smiled back at him. Clearly Chad's choice of words hadn't been lost on him.

"Then let's look," Jonathan said.

"You just took a shower. It's all dusty in there."

"Dude, dust rinses off. I'll take another shower afterward."

"Sounds like a good reason for me to get dirty, then," Chad said.

After Jonathan put on a T-shirt, they prowled through the stacks of junk on Mona's desk: bills, bills, and more bills, most unpaid. *Like mother, like son,* Chad thought blackly, staring at a stack of "pay or else" notices from collection agencies. How much debt was she in? Chad wondered how she had hoarded the money on a fixed government income, and decided he didn't want to know. She had always attracted the sort of men who needed getaway cars driven and drug stashes concealed for a couple of days. Chad felt sure one of them had been his father. The stash of money wouldn't cover Mona's outstanding debts, Chad suspected, especially if her medical bills were taken into account. It also wouldn't pay off of his own debts, but it might knock them down to manageable proportions.

On the other hand, when Mona was dead nobody would know about the money. Chad suspected she had come to be swamped with bills the same way he had: credit card companies kept issuing her cards and raising her credit limits, despite indications she was over her head and could never pay off what she owed. He flipped through a few of the collections notices, then asked Jonathan to hand over a couple of Visa bills. Sure enough. *Fucking loan sharks,* he thought. *Predators.* That's all they were. Loan sharks with offices in Wilmington, Delaware, where state laws let lenders charge usurious interest rates not permitted elsewhere.

If she had a will, and had named him executor of her estate, he guessed that meant he had a legal obligation to settle her debts. He looked down at the collections notices again and decided the Visa and MasterCard people could go fuck themselves.

"Your mother likes to save her junk mail," Jonathan observed, after digging through a foot of the detritus on her desk.

"She never used to. I'm going to the kitchen for garbage bags."

Magazines whose subscriptions Mona had allowed to lapse years before kept sending plaintive cardboard pleas for her to renew. Chad started with a desultory look at the envelopes and pieces of paper he picked up and realized he had gotten distracted.

"We should check in here," Chad said, opening a filing cabinet door—unlocked, thank God, because the key could have been anywhere. "Although I doubt she'd have been so logical as to keep the will in a manila folder with a legible label."

To his shock, the contents of the cabinet were arranged in alphabetical order, A through G. The files, though untidy, were labeled clearly.

"She never ceases to amaze me. Look at that." Chad did a Vanna White sweep of the cabinet. "Would you like to buy a vowel?"

"A consonant," Jonathan said. "Those are free. I never liked vowels enough to want to spend money on one."

"I can guess which one you want to see." Chad stooped to open the bottom drawer, where W ought to be.

"Will," Chad and Jonathan said, simultaneously.

Chad reached for the folder.

"It can't have been that easy."

Of course it wasn't. Not a second time.

The folder was empty.

Chad looked at Jonathan. Jonathan looked at Chad.

"Fuck," Chad said.

Jonathan nodded. "Fuck," he said, solemnly. Amazing how well a somewhat plummy British boarding school accent could brighten up the most vulgar words in the English language.

"I guess we keep looking."

"Is there anything to drink?"

Chad checked the refrigerator and found a plastic pitcher of suspicious-smelling iced tea and another pitcher, glass, of water, also somewhat questionable when he sniffed. Mona had not been one to keep boxes of baking soda in the fridge, to eliminate odors. Nor, evidently, had she been one to throw away leftovers, no matter how long ago she had cooked them the first time. "I'm not sure there's anything here you'd want to put in your mouth," Chad called back to Jonathan.

"I can think of one thing!" Jonathan replied. "But it isn't in the fridge!"

Chad returned to Mona's study empty handed. Jonathan had his back to Chad and was flipping through something, although Chad couldn't see quite what he had in hand. Chad admired the view for a minute—broad shoulders making a triangle of his back, tapering to a point at his narrow waist. The jeans concealed his ass, but that was OK. Chad already knew what it looked like. Sooner or later he meant to slide his tongue between Jonathan's cheeks to find out how it tasted, as well.

"Card file," Jonathan said when Chad took a break from his mental pornography and asked what he was looking at. "I found a business card from a lawyer. Did your mother have a lawyer, to the best of your knowledge?"

"Until today, I'd have said I didn't think she could afford one, but now, anything is possible."

"Check this out." Jonathan gave Chad the card, which was printed on plain white stock with tiny words embossed in black ink.

"Linda Grossman, Attorney at Law. *Wills, estate planning, retirement, Social Security cases.*" Chad looked up. "I need to call her. Now." He started to say "we" instead of "I," but stopped himself before the word could come out. This was still his game, not Jonathan's, although the gap between them was closing.

After explaining who he was to a receptionist, then an assistant, then waiting on hold for what felt like hours with Muzak numbing his brain like a Thorazine drip, Chad finally got Ms. Grossman on the phone. He went through the spiel again.

"I remember your name. Your mother always spoke well of you," said Linda Grossman. Her dense Long Island accent was a breath of fresh snowy air now that Chad had spent almost forty-eight hours in the humid muck of eastern North Carolina. Reminded him of civilization—corner delis, subways, good coffee—if not of home, per se. "She had revised her will, and I hadn't quite gotten around to putting it in the mail back to her. I'm very sorry to hear about her condition, but we all knew her time was coming up. Is there anything I can do for you?"

"Well, not to be too blunt, but I need to know if the will said anything about final arrangements. Or maybe she said something to you about that. I'm flying blind, over here, and I have a half brother, Martin . . ."

She interrupted him: "Martin has been cut out of the will. Your mother wanted it worded strongly enough to keep her estate away from him. You don't need to worry about Martin."

"Has she talked about final arrangements?" Chad couldn't believe his mother's attorney hadn't demanded he trek down to her office, present photo ID, a birth certificate, DNA, fingerprints, a urination test. He wasn't in Washington anymore. "I've just learned she was financially better off than she let on, and now I kind of wonder, you know, if there were other things she had planned out and then not told me."

"I can answer most of those questions for you. She said she had communicated her wishes to you very clearly. When the time came, she said, you would know exactly what she wanted done with her remains." Ms. Grossman's voice showed the first hint of suspicion.

"Christ. Then the cancer must have caught her before she could tell me, because I'm without a clue here." Jonathan scribbled a note and handed it to him. *Tell her about the money and ask if she's holding anything in addition to the will.* Chad almost dropped the phone. That would never have occurred to him. As carefully as possible, he said he had found something under the mattress and wondered if Ms. Grossman might know anything about its origins, and whether there might be anything more in a safe deposit box somewhere.

"That's where I have to draw the line, Mr.—I'm sorry, I'm not sure if your last name was the same as your mother's. It was? Sobran? Good. Sorry. OK, as I was saying, I don't mind going into this on the phone, up to a point, but I have an appointment in five minutes, and I can tell you only so much without seeing you for myself, to establish who you are. Can you drop by my office this afternoon? I've got a packed schedule, but I'll see you for a few minutes. I'd like to be able to offer more, but the timing's lousy."

Chad knew she was going to say something like that but didn't mind. Much. It wasn't like he had an office to get back to, a phone ringing off the hook, and meetings booked all afternoon.

She wouldn't say, he mouthed to Jonathan. "Sure, I'll be glad to stop by. We can do that on the way to the hospital, if you'll just give me directions."

Jonathan drove. Chad navigated.

"I feel like Thelma and Louise, only with penises," Jonathan said. He stopped for a red light and fiddled with the stereo.

"Did you know I've seen that movie three times and still don't know which one was which? It should have been called *Susan and Geena*. Or *Geena and Susan*."

"You know what I mean, though, don't you? Us against the rest of the world."

Chad looked at him. Jonathan looked his age for a second, young and vulnerable, too small to be driving this gigantic SUV through an unfamiliar town. He had to scoot the seat forward to reach the pedals, Chad noticed, feeling rather like a pedophile. Jonathan brushed a lock of dark hair out of his eye and squinted at the map Chad had drawn on a pink sticky note.

"Of course, I know. That's always been part of the appeal," Chad said.

"I'm not always as confident as I seem," Jonathan said.

Chad thought, *What brought this on?* Where was Jonathan going with this?

"I like you a lot," Jonathan said, looking straight ahead. "You make sense right now. Not much else does. I'm not saying I want us to, like, get married or whatever. Just don't turn psycho on me or take off and not tell me why. OK?"

"Cross my heart," Chad said. "Now drive. The light's green."

Linda Grossman occupied a small suite of offices in a strip mall near the hospital. Her corporate neighbors were a pager and prepaid cell phone dealer, a down-at-the-heels pharmacy, and an empty storefront with papered-over windows and a sign indicating that Treesha's Hair + Nails would be opening in a month.

"Not exactly K Street," Chad remarked, as Jonathan parked in a spot outside the door.

"K Street?" Jonathan asked. "I'm from Connecticut. What's a K Street?"

"The street in DC where the legal eagles roost," Chad replied, getting out of the car.

The receptionist who greeted them—a mushroom-pallid woman whose orange blusher ended in a line halfway down her neck and whose bleached hair showed a wide stripe of black roots where it parted—quacked, "How can I help you?" in a two-packs-a-day voice. She gave them a look that dripped with bored disdain.

By using any color other than blue for your eye shadow, Chad thought.

"My name is Chad Sobran. I'm here to see Linda Grossman."

"Is she expecting you?"

"Yes. We spoke on the phone about an hour ago. My mother is a client." Chad mentally kicked himself for explaining too much again. He felt Jonathan looking at him but didn't turn to meet his gaze.

"Have a seat right there,"—she indicated an uncomfortable-looking vinyl sofa with wooden arms—"and I'll just call to let her know you're here. Your name again? Chad Something?"

Jonathan took a seat in the sofa opposite the one the receptionist had indicated. Chad sat beside him.

"Sobran," he said.

"Interesting name," the receptionist quacked, pressing a button.

"I know," Chad said.

– 16 –

Thursday, Late Afternoon

"You resemble your mother," Linda Grossman said. With her Long Island accent, it sounded like, "Yew resemble yah muthah." Chad tried to imagine what circumstances had brought her to the waterlogged edge of North Carolina, where the natives put several extra syllables into every vowel and looked with open skepticism on anyone from farther north than Maryland's Eastern Shore.

"My figure's a bit different," Chad replied. "But I think we have the same facial features."

Ms. Grossman gave him the eye. She had on a severe brown pantsuit, accented with a gold brooch, and she wore her greying hair in a chignon the approximate size and shape of a toaster.

She offered them water from a cooler by the door. The garbage can next to it overflowed with paper cones.

"I only have to take a look at you to tell you're her son. And I don't doubt for a second she's in the hospital, in very bad shape. So I'm going to give you a copy of the will, and I don't mind telling you now, because I know you've got to be wondering, you're getting everything, but she has given you a lot of responsibility as well. I hope you're up for it."

Chad blinked in surprise.

"It seems your brother Martin has called her several times in the last six months . . ."

"No fucking way!"

Ms. Grossman looked up from the stack of papers she was rifling through on her desk and blinked a few times.

"Yes fucking way. He called her several times. Your mother got the impression he was trying to worm his way back into her good graces. She told me he was kvetching about having to put his children through college and wanting money for the down payment on a townhouse. No shame, your mother told me. He had no shame. *Has no shame*," she said, still rummaging. "He's in the military, I understand. There are programs available. Neither your mother nor I could figure out what he was up to, but I doubt he's going to write us a memo and fax it over. My God, I just had my hands on that piece of paper, and now where is it? I'm being honest with you: I am not normally a disorganized woman, but I started purging files this morning, and the pieces of paper must have multiplied while my back was turned!"

Chad reeled. Mona had never mentioned any contact from Martin. He said so.

"It doesn't surprise me. I think Mona—she told me you call her that, by the way, and I think it's kind of cute—decided if he didn't want anything further to do with her, she didn't want anything further to do with him. It was obvious what he was up to. I don't think he knows about the cash she had hoarded—there's no way he could—but he knows she had clear title on the house, and a small life insurance policy. That's what he was after."

Chad stared out the window wondering what else Ms. Grossman was going to drop on him. There are only so many shocking revelations a person can take before his head explodes like a jack o' lantern with a grenade inside.

"Got it!" Ms. Grossman handed Chad a several-page document. "The basics you need to know are that she wants to be cremated and doesn't give a damn what you do with the ashes, as long as you don't use them to line her cat box."

"How is this version of the will different from the previous one?" Chad asked, flipping through it. The document contained a list of items that he expected to see—title on the house, life insurance policy, set of china, television—but nothing out of the ordinary.

"Different language. Stronger. If he challenges it in court, it'll be almost impossible for him to win. He appears to think he's entitled to his fair share of the estate, and your mother disagrees with him."

"I'll have to take your word for it."

Ms. Grossman opened a safe on the floor next to her desk, next to a small refrigerator. Bending forward with an unladylike grunt, she withdrew a thick envelope much like the one from beneath Mona's mattress.

"Tell me that's not another stack of cash," Chad said.

"OK, I won't tell you. Look for yourself."

"Where did she get this? Did she say?" Chad opened the clasp and tore the adhesive. This time, a sheaf of smaller bills—twenties mostly, a few fifties—could be seen when he peered inside. "We barely had enough to make ends meet all my life, and now this? I don't know whether to jump for joy or throw up."

"She never talked about where she got it, although I don't mind telling you sources may not have been one hundred percent legal. Not the kind of thing you tell your kids about. And she didn't trust banks with more than the minimum necessary to maintain a checking account."

"Jesus Christ."

Chad looked around for a chair, a coffee table—something he could sit on. Jonathan interpreted Chad's look correctly and stood up, with a gesture for him to take the armchair. Chad fanned himself with the money as sweat formed on his brow. He crumpled a twenty-dollar bill to soften it, then used it to mop his forehead.

"Mona doesn't trust the government, period," Chad said. "Nor the police, nor anyone else. I guess it makes sense that she'd stash money away."

He thought back and remembered purchases that now made more sense: quality liquor instead of the rubbing alcohol to which he had assumed her budget would restrict her; her televisions, always more expensive than he had thought she could afford; her car, a late-model Mercury station wagon (still prone to frequent breakdowns, but fairly new). Every couple of weeks, when Martin and he were young, she would take them to a steak house or a buffet for dinner—her idea (consistent with much of the populace of New Bern) of fine dining.

"May I ask something?" Jonathan spoke for the first time.

Chad nodded. Ms. Grossman looked more curious than anything else.

"Do we know if she ever filed income taxes? When we were looking for the will earlier, I never noticed any tax-related information among her files."

The bottom dropped out of Chad's stomach.

"She probably didn't," he said. "That would be in character."

"I suggest you take another good look through her things after you visit her in the hospital," Ms. Grossman said. "And find out if she had an accountant."

"One other question," Jonathan said.

"You're going to make a fine lawyer someday, I can already tell," Ms. Grossman said, sounding a bit awed.

"Why doesn't Chad have a medical power of attorney?"

"He does," Ms. Grossman astonished them by saying. She turned to Chad. "I prepared it for her, but she went into the hospital before she could sign it."

"So she left no official instructions for me? No word on whether she wanted life support, heroic measures, respirator or no respirator, whatever?"

"Nothing official," Ms. Grossman said. She frowned at him. "But she said you would know what she wanted you to do. You don't, I take it?"

"Haven't got a clue," Chad lied. He stared at his feet.

Chad had little to say on the drive to the hospital, and Jonathan left him alone to sort through the piles of garbage in his head. He kept the volume low on the stereo, the air-conditioning high, and occasionally hummed a tune Chad couldn't identify.

"It's a good thing you're here," said Dwayne, the nurse Chad had seen earlier, the second he and Jonathan stepped from the elevator into the ward.

For the second time that day, a trapdoor opened in Chad's stomach. His legs went flaccid for a second.

"What's going on?" he said.

"The doctor will be around later to explain the details, but I can tell you this: her blood gases are dropping rapidly," Dwayne said. "She doesn't have long."

He noticed an empty chair by the nurse's station and sat in it, elbow knocking over a couple of charts. After a second's deliberation, he put his head between his knees, closed his eyes, and took deep breaths: in through the nose, out through the mouth. One of the nurses told him he wasn't supposed to sit there. He sat up, speared her with a look, and asked if she thought the floor was a better alternative.

"I have to get my shit together before I go in and see her," Chad said.

"Take your time," the nurse said.

"How long could she linger like this?" He knew he had asked the same question several times, but he likened it to looking into an empty refrigerator when he was hungry: there might be something new inside, something that hadn't been there the last time he looked. You could never tell what you'd find when you opened the door.

"She's very unstable. She could last for a couple more weeks at the outside, but that would be a miracle. Or she could be gone by the time we walk into the room."

Another nurse wheeled an emaciated person down the hall, past them, on a gurney. Chad caught a quick glimpse of blotchy skin, sunken mouth and cheeks, tissue-paper wisps of white hair floating this way and that. He couldn't tell the sex of the patient as the barely living body whisked by, an acrid smell trailing in its wake.

Even if the will says Mona wants life support I'm turning it off. Note or no note. Money or no money. A black epiphany, he realized, but an epiphany nonetheless.

Jonathan offered to fetch the paperwork from the car. Chad had a few moments alone with Mona. He supposed he ought to say some last words to her, something along the lines of "Fuck you for putting me in this position, you bitch. I hope Satan turns up the thermostat in your cell." Only he couldn't get those words out, or any others. The time for accusations and recriminations had passed. So when he was a kid he went hungry and always had bruises from big brother Martin and sneezed out smoke-blackened snot from morning till night. So what? It all ended here. He sat in the armchair by her bed and stared at her chest as the respirator hissed, pumping air in and out. If he had a cat, he could put it on her chest. According to myth, cats can suck the breath out of sleeping babies. Maybe it would work on Mona, and nobody would be the wiser. Where could he get a cat? Would the nurses let him bring Martini to Mona's room for a permanent farewell? Or, hell, Chad could simply press down on Mona's chest, and stop her breath himself.

He shuddered.

He would never know where she had gotten the money now burning a hole in his backpack. Had she really driven getaway cars and smuggled drugs, as she had occasionally hinted while drunk? No reason to suspect she hadn't done all that and more. Chad scratched his head, checked to make sure nobody could see him, then scratched his balls.

The respirator is plugged into an outlet.

He noticed it, and the knowledge trickled down his spine like a drop of cold water.

The respirator can be unplugged, if necessary. Simple as that.

Like the money under the mattress, it couldn't be as simple as that, but it probably was. Chad knew he had a long history of making things harder than they had to be.

Simple as that.

But not now.

Chad's conscience caught up with the front of his brain just then: a knife of pain in the gut, a twisting feeling, moray eels writhing in his belly. He dashed to the rest room adjoining Mona's room and threw the door shut behind him; he barely got the lid up before his stomach sent a spume that was half coffee, half sulfuric acid into the toilet. He threw up three times. *I've really got to take something for this,* he thought.

In addition to Chad's digestive system, wrecked from stress, he had a pervasive, clammy fear that Jonathan would come to his senses, toss Chad's belongings onto the hospital parking lot pavement, and speed out of there. Why he would want to entangle himself with this Southern Gothic homodrama, Chad couldn't imagine. Why stay?

It's not like he doesn't have legal issues of his own. He's had how many conversations with the DC and Connecticut police?

Jonathan returned with the paperwork. The sound of him taking a seat in the armchair by Mona's bed gave Chad a curious sense of relief. Nice counterpoint to his burning throat. When Chad emerged from the bathroom, trembling slightly, he reviewed the will. It contained nothing useful.

What if hell exists and I'm buying myself a one-way ticket by even thinking these thoughts?

He thought for a second.

Probably no big deal. Everyone I know will be there. We'll take over and re-decorate.

"Damn you," he said to Mona.

No reply. Not even the twitch of an eyelid. Chad looked a little closer, for signs of rapid eye movement beneath the lids. What could she dream about in this state? What do your dreams look like when your fondest hope is for someone to pull the fucking plug? A blank screen in a dark movie theater? Surround-sound silence? Mona's machines beeped, hissed, hummed, and whirred.

"You feeling OK?" Jonathan asked.

"Upset stomach. I puked. Too much stress." Admitting this to Jonathan bothered Chad very little. He took that as a good sign. He didn't have to self-censor for fear of making Jonathan go, *Ick*. He came back this time, when he had the chance to run. The chances he'd stick around a bit longer seemed to have improved. *At least until he decides I'm only in it for the money.* Flipping through the pages of the will, Chad found nothing that specified whether Mona wanted to be put on a respirator. She was already on one. It was a moot point now. The question remained. Turn it off? "Fuck. Looks like it's up to me."

"Want to get out of here? Take a walk or something?"

"Yeah. We might as well go. If I do the dutiful son thing and wait by her side, the sound of that machine will drive me out of my fucking mind. Right now I do not have a clue what I'm doing."

On the way out, Dwayne intercepted them again. He restated his concern that there may not be much time and suggested they have a word with the doctor when she made rounds later that evening.

"I need more information," Chad said. "And then I want to sleep on it. If she goes in her sleep and I'm not here for it, then that's a risk I'll have to take."

I should be so lucky. If she goes and I'm not here for it, then I'm off the hook.

Jonathan insisted on taking Chad out to eat "somewhere good." Chad warned him that New Bern, North Carolina, had a limited view of what "good" meant where restaurants were concerned. If you wanted barbecue and hush puppies, fine. Fried chicken and french fries, you could get. Chad had a feeling Jonathan wasn't talking about the steak houses and family-style buffets with their slimy metal serving bowls of string beans, chicken-fried steak patties like stacks of hockey pucks, and iced tea sweet enough to induce diabetes with one sip. Growing up on that kind of food, Chad failed to understand why he didn't have an ass the same size and shape as two Volkswagen New Beetles.

"Whatever. There has to be something. Would you drive? Are you up for it?" Jonathan asked. "I'm knackered from the drive down, and I've never been in this state before."

"You haven't missed much. We'll find something. If I remember, there are a couple of decent places downtown, near the waterfront."

"Let me shut my eyes for a few minutes and I'll feel like a human being when we get there. Hey—the mobile phone in this thing still works. I haven't disconnected it yet. Why not call Ms. Grossman from the car, while you're driving? Don't worry about running the bill up—it's not like we can't afford it."

We.

Chad hoped he wouldn't get in a wreck but kept his fears to himself. It's one thing to know a city like the back of your hand; it's another thing to be driving through it in a car worth more money than you've made in the last two or three years combined. Chad, still unsteady inside from vomiting, broke into a light sweat again when he turned the ignition key. *It's just a car,* he told himself. *And there's enough cash in your backpack to buy a new one outright. Grow a dick and drive.*

Emboldened, he reversed out of the parking spot, then inched forward like an old lady for a few minutes before placing the call, assuming he could at least leave a message with Ms. Grossman's answering service.

Jonathan began to snore. Again, he looked like a pedophile organization's poster child, fresh and young, his hair falling in his eyes, mouth slightly open. Torn-up old jeans, faded Marilyn Manson T-shirt, battered Nike trainers. Did Jonathan have any idea what a sexy little bastard he was? If so, he didn't let on.

Linda Grossman answered on the second ring.

"Hello," Chad said, surprised. "I was expecting your receptionist."

"Left for the day. May I ask who's calling?"

Chad introduced himself again and outlined what had happened. "So it looks like I'm going to have to make the decision whether to pull the plug, right?"

"I'd say that's a fair assessment. I'm sorry your mother was so vague on that point. I tried to talk her into being specific, but she insisted you knew what to do." She sounded like she might be saying *Oy* inside her head.

"Yes," Chad said. *We've established that.* "What I'm really getting at is this. Martin, my brother, is trying to have me committed. I got hurt in a fall late last week and he turned it into a drunken suicide attempt when the ambulance came. Next thing I knew, I was in the psych ward. According to my doctor, Martin's not just trying to get me put away, he's also trying to have me declared incompetent, with himself appointed as my guardian. Which I guess would cause control of Mona's estate to revert back to him, wouldn't it?"

"Christ Jesus," Linda Grossman said. "So was it a suicide attempt?"

"No, but arguing otherwise has been like pissing into the wind, if you'll pardon my language. My psychiatrist says I don't have much to worry about, because the hospital did release me after only the seventy-two-hour observation period, but still, there's no telling what the judge will decide. I feel like Sisyphus pushing his boulder up the hill."

"With good reason. Here's the answer to your question where the estate is concerned: it depends. Jurisdiction is one issue—he's trying to have you declared incompetent in the District of Columbia, but the estate is here. Like you said, it depends on the judge. Have you thought of leaving the District? That would muddy the waters and buy you some time."

"Not really, but you're the second person to suggest that to me. The idea crossed my mind, but I'm not crazy about it."

"Give it some thought," Linda Grossman said. "If you're not tied to the area, that will make Martin's life more difficult. As things stand, he might be able to do it if he finds enough evidence to satisfy a judge. All he needs is a good witness or two to testify that you're a danger to yourself and not capable of executing your mother's estate, and you're· in duck soup. You then have to get people to testify you're not the mess he claims you are. The legal bills skyrocket while you duke it out. It's just not a pretty sight. So what if it's technically a little unethical for me to suggest this? Attorneys have suggested worse things. Move out of the DC area as fast as you can pack a U-Haul. I hear the young people are moving to Austin, Texas, these days. And Atlanta. My cousin Herbert lives down in Atlanta and loves it. Give it some thought. It's a more expedient and less stressful solution than sticking around to let him drag you over hot coals."

Chad understood why Mona had hired this woman. He liked her too.

"Which he wants to do, because he's the Prince of Darkness."

Jonathan opened one eye, looked over at him, then shut the eye again and went back to sleep.

"Which he does, right? So my advice to you, where the estate is concerned, is that you talk to your attorney in DC. You'll get better answers with regard to the local jurisdiction. I can speak in generalities, but I don't know local precedent up there. I don't know the judges. However, I can represent you down here if there's a need and you'd like me to."

Next she was going to offer him a bagel. He loved this. Maybe he should move to New York. He could afford both the deposit on an apartment and the bribe necessary to get a good one.

"What about the life support thing? I stand to inherit if I take Mona off her life support and that finishes her. Could that be used as ammunition against me in court later?"

Silence.

Chad wondered whether he had lost the connection, and held the phone away from his head to look at the transmission bars. They showed he still had sufficient network coverage for the call not to have been dropped. When he pressed the phone to his ear again, Ms. Grossman resumed speaking, as if she knew he'd need a look at the phone to convince herself she was there.

"You're smart to think of that. It could happen, and you ought to be prepared for it. But don't let that dissuade you from doing the right thing and then trying to get away with it if you can."

17

Thursday Night

Jonathan produced a fake Texas driver's license when he ordered a glass of Sangiovese and the waitress carded him. After arranging their glasses of water, plate of bread, and saucer for olive oil, she gave Jonathan a dubious look—eyebrows arched, eyes narrowed just a tad. Chad saw her weighing her options—question Jonathan's ID, make a scene, or let the issue drop?

"Honey," Jonathan drawled, all traces of London gone from his accent, pure San Antonio now. "I get that look you're givin' me *all the time*. Next thing I know you're gonna ask me to drop my pants and check whether I've got hair down there yet."

Even in the dim light of the restaurant, the waitress could be seen to blush a deep red, the same color as the wine Jonathan had just ordered. She returned his license (Chad reminded himself to ask for a closer look later, when his examination wouldn't get them in trouble) and took half a step away from the table, now embarrassed.

"Umm . . ."

In his regular London-by-way-of-LA voice, Jonathan said, "Don't worry about it. I get that reaction all the time. And I really do have hair down there. I know you were wondering."

She laughed and made her way toward the kitchen after taking their order.

"Silver-tongued bastard," Chad said. "I'm terribly impressed. When we get out of here, you'll have to show me that thing."

"Which thing?" Jonathan winked. "You're really going to have to be more specific, Chad." He sipped water, then dipped a piece of bread in oil. "I'll show either thing to you later if you'll remind me," Jonathan answered. He yawned. "As sleepy as I am, I'm likely to forget."

"Where did you get your ID?"

Jonathan spoke with his mouth full. "Promise not to shit on yourself when I tell you?"

Chad crossed his heart and idly looked at the menu. He wanted something with shrimp.

"Cross your heart, hope to die, stick my penis in your eye?" Jonathan asked, eyebrows raised, mouth no longer full.

"Couple of inches lower down," Chad said. "Getting socket-fucked doesn't sound like much fun. So where did you get it?"

"Harry. My lawyer. That man is a gift from the gods. How he put up with my father, I'll never know. The money, I guess. He's been keeping an eye on me. I told you that. When I asked him about emancipation, he told me he'd been expecting that request for some time . . ."

"Even though you'll turn legal—God, keep an eye out for the waitress, this is not a conversation we want her to overhear—in a few weeks anyway."

"Right," Jonathan said. "Harry actually got the ID for me right after my father . . . you know. He has some contacts with people who make things like driver's licenses. Real ones. If someone decides to check the DMV in Texas, you know, if I get pulled over for speeding or running a red light, the identity will hold up under examination. Unless I'm stupid enough to carry ID under both names at the same time, I won't get caught."

Chad gaped.

Jonathan went on. "It was bloody expensive, but so far well worth what I spent."

"No fucking way. I'm surprised your lawyer would go for something like that. He could get disbarred if he got caught."

"He told me that. He's kind of an old guy, and he's worth a fuckload of money, and the bonus is that he's gay too. Total outlaw. He looks like a run-of-the-mill high-powered lawyer, but in reality he's way out there on the bleeding edge. The way you'd wish your grandfather would be, if you could order one from a catalog. Both of mine died when I was little, so I wouldn't know. Harry told me he's going to retire and move down to Costa Rica in a couple of years and drink margaritas on the beach with his partner. He doesn't give a damn about breaking a law or two. Besides, he isn't doing all this work pro bono."

"I think I like this guy." Chad thought about it. "We're pretty far out on the bleeding edge, ourselves."

Their wine arrived and, rather than sending the waitress away for another few minutes, they ordered quickly. Chad stared into the votive candle flickering behind red glass. This was the first moment in days where Chad felt he hadn't been swallowed by a gigantic beast. He tore off a piece of bread, swirled one end in the oil, and devoured it. Jonathan did the same thing. Chad's appetite surprised him. He hadn't felt hungry all day.

"You know," Jonathan said. "It occurs to me that I might as well tell you the rest of it. I think this is the right time. I'm just tired enough to want to lighten the load a little bit."

"The rest of what?" Chad sipped his wine, his hands shaking a little.

"Me. How I ended up here."

"Here?"

"In DC, I meant. But I ended up here in North Carolina with you, so it's an extension of the same story."

"Is this something I'm not going to enjoy hearing?" Chad had sucked down half the wine in his glass. Half-empty. He'd order another when the waitress returned. To hell with his meds and the drunk-driving laws.

Jonathan shrugged. "It's not a nice story, but I'm not going to admit to being Charles Manson's little brother." He traced a swastika on his forehead with his index finger, then crossed his eyes and stuck out his tongue. "This is one of those stories where you wish you were a smoker so you could suck on a cigarette while you're telling it.

"When we were in the hospital I told you I had been at one of those military schools where everything is strictly regimented, where you're under close supervision twenty-four hours a day, where the upperclassmen torture younger kids. That was true, and it was a terrible place, but I didn't mention where I was before that."

"You said you were in a European boarding school. Schools. I'd have assumed it anyway, even if you hadn't told me." Chad sipped more wine and felt like Sherlock Holmes. "Anyone with a few brain cells still firing could have figured it out. Your accent. And if you'd been to school in the States, you wouldn't be as articulate and sophisticated. Schools in this country mostly turn out brainless media junkies who think *The Real World* on MTV is an accurate depiction of life."

"You're exactly right. When I was young, in elementary school, I was closer to home. My parents enrolled me in a day program in Connecticut, but once I got older they packed me off to this school in Gstaad. Gstaad is the size of a postage stamp, but it's not far from Lausanne, which I liked. For high school, I transferred to another school in London, and I fucking loved it there. Every time I flew back to Connecticut for a holiday with my parents, it was like being . . ." Jonathan shook his head, searching for the words. "They were strangers, and I lost interest in getting to know them. Of course, I was related to them, and when I looked at their faces it was obvious I had similar features, but they had almost nothing to do with my life. When my father was around, he'd ask how my studies were going, without having a clue what I was studying. Even when I had told him half a dozen times.

"So I'd tell him I was taking French, and he'd ask if I was conjugating verbs yet. A pleased look would flit across his face. After I saw that look a few times, I realized he was congratulating himself for pulling a rabbit out of a hat. He had come up with a question to ask me, to make it look like he was paying attention to my life. I speak French like a native. I grew up in Switzerland. I remember the last time he asked me about that, earlier this year, before . . . before I left London. I was in a literature class reading Celine. Untranslated. That helped me decide I needed to live my life like an orphan, because my parents were never going to contribute anything to my well-being. Except for money. So I said 'Yes, we're doing some of the more complex verbs this year, and I'm studying Spanish, too. You'd be so proud, at the end of the term some friends and I are going down to the Costa del Sol and we'll fit right in.' "

"Somehow I didn't know you speak Spanish," Chad said. Switching languages, he asked if Jonathan had been to Sitges.

Jonathan chewed bread and nodded. "Just once," he replied, also in good Spanish. He had a convincing Iberian lisp on his sibilants. Chad was impressed. "I liked it, but we weren't there for long. We spent a few days in Barcelona on our way to Ibiza. We just stopped in Sitges for the day. I never told my father about that trip."

Chad had been to Ibiza during his year in Spain. Party capital of the planet, not for the faint-hearted. Made Daytona Beach during Spring Break look like Sesame Street. Only the drunk college kids passing out in the discotheques at five in the morning were from Salamanca and Bologna and Toulouse, not Mobile and Knoxville and Charlotte. "Ibiza is not the kind of place you tell your parents you're going to visit."

"Right." Jonathan switched back to English. "Well, on second thought, they're unlikely to have heard of Ibiza. Where's our food? I'm going to finish my half of the bread and start on the tablecloth if that waitress doesn't appear with our food in three minutes or less. Where was I? School. So I was there until halfway through my senior year, this school in London. You've been to London, haven't you?"

Chad nodded. During his year abroad, he had made two trips to London, for a total of about two weeks. He and his German friend Lionel haunted Soho; dove into underground clubs down in Brixton, south of the Thames; wandered the gentrifying areas of Battersea one night, on the way to a party they never found; got caught in the rain dashing to Wembley Arena from the tube stop, late for a concert; spent a romantic night together in the narrow bed of their hostel near the tourist-infested Piccadilly Circus . . .

"I could live there," Chad said. "I just had a nostalgic moment. I spent some time there with a friend. I'm not sure what else to call him. You know."

"Yes, I noticed."

The food arrived, borne on a big round tray by a big round man dressed in white things. He set a steaming mountain of pasta before Chad and a salmon fillet the size of Rhode Island in front of Jonathan, then promised to send the waitress back to refill their empty wine glasses.

"I could too. So where was I—oh yeah, my total lack of morals. Technically I wasn't kicked out of this school, but my parents re-moved me after I was caught having an affair with this guy who worked there. Bart. His name was Bart. He was thirty-four and should have known better. The age of consent is lower in the United Kingdom, but the school still saw fit to contact my parents. Everyone knows what prudes Americans are when it comes to sexuality. Legally it was murky, what the school officials did. I hadn't broken any laws. No matter, my parents still acted as if I had stolen the Crown Jewels. Next thing I knew I was on a plane back to the States, and they had arranged for me to go to that military school place. As if I wouldn't be around a bunch of horny young guys.

"Bart was my first lover, if you want to know. Do you want me to tell you about him? Does that freak you out?"

Chad motioned for him to continue. "You're not Venus emerging from the foam. Neither am I. Go ahead. It's fine."

"Venus from the foam." Jonathan licked a pink slice of salmon lasciviously. "If I were in that picture, you'd see me standing on that shell with my dick in my hand. You know that's what she's doing in that picture, don't you? Touching herself?"

Chad nodded, enjoying the mental picture.

"So—Bart—I'm trying to think when it started. The equivalent of my junior year, near the beginning. How we managed to keep it quiet that long in a residential school, I'll never know. But we did."

"How did it start?" Chad slurped a strand of linguine and hoped he didn't look too gauche. As surreptitiously as he could, he checked his shirt for drops of tomato sauce. What had he been thinking, ordering pasta when he was wearing a white shirt?

"The usual way: meaningful looks. I spent loads of time in the library studying—I actually had really good grades, although you probably think I'm a juvenile delinquent—"

"They're not mutually exclusive," Chad interrupted. "I'm kind of a delinquent myself."

"You're a big delinquent, not a little one. You have a big, wide, thick streak of delinquency. As I was saying," he said, with a wink, returning to normal speed. The couple at the next table, a black man and woman dressed as if their next stop was the theater, had begun to bicker. Chad eavesdropped just enough to understand that the woman didn't like the man's propensity to order wine without consulting her first. His taste wasn't *all that*. His attention returned to Jonathan. "Bart looks a bit like you, believe it or not. That's one reason I snuck into your room that morning. When they brought you in the night before, I got a glimpse and thought, *Jesus Christ, they're twins.* I had to get a closer look. Having a guy on the ward who looked that much like Bart would have really fucked with my head. But the resemblance is only superficial. You're better looking."

"Thank you, kind sir." Chad lifted his glass to Jonathan and took a sip, as salute.

"Bart was subtle. I got this vibe from him that he was attracted to me, and I thought he was hot—not like the other guys my age, who still thought having a wank was a big deal. Red hair, freckles, nice features, and this great Scottish burr. From his voice I could tell he smoked. He would chat with me when I checked books out, and it kind of started there. I'd never been with a guy before, and he made me nervous and excited and horny at the same time. But he was great for my grades, because I went to the library all the time to study. And there he'd be, shelving books or doing whatever behind the circulation desk. And when I came in, he'd look at me a certain way."

"Like the Big Bad Wolf checking out Little Red Riding Hood's sweet scrumptious ass, I'm sure," Chad said. "Bart was probably saying *Yum yum* under his breath, and drooling over your cuteness."

"Thanks, I think. God, my food's getting cold."

"I won't run away if you talk with your mouth full."

Jonathan stuffed salmon into his mouth, chewed, then stuck out his tongue.

After swallowing his fish, Jonathan went on to say, "So Bart finally suggested I read *Maurice,* and that's what started it."

"That Forster. Despoiler of youth, corrupter of morals. I'm done eating now, and you're only half-finished with your salmon. Do you want to tell the rest of the story later?"

"No, it's OK. I think I ate too much bread anyway. I'm almost done."

"I thought you had realized you were gay long before Bart came along."

"Yes and no. You know how you can be aware of it, and then set up patterns of—I'm not sure what the best word is—doublethink, if you can stand the George Orwell reference, to shield yourself from the idea that you're attracted to other guys? So I knew I was gay, and I had experimented, a wank here, a kiss there. Nothing you'd see published in one of those *Best Gay Erotica* anthologies. Bart was really the one who showed me the ropes."

"He was a good teacher," Chad observed. "He knew what the hell he was doing. I thank him for it."

"You can say that again," Jonathan said. "I read *Maurice* and enjoyed it, but I also saw it for the gesture it was. The next time I was in the library, he asked if I'd have a coffee with him. Inappropriate, but it was possible to leave the school. And once you were off the grounds, London was yours. The school was strict in some senses, but there were so many students that I could slip away without being noticed.

"I agreed to meet him at a coffee shop far enough from the school to be safe. 'I'm the only school employee who lives around here. You won't have to worry someone will see us,' he told me. Scared me to death, but I went. At school we had to wear uniforms, and the faculty and staff had to wear suits. So when I got to this coffee shop and saw Bart in corduroy pants and a big cable-knit fisherman's sweater, I almost died on the spot."

"How long did it take for you two to . . ." Chad searched for the word. When he came up with *connect,* Jonathan said *fuck* at the same time. They looked at each other and laughed.

"I wasn't going to be quite that crass," Chad said.

"Crass is fine. I guess I started seeing Bart after that night. I still made the trips to the library and still studied assiduously. Even then, I had sense enough to realize that whatever was going on, I was better off in England than Connecticut, and I wasn't about to jeopardize it. Bart took his time. He wasn't in a hurry. He also knew what the stakes were and he wanted to make sure I wasn't some immature prat who'd panic after the first time he'd gotten off with another guy and go screaming rape to the headmaster.

"So he didn't push. I was dying to get to bed with him long before he finally relented. Took us a month. Took *him* a month; I'd have done it a lot sooner. We timed the occasion with a public holiday. He took a couple of days off and we slipped away to this house in the Cotswolds together. It was like driving a Lamborghini after you've been putting around on a Vespa. My first man after several clumsy boys. He knew what he was doing. He took his time, and by the end of that trip we were both walking funny—it was incredible, affirming, overwhelming, you know. You've been there."

"Not the Cotswolds," Chad said.

"We kept seeing each other for—well, until we got caught. We were subtle. For a kid as young as I was then—" Chad couldn't help smirking a little; Jonathan noticed, smiled angelically, and gave him the finger "—I did a good job of keeping my mouth shut. Bart had more at stake, so he was even more discreet."

Jonathan paused when their waitress brought the check and smiled in that *It's-time-you-surrendered-the-table, guys* way Chad always found annoying.

"We can finish this in the car and back at Mona's house, can't we? I need to feed her cat, anyway. Hell, I need to find a home for it."

"Sure. I want to crawl in bed next to you right now, curl up, and pass out," Jonathan said.

"Just when your story was getting to the exciting part."

"I know." Jonathan put a fifty-dollar bill under the check and said he didn't require change; they rose to leave.

Jonathan fell asleep before he could finish the story. He yawned his way through a few sentences once he and Chad were naked in bed together, spooning, the small of Jonathan's back against Chad's stomach. His last words before starting to snore were, "We even did it in the stacks once, after school let out one day . . ."

Late in the night, while Jonathan snored and Chad lay awake watching him, dark thoughts intruded.

Am I in love with him? Or is it just infatuation? Lust?

Why isn't there a dictionary where you can look these things up? Some kind of encyclopedia, with charts and pictures?

Is he in love with me? Christ, he's so young. He barely needs to shave.
Reality check. He's older than I am in a number of significant ways.
He's certainly hung like a grown man.
Jesus, Chad, get your mind out of the gutter for three minutes.

Chad had trouble with that one. The gutter? Hard for his mind to go anywhere else with Jonathan lying naked next to him.

This is too easy.
No, there's nothing easy about this.
Do I like him? Well, yes. That's an easy one. Of course I do. I like him a lot more than I like anyone else I can think of off the top of my head. And the more I'm around him, the more I like him. But it's more atavistic than that. It's certainly not about his money. I just like the guy.
Do I trust him?

A stillness of the mind followed that. Jonathan stirred in his sleep, mumbled something, then settled down again.

Then:

I suppose I do. No way he killed all those people. It just doesn't make sense. He drove down from Connecticut and took a risk of missing me. He could have done different things. He could have just hopped on a plane, never to be heard from again. Simple as that. Fuck it, we're going to Jamaica. Or back to London, or Ibiza, or Cape Town, or Tashkent, or wherever the hell else he fucking wants to go. It's not like I have anything for him to fleece me out of.
Well, I do now.
He's worth how many millions?
He's not the fleecing type. My backpack full of illicit cash isn't going to give him a hard-on. It's just the sort of thing he'd look at as a little challenge. Like figuring out how to sneak through customs with it, to deposit in his offshore accounts.

Chad put an arm around him, snuggled closer, and pressed his face against the back of Jonathan's neck, to silence his worries with the smell of Jonathan's hair.

Being together right now is easier than being apart, and it makes more sense. There doesn't have to be anything else to the decision. I don't have to make it more difficult than it already is.

That thought provided the spark of comfort Chad was looking for. He drifted, relaxed, and began to dream.

18

Friday Morning

The phone woke them. Chad let it ring. He lay in bed, a squint not protecting him from too-bright hangover sunlight. Covering his eyes with his hands helped but didn't stop the phone ringing. *Eck.* He had thrown all the covers off himself in the night. Too hot in here. He dropped the phone on the floor, cussed, and reached down to pick it up. Under the bed, he glimpsed a menagerie of dust bunnies. Another project. He moved the hand with the phone a safe distance away from them in case Mona had left them unswept long enough to evolve and acquire an appetite for boy.

"I woke you up. Sorry it's so fucking early, but this couldn't wait," Rose said. "Chad, your fucking brother is a fucking nut, and his wife's almost as bad."

Chad took advantage of her pause for breath to point out that she had used the word "fucking" three times in two sentences. Jonathan stroked Chad's thigh. A squadron of exclamation points zinged all the way up his spine. Jonathan yawned with red-wine morning breath, mumbled something, and fell asleep again. His body twitched, then was still.

"What have they done this time? Did they roast their kids on a spit and invite the neighborhood over for beer and baby buttocks, or something?"

"Cindy called last night. She was looking for you, but I told her you were out of town. So she asked if I had seen Martin. Said they had been in a fight and he had taken off."

"I think he hits her," Chad said.

"You've got a bright future with the Psychic Friends Network," Rose said. "It's vile, this thing with Martin and Cindy. She said one of the kids blurted out that she was planning to leave him. God knows how that happened. Maybe she thought they could keep it a secret."

Chad sat bolt upright, hangover fuzziness gone in a snap.

"Jesus Christ. What else do you know?"

"It's pretty grim. Cindy said Martin lost his shit. It was Alexander. Martin got pissed off at him, went totally berserk, started beating the crap out of him. When Cindy yelled at him to stop, he hit her. She said the only reason he stopped was because his arm got tired. She asked him if he wanted their kids to grow up remembering their father like this. She'd leave with them right now, take them to the hospital, and call every social worker in Maryland, whatever. She just gushed all of this out at me. I didn't know what the fuck to say, so I just sat there and let her talk."

"You did the right thing." Chad felt ill. "What happened next? What else did she say? Is she OK now?"

Again, Chad felt torn, as he did with Mona. He didn't like Cindy, but didn't want Martin to beat her up. And the kids should never have been put through that.

He wished he weren't related to any of them. But his heart broke when he thought about Brittany (who deserved a better name) and Alexander growing up with Cindy and Martin for parents. At this rate, they'd commit suicide or grow up to be serial killers.

Rose continued. "Cindy told me she threatened to call the military police, and that brought him back down to earth for a little while. He took off. No idea where he went."

"Did she report him?"

"Unfortunately, no. She threatened him with it, but she doesn't really want to report him. Stupid cunt. I think she's serious about her threat to leave him, though. After this. Jesus, Chad, I can't believe women let that happen to their children and don't get a gun and blow a hole the size of the Grand Canyon in the assholes who do it." Rose spat out the words.

"Jesus."

"Chad, it gets worse. The piece of shit showed up banging on the door at six o'clock this morning. Drunk off his ass. He was yelling for me to let him in. He said he knew I was lying about where you were, and that I had better fucking tell him or he'd make me wish I had never been born. I called nine-one-one and got put on hold."

"Oh my God, Rose. Are you safe now? Do you feel safe?" Chad drew his knees up close to his chest and wrapped his arms around them.

"Safe now? Yes, I think so. For the moment. But you need to do something about him, because this shit cannot keep happening. It just can't. It's fucking scary. I don't like being scared in my own home." Chad wasn't sure but he thought her voice was trailing off toward the end, as if she had had an idea, or thought of something.

"Did he leave?"

"No, he's lying in bed next to me smoking a cigarette. We're naked and covered with honey and maraschino cherry juice. He eats pussy like a lesbian."

"I have a hangover, Rose. Joke with me after I've had coffee. What happened next?"

"He left. Then I called one of the partners at my office to ask about a temporary protection order."

"I'm sorry," was all Chad could think of to say.

"It's not your fault your brother is a monster," Rose said. "If you have to be sorry about anything, be sorry because he hasn't done enough for a judge to actually *grant* one. And even if he had, TPOs aren't always worth the paper they're printed on. That's what I was told. If Martin wants to bother you—us—he will. And there's no way to stop him."

Chad thought of the wad of cash in his backpack. He imagined a blow with a blunt instrument, cinder blocks to weigh the body down, and a boat ride out beyond the edge of the continental shelf. That would stop Martin. How much would all that cost, if he were to hire professionals? Would an all-inclusive package deal be available, like a cruise? Execution, corpse removal, and a guarantee of discretion, all for one low price? Where did one find hit men, anyway? The yellow pages?

"What are you going to do?" he asked.

"The things I usually do," Rose said. "I fucking refuse to be chased out of my house by that psychotic piece of shit. I'm going to go to work tomorrow morning, looking absolutely fabulous even if I am working on a goddamn weekend. And I'm going to come home at the end of the day, looking slightly rumpled but equally fabulous. If he gives me any crap I'm going to remind him I work for one of the evilest law firms in the District. So many of the attorneys there want to fuck me that I can always work some pro bono revenge action. I'll law his ass until he squeals like the fat boy in *Deliverance*."

"Are you sure you're not from Alabama?" Chad asked.

"Mississippi."

"Same difference. Doesn't answer my question, though. Are you safe? I'm still not convinced."

"Do I have a choice? I'm not going to be held hostage in my own house. I'm not going to act like one of those cringing pussies who won't step outside her own front door to pick up the newspaper without a floodlight, two Dobermans, and a police escort. This is too much." Chad heard a click and whirr. Rose was smoking a bowl, he guessed. Awfully early in the morning for pot, but under the circumstances he didn't blame her. If he had a joint he'd light up, too. Jonathan grumbled in his sleep again. "But that's not all I called to tell you. The DC police called last night. The detectives looking into those deaths at the hospital? They want to talk to you. I told them you were in North Carolina dealing with a gravely ill mother, and that you'd be back in town in a couple of days. So there's that. The one I talked to said he wants to interview you as soon as you get back to DC. Plus, your shrink called about ten minutes ago. Dr. Perkins? He wouldn't tell me what was going on, but said to tell you it was urgent. You should give him a call. You've turned into a popular guy. You should jump off balconies more often."

"I fell, bitch. Jesus. Rose, look, I feel awful for putting you in the middle of this."

"I'm not in the middle. If this were a hurricane I'd be in one of the outer bands."

"Whatever. Can you blow out of town for a few days? Erode a few beaches in some other part of the country? Get yourself another passport stamp?"

Rose paused a long time, then said, "Of course. Never mind that I just got back from a three-week trip to the Mediterranean. No problem. I'm sure my boss will approve another few days away from the office. Why would I need to leave town, Chad? Martin is a sick fucker. We know that. He beat up his wife and kids, but I think past that he's all talk. He isn't a knife-waving psycho."

"I don't know. I don't think you should be too sure. Maybe I'm just overreacting. I hope I am. When he gets like this, he can do stupid shit. And if he's been out all night drinking, there's no way to guess what he'll do. I think you should play it safe."

Jonathan rolled over on his side. Chad was not surprised to see that he was wide awake and watching, eyes a little bloodshot but alert enough.

"Look, I'll be fine. I'm meeting Gloria and Ellen for the drag brunch at Perry's, so I have to motor. Don't worry about me. Just—look. Umm. I haven't even asked about your mother. You must think I have the manners of a trapdoor spider." When Chad had filled her in ("As of last night, bad and getting worse. That's all I know."), she continued. "You're going to have to do something about Martin. It's just that simple. I know your hands are tied, with Mona in the state she's in, but you may be needed here too."

"I'll try to figure out what to do," Chad said. "In the meantime, take care of yourself. Be careful. I want you to stay near people until Martin chills out."

"Chills out?"

"I didn't know what else to say. *Until he drinks a quart of unleaded and swallows a match* would be too much to hope for," Chad said.

"Drama queen," said Rose.

She hung up on him.

Jonathan snuggled closer.

"Do you know what you did when the phone rang?" he asked.

"How would you know what I did?" Chad asked. The words sounded like a protest, so he tried to soften what he had said. "You were asleep, weren't you?"

"I was sort of awake. The first ring woke me up all the way." He pressed his lips to Chad's shoulder.

"Tell me what I did, then," Chad said.

"You flinched like you had been burned," Jonathan said. "You sucked in your breath and your entire body went rigid. Do you always do that when the phone rings?"

"I don't know." Chad mused. "Probably."

"What is it with you and telephones? Did Ma Bell abuse you as a child?"

"Not in any way that you want to hear about," Chad said. "So I flinch, do I? Nobody has ever pointed that out before."

"Not the hundreds of men you've slept with?" Jonathan asked, poking him in the ribs. "Not even one? The phone must have rung at least once!"

"You're going to get tickled if you keep that up, buddy," Chad said.

"I'm kidding about the hundreds of men. I'm sure it's only dozens. So are you going to tell me why you jump like someone has shot a gun outside when you hear the phone ring?"

"Creditors," Chad said. "Debt." He recounted the story he had told the Intake Team a few endless yearlike days before, and omitted other parts. "After awhile, you get used to spending money you don't have. It's like putting off a trip to the dentist when you know you need to go, or not filing taxes one year, and then the next, and then the next. You sort of know it'll catch up with you eventually, but you don't have to obsess over it every hour of the day. You need something, you want something, you buy it and worry about unpleasant realities later."

"Sounds like fun," Jonathan said. "But there's nothing I can say because my experience has always been just the opposite. If I don't say much will you believe me when I tell you I just want to listen?"

"There's not much else to add," Chad said. "I guess I've told you everything. Never got around to declaring bankruptcy, because of pride. For a long time I maintained this illusion that I could pay everything off, but the debt continued to mount up. Every time the phone would ring it was some asshole who wanted to shout at me if I didn't send them hundreds of dollars yesterday."

"And now?"

"The assholes are still calling my home in DC, I'm sure. I think Rose only puts up with it because she uses her cell phone for everything."

"Well, no. I meant to say, *And now?* In that you could pay all that debt off if you wanted to. Couldn't you?"

"Most of it," Chad said. "But then I'd be left with nothing. OK, let me amend that. The debt would be gone, and that's not insignificant. You could call it a chance to start over. But there's another side to this. I have a grudge. And maybe this puts me in the position to do something about it."

"You'd walk away from the debt?" Jonathan sounded as if he approved. He nestled closer and pressed his rigid dick against Chad's side.

"In a heartbeat. This may sound like the height of petulance, but I'm physically sick of hearing from collections assholes. They work for the same companies that kept issuing new cards and raising my credit limits even after I was too deep in debt to pay it all off. I didn't ask for it. I've thought about that angle. I was just trying to stay in school and hold on to my apartment.

"First you get a card in the mail with a five-thousand-dollar limit, without even applying. Or you get your statement, look at the available credit line, and presto, they gave you another thousand dollars. Then these people call and threaten you. Yell at you. I'm not kidding, it's horrible. And they want their money back."

"But resistance requires more energy than you think you have, right?"

"I couldn't have put it any better, myself."

"So you want to fuck them?" Jonathan asked.

"Like I want oxygen," Chad said, surprised to hear the words come out of his mouth. He had never articulated this sentiment before, and told Jonathan so.

"Then celebrate by fucking *me* first," Jonathan said, straddling him, then bending down for a kiss. "But turn the ringer off, OK?"

Chad called Dr. Perkins from the car as Jonathan drove to the hospital. Jonathan said he remembered the way now, here's the mobile, go for it.

He got the receptionist. "He's with a patient, but he said to put you through. Hold on."

Chad heard a polite rap in the background, murmurs, then: "I don't have long to talk, Chad, but I needed to tell you this as soon as possible. Your hearing date has been moved forward to next week. The new judge in the District has decided she wants a reputation for clearing the docket, and she's disposing of cases at an unprecedented rate. Martin put in a request to move the hearing to a closer date and it was approved."

"Oh, fuck." Chad's head swam. "When did that happen?"

"Yesterday, apparently."

"Oh, fuck. I did not need this."

"Breathe." Dr. Perkins sounded kind but firm. "Here's the bottom line. We released you. You're not crazy. I'll put it that bluntly. I don't support what your brother is trying to do and, to be honest, it's unlikely he'll get very far without me on board. Keep that in mind."

"I'm on my way to the hospital to see my dying mother. My brother who wants to have me committed and declared incompetent went on a drinking binge last night, beat up his wife and one of his kids, took off into the night for God knows where. She didn't report him, so there's nothing we can use. This morning he showed up on my doorstep and threatened my roommate if she didn't tell him where I was. The police want to talk to me about the deaths that happened in the hospital while I was there. Please put something else on my plate. It isn't overflowing yet." Chad thought about adding, *I'm broke,* and smiled when he remembered he wasn't. He had his backpack with him. With every filthy hundred-dollar bill. He didn't want to let the stash out of his sight.

"Chad, for now, all I can tell you is that you're going to be fine. Your medication will keep you stable through all of this. If you start to feel like you can't handle what's going on, I want you to call me. Immediately. Can you write down phone numbers right now?"

Chad found a pen and an envelope in the glove box.

Dr. Perkins recited his numbers (answering service, pager, voice mail) and hung up.

"That was the cherry on the cake of my day," Chad said.

"Chad, it's only ten in the morning."

"It's already been a long day. At least one good thing happened."
He squeezed Jonathan's knee.

"We've been trying to call you," said the red-haired, zaftig nurse
the second she recognized Chad.

He and Jonathan had just stepped off the elevator.

Chad couldn't remember the nurse's name. She wasn't close enough
for him to read her name tag. He'd given up trying to remember their
names. He knew her face. She had a mole on her left cheek the same
size and shape as Albania and red hair that didn't look natural.

The nurse approached him, eyes wide. She clutched the pen she
wore on a pink ribbon around her neck as if it were the pendant on a
rope of pearls. "I've been trying to call the number at your mother's
house, but it kept ringing, and there wasn't an answering machine . . ."

He felt himself slump—shoulders forward, spine hunched—as the
nurse's face broadcast the news he supposed had to come sooner or
later.

"What time?" he asked.

"I'm so sorry," the nurse went on to say, now wringing her hands.
Everyone at the nurse's station was staring.

"What time?" Chad asked again.

Jonathan took his hand. Inside, Chad gave a tiny cheer on account
of Jonathan's audacity.

"About an hour and a half ago."

Jonathan and Chad exchanged a look.

Chad felt a twinge of guilt when his first thought was, *Thank God, I
didn't have to kill her myself.* The guilt didn't last long. Life had just gotten much less complicated.

"The hospital has someone on staff to help with arrangements," the
nurse said.

"I just blew a couple of fuses," Chad said. "I don't have a clue what
to say or do next. I think . . ." He stopped to think. "I think she made
most of her own arrangements herself. She was very Southern Gothic
like that."

"If I could ask a question?" Jonathan said.

The nurse turned to look at him. Chad couldn't read her expression: surprised or indignant. He assumed she hadn't noticed Jonathan before. Remarkable, how he could be handsome yet invisible at the same time.

"Go ahead," Chad said.

"Where is she? Her remains, I mean. Not still in the room, right?"

"Oh right. Yes, the remains are downstairs in the morgue. Did you want to have a moment with her?"

Chad nodded. He had no idea whether he wanted a moment with Mona's earthly remains or not. Might as well. He wouldn't get another chance.

When you view the remains of your newly dead mother, you're supposed to experience an epiphany. Tender moments are supposed to flash before your eyes—those delicious key lime pies she made in a kitchen that smelled like heaven, the chicken soup when you had the flu and couldn't go to school, the rides to Little League practice in her station wagon. Or, on the other hand, you stand over the body and tell her what a gorgon she was, how she poisoned your childhood, ruined your life, set you up to fail as an adult, and should have done the world a favor and died years sooner. Chad supposed the second option came closer to matching life as he remembered it, but in the end he had very little to say to Mona, good or bad. If she was even around to hear. Which he doubted. If she was anywhere, she was getting her roots done and a facial in hell.

Chad saw his train of thought derailing and applied the brakes.

If Mona had looked wasted before, death hadn't done her any favors. When the morgue attendant pulled back the white sheet covering Mona's body, revealing her head and neck and an embarrassing biscuit of shriveled breast, Chad shut his eyes and turned away. Mona looked like an unwrapped mummy. Desiccated almost past recognition. Skin an unnatural bluish color. Broken veins in her face. Chad smelled something putrid beneath the antiseptic sting in the air and pulled up the collar of his shirt to breathe through the fabric. He hurried out of the morgue, to the anteroom where Jonathan was waiting.

"This was a mistake," Chad said, hands over his eyes, stomach roiling. How much wine had he drunk last night?

"Let's get out of here, then." Jonathan walked out with his hand around Chad's elbow.

Chad felt like a wimp again. Jonathan had seen his father shoot his mother. Had almost been shot himself. How much more wretched could things get, for either of them?

"I know what you're thinking," Jonathan said. "Don't. It's all right to be disturbed. What happened to me doesn't have anything to do with it."

– 19 –

Friday Morning

Jonathan started the engine but didn't put the truck in gear. He switched on the air-conditioning and stared over at Chad from the driver's seat.

"How are you handling this?" Jonathan asked. "Trite question, I know, but I can't tell."

Chad shrugged. His mind kept drifting back to Mona's lifeless face. She had been washed since he last saw her alive, he realized. Someone had cleaned the dried saliva away from her mouth. Grief glowed in the center of him, small orange embers, mostly harmless. He turned the nearest dashboard vent to direct more cold air at himself.

"As well as can be expected, under the circumstances." Chad stopped himself. "Look, would you mind if we drove around, instead of going straight back to Mona's place? I can't deal with being there right now."

The thought of going back to her house made him want to plunge into traffic and run as far as he could. Oncoming cars? Either they'd hit him or they wouldn't.

"Sure. Will you tell me where we're going, or will I find out when we get there?"

"I don't even know, myself. We'll figure it out as we go. Take a left as you leave the parking lot."

Might as well tell him all of it. He's come this far with me, and hasn't run away yet. If Mona and Martin haven't driven him off, Barry won't.

Chad resisted the idea of talking about Barry, and now he searched for the reasons why. Who was he protecting? Barry? Unlikely. Barry had moved away and recovered from what had happened and gotten on with his life. In Seattle most likely, or Portland. Vancouver if he had decided to cross the border. He loved the Pacific Northwest. They had talked about moving there together. Martin? Chad couldn't find the words for Martin's role in all of this. Mona's death, while not unexpected—and even, if Chad wanted to be completely honest with himself, long overdue—had knocked the wind out of him. Chad had no reason to protect Martin. Chad felt he and Jonathan needed protection from Martin, not to protect him by keeping secrets. Jonathan, then?

Or am I protecting myself?

Chad directed Jonathan through several more lights, to an on-ramp. At this time of day, in the middle of the week, traffic on the highway to Morehead City and Atlantic Beach wouldn't be heavy. But then, by DC and suburban Connecticut standards, traffic here was never heavy.

"The beach is less than an hour away," Chad said. "I could use an ocean right now."

"Oceans are good."

"It's funny, how your perspective shifts. People here don't move around much. Driving half an hour to the beach feels like a trip out of town. In Beltway terms, that's nothing. If you live in DC, an hour is a reasonable commute to work. One way." Chad trailed off. He felt an odd pang of relief at his exemption from caring about school districts and property values. He thought about trains. The idea of going places. Somewhere else. *Anywhere but here.* "There's not really a point to that. I was just thinking about how driving to the Outer Banks for lunch is no big deal when you're used to the time it takes to get around the city."

Jonathan fed the stereo a CD, and they drove in musically enhanced silence for ten minutes or so. Chad measured time by the tracks on the disc.

"There's something I haven't told you," he said.

Jonathan glanced over and cut his speed from seventy-five to a bit less than seventy.

"Why are you slowing down?" Chad asked.

"To listen better," Jonathan said. "I don't know if there's any relationship between driving slower and listening better, but it feels like there is."

"You're so adorable and such a nut." Chad took a deep breath and twisted his thumb ring. "This is one of those things you just dive into. The thing with Martin. You probably guessed there's a little more going on than I've talked about."

Jonathan nodded. He grumbled, overtook a rusty blue El Camino, sped up again. The driver of the El Camino, a fat bearded man in a baseball cap, gave them the finger.

"Go ahead."

"Martin was stationed at Andrews after several years in Germany. I could never tell if he arranged it. He knew I was at GW. It probably doesn't matter. As soon as he got here, he forced his way back into my life. I had just moved back to DC after recovering from the car wreck. It was a tough time. I was still strung out on painkillers all the time. I barely knew what I was doing. I was renting a room in this group house in Mount Unpleasant. My roommates were all horrible self-righteous let's-change-the-world Nazi vegans who worked for nonprofit organizations. It was hell. I mean, every minute I spent in the 'commons room,' as they called it, opinions got shoved down my throat like dicks in a gang rape. *You take too much medication. You created your own problems. You'd feel better if you gave up meat.* I was like, *Suck my ass.* I lasted three months. Then I moved out one weekend when they were all at some save-the-chinchillas march on the Mall. I could only take hearing I was the Antichrist every time they caught me eating a ham sandwich for so long. I wanted to bite their noses off.

"Sorry, too much detail. I found a roommate through the *Blade*—that's the DC gay newspaper—and everything calmed down after I moved. Martin didn't know my phone number yet. This guy I was rooming with, Diego, was great. He was this fortyish composer from Chile who had lived in DC for years and knew everybody. He saved my life. He had a party to introduce me to some of his friends. I ended up hooking up with this guy Barry that night.

"Barry was in the Air Force, too, like Martin. Diego had dated him for about five minutes, or something. They sort of segued into being friends when the sex evaporated. You know how gay friendships are."

"Well, no, actually, I don't," Jonathan said. "But I'll take your word for it."

Chad chuckled. "Barry and I hit it off the first time we looked at each other. He was a handsome guy. Big brown eyes. He was a couple of years older than me, worked out a lot, so you can imagine how he was built."

"You don't seem like the sort who would go for the military look," Jonathan said. "I certainly don't look like that."

"Now and then, it's OK. Depends on the guy. Anyway, you get used to it, living down here. This half of the state is one big military base. The Army's over in Fayetteville. The Air Force base is in Goldsboro, about an hour from here. The Navy and the Marines are just down the highway in Jacksonville and Havelock. Go to the beach in the summer and half the guys you see have buzz cuts and dog tags."

"That's also true in Soho," Jonathan said.

"Somebody's giving me a hard time," Chad said. "I'd tickle you, but you'd run off the road and we'd die. I've had enough death for one day."

A pang of sadness speared him. He shut his eyes and counted breaths, then continued his story.

"Barry had the regulation chopped-off hair and all, and he was covered with incredible tattoos. He was really well-read and smart and articulate. From this postcard-sized town in Washington State. Seattle later. Poor family. No money for college. Used the military as a way out. It beat taking out a million dollars in student loans.

"So we hit it off. We ignored everybody else at the party and spent a couple of hours outside talking with our own bottle of wine. Diego announced the party was officially over and he was dragging everyone down to Dupont Circle for drinks so the new lovebirds could be left alone to make a nest.

"You can guess the rest. Barry spent the night. And he never really left. We'd both had boyfriends before, but not like that."

"Tell me something," Jonathan said. "I didn't grow up here, so I don't understand the bit about being gay in the military. You make it all sound very matter of fact. In Europe, the stories about the witch-hunts make the States look like a . . . theocratic, medieval backwater. And the military sounds barbaric."

"This is a barbarous country. It just pretends otherwise," Chad said. "*Theocratic, medieval backwater?* I love that. It's so apt."

"Well, yes, but the gay thing. Wasn't Barry scared to death?"

"No. He told me a lot of the old guys, the career officers who have been there all their adult lives, generally can't deal with the idea of fags in uniform. And you get the redneck trash who bellow about being afraid to take a shower with a hummasexshul. As if any self-respecting 'mo would give those guys a second look. But there's a huge gay underground, so to speak. Think about it. Lots of guys in close quarters, sharing living space and exercising all the time. Group showers and uniforms. Of course it's going to be wall-to-wall queers.

"The witch-hunts were real, but Barry's attitude was, *Let them kick me out.* He wasn't in it for a career, and he had his degree. Business and computer science. With his job skills, he was like, *Fuck you. I'll leave and make four times as much money.* We had to be careful, though. Don't get me wrong. I'm not trying to make light of it. But there are lots more gay people staying in the military than getting tossed out.

"The bigger problem was Martin. He couldn't deal with the gay thing to begin with. Martin's warped little mind couldn't cope with that much reality. At first we tried to sneak around. That took too much energy. So we didn't confront him, but we quit hiding and let him come to his own conclusions.

"I put extra effort into avoiding Martin, myself, though, and I didn't talk about it with Barry. It was just something I did. That's when I quit answering Martin's calls. Stubborn fucker still hasn't figured that out and given up. That's part of the phone thing, why I hate it so much. Habit. Most of my calls were from creditors by that time, and another 25 percent or so were from the Prince of Darkness, which by the way is a nickname Barry made up. So why answer the god-damn phone? Martin would ring the doorbell and I'd lie very still on the sofa, where he couldn't see. Eventually he'd give up and go away.

"It took over a year for him to figure everything out, and of course he reported Barry to get him in trouble. It would have worked, but Barry was up for reenlistment anyway and decided to get out.

"Now, during all of this, I had lost my scholarship at GW and had gone to work full-time. So it wasn't the greatest period of my life, but Barry was good for me. I think he's the one thing that kept me from falling apart.

"We one-upped Martin that time. Barry agreed that the best way to deal with Martin was to avoid him. It didn't take long to see how nuts he was.

"Things were getting pretty serious. The gay thing worked to Barry's advantage: his discharge went through in record time. He got a job with no problem. We started talking about moving in together. And you're probably wondering where I'm going with all this happily-ever-after shit. Martin fucked it all up, of course. When he found out Barry and I were looking for an apartment together, all hell broke loose.

"He showed up at Diego's place one night. Barry and I were there watching a video. Diego and his gang were off seeing some play.

"Martin was yelling and pounding on the door, and Barry decided to put an end to it then and there. He opened the door and Martin immediately punched him. Broke his nose, knocked him out cold. He forced his way past me, like I could put up much of a fight. He was screaming and yelling, and his face was all red, and he was piss-drunk.

"He was screaming at me, calling me a fag, asking me if I liked getting it up the ass, or was my fucking fairy boyfriend the one who liked getting his hole hammered. Shit like that. Martin beat the crap out of me and tied me up with the extra telephone cord from Diego's utility cabinet while I was lying there half-unconscious."

"Oh, fuck. Chad." Jonathan reached over and took Chad's hand.

"But wait. There's more. Martin tied me to a chair so I would see what he was doing next. He said, 'Keep this in mind if you're going to keep on with all this faggot bullshit.' He then tied Barry's wrists together, gagged him, pulled his pants off, and—fucked him. Raped him. He climbed on top of Barry, who was writhing and trying to fight him off, because he knew what was about to happen, and pushed his legs apart and, umm . . . shoved it in. Barry couldn't put up too much of a fight. He was tied up, and Martin was bigger. And Martin had been hitting him and kicking him before he . . . you know, before he did it." Chad shut his eyes, seeing it all again, and gave himself a second to think. "And that—how can I say this without being gross—that particular act wasn't something Barry had a lot of experience with. His face was almost purple, he was in so much pain. I was crying and screaming at Martin, and it didn't do a fucking bit of good. Obviously he was getting off on the violence. Plus whatever else he was getting off on. I don't want to describe the details too vividly, but you get the idea. He did some damage to some very personal parts of Barry's body."

The Range Rover lurched to the right as Jonathan recoiled.

"Please tell me you called the police."

Chad shook his head no, sick from remembering all this, seeing it again.

"Martin kept at it and came inside Barry, then pulled out, stood up, and gave me this evil look. He then pissed all over Barry and left."

"Barry had to go to the hospital. In addition to his physical injuries, his spirit was broken. A detective was assigned to the case. He got in touch with the military police at Andrews, and they investigated, sort of. Never mind the evidence that was leaking out of Barry's ass, as soon as the homosexual angle came up, Martin denied everything and the MPs were only too happy to believe him. The detective was no paragon of sensitivity either. Faggots get what they deserve. God bless America. You can kind of see why I'm not so crazy about dealing with the police. And Barry refused to press charges. He said it would be worse for us both if he did. He couldn't deal with being involved with me if that much risk went along with it. The worst part was, I kind of agreed with him at the time. So he got out of the hospital and left without saying goodbye. I haven't heard from him since. Well, I take that back. I got a Valentine's Day card about six months later, ironically just after my suicide attempt. He didn't say where he was, just that he was doing OK and still thought of me. The postmark said Salem, Oregon.

"If I was a mess before that, I was hopeless after. Couldn't keep a job. Racked up debt. Maxed out credit cards left, right, and sideways. Finally decided I'd had it, and tried to OD. Martin found me, of course, and carted me to the hospital. At the time, I was pissed off that I'd lived, but I got over it."

"Why do you still live near him?" Jonathan asked.

"Funny. Rose was just asking me the same question." Chad thought about it for a second. "I guess Barry wasn't the only one whose spirit broke that night. I figured there was no point in running, or maybe I didn't have the energy, or something. Martin would have turned up sooner or later. I don't really know."

Jonathan shook his head, eyes wide with disbelief. "I am so sorry. I feel nauseated now, hearing that."

"I feel nauseated myself, recounting it."

"You didn't have to." He hadn't let go of Chad's hand. Now he squeezed it.

"I think I did," Chad said. "I wanted you to know. You needed to know."

The rest of the day, they walked the empty midweek beach, tossed shells into the surf, and ate a seafood lunch in Morehead City. They said very little, each lost in thought.

The police car in Mona's driveway couldn't be a good sign. Two head-shaped shadows inside. Chad flashed back to the hospital, a few days before—the two detectives from the DC Police, emanating that odd, beige sort of competence. As if they had x-ray eyes.

"What do you suppose *they* want?" Chad asked.

Jonathan parked the Range Rover in the front yard, to allow the cops space to leave, which Chad hoped would happen soon. He felt disinclined to talk. He had said more than enough for one day. Having spent the afternoon on the beach, he felt drained. The story about Barry, the sun, the gigantic plate of steamed shrimp he'd eaten for lunch, and the drive home had leached away what energy he had left. Mona's death preyed on him, and he couldn't decide what he was feeling in the aftermath, if anything.

Two male officers stepped out of the car as soon as Chad and Jonathan opened the doors of the Range Rover.

"Which one of you is Chad Sobran?" asked the one from the driver's seat, a stout guy with a round, ruddy North Carolina face and a stain on his uniform. He mispronounced Chad's last name by putting the stress on the first syllable.

Chad half-raised his castless hand and vaguely waved. He didn't trust himself to speak.

"We have a couple of questions for you, and some rather unfortunate news. Could we talk about this inside?"

Chad's stomach felt as if he had swallowed a handful of cracked marbles. Shooters.

"Sure," he said, in the same sort of breathless croak a frog would make after an hour in a tanning bed.

In Mona's now-less-fetid living room, after introductions, the two cops took their seats (Chad brought an extra chair from the dining room). They didn't waste time delivering the next blow. Mona had not died of natural causes. Somebody put a pillow over her face that morning.

"That's ridiculous," Chad blurted. "She would have been dead in a few hours anyway, right? Why fucking bother?"

"You don't seem too grief-stricken," drawled Cop No. 2, who up until now had been silent. He had the dapper, groomed appearance of a dadlike local news personality. Sports or weather maybe. Fortyish, mustache, looked like a guy who took his two sons camping every couple of weeks or so and probably didn't fuck them.

"Mona had been sick and getting sicker for a couple of years," Chad said. "I'm concerned, but the grief stage is long gone, and the idea that somebody went and killed her is just too stupid to get my mind around."

"So it's not something you would have done yourself, to ease her suffering? Lot of people out there would think such a thing was perfectly all right, never mind what the law says."

"Have you lost your fucking mind?" Something very cold slithered around Chad's insides.

No, I didn't do it myself, but I would have. I was trying to work up the nerve.

How on earth could they possibly fucking know?

Be rational, Chad. They couldn't.

A pillow? When all they had to do was unplug the goddamn respirator?

"No, I haven't. Your mother was in a great deal of pain. You might have seen it as an act of mercy." Bad Cop (as Chad thought of him) had the hands of a smoker. Chad noticed fingers moving as if they had minds of their own and wanted to pick up a cigarette.

"She was pumped full of morphine. I doubt she was suffering . . ." Chad's voice trailed off. He had no idea whether Mona had suffered or not. He suspected she had and the truth made him feel dirty. She had lain in her horrible hospital bed being eaten alive from the inside out while he hemmed and hawed over what to do about her.

Somebody had killed her?

"What we're not saying, Chad, is that one of the hospital staff saw someone fitting your description, leaving your mother's room this morning around six."

"I wasn't there," Chad said.

"Where were you?"

"Here, in bed."

"With me." Jonathan spoke for the first time.

Both officers' eyes widened. They turned to look at Jonathan as if he had just opened his mouth and meowed. A blue jay's caw outside broke the bubble of silence that followed.

"I got up around that time to use the bathroom. Chad was still asleep. I went to the kitchen and got a glass of water, then came back to bed."

"With Chad," Newscaster Cop said. He sounded skeptical. Chad couldn't tell whether he was dubious or disgusted.

"That's right."

"Help me understand why you were sharing a bed and not sleeping on the couch, or somewhere else."

Good Cop, Bad Cop again.

"He's my boyfriend," Jonathan said. "Where else would I sleep?"

This time both officers looked at Chad for confirmation.

"He hogs the sheets," Chad said. "I was here all night."

The questions continued for another hour and a half, dull repetitive questions about where Chad lived, what he did, what Mona had been like, her illness. The story about the hospital aroused keen interest. Why had he landed in the psych ward? What was his diagnosis? *Psychotic Older Sibling Syndrome,* Chad answered. Chad suggested that if anyone had killed Mona, Martin had done it.

"With me in the hospital and declared incompetent, and her dead, he'd get everything," Chad said. "There's not much, but he's more interested in having it than having live relatives."

"We'll need his phone number. We'd like to talk to your doctors, as well," Good Cop said.

"Am I a suspect?"

"Your *friend* here says you were at home when your mother was murdered, but we have a nurse with almost twenty years of distinguished service at the hospital saying she saw you there," Bad Cop said. "We have to investigate all the possibilities."

"Saw him, or someone who looked like him?" Jonathan asked.

"We don't need that pointed out, thank you," Bad Cop said.

"Perhaps you do."

Chad couldn't believe Jonathan's nerve and wanted to tell him to shut up. On the other hand, Jonathan was dead right.

"Are you a lawyer or something? You can't be more than sixteen," Bad Cop said.

"Speaking of lawyers," Chad said, as if the idea had just occurred to him. "I should give mine a call. This is getting scary."

"That's your prerogative," Good Cop said. "We don't mean to scare you, but we want you to be very clear on the circumstances here. At this time, there are no charges. We're still doing the preliminary work. But you could become a suspect once we interview this nurse and her supervisor again." He looked at Jonathan. "And you, Jonathan, we might like to talk to you again, too."

Jonathan replied with a curt nod.

Both officers scribbled phone numbers (cell, pager, voice mail) on their business cards, then left. In their wake, the house had a residue of loudness and intrusion. Rose would have recommended burning a bundle of sage, but Chad felt sure Mona didn't keep ritual purification herbs around the house. Didn't keep? *Hadn't kept.* That pang of sadness jabbed him again.

"What a fucking horror show," Chad said.

"May I suggest you call your lawyer now? Whichever one that is? Or one of mine?" Jonathan asked. "My read on this is very bad."

"How so?"

"Two gayboys in eastern North Carolina. We met in the mental hospital. My parents just died splashily, and I witnessed it. There might be enough to convince them we're Leopold and Loeb."

Chad thought, *Aren't we? Or wouldn't we have been?*

"Which one was cuter, Leopold or Loeb?" he asked. "I've never seen pictures of them. Just *Swoon*."

"They were both hideous in real life, I think," Jonathan said. "We don't want to be the next Leopold and Loeb. Please call your lawyer. I have a bad feeling about this."

Linda Grossman didn't specialize in criminal cases but gave advice. "Don't say anything else to the police. Not one more word. Nothing. You know you didn't do it, and that's fine, and I believe you, but this is a state whose voters kept Jesse Helms in office for more years than I can think about without wanting to burn a Bible on the steps of the state capitol building. Don't expect to be treated well now that they know you're gay.

"Should you leave the state? They can't keep you here yet, but they could strongly advise you to stay. Make a big show of giving them phone numbers if you have to go back to DC.

"Call me if you hear from them again. I'll give you the name of a criminal lawyer who will strike fear into their black little hearts, don't you worry."

She apologized for Chad's loss, asked when the funeral was and if he needed help with the arrangements, and gave a respectful bark of laughter when he said he just wanted to get the whole thing over with as soon as possible.

"Auction," Ms. Grossman said. Chad heard a siren on the other end of the line. His heart beat faster. "Pick out what you want to keep, if anything, and auction the rest. I know a good auctioneer. When you're ready to talk about that give me a call. Gotta run now, client just walked in, she's tapping her foot like she's waiting outside the ladies' room."

Chad knew that deep down in the crevasses of Mona's own black little heart, she would have loved nothing better than an elaborate funeral with mourners fainting from grief, as screams and cries rent the air. Mountain ranges of flowers, overflowing from the church into the parking lot. If two or three hysterical friends didn't fling themselves at the coffin (where she herself lay resplendent, even more radiant than in life) wailing like banshees, then the whole goddamn dying thing wouldn't have been worth the trouble. Mona would take grave offense.

On a more realistic note, Mona didn't have any friends that Chad knew of. She had a sister, but Chad didn't know the woman's name or where she might live. His own father had contributed nothing more than a few pelvic thrusts and one spermatozoon. Not something to warrant a card in Mona's Rolodex, if she'd had one, much less an invitation to her funeral. Martin? No, Chad didn't think he'd call Martin. Mona wouldn't turn over in her grave, but her ashes would spin in their urn like cat litter being flushed down the toilet.

"Cremate the remains," Chad told the funeral director. He looked around Mona's house—stained furniture, monster TV looming like the obelisk in *2001: A Space Odyssey,* slants of sunlight with motes of dust floating, cat box and cigarette smells now down to tolerable levels but still gross—and decided if the place couldn't be auctioned he'd pour gasoline in every room of the place and throw a match.

"Once the morgue releases them, we'll see to it. Shouldn't take long."

Handle this all expediently, that was Chad's bottom line. He had spent enough time here. More than enough. He had no more energy for this. He wanted nothing in the house. The pictures meant nothing. The furniture reeked. He wanted the cat to have a good home and was at a loss how to provide one. The beast could go to the animal shelter, for all Chad cared.

The funeral director murmured apologetic blandishments. Chad tuned out and hung up.

Jonathan perched on the arm of Mona's recliner as if the stains on the cushions were still wet.

"Feels like late afternoon," Jonathan said, teetering. "It's not even lunchtime."

Chad nodded. "It's been a long day."

"Where do we go from here?" Jonathan asked.

"I think we just had a telepathic moment. I was going to ask you the same thing." Chad sat on the coffee table, daring it to break. "I vote for tying up loose ends here as quickly as I can—calling an auctioneer, arranging for the hospital to release the remains for cremation as soon as possible, making sure the cops have my numbers in DC, taking the cat to the animal shelter, and blowing this town. I don't give a shit if I ever come back here again."

Jonathan nodded. "I feel that way about Connecticut. If I never set foot in that state again it'll be too soon."

"Not that there's anything here, but I want to liquidate it all and never come back."

Jonathan looked at Chad for a long time before speaking. "Great minds think alike," he said, as Chad began to squirm under his stare. "While you've been busy, like at the hospital in the last couple of days, I've been on the phone with Harry, arranging the same thing with my parents' properties. Sell everything and wire the funds to an account in the Caymans. It's not like I'm ever going to live in Connecticut again." He stared off into space. "Connecticut. The idea."

"Great minds think alike. So where do you want to go next?" Chad asked.

Five or six years melted off Jonathan's face. He looked like a little boy. "I was kind of hoping I could hang out with you more in DC. I mean, if you don't want me to, it's cool—I'll go to London; I have friends there—but I like what we've got going on, you know . . ."

"You have to ask?" Chad heard himself saying. "I'm surprised you're still around. I'd run if it weren't my life and therefore impossible to run from."

"Not impossible." Jonathan looked dark. "Anyway, isn't running from our lives the thing we've been talking about for the past two days?"

Chad had to concede it was. Indirectly.

"There's nothing wrong with wiping the slate clean when it's too covered with dust to be useful," Jonathan went on.

"I think I can wrap everything up in a couple of hours," Chad said. "There's this terrific Brazilian restaurant in Adams Morgan, in DC. The Grill From Ipanema. Their paella is sublime. Dinner there work for you?"

– 20 –

Friday Afternoon

"I have an idea," Jonathan said on the way out of town.

They had stopped at a Wendy's to pick up burgers for the road. Around them a crowd shifted and babbled in line. Chad felt as if he and Jonathan were the only people there. The romance of the moment evaporated when they got to the cash register to order their food and the pimply teenager on the other side of the counter asked in a robotic lisp, "Is that for the dining room?" and "Would you like · to biggie-size that?"

Phone calls had been made, numbers left. The New Bern police didn't like the idea of Chad leaving town, but when he pointed out that he had settled Mona's estate as best he could and needed to go home (they didn't need to know about the stash of money or his plans to auction the house), they relented. Chad said he had to go back to work. He promised to stay in touch. They couldn't argue.

The auctioneer had a cancellation for the following week. In exchange for letting the man keep more than his usual 10 percent commission, Chad got a guarantee of expedient service. The title and so forth would be taken care of, nod nod wink wink. "You'll FedEx me the check in DC? Quick turnaround time? Great." This couldn't be strictly legal, but Chad didn't care. In the last week, how many laws had he broken? Why stop now? Ms. Grossman had promised to take care of all the paperwork associated with Mona's estate as soon as possible. The sooner that could be done, she had explained, the worse Martin's odds of interfering. "As for her creditors, to hell with them," she said in that great Long Island brogue. "Once you sell the house, there'll be plenty left over. They'll get it when they get it, and they don't need to know about her envelope of money. Neither does the damn IRS. Have a party, sweetheart."

Chad said he'd call the auctioneer with a fax number for the paperwork as soon as he got to DC. Martini, the final, fuzzy detail, caused
Chad a few minutes' stress until Ms. Grossman offered to find a home
for him. Chad supposed she'd donate the cat to a home for the re-
tarded, or a halfway house for crack whores, or some such charitable
organization. So much for that.

"What?" Chad had drifted off into space. He looked at Jonathan in
faint surprise, as if seeing him for the first time. Jonathan had said
something.

"I saw a place on the way in. Follow me for a while, OK? This is the
same road I took coming from the interstate. There's a stop we need
to make first."

Chad ate his burger, eavesdropped on the conversation at the next
table (a young woman who looked as if she had never ventured ten
miles beyond the trailer park where she'd grown up was trying to feed
a baby and two squirmy little children, without much success), and
tried to predict what Jonathan was up to.

When Jonathan turned into a used car lot ("Dale's Auto's—We
Buy Cars"), Chad was confused. He parked next to a newish, garish
Camaro Firebird thing, white with ground effects, a gigantic spoiler,
and dark-tinted windows, and got out.

"I know this is the height of presumption," Jonathan said. "But I
had the idea you might like a Mercedes E-Class, barely driven, a bit
more than you like the Toyota. Do you owe less on it than it's worth?"

Chad nodded, dumbstruck. A plaid-suited salesman with shark
teeth made his way over to them, and said it would be no problem to
buy Chad's Toyota. No paperwork? Just the registration? Title still
with the finance company? No problemo! Not upside down on the
loan? Just about even? Well, if your nice friend wants to give you a
ride back to Washington in his Range Rover, hell, man, more power
to you! Want a cigarette? Mind if I smoke?

In a whirl of used-car salesman slime and cigarette smoke, the Toyota was gone, just like that. Chad put his CDs and overnight bag in
the back of the Range Rover. He felt numb. First Mona had slipped
out of his life and now the car.

"I'm in shock," he said, throwing his bags into the back of the truck. "Forgive me if I seem slow and dumb right now." The lump in Chad's throat offended him. He wasn't supposed to feel more choked up at the loss of his car than he did on account of his mother's death. Even allowing for the strange nature of his relationship with Mona, his reaction went against the natural order of things.

"You're sure of this?" he asked Jonathan. "The car, I mean. You barely know me."

"Of course I'm sure. To what better use could it be put? I'll call Harry from the road and ask him to take care of the paperwork. The Mercedes is white. It has a V-8 and goes really fast and slurps high-octane gas. It'll make you an official, card-carrying enemy of the environment. You're OK with that?"

Chad didn't look back at the Toyota. He felt as if he had betrayed it. It was a nice, humble, unassuming little car. It would either be sold to a family with teenagers who would flog it until it collapsed, or it would go to a chop shop, be dismantled for parts, and shipped to China in microwave boxes. He didn't look back because he was afraid he would turn into a pillar of salt. He took another look at the thousand-dollar check from the dealership and gave fleeting thought to tearing it to shreds, which he would then throw out the window. His car for a measly thousand dollars. Again, shame burned him. Another remnant from his old life gone like a soap bubble in a sudden gust of wind.

Jonathan merged with traffic, stopped for petrol as he called it, charming Chad out of his blue funk, then hit Highway 70 at eighty miles per hour and never slowed down.

"Finish your story," Chad told him as New Bern, which wasn't big enough to have suburbs, gave way to the farms and pine forests of the North Carolina coastal plain. The cement-colored sky bore down on them. Haze and muck. Acres of tobacco and cotton wilting under the harsh white light. Ramshackle houses, rusty trucks in driveways, listless people on porches. *God, I hate this place,* Chad thought. He told

Jonathan, "You never got to what happened after you were caught with the Scottish guy."

Jonathan turned down the volume on the stereo, a relief to Chad because although he liked the CD they were listening to, he couldn't hear himself think.

"Mmm. You're right. Tell me where I left off."

"Cotswolds, if I remember. Driving a Lamborghini after putting around on a Vespa."

"Right." Jonathan frowned. Their speed dipped to sixty-five as he collected his thoughts. Jonathan noticed how slow he was going and stepped on the gas again; the Range Rover surged forward, swerving to avoid a glistening mound of roadkill. Chad reconsidered his burger. "Bart. We got caught. I was so naive to permit that to happen. My German teacher wanted to fuck me."

"You speak German?"

"Not after what happened with Herr Schroedinger. He wasn't bad-looking, I guess. Older than Bart, nice enough build. I don't think I'd have minded shagging him too much, but I was so taken with Bart. I didn't want anybody else. And stupid fuck that I was, I told Herr Schroedinger I was seeing somebody and didn't want to be unfaithful. I was sure he'd understand. Instead he had me watched to find out who I was sleeping with. Didn't take him long.

"I found out later that half a dozen people were spying on me. He told a couple of my teachers he thought I was in some kind of trouble, drugs maybe, and my marks were starting to slip. Which was a lie, of course. I was at the top of my class. What do people here say? The head of my class? It was a blatant lie, what he said about me, but it worked. It wasn't a secret that Bart was gay; plenty of people knew, so it was only a matter of time. One of the teachers noticed how much time I was spending in the library and put two and two together. Whoever it was asked Herr Shithead if there might be something going on with Bart. Schroedinger kept an eye on us. Next time we had a holiday, I told everyone I was going up to Leeds with a friend who had agreed to cover for me. He dropped me off at the train station after we left school. I showed up at Bart's house less than an hour before a whole contingent of administrators from the school did. We were in a very compromising position when we heard the knock on the door. Bart wouldn't have answered, but the Headmaster shouted through the door that he knew we were in there.

"It was foul. It was a very un-British thing they did. Normally I think there would have been a polite inquiry. Once the administrative types had all the evidence they needed, they'd have called a few discreet meetings: one with Bart, one with me, one with my parents and me. I don't understand the sequence of events, even now. I know what happened behind the scenes, why they gave a damn. I assume my parents had something to do with it. Next thing I know the Head's there in Bart's bedroom telling me to get up and get dressed, and I'm naked under the sheets, and I won't do it. He's barking at me like he's the fucking Gestapo. Bart has this big blue duvet he got from somewhere up in the Hebrides, and I'm hiding under it, my dick shrunken to the size of a dead cocktail prawn, crying, seeing my whole future flash before my eyes. I think the headmaster sold me out because he was an old poof, himself. Wanted to see me naked. I'm sure of it. Who fucking knows.

"My parents flew in as soon as they could get on a plane. I was kept in my room at school. Bart went back to Scotland, and I lost track of him. So I can appreciate the way things with Barry ended, because I went through something very similar. At the time, I was already above the age of consent in Britain, so they couldn't do much to Bart other than make his life hell. He saw the handwriting on the wall and left. I think he got a job at a library in Glasgow but I'm not sure. I wanted to find out how he was doing, but I've never been able to track him down. Never got to travel up to Scotland after that, to find out for myself.

"If the scene at Bart's flat was horrible, the confrontation with my parents was worse. They came straight from Heathrow. It was obvious my mother had been quaffing Bloody Marys all the way from Kennedy. She had that smeary look women of a certain age get when they're full of cocktails. My father smelled like he was off his face, too. They were apologizing to everyone in the room as if they had personally committed some offense. They kept looking at me like I'd been caught selling drugs, you know, or shoplifting at Harrods.

"They threatened it, by the way. Said they'd disown me if I was ever caught doing such a thing again. They'd send me to one of those places in Utah where they deprogram gay kids."

"Jesus," Chad said. "I thought Mona was the queen of dysfunction."

Jonathan shook his head. His accent had thickened. "I'm sure she could have taught my parents a thing or two about dysfunction, but . . ." he seemed to lose the thread. A highway patrol car careened past them, lights and sirens blaring. Chad's heart raced. His palms filmed. He wanted to see another cop about as much as he wanted to see another nurse.

"What happened then?"

"I had just started the equivalent of my senior year. I told my parents I wanted to go back to the States, get a GED, and enroll in community college. They wouldn't hear of it. They wanted me in an Ivy League school, or Stanford, or at the very least one of the wannabes like Tulane or Pepperdine. It didn't matter to me, but they wouldn't hear of it. In fact, they tried to tighten the screws. They. My father. Let me be very clear about this point: it was all about what my father wanted. My mother doubled her booze intake but otherwise carried on as normal—sessions at the country club with the tennis pro, golf with the other exurban bitches, charity events, and more booze and busy uselessness.

"I was sent to a military school in upstate New York. I told you about that place. It has a solid reputation, for people who care about such things, but its real raison d'être is to incarcerate kids like me who've fucked up in more prestigious schools. Your parents send you there to be whipped into shape.

"My father drove me up there himself, and the whole two-hour drive was a lecture on taking care of myself. How I had disgraced him and my mother by fagging around with another man. That's what he called it. How unnatural that was. It was beyond belief. If I was ever caught or even suspected of doing something like that again so help him God he'd ship my ass to Utah so fast I wouldn't know what hit me. Deprogramming. Electroshock treatments. Have you ever seen A Clockwork Orange? I've heard that's what they do to gay kids. They prop your eyelids open and inject you with medication to make you nauseated. You're forced to watch film clips of men having sex. Or they put electrodes on your balls and zap them. It's bloody horrifying.

"He went on to say if I got constipated he'd make sure a nurse came in to give me enemas, so I'd better eat enough roughage in my diet. If I got any cavities he'd have the teeth pulled if he found out. On and on like that. I was holding back tears when I got there, but you know what would have happened if I had let him see me cry. One-way ticket to Salt Lake City.

"So I got there, and it was as awful as it sounds. Dorms. No privacy. I transferred in as an upperclassman so I was exempt from the worst of the hazing, but I got beaten up a couple of times for trying to stop it. They'd pick on the younger guys, the frail ones . . ."

"The ones who were obviously gay."

"Right. I don't think it took people long to figure out which team I was on, but I was careful, at least at first. I had a buzz cut, same as everyone else. I'm not too obvious, you know, but I refused to hide. I didn't want to be there, and I didn't care what people thought. In the changing room, I didn't pretend not to look."

"Grew back fast," Chad said, touching a lock of Jonathan's long hair.

Jonathan nodded.

"It does grow fast. Plus, the short-hair requirement wasn't strictly adhered to. New kids get buzzed, but after that, as long as it looks short, you're fine. Nobody checks. Judicious use of gel made it look shorter than it was.

"So I got used to the regimentation. Faked the necessary enthusiasm. In England, I had considered my parents a necessary evil . At the academy I fell in hate with them. Which is the reason I let down my guard. It wasn't that I was so interested in Antonio, the guy I ended up being caught with—again, same thing; you'd think I'd learn to keep my dick in my pants—but it was a way of saying, *Fuck you, you're not telling me what to be.*

"Antonio couldn't have been more different from Bart. He was the same age and grade in school as me. Same build, too. Same height. Puerto Rican. Apart from the accent it was very autoerotic, being with him. Sweet guy, but I was heartbroken over the break with Bart. Antonio cared. I liked him. The inevitable things happened sooner or later, and we kept them quiet as long as we could. And then of course we got caught. I was being watched more closely than I knew at the time. And I was allowed to dig my own grave. Per my father's orders.

"Antonio got a slap on the wrist. He was one of the academy's top students, never been in any kind of trouble, and I was easy to scapegoat, having transferred in with a few big black marks on my record. My father was called. I'd only been there four months, and the shit was already hitting the fan again.

"Once I found out what was going on, I ran. He was totally serious about the threat to have me deprogrammed. I got away from the school and went to Manhattan to hide. I've always hoarded my money, so I had enough to get to the city, buy clothes, and take a room in a hostel for a few days. I had left everything and nothing behind. Never had many clothes because my boarding schools required uniforms. Never accumulated many personal items because I moved around too much.

"That's when I started having conversations with Harry. I'd seen how he looked at me. It wasn't that he wanted to fuck me—nice change, that—but the times he'd seen me with my parents, I could tell he felt sorry for me. He didn't like my parents and he could see I didn't like them either. He slipped me his business card once and told me to call him if things at home got too intense. I kept that card. On impulse, I gave him a call from New York. Told him what had happened. He was pretty disgusted.

"The first thing Harry said after I had told him my story was, 'I'm not going to fuck you by telling your father where you are. Put that out of your mind now. But he's a resourceful man, and he has a lot of money. New York is one of the first places he'll look. Get the hell out, go somewhere safer.'

"That's when he told me about the fake-ID option. That's how I got the Texas driver's license. He asked if I felt safe staying put for a few more days. And I said of course I did. Manhattan is a big place. Harry told me to get pictures taken at one of those passport photos places. Then change my appearance somehow—like get glasses with dummy frames, or bleach my hair—and get another set taken. FedEx him the pictures.

"So I did. That day. He gave me the address and told me he'd send the package back to me via general delivery if I didn't feel comfortable telling him where I was staying. He had the Texas driver's license and the Social Security card fabricated within seventy-two hours. Wouldn't tell me where he'd had it done, or how.

"The only time he ever actually said anything to me about my father was during this time. 'He's not a healthy man. You're better off staying as far away from him as you can.' He went on to ask if the ID had caused any questions to be asked. Which of course it had. I act older than my age, but I don't look it. That took some getting used to.

"So my plan was just to adopt this false identity and avoid my parents altogether. I'm good with computers, so I knew I could make my own money. I figured I'd get Harry to help with a passport and a GED, then maybe fly back to the United Kingdom. I wanted to track Bart down, but my father found me before I could get away.

"This was only a few weeks ago. It was horrible. It was beyond horrible. It was a whole new word that hasn't been invented yet."

"How'd you keep the fake ID?"

"Combination of luck and stupidity. I don't think he knew where I was staying, only that someone matching my description had been seen in the area. I had a room in the Meat Packing District, and it was paid through the rest of the month. For some reason that day I was carrying my Jonathan Fairbanks ID. Some instinct told me to. I shouldn't have listened. I went shopping for clothes—they're addictive, when you've been wearing uniforms all your life—and got nabbed at Macy's of all places. Store security detained me. They called the NYPD, who called my father, and he took the first train.

"This time, he had hired a couple of private security guys to physically detain me and accompany us back to Connecticut. Big hulking bodybuilder rent-a-cops. They didn't let me out of their sight. Not even to take a shower. My father said I was going to be sent to a clinic in Utah but not for another two weeks, so he'd keep me at home under close supervision in the meantime. So these guys and a couple of others were on duty twenty-four hours a day, seven days a week.

Watching me. One physically in the room. The other in the hall. The third on the grounds somewhere. But I can't really explain what happened next," Jonathan said. "Inasmuch as I was kept locked in my room with Larry, Curly, and Moe. Ever read Tennessee Williams?"

Chad nodded.

Jonathan paraphrased a line: " 'An awful flower grew in his head.' It was the day I was supposed to leave for Utah. I was going to be flown from Hartford to Salt Lake City. Two of these guys were going with us. I was going to be tethered to one of them at all times, on some sort of nylon leash so I couldn't run. My father explained that personnel from the clinic would meet us at the airport. The paperwork had already been taken care of. The security goons would be released after handing me over, to fly back to Connecticut or rape local teenagers or whatever they did for fun. The clinic people would drive me to their facility, pump me full of drugs, burn off my dick, give me a lobotomy, God knows what. I was shitting myself. And I was running out of time. I was pacing my room, trying to figure out how to get away, what I'd have to do, but I couldn't think of anything. And my father solved the problem for me. He lost his mind. If he'd ever had one. He came home from work that day and dismissed the security guys. I didn't see or hear it, but from the reports I read, one left right away, but the other one questioned him. My father just shot the son of a bitch in the face, right in front of my mother."

"Oh Christ. Nobody told me there was a third murder." Chad's stomach knotted. The burger, not the best digestive choice to begin with, turned into a chunk of dirty granite.

"I don't feel much sympathy," Jonathan said. "In fact, I feel none at all. I'd have done it myself if I could have gotten my hands on a gun."

"Don't blame you," Chad said. "I think I would have, too." He shuddered. The day, boiling outside, seemed midwinter cold all of a sudden. Chad directed the flow of chilly air from the vent in the dashboard away from himself.

"I was getting ready to run, when it happened. They'd left me alone, and I was going to break my bedroom window with a chair. It was a window of opportunity I'd never see again, before some crazed Mormon doctor in Utah took a swizzle stick to my brain, and I was going to make the best of the chance, even if it meant I'd be on foot. Then I heard the first shot and froze. I snuck downstairs, where I could hear my mother screaming and my father shouting at her. They were in the front room. I was going out the back way, through the kitchen.

"My mother was screaming and crying and praying for her life. If she was drunk, she didn't sound like it. I expect a gun in your face sobers you up fast. I had a stupid moment and stuck my head into the room long enough to take a look. I saw blood everywhere, saw the body of the security guy, and was just in time to see my father shoot my mother. Her brains splattered the wall. It looked like red vomit coming out the wrong side of her head. I turned and ran, and heard a shot behind me. He was shooting at me."

"Thank God he missed," Chad said.

"Yeah, no shit. Thank God he missed. He was chasing me through the house. I got outside, and he stayed in the doorway to reload his gun, then started shooting again. A couple of bullets hit the ground near me. I ducked behind the security company's Taurus, and he shot the windows out. When he emptied the chamber again, I took off down the drive, literally running for my life. I could already hear sirens in the distance.

"You know the rest of the story from there. He reloaded the gun, sat down in a Louis XIV armchair, and put the gun in his mouth. Ruined the chair. I never stopped running. Stopped in New York and hid out in my room there for a couple of days. I freaked out or had a nervous breakdown or something. I couldn't stay still. I wandered all over the city for a couple of days. I went to the museums—the Met, the MOMA, the Guggenheim, the Frick—and just wandered around. I wanted to see the great works of art, all of a sudden. They'd have all the answers. But the thing is, I never really saw those paintings. I remember swirls of color. I know I stood in front of that gigantic Monet in the MOMA, *Water Lilies,* and half an hour slipped away while I stared off into space. I never stayed in one place long enough to see what was right there in front of me—I just kept moving.

"I couldn't stay in New York. On impulse I bought a ticket on the high-speed train to Baltimore. Left just like that. Left all my gear in my room. Even the ID. It never occurred to me to take the fake one with me. I was used to living frugally, so I'd been using my real ID for youth discounts. So I fucked off to Baltimore, where I spent a couple of hours. Hated it. Hated the feel of the place. Not because there's anything wrong with Baltimore, but I just couldn't be there. I took a cab to the Inner Harbor, walked around, ate a crabcake sandwich, threw it up into the Chesapeake Bay, took another cab back to Penn Station, and boarded the first train to Washington. Wearing only the clothes on my back.

"By this time I hadn't digested anything in about twenty-four hours. Maybe more. It's all a blur. Knowing what my father was about to do—the clinic, I mean, not the murder/suicide—had wrecked my appetite. I got off the train at Union Station and was in a total daze. I vaguely remembered someone telling me Dupont Circle was the gay village in DC, so I got on the Metro and rode over there. I tried to eat, couldn't, threw up again in the lobby of the Mayflower. And that was when I fell apart myself. Somebody called the cops. Somebody else called an ambulance. I ended up in the hospital with a diagnosis of severe post-traumatic stress disorder. As if the thing with my parents weren't horrible enough, I was about to keel over from hunger."

"I can't imagine," Chad said.

"Well, there's one other thing I never confessed in the hospital. I wanted them dead, and I wasn't sorry. That was one of the hardest things to admit to myself. The thing was, while I was locked up under arrest in my own bedroom, I decided I wanted to kill my father. If he had actually sent me to Utah, I was going to try to escape, make my way back to Connecticut, and kill him. Assuming the lobotomy or the electroshocks didn't turn me into a vegetable. Ideally, I'd have made it look like my mother did it. She would have been too drunk to testify coherently. Then he went and saved me the trouble." He looked at Chad. "Does that make me a terrible person?"

Chad shrugged. "Not in my book. But I might not be the best person to ask. I was going to kill my mother this morning, so I might be a bit biased."

21

Friday Afternoon (Later)

"How did you keep your ID, then? If you ended up in the hospital at GW? They go through all your shit when you check in." This part mystified Chad.

"My room in New York was paid through the month. When I checked out of the hospital the day before yesterday, that's the first place I went. On the train, I was scared shitless the whole way back. I couldn't concentrate on the book I was reading. My hands were shaking when I unlocked the door to my place. But everything was fine, just where I had left it.

"I kept the clothes I'd bought there in New York, and the ones Harry got sent me in DC when I didn't have anything else to wear—they're in that suitcase in the back, which is also new—and a few books, nothing else," Jonathan shrugged. The flinty expression on his face as he stared ahead at the highway troubled Chad. "That's it. All the worldly possessions I care about."

"Kind of a light load for a seventeen-year-old," Chad said, feeling lame. He admitted he felt lame. Sounded kind of lame.

"Well, you can add the Range Rover and an estate valued in the mid-to-high eight digits," Jonathan said. "And I have a few CDs. When I have time I want to pick up a new laptop."

"Oh, well, in that case, you're normal after all." Chad wanted to tickle him but the timing was wrong. Something in the air didn't quite feel right. That thought surfaced again. *Only in it for the money? The mid-to-high eight digits?*

"Right, every twenty-two-year-old teenage boy has to have a Range Rover," Jonathan said. "If not, send him to the counselors at once!"

"Lock him in the psych ward!"

"Ritalin!"

Chad breathed easier. "So you picked up your ID, went to Connecticut, signed papers, and stopped by your parents' house to grab the truck?"

"That's pretty much where the story ends," Jonathan said. "Harry is my guardian angel. For a healthy fee, of course. He's not totally altruistic. He hired a cleaning team to go in and remove the bloody mess. He assured me they are the best around, came all the way from Manhattan. 'We guarantee you will not find clumps of brain matter on the sofa or your money back.' "

"Ew."

"Yeah. I stuck around long enough to find the keys to the Range Rover, wash my clothes, drink a cup of coffee, figure out where Mona's house was, and run. As far as I'm concerned I never need to enter my parents' house again. Harry can have one of his paralegals or servants or whatever they're called pick up the keys to the Mercedes for you. Apart from that, to hell with the place. It could burn to the ground and I would not care. I wouldn't feel as if I had lost anything."

"That's how I feel about Mona's house. Fuck it. Let them auction it off and send me a check."

"Amen. So we're at the end of my story and back to yours. What do you do now? What do you do about Martin? What do you do with the money?"

Chad thought. Carefully, he said, "That depends on how much there is. I guess if there's going to be enough left over, I can get rid of my debt and be left with something in the bank. Enough to buy a bagel and a cup of coffee, maybe. I don't know. I haven't had the money long enough to think about it seriously. It's still a fictional construct."

"Mmm. A fictional construct," Jonathan said. "What about Martin?"

"I can't begin to tell you. I guess it depends on the outcome of this competency hearing and all the rest."

"Have you thought about not sticking around for it?"

"What do you mean?" Chad thought he knew but wanted to hear the words spoken out loud.

"You have how much money in that backpack? Seventy-five thousand dollars? Why not just—go? You can't be institutionalized if you're not home when the men in the white coats come."

"He'll find me." Chad's response came immediately, but as soon as he closed his mouth after speaking the second thoughts surfaced. Could Martin find him if he ran far enough? No, probably not.

"My father could have found you. Martin is not my father."

"I don't know. I make him sound like the bogeyman, you know, or like Freddy Krueger, showing up every time I shut my eyes. He's not. I don't even know that he's as evil as I make him sound. It's more like he's so rigid, that my existence is a terrible threat to the order in his little universe."

"Do I need to remind you that he beat the crap out of you and raped your boyfriend and made you watch?" Jonathan asked. "You can stop sticking up for him. He's a sick fuck who needs to be out of your life. It's OK. He's not going to be a problem for you forever. One day you will be able to discuss him without getting sick to your stomach. That's something to work toward, right?"

"You have a point," Chad said. "I have a passport, money, and a respectable lack of job skills. The world is my bottle of oyster sauce. Maybe I should leave," he mused. "Want to go to Canada for a few weeks? Toronto's cool."

"Sure," Jonathan said. "Any place where the money comes in different colors is better than here."

The mid-to-high eight digits?

Finding a place to park on Capitol Hill, in the vicinity of Eastern Market, was the same shade of unlikely as driving to the South Pole. Jonathan circled, swearing, for twenty minutes before finding a spot close enough to Chad's house that they wouldn't drop dead from heat prostration walking back.

"This is when driving a Range Rover sucks," he muttered, backing up until the fender rapped the car behind them hard enough that Chad could see it move. He pulled forward, turned the wheel, said "fuck" several times, and parked. The imprecations continued. "Why didn't I trade it in for a Civic hatchback? Why don't Range Rovers accordion-fold when you park them? Why isn't there a sonar to help find the car behind you?"

"You're a mile from the curb," Chad said.

"So tow me."

"At least you didn't dent this Ford."

"They're made of aluminum foil. I'm surprised I didn't."

Back at the house they found Rose crashing and banging into things upstairs. Madonna blared from the stereo. Something glass smashed, Rose spewed profanity, and for a second Chad was wreathed in a beautiful glow of life going on just as it ever had.

"Disaster follows me everywhere I go," Chad said, motioning for Jonathan to dump his bag on the floor. "You and Rose are going to love each other." He shouted for Rose to stop knocking a hole in the side of the house and to come meet Jonathan before she got brained by a chunk of falling masonry.

Rose was dusting her hands as she came down the stairs.

"What on earth were you doing up there?" Chad asked.

"Your brother surprised me when I got home," Rose said. "He tried to ambush me. Of course I was forced to kill him, dissolve his body in sulfuric acid, and refinish the tub after ruining the glaze."

"That's just ducky," Chad said. "I believe I am now one hundred percent relative free. I feel all warm and tingly inside."

"It's just gas," Rose said. "Couple of good farts and you'll be fine. You can't be anyone but Jonathan."

"Should I shake that hand? You were just dunking someone in acid."

"I washed it."

They shook.

The phone rang. Chad could tell Jonathan had turned to catch him when he flinched.

"Where's the caller ID box?" Chad asked, surveying the mess Rose had created and noticing a number of things missing. "For that matter, where's . . ."

"It's the cops," Rose said. "Chad, I think you ought to take this." She handed him the cordless.

"I'm not sure I want to." Chad pressed talk. "Hello?"

"Chad Sobran, please. This is Detective Vargas, with the DC Police."

"Speaking."

"I have to be blunt, because there isn't much time. We're aware of the reason for your trip to North Carolina, and we're all very sorry for your loss." Before Chad could murmur *Thank you,* Vargas steamrollered on. "There have been a few developments in the case at GW, and we want to ask both you and Jonathan Fairbanks more questions. He's with you, isn't he?"

Chad blurted *yes* before he could think of anything else to say.

"How soon can you come down to the station?"

"We've just driven in from North Carolina."

"I understand that, but this is . . ."

"I get the idea," Chad interrupted. He shifted from one foot to the other, acutely needing a toilet. "We need a couple of minutes here, and then we'll be right over."

Rose and Jonathan stared with wide eyes when Chad switched off the phone.

"What the hell was that?" Jonathan asked.

"Our beige friends from the DC Police want us to pay a call down at the station, as soon as we can get there."

"Fuck," Rose said. "Who are you dating here, Ted Bundy?"

"They seem to think so," Jonathan answered for Chad. "It's all right. This shit was inevitable. You can't have as many people drop dead in your presence as I have without being asked a few questions."

"Right. Look, I'm about to piss on the floor. I'll be right back. Talk among yourselves." Chad hurried into the powder room under the stairs.

After using the toilet and washing his hands with vanilla soap he hadn't seen before—must have been a by-product of Rose's retail therapy regimen—Chad stared into the mirror. Had there been so many shadows and wrinkles in his face this time last week? Two weeks ago?

Jonathan really could have done some of the murders. He had opportunities. He had motive, and he is cool enough to at least think he could get away with it. What have I been sleeping with for the last week?

Chad splashed his face with cold water—one handful, then another, then a third. He squirted soap from the pump dispenser into his hand, washed his face, took another look. He still looked like Chad.

"Be real," he told himself. "Jonathan has not killed anybody."

A voice at the back of his mind added: *who didn't have it coming.*

That gave him the boost he needed. When he finished with the bathroom, Jonathan and Rose were nowhere to be seen. Upstairs, a toilet flushed.

Disaster follows me everywhere, Chad thought.

On the way to the police station.

"Rose is a nut. I like her." Jonathan seemed uncomfortable. "Is her room always that messy?"

Chad shook his head no. Rose tended to be pretty clean. More so than he himself could ever be.

Jonathan rubbed the tattoo between his thumb and forefinger with the other thumb. He was holding the wheel with one hand, driving up narrow streets to the police station, with Chad telling him when to turn left and right.

This feels so natural, Chad thought. *I'm not grinding my teeth behind a smile and looking forward to him leaving. Now if we were going anywhere other than to see those two detectives . . .*

"She looks like she's packing," Jonathan said. "She clearly didn't want me to get more than a glimpse of her room. There were a couple of suitcases open and some cardboard boxes."

"She just got back from overseas," Chad said. "Right at the next light. It's probably crap she bought while she was away. She's boxing up her old shit so she can put out the new."

Jonathan nodded. "Could be. But that wasn't the sense I got. She's not really the tense type, you know?"

"Maybe she shipped herself some opium from Turkey."

"Could be. Is Turkey a big opium producer? I'd never really thought about it. Thailand or Laos, maybe, but . . ."

"We're here. Turn into that parking lot."

Two separate rooms, one for each witness—or was it victim? Detective Vargas, whom Chad remembered from GW, showed Chad into a small light-green room with an eyehook in the floor next to the rickety desk and two chairs. The paint on the walls looked and smelled like the inside of a smoker's lungs. Two breaths and Chad could feel emphysema setting in.

"How long am I going to be here?" Chad asked.

"Until it's time for you to leave."

They left Chad waiting half an hour while they talked to Jonathan.

He had to bang on the door to be allowed a trip to the rest room and a Coke from the vending machine. His head started to throb from the cigarette stink in the walls and the mottled carpet.

Chad had a book in his backpack, but he couldn't read at a time like this. Not even Richard North Patterson.

Some ten minutes after the rest room trip, Vargas and his partner Gonzalez returned.

Chad already had to piss again, and he wanted a breath of air that didn't smell like Jesse Helms had just exhaled it.

Some of the things Vargas and Gonzalez asked.

"Do you know your friend Jonathan well?"

"Yes and no. I mean, we've spent a lot of time together over the past week . . ."

"Intimate time, right? You're sleeping together."

"Well, yes. I won't deny it."

"Good. So do you know him well? Would you say you have a good insight into his character? Or just his dick?"

"Christ, are we back to the Good Cop, Bad Cop thing? I just went through that in North Carolina."

"And now you're in Washington. Going through it again. And you're going to keep going through it until we finish with you."

"We've been in touch with the police in New Bern. That's one reason you're here. You understand all that, don't you?"

"Of course I do. Look, will you just tell me what you think I did? Or what Jonathan did? That seems to be the point of all this."

"You want to remember something. We're the ones asking the questions, not you. We have enough evidence to press charges. We already know everything, and we're just confirming it all."

"There's not anything to know. His parents shot each other, or something. His father almost shot him. I didn't think there was any question about that."

"Do you feel safe, being around him?"

"I feel safer with him than with my brother Martin. I assume you've talked to him, too."

"He killed both of those patients at GW. You know that, don't you?"

"He couldn't have killed Linda. He was in the room with me all night."

"Were you awake, watching him?"

"OK, so he admitted he sprinkled pepper in her panties that evening before she went to bed. But he didn't throw her down an elevator shaft in the night. He'd have woken me up getting out of bed and leaving the room. Those door hinges needed WD-40."

"Doesn't that bother you, Chad? That your *friend* would do something like that to a mentally ill woman who couldn't help herself? Sprinkle chili pepper into the crotch of her panties and cause her terrible pain?"

"She was a pain in the ass. I hadn't really thought about it."

"*You better fucking think about it!* She is fucking dead with her fucking neck broken, compound fractures in her legs, just smashed all to shit . . ."

"I get the picture."

"No, I don't think you do. We have pictures here. Why don't you take a look?"

"No thanks. I'd rather not."

"No, I think you're going to see them whether you want to or not. Get an idea what you're dealing with here. What you're sleeping with."

This went on for hours. Maybe it wasn't hours, but it felt like hours. It felt like eternity. It was hell in advance, freeing Chad's soul to do whatever horrible things he wanted, without fear of retribution from on high.

"And you didn't get up in the night and go to your mother's hospital room yourself. Why not? You're at least one hundred thousand dollars in debt. The house is worth enough to pay off some of your bills. With the insurance, there's enough for you to go back to school, get another degree, get a new start . . .

"So who can say Jonathan didn't? You were asleep. He's not a big guy. He could have climbed out of bed. If you woke up at all you'd have thought he was going to take a leak or something. You didn't lie there watching him all night like a hawk, did you?"

"Do you know where Martin was the whole time? How do you know he didn't do it?"

"*Do not ask questions—answer them! Which side of the table do you think you're on, here?*"

Several times Chad found himself near tears.

He kept looking down at the eyehook bolted to the floor. For leg irons. How far away from arrest was he? How much would he get raped in prison? Would there come a point when he would find he liked it? When his asshole had stretched enough that the big burly drug dealers and bank robbers could shove in their baseball bat dicks and he wouldn't even blink? Chad shuddered. He didn't want to be somebody's bitch behind bars. Not even in his most lurid jack-off fantasies.

When Vargas announced there were no more questions and he could leave, Chad forgot Jonathan was still there. He wasn't sure of his own name, in fact, or what day of the week it was, or where he lived. Chad had no idea whether he had told the detectives anything useful. He had no idea whether he had given them anything they could use against Jonathan. Chad felt as if the top of his cranium had been sawed open, his brain sucked out, and clumps of wet newspaper dropped into his skull.

Jonathan sat outside on the front steps, his head in his hands.

"We should get out of here," Jonathan said quietly. "I've already called Harry about this. I told him we're in so much trouble right now, I'd finance his entire retirement if he'd clear his schedule and get his ass down here. He's on his way."

Chad sat down next to him.

"I didn't want to cooperate with them. I don't want to be here at all. I just want—I want us not to be in this situation. I don't think you did any of these murders, OK? Let me reassure you of that. I don't think you did them."

Jonathan put his arms around Chad. Again, that sense of Jonathan being a lost little boy.

"That's what I was hoping you would say," Jonathan said. "I needed to hear that. I feel totally overwhelmed right now. Can we get the fuck out of here?"

22

Friday Afternoon (Even Later)

"Princess parking," Chad said, smiling through the dentist's drill sensation of a tension headache that buzzed at the base of his skull.

He eased the Range Rover (Jonathan didn't feel like navigating the maze of little streets back to Chad's home; the detectives had gone a lot harder on him than Chad) into the spot across from his house, lightly tapping a Saab's front bumper as he struggled, as Jonathan had, with the cumbersome dimensions of the truck.

"I don't think I'd have the nerve to drive this thing off road," Chad said.

"You'd surprise yourself," Jonathan said. "Once you crossed a few streams in it and realized you were driving a tank, your confidence would soar. Do you have any pot? I could use a big fat spliff."

"No, but Rose probably does."

"I doubt she's going to be here when we get inside," Jonathan said, climbing out of the truck. "She was packing and trying to hide it from us."

"You're on crack," Chad said.

"I wish I was on something. God, I can't deal with any more cops." He waited for a car to pass, then jaywalked across the street at a brisk jog. "Dibs on the downstairs bathroom!"

"Hey, no problem." Chad waited for a taxi to pass, then jogged to catch up with him. He tossed the keys.

Jonathan snatched them neatly out of the air. Chad felt a spark of awe; he'd have missed them himself. Jonathan unlocked the front door and scooted inside.

Rose isn't home, Chad thought as he climbed the stairs. He couldn't hear a thing. If she had been here alone, music would be blasting and she'd be destroying things or dancing like a Middle Eastern Madonna on the sofa. Maybe Jonathan was onto something after all.

From downstairs, Chad heard a thump and a small cry as if Jonathan had knocked something over on the way to the bathroom. Something heavy, from the sound. Whatever. Chad hoped Jonathan hadn't hurt himself.

He stuck his head into Rose's room and stepped back in shock, from the mess. A tornado had hit her bedroom. Someone had detonated an egg carton of hand grenades under the bed. The Tasmanian Devil had flown in from Down Under and thrown a party for a hundred of his closest friends.

Several perfume bottles must have been dropped, from the overpowering whorehouse stink. Clothes lay in garish heaps on the floor and were strewn across the bed. A tower block of cardboard boxes had sprouted along one wall. Bills and envelopes and enough miscellaneous bits of paper to establish a stationery store littered every flat surface. Her computer keyboard could not be seen beneath a layer of bras and panties. The monitor above the stack of unmentionables swam with screensaver fish. Digital sharks and stingrays drifted across the screen. The name of that screensaver, Chad remembered, was *Dangerous Creatures*. In the middle of the vortex lay a stack of unmarked manila envelopes and folders.

"Fuck me," Chad said under his breath. "Jonathan was right. She's going somewhere, or she's already gone. There's no other explanation for it."

When he stepped into his bedroom something shoved him from behind and sent him sprawling face-down across his bed.

What the fuck? Chad couldn't tell whether he'd thought it or said it. He pulled the fabric of his comforter out of his mouth and took a deep breath, confused. Something pricked at the back of his mind. He knew what was going on here and wished he didn't.

He looked up.

Martin stood between him and the door.

"Shit."

"Nice to see you, too, asshole," Martin said, taking a swig from a flask Chad didn't recognize.

In dumb panic, his mind sidetracked toward the thought that he hadn't visited Martin's home in almost six months. No, more like seven. It was that time Cindy insisted on barbecuing chicken she'd bought on sale at Giant. She went a little overboard in her event-planning efforts and ended up with approximately 75,421 thighs and drumsticks drowning in cheap sauce, a kiddie-pool bowl of limp salad, and a case of watery beer to wash everything down. If Chad hadn't been desperately broke at the time, he'd have never shown up. All these Air Force guys had been there—huge, hunky jock types with big-haired girlfriends who had on too much makeup—along with skinny, brainy gay Chad who had been perfectly miserable, counting time until he could vanish without incurring Martin's wrath and hearing about it for the rest of his tormented life.

"What the fuck are you doing here, Martin?" Chad asked, forcing himself back to the present.

"Came to find you. Your fucking bitch of a roommate kept putting me off with this bullshit about you being in fucking Boston. Man, that was such an obvious fucking lie. She must have thought I was stupider than I look."

He stopped for another swig and the first awful flowers of panic bloomed in Chad's head. Chad saw broken blood vessels in Martin's nose. His eyes were bloodshot, his face florid, his hair clotted and un-washed. When was the last time Chad had seen him up close like this? Not recently.

He's shitfaced, and he's using the past tense when he talks about Rose.

"Martin, what are you really doing here?" Chad couldn't run; Martin had positioned himself between the bed and the door for a reason. He had been trained to fight. Built like a boxer, with the temper to match, Martin stood glaring at Chad, daring him to do so much as blink.

"Like I said." Swig. "Came to find you. My lawyer convinced that new judge to move up the date of your hearing . . ."

Chad shook his head no. "That's not why you're here, Martin. Where is Rose? Why isn't she here?" The panic spread through him like blood pooling around the corpse of a murder victim.

"I just came to take you back to my house until the hearing, to make sure you showed up for it," Martin said. "I didn't mean for . . ." He stopped.

"You didn't mean for what?" Chad forced the words out.

Jonathan's downstairs. Yell for him to get out of the house. Martin will do something to him.

"She attacked me," Martin said. "Didn't she fucking know what a stupid goddamn idea that was? Attacking me? Like, duh, look at me, and she's like this tiny-ass little dyke in heels. I mean, come on. She didn't have a fucking chance in hell."

"What did she attack you with?"

Martin bent down and picked up a brass fireplace poker. Even with the blinds shut Chad could see that the sharp end of the poker had a reddish cast.

Chad shut his eyes.

"You fucking killed her. Jesus Christ, Martin. You killed her. You killed Rose."

"Wasn't supposed to happen," Martin said. "She attacked me with this thing. I just wanted to get it out of her—you know, where you were and shit. And she tried to hit me over the head."

Veins bulged at his temples. Veins grew like the roots of trees down his arms. The sweat stains at the armpits of his Polo shirt extended halfway to his waist. His face glowed a mean drunk red.

White noise roared in Chad's head. There was a good chance he was about to die.

His mind went away for a second: *But I can't be about to die. I want to spend more time with Jonathan. I've never been to Barbados. No.*

Then it came back. "You killed her. You piece of shit."

"You're right, I fucking killed her. I'm just a dumb piece of shit Air Force fuckhead. What the fuck do I know other than how to fly a plane and shoot shit down? All I ever fucking wanted was to make sure my little brother was OK, and what did you do but treat me like I was a goddamn retard? Run away from me?"

A snapshot of Martin unzipping his khakis and forcing Barry's legs apart strobed through Chad's mind. Barry screaming. Snot coming out of his nose. The glimpse of blood and shit smeared on Martin's dick afterward. *His looks like mine—I didn't want to know that,* Chad remembered thinking. The dead look in Barry's eyes before he went to the hospital. Chad closed his eyes against the memory, but it wouldn't go away.

"You can't fucking take care of yourself. You're mentally—I don't know what the word is. There's something going on with you, man, and I was only doing this thing with the hospital for your own fucking good. You're not healthy."

"You don't have a clue," Chad said. "You wouldn't know healthy if it threw you down and fucked you like you fucked Barry."

Chad expected Martin to respond by swinging the fireplace poker and putting the lights out once and for all, but instead, Martin shrugged. Took another long swig from the flask. Wiped his mouth with the back of his hand. He swayed a little. "Doesn't matter now. Yell for your friend to come upstairs."

"No."

Chad had half a second to register what was going to happen. Martin smashed his right leg with the poker. The scream tore itself out of Chad's lungs like a flock of bats. Like something red and alive and angry. He curled into a fetal ball immediately.

"Jonathan! Get out!"

Another blow, across the side this time.

Riots of pain across Chad's side.

God, not the cast, don't hit me where the bone is already broken, he thought, sheltering his broken wrist with the rest of his body.

Another blow. Chad screamed.

Then he blacked out.

"Chad." Jonathan's voice came through the darkness, circled around Chad, nudged him out of himself. A hand was stroking his head, gently. "Chad."

Jonathan rocked him awake. Chad realized the soft thing happening on the side of his face was Jonathan kissing him every couple of seconds, delicately, like Chad's skull was an eggshell.

Pain jabbered through Chad—a senseless network of agony and
stiffness and things that screamed, *"Oh shit, don't do that!"* when he
tried to sit up.

"Chad, are you OK?"

Chad nodded. He felt dizzier than he'd ever felt in his life, nauseated. He was going to throw up—

It happened a second after he recognized the need. His abdomen
knotted, his stomach contorted, bile and chunks flew. Pain rocked
him—he tried to recoil from it and couldn't get away. He was made of
it. Solid pain. *I hurt, therefore I am.* It came from inside him. Things had
been broken in there. Organs splattered like pomegranates dropped
off tall buildings. Red meaty stuff everywhere. His lungs probably
had big holes in them.

"Chad, say something if you can. He hit you pretty hard. You're
very pale. I need you to wake up. Can you do that?"

Chad nodded. His tongue had turned into a pine cone. He nodded
again. "Gblergh," he said.

His head cleared after a moment. Jonathan held him. Time moved
in syrupy clots and bumps.

"He did something to Rose, didn't he?" Chad asked. Who had
wrapped a scarf around his tongue? He knew what Martin had said.
Maybe Jonathan would tell him something to make it all not be true.
Jonathan would make it all go away.

"Shh. Just finish waking up."

Alarms started going off somewhere in the outer reaches of Chad's
mind. He swam the rest of the way toward consciousness.

"Where's Martin?"

"On the floor by the bed, tied up and bleeding where I stabbed
him," Jonathan said.

Chad sat bolt upright. "From where you *what?*"

"Stabbed him. You know that big knife in the rack on the kitchen
counter? It's still sticking out of his ass. I told him if he pulled it out
he'd blow his intestines all over the floor, and bleed to death as well.
He stayed very still when I tied him up."

"What the fuck did you do that for?" Chad asked.

"He was beating the crap out of you with a fireplace poker. I'd have stabbed him in the back, but he was bent over you. His ass was closer."

"Umm . . . I missed that. I must have blacked out or something, after he hit me a couple of times."

"Chad, listen to me. He killed Rose. Her body is in the bathroom downstairs. He broke her neck."

The words ripped through Chad's guts like a flenser's hook tearing hunks of blubbery flesh off a whale. He shut his eyes and leaned against Jonathan. It was awfully cold for late summer. Chad couldn't stop shaking.

"There's more. He had a gun in his pocket. From what I heard him saying to you, I think he was going to kill both of us, too, and try to pin it all on me when the cops came."

"He wouldn't have gotten away with it. I mean, it would have been easy enough to prove who did what to whom," Chad said, struggling not to throw up again.

"He's piss-drunk," Jonathan said. "I doubt he was thinking before he acted. Bottom line, though: I crept up the stairs after taking my shoes off. I had the knife from the kitchen, and I was scared shitless that he might have killed you, that he might catch me sneaking up on him or get the knife away from me. When I saw him hitting you I rushed in and stabbed him in the ass. *Up* the ass. He howled and dropped like a sack of potatoes."

Chad swallowed. "I guess now we have to figure out what to do with him."

"I haven't called the police yet, but the neighbors probably have," Jonathan said. "We need nine-one-one for you, though. I'm not sure you aren't in shock. I don't know. You're pretty banged up, and you need to see a doctor."

Chad nodded, feeling dull. With effort, he swung his legs off the bed to stand up. For the first time, he noticed splashes of blood—his own?—on his bedspread.

"Christ, I didn't need to see that," he said, taking a deep breath.

"You're going to be OK," Jonathan told him.

"I wonder if he thinks this is for my own good. Beating me up. Killing Rose."

"I don't think you should stand up," Jonathan cautioned. He looked alarmed. Behind his bangs, beads of sweat covered his forehead. His face was white as chalk.

"I'm going to anyway, if you'll hold still so I can keep my balance." Chad carefully stood. The leg Martin had struck screamed in protest, almost giving out. He swore, sucked in his breath when he took the first step, swore again.

This is how the Little Mermaid must have felt.

Martin lay bound and gagged on the floor. With telephone cord.

"God, you're thorough," Chad said to Jonathan.

"It was handy." Jonathan gave a modest shrug. "He didn't put up much of a fight. I suspect it's hard to struggle when there's a machete sticking out of your rectum."

"Good point." Chad's head felt a bit clearer.

"Chad, what are you about to do?"

"Would you come over here a minute? I need to kneel down next to him."

Martin muttered something through his gag. The belligerence had gone out of him, Chad saw. A feral cat that arches its back and porcupines its fur to frighten an enemy looks pathetic when it's tossed into a stream. It remembers how small it is.

"Phone cord," Chad said again, his amazement exaggerated by the amount of pain he was in. "You used phone cord. I want to be you when I grow up."

He wanted to say something to Martin but found he didn't have the words. There wasn't anything to say. *Fuck you* was the first thing to come to mind, but it didn't even begin to express how he felt.

"He'll either bleed to death or die of some nasty infection if one of us pulls the knife out, right?" Chad asked Jonathan. He still felt dull and slow. A cup of coffee would do him right. Make that two cups, some Mylanta, a lot of codeine, and about a month on a tropical beach with nothing more strenuous to do than watch Jonathan run naked in the surf, if he could be convinced to take off his swimsuit.

Jonathan looked skeptical. "I think that's how it works."

"I think so too," Chad said, his mind coming back again.

He reached around behind Martin, grasped the knife as firmly as he could with one hand that shook and the other still in a cast, and jiggled it. Martin cried out behind his gag. He sort of coughed. Chad jiggled the knife again.

"Like that?" he asked Martin, whose face had gone waxy white. Tears streamed out of his eyes. "Like having something stuck in you? Think how Barry must have felt."

Chad withdrew the knife. Pulling it out took effort, and smelled bad. Chad couldn't get a great grip since he was limited to one hand, but he jiggled it and pulled and coaxed the blade out of Martin's body. Made sense, he supposed, that it should require more effort than pulling a toothpick out of a cake to see if it's done in the middle. There's a first time for everything. Martin's muffled whimpers and yelps should have affected him but didn't.

Blood pooled on the floor.

Turning to Jonathan, Chad asked, "How long do you think it'll take?"

"Until what takes? Until he dies? I don't know. Maybe he won't."

"Let him lie there and bleed some, then. We can call nine-one-one in a minute or two. We'll say I pulled out the knife because I thought it would help. What can they say? It's not like anyone will believe him."

Chad lay with his head in Jonathan's lap to wait for the ambulance.

– 23 –

Friday Night, but Mostly Sunday

In the ambulance, Chad's mind drifted. Sometimes he went away. Then he came back.

Barry had been carried away in an ambulance like this, with blood coming out of his nose and his ass. That time, the EMTs wouldn't let Chad accompany them to the hospital. One had jostled Barry, eliciting a gasp of pain, and Chad had called the guy a fucking incompetent shit. "If you say you don't need medical treatment, buddy, then you can stay home and wait for a call when the docs finish with your friend. Or drive to the hospital yourself."

This time, the EMTs said he was in shock. Possible internal bleeding. He hadn't been hit in the head, had he? Could he remember? Chad had no idea. What about the broken wrist? Had that been hit? X rays would have to be taken, to be sure. And a new cast that didn't have blood on it.

"Am I OK?" Chad asked.

"You will be," they assured him. They. He. A guy. He was Asian. Handsome, too. Looked Jonathan's age but had to be older.

The handsome Asian EMT had given him a shot.

Beautiful billowing white clouds blew across Chad's mind. He remembered them. Must be the same drug again. This felt like being in the movie *Brazil*. At the beginning or the end, when the hero has left the dreary real world and gone someplace else in his head.

Am I a murderer now? He didn't know whether he thought this or spoke it.

Where the hell was Jonathan?

Chad had a dim memory of blacking out again after Martin . . .

Jesus.

The ambulance was speeding toward another hospital.

Rose was dead. Martin had killed her.

Had they killed Martin? Chad hoped not. He also hoped so.

But Martin was going to kill me. And Jonathan. He was going to kill us both.

More clouds drifted across the mental sky. He swam in the breathtaking blue for a little while.

Where the hell was Jonathan?

At one point Chad heard someone say, "We've got him stabilized. His injuries are mostly superficial. He's out of the woods now."

Then he fell asleep again.

Where the hell was Jonathan?

"Chad?"

Chad opened one eye. He saw a hospital room, blindingly white, a horrible absence of color after the clear Caribbean blue in his head. From the table next to him, a bouquet of lilies and orchids perfumed the air and helped to mitigate the antiseptic hospital stink. Detective Vargas sat at the end of the bed, with an attentive-but-bored expression Chad took to mean he had been there for some time.

The mental clouds had dissipated. Another hospital room. No fake Georgia O'Keeffe print this time. Just a bored detective with sweat circles at his armpits and a Styrofoam cup of coffee in one hand.

"Hello," Chad said.

Vargas nodded his head in greeting.

"I doubt you came here just to make sure I was OK," Chad said. He wondered what day it was.

"Well, that was a part of it, but you're right. I have a few questions. So do a lot of other people. Are you up to answering them?"

Chad nodded. He supposed a lawyer would be a good thing to have, but he nodded anyway. They were all off the edge of the world now, weren't they? Everything was too far out of control to be brought back. They were speeding on the freeway with their eyes shut. Abyss, here we come. Chad realized he hadn't stopped nodding yet. He stopped.

"Your friend said he stabbed your brother during an attack on you. Your brother is in the ICU downstairs. The docs aren't sure he's going to live. The problem with your friend is, he's also a suspect in at least two other deaths, one of which has been ruled a homicide. Then there are questions about your roommate and your mother. We can't be sure things didn't happen the other way around until you tell us who beat the shit out of whom."

"Martin was trying to kill me."

"Why would he want to do that?"

"Why would I lie?"

Vargas nodded. "You're facing a competency hearing. We're bringing in a psychiatrist to determine whether you're well enough—mentally, I mean—to know the difference."

"Oh Jesus Fucking Christ," Chad spat. Anger burst through his narcotized surface. Calm, sudden lava from a dormant volcano. "Have you lost your goddamn mind?"

"I wouldn't say that. The question is whether you have lost yours."

"The hospital released me. I am not a goddamn psycho."

"Just to let you know, your friend out there, Jonathan, we're like ten minutes away from Mirandizing him and taking him down to the station. The cops in Connecticut would like to talk to him about how his parents died. Like who shot who, that kind of thing? The ballistics people had some questions about that. It all looked kind of funny. And at GW, when those patients died? He was there. Both of them were bothering him. He looks bad, Chad, and you're blind if you don't see it. He's been around a lot of death. Look at what happened in North Carolina. Are you absolutely sure he was in bed with you all night? He could have gone to the hospital and put a pillow over your mother's face, couldn't he? Done a little Dr. Kevorkian job on her, so he could have you all to himself? That goes for your brother, too. It just doesn't look like self-defense, man. Tied up with a phone cord? Stabbed up his ass? Man, that sounds like a fucking assassination attempt to me, not self-defense."

"It's what was on hand," Chad said. He took stock. Reports came in like news flashes from the front lines of a battle between countries he'd never visited: His leg ached, distantly, where Martin had clobbered it. His head hurt as if remembering a headache rather than still feeling one. "He was trying to do something. I'm half beaten to death, here."

"You're a smart guy. You know where I'm going with this. Help us out, here. You're not in such great shape yourself. You're looking at a competency hearing. You're probably going to get there with a criminal record. Depending on what Jonathan gets charged with, accomplice to murder. You're also in debt up to your eyeballs. Do you really think you're going to stay out of Saint E's?"

"I just woke up after my brother beat the shit out of me with a fireplace poker," Chad said. "I haven't had time to really think about it."

A knock at the door punctuated his sentence.

"Can I help you?" Vargas snapped, when a sixtyish man with movie-star coiffure stepped into the room.

"You can leave," said the man. "My name's Harry Green, and this is my client." He raised his eyebrows just enough to mean, *Fuck you,* and smiled politely.

"Is he your lawyer?" Vargas asked.

Chad had never actually heard Harry's last name. "Yes," he said. "Hi, Harry. What took you so long?"

"Thank you, Detective," Harry said, stepping aside to allow access to the open doorway. He reminded Chad of James Woods with the sharp edges filed down. "We'll talk to you again very soon. Don't worry. We all want to get to the bottom of this."

As soon as the door was shut and hands had been shaken, Harry said, "I've convinced the police that arresting Jonathan would be a mistake of titanic proportions. James Cameron would make a movie about it. He'd sink tens of millions of dollars into the production."

"I like you already," Chad said. "I can see why Jonathan does."

"He may change his mind when he gets my bill," Harry said. "I'm going to attach a handwritten note to the invoice: 'Remember how much you're worth, especially after your estate gets through probate.' "

"Fat lot of good his funds will do him in jail," Chad said, wondering what had happened to Mona's stash. He assumed the police were taking apart his home piece by piece, investigating. The envelope full of

cash was bound to be discovered and impounded, and would go toward financing some crooked cop's cocaine habit. He felt hollow.

"Which is why he called me when he did. After your meeting with
the police yesterday, he saw this whole situation going south fast.
He's sharp like that."

"I'll say." Chad thought for a second. "Yesterday?"

Harry nodded. "You've been napping."

Chad wondered what to say next. He sensed this wasn't a social call
but was too far over his head to know how to proceed. The safest option seemed to be staying right where he was, under the covers.

He could see why Jonathan liked Harry. He emanated a subtle
nonchalance that just avoided being smug. His clothes didn't draw
attention to themselves but if you had a good eye you could tell he
shopped well. The clean lines of his shirt and trousers looked like
Hugo Boss. If his loafers weren't Ferragamo, Chad decided he would
swallow his hospital gown whole, without salt or ketchup.

"I heard enough of what the detective was saying to know you've
gotten the full story," Harry said. "The police don't have any rock-
solid evidence. They don't have enough to convince a jury beyond a
reasonable doubt. So they're pushing him to make a deal and confess
to something—once they decide what they can charge him with."

"So they're trying to intimidate him by telling him how horrible
the worst-case-scenario charges are, right?"

"Something like that. Detective Vargas has given him a laundry list
of things that could be evidence in each case. He's had a lot to say
about motive because he has a lack of material evidence. That's all
sort of tangential to the point. Jonathan didn't exactly help himself by
putting pepper in that woman's underwear drawer. Whether that
pushed her over the edge, literally, is anyone's guess. Maybe so; maybe
not. From what I've heard about her, I doubt it. I don't believe for a
second that Jonathan was responsible for any of their deaths, but the
police don't agree with me."

"What about Martin?"

"That's the stickiest of all. Just like the case with your mother's
death, things don't look good for either of you. The prosecutor is going to make a case for you being mentally ill. Never mind that you

were released from the hospital. Your involvement in this isn't going to help you, not one bit. It's going to follow that either Jonathan snuck out in the middle of the night and smothered her or you did, and the other one is lying. The attack on Martin is going to be seen the same way. There's not much question that he killed Rose, but after you were knocked unconscious Jonathan stabbed him with a knife that looked like something Indiana Jones would use to carve his way through a jungle. Up the ass, too, which raises sex crime questions, because you're both gay. Don't look at me like that; this is America and we hate fags here and the question is going to come up. Then Jonathan trussed Martin up with telephone cord and gagged him."

"And the police say it looked like an execution," Chad said. "What happened to self-defense?"

"I think they're going to say the knife was enough. But to tie him up, gag him, and pull out the knife?"

"Even if we thought pulling out the knife was better than leaving it in?"

Harry seemed to be studying him. "You're going to have to trust me when I say I've heard enough about Martin in the last few days to have stabbed him myself if I thought I could have gotten away with it. I also know Jonathan well enough to say he knew exactly what pulling out that knife would do. Whichever one of you actually did it, *he* knew. You may be able to convince a jury that you thought . . ." He seemed to be reconsidering. "If this were ever to get to trial, yes, you may get away with that one."

"You're heading toward something," Chad said, noticing it for the first time.

Harry nodded.

"Jonathan got an idea while he was waiting for the police and the ambulance to come. He looked through Rose's room and found some very interesting things. I don't know if you're aware she was embezzling money from the law firm where she worked?"

"What?"

"I'm not kidding. She started at least a year ago. She also seemed to know someone in the mortgage business. She used her own monies to purchase four HUD houses here in DC, and then she took out one hundred twenty-five percent mortgages on each property."

"Holy shit."

"She had a Turkish passport, too. Bet you didn't know that. Chad, she was going to run. There's no sign anyone had figured out what she was up to, but she was going to leave the country. She had tickets for a flight to Istanbul. This time tomorrow, she would have been on a plane."

"I think I'm beginning to see where you're going with all of this."

"I think you're going to owe Jonathan a huge debt of thanks for calling me when he did, because I got to the scene just before DC's Finest did. I have your backpack with your mother's money. There's also an envelope full of cash from Rose, with your name on it. I think she intended to leave you a going-away present."

The room magically contained oxygen again. Chad sank into his pillows.

"I also have all the paperwork pertaining to Rose's transactions. They're in your backpack, too. Jonathan thought you might like to have them. She should never have written down her account numbers and passwords, not if she wanted to make a clean get-away, but you can profit from her stupidity. Somebody ought to. Jonathan thought you might want to throw some flowers into the Bosphorus someday in gratitude."

"You don't mean . . ."

"That's exactly what I mean."

"The money's dirty," Chad protested, more because he thought he was supposed to than because he truly objected.

"We're all dirty," Harry said. "And every cent you and Jonathan have is dirty, too, at this point. We're running out of time. You're going to go before a judge in about a week's time, with all of this shit behind you, and you're going to have to convince her you're healthy and sane and capable of taking care of yourself. You may stay out of Saint Elizabeth's. You may not. Do you want to find out the hard way? I think you'll agree it's better to stay out of a witch-hunt than to stick around and be burned at the stake."

"Get me out of here."

"Attaboy. I've convinced the police that if they arrest Jonathan right now, the media will crucify them and so will I. But that's beside the point. I don't see why you should stick around for this legal shitstorm when you both have an alternative."

"We can run."

"I've chartered a plane and bribed a few officials, so there'll be no record of your takeoff. The airports will be under surveillance when you two disappear, but Jonathan's in a position not to require a commercial flight."

"Jesus Christ. How much is this costing?"

Harry chuckled. His eyes looked hurt for a second, as if it nauseated him to be a part of all this. "Ask him when I send the bill," he said.

"You're going to get tarred and feathered because of this, aren't· you?"

Harry looked away. "Why don't we look at it this way. I own a house in Costa Rica and have been looking forward to spending more time there. The timing of all this isn't great, but what the hell. I'm not going to let Jonathan and you get fucked like this." As an afterthought, he added, "Anyway, my partner already lives there. He's Costa Rican, himself. He's only too glad to hear I'll be moving down for good."

"All I have is the clothes on my back," Chad said. "Or in the closet, or wherever they are."

"Then I suggest you put them on. Do you think you can walk?"

"Slowly, but yes."

"If you need help getting dressed, I'm willing. Otherwise, I'll turn around if you want privacy. I'm going to leave as soon as you're dressed."

"I don't care." Chad stood, hobbled across the room to retrieve his clothes from the stack on the dresser. He didn't care if Harry saw him change—there were other things to worry about. And Harry was tasty in that older-guy-in-good-shape way Chad had the occasional fantasy about.

"I'm glad you're not shy," Harry remarked. "I hope you're not offended when I say I can understand why Jonathan's so taken with you. If I weren't an old married guy I'd have a couple of lecherous thoughts myself."

The blush made Chad's knees glow.

"Are you sure you're up for this?" Harry asked. "You have an alternative. I can shelter the money—what you're going to inherit from your mother, as well as the cash. I can refer you to a colleague who can fight the charges. Jonathan's still going to run. You are both going to be fugitives living under false identities—at least until the furor dies down. It sounds glamorous, but it isn't. Are you absolutely sure?"

Chad nodded. "It's weird, but I want to be with Jonathan. Even though I haven't known him long." He shrugged. "I can't predict the future but the present works, you know? And it beats the hell out of staying here."

"Good boy. You've got balls. When I walk out of here I'm going to pull a fire alarm on this floor and the floor under it. You're on the third floor, by the way. In the ensuing mayhem, you're going to have to get out."

"Aren't the cops still here?"

"Vargas and his partner left, but I expect there's someone nearby. It's a chance we'll have to take. I'm afraid I can't arrange a better diversion."

Chad nodded.

A strange squawk outside broke his train of thought. He and Harry turned to look at the door, as if it had a window. They smiled, catching each other in the same mistake. Chad's tension decreased a notch.

"There's a fire door about five doors down. When you step out of this room, just go to the left, down the stairs, and outside. I'll be in the black Lincoln. Jonathan will be there with me. You understand we're going straight to a private airfield and there's no time to stop by your house."

Chad nodded again. "There's nothing I'm so attached to that I can't leave it behind."

What the hell? He'd lost almost everything else already. Why not dispose of the rest of his life in one fell swoop? Wasn't that what he'd always wanted?

"Good. Then let's do it."

With that, Harry stepped outside.

Cindy exploded into the room, trailing two flustered nurses.

"They told me you were talking to your lawyer," Cindy spat. "They wouldn't let me in to see my own family."

"First time I've ever seen you eager to claim me as family," Chad said, glad she hadn't caught him changing clothes. He didn't mind if Harry caught a glimpse of his ass but with Cindy present, it was better to stay in purdah.

Harry stepped into the room.

"Can I be of assistance?" he asked.

"No," Cindy said, before Chad could open his mouth. "I don't know who you are, but you are not needed here."

"I believe my client is the best judge of that," Harry said.

Chad admired the man's poker face.

"This is Harry Green, my attorney," Chad said. He tried to project an air of calm. The thought of choking Cindy and sending her to hell—there to spend eternity nagging Martin—while fun, would have to wait until some other time. Harry looked calm, and Chad needed to look calm almost as much as he needed more painkillers if he was going to get through the next couple of hours. Maybe Harry had some of those, too. Chad wished he could concentrate. "If you can stay an extra minute, Harry, I'd appreciate it."

"You tried to kill Martin, you little shit." Cindy's face looked like Martin's for a second: the angry vein that throbbed at her temple linked them. Which spouse was worse? How on earth were their kids going to turn out? "I don't care what the police say, or whether you or your *friend* actually did it, but you stabbed him."

"Cindy, he's not dead. And no matter what happens to him, we saved you the trouble of divorcing him, right? After he beat the crap out of you the other night? The bruises haven't even faded yet. Have you forgotten that part? Jesus, why aren't you thanking me, you stupid cunt?"

Cindy's mouth opened and closed. If her face got any redder it was going to turn into one gigantic scab.

"You . . . fucking . . ."

"Save it, Cindy. I don't want to hear it. Tell me whatever you came here to tell me, and then get the fuck out." Chad had been standing too long; he sat on his bed again to conserve his strength. He needed Cindy out of his way soon if he and Jonathan were going to escape.

Cindy stared at him as if she couldn't think of what to say next.

"I'm going to give you fifteen seconds, Cindy, and then I'm going to ask Harry to call a nurse for me. You'll be escorted out of the hospital by security if it comes to that. I did it to Martin when he came to the psych ward last week and I'll do it to you now. What the fuck do you want?"

She shook her head. "You arrogant little . . ."

Chad sighed. "I know what you want, and you aren't capable of saying so directly because you're afraid of what I'll say next." Time to bluff a little. The best lies are the ones you've seasoned with elements of truth. "There isn't going to be any competency hearing without Martin around to push for one. Harry has already started working on that."

Harry allowed an *I have?* expression to cross his face. Cindy, still glaring at Chad, missed it.

"I know the bottom line with you is money. And since you have two kids to raise, I'm not going to criticize you for that. Martin had insurance through the Air Force but I bet you think it's not enough, right?"

"I hadn't even thought that far," Cindy finally said.

"You're lying," Chad said. "But it's OK because I don't care. Don't give me that look. Harry, can you arrange for the proceeds from Mona's estate to be put in an airtight trust for my niece and nephew? So there will be funds available when it's time for them to go to college?"

Harry nodded, a smile cracking his stoic veneer. Chad got the impression he'd scored a home run.

"Cindy, my money is what you really came here for, even if you were expecting to jump through more hoops to get it," Chad said.

"You can't be serious," Cindy said. She looked like she'd been slapped.

"Never more serious in my life. I want you to call Martin's lawyer and tell him to drop the case. All of it. Tell him you saw me in the hospital and you thought all along that Martin was just out to fuck with me. Use better language. You're bright enough to come up with something. Say you refuse to testify that I'm incompetent. You agree I should be left the hell alone, so we can all get on with our lives. Will you do that for me?"

"This is a bribe," Cindy said. "You're trying to bribe me."

"You're coming out on top, here, Cindy. Do you care?"

She nodded.

"It's settled, then. Will you excuse us?"

Harry held the door for her, and she hesitated. She turned back, as if she meant to say something else.

"Get out," said Chad.

"You'll go far," Harry told Chad, smiling when Cindy gave an exasperated sigh and stormed out of the room, elbowing a nurse who got too close.

"I hope so. Preferably by tonight."

Please let this not be the stupidest thing I have ever done.

Please let there be no cops in the hallway.

Please let me not trip and fall down the stairs.

Please let Harry and Jonathan be there. If they're gone, if this is all a big mind-fuck, I have nothing. Less than nothing.

When the alarms began to blare and the emergency strobe lights started flashing, Chad shoved his door open and stepped into the hall. Doctors and nurses scrambled around like World War II Londoners in an air raid. Chad saw a police officer out of the corner of his eye and kept going.

What hospital was this? For the first time, it occurred to Chad that he didn't know where he was. Providence? DC General? He didn't have a clue.

His clothes stank of fear and sweat.

The fire door wouldn't open at first. When he pulled on it, his arms screamed in pain. The world shimmered for a second. His stomach turned cartwheels.

Behind him, someone started yelling, "Hey! Hey! Where are you going!"

The door opened, and Chad stepped into the stairwell.

He hurried.

There was someone behind him.

He wasn't going to make it.

The angry red face one flight up could have belonged to a man or a woman, impossible to tell, just enough time to see that the officer was overweight and clumsy and gaining on him, heavy feet clomping down the stairs, now only a dozen steps behind him, then . . .

"*Fuck!*"

Small miracles do sometimes happen.

The cop tripped and fell down the stairs, hitting the landing above and behind him with a thud. *It's a woman.* The news took a moment to register. *She's female.* It was like hearing someone say, *The sky is blue,* or, *The air contains oxygen,* as if this fact had just been discovered by Nobel laureates. *Really? Oh, that's interesting, and I have to escape now.* Chad didn't stop to check whether she had broken her neck. He had seen more than enough dead people lately, and this was a hospital, after all. It wasn't as if there were no doctors around. The exit door lay just one flight down.

He hobbled outside, blinking in the sun, alarms and sirens blaring. People on the sidewalk were staring at the hospital as if a flying saucer had landed on the roof instead of the Medivac helicopter. A black Lincoln pulled up to the curb, and the passenger-side window buzzed down.

"Do you party?" Jonathan asked.

"Hard," Chad said. "Want a date?"

"Can I afford you?"

"I'm not cheap," Chad said. "How much have you got?"

"Countless millions. Think that's enough?"

Chad nodded. He heard the doorlocks click.

"Get in," Jonathan said.

On the way out of DC, Harry stopped at National Airport and parked in the long-term lot.

"I've rented another car," he said. "I assume the police know to look for this one. It's not very inconspicuous. I want you guys to come with me, but wait outside the rental office, OK? I'll be fast."

An agonizing twenty minutes later, they had a Sebring convertible. Chad clutched his backpack as if his life depended on the thing. Which, in a way, it did.

"It's not as fast as I'd like, but it'll do. Nobody who knows me would ever picture me behind the wheel of one of these things."

Chad directed him out the GW Parkway, then to I-66 and the Dulles Toll Road.

"Be careful here. It's heavily patrolled."

Harry drove like someone's grandmother.

"So," he asked after they all held their breath at the toll plaza. "What Latin American country would you guys like to be citizens of?"

"What are our options?" Chad asked.

"My friend in Miami says the best bets right now are Venezuela, Chile, Argentina, and Panama. He's had the most luck getting into their systems. Costa Rica's also a good one, but I'm biased."

Chad had an idea: "Didn't the Venezuelans elect a dictator a few years back?"

"Hugo Chavez. Yes, they did, didn't they?" Jonathan said.

"Very good," Harry said, anticipating what Chad was getting at. "As long as Chavez is in office, and doing things like dissolving the Venezuelan Senate, the U.S. government will keep him at arm's length."

"And vice versa," Jonathan said. "So you think we'll stand a better chance there than anywhere else?"

"It makes sense. Anyway, I have a couple of friends in Caracas," Chad said. "Or I used to. From when I was on exchange in Spain."

"Be careful looking them up," Harry cautioned. "I can't emphasize that enough. You don't want to be found after you disappear."

"So we're going to become Venezuelans, are we?" Jonathan asked.

"I always thought the *caraqueños* I knew were cool," Chad said. "Wouldn't hurt to try being one."

"Are you guys sure?" Harry asked.

They looked at each other and nodded.

"Then I'll take care of it."

An hour later, they were on a small jet that would take them to San José, Costa Rica. Pablo, Harry's partner, would meet them at the airport; they'd stay at Harry and Pablo's home for several days until Venezuelan papers could be arranged. Then the world was theirs. They could proceed on to Caracas if they wanted. Or stay in Costa Rica. Permanent-resident status would be easy to obtain, Harry told them. The government there made it easy for wealthy people to be comfortable. Few questions would be asked.

"We'll figure it out when we get there, won't we?" Chad asked Jonathan.

They took their seats.

Harry shook their hands, then had a second thought and hugged them both before exiting the plane.

"I'm sorry to see him go," Jonathan said. "You're smiling. Why in the world are you smiling?"

Chad took Jonathan's hand.

Up front, the pilot started the plane's engines.

"An old thought I had just came back to me. It was a phrase I thought of when I was leaving for Spain for my year on exchange. *The inherent consolation of liftoff.*"

"That's lovely," Jonathan said, giving Chad's hand a squeeze. "Even lovelier would be the inherent consolation of vodka. Where's the flight attendant?"

Twenty minutes later they were airborne, flying south through darkening turquoise skies.

Epilogue

Eight Weeks Later

Chad had no trouble convincing Jonathan to frolic naked in the surf. Everyone else was doing it. People on beaches here in Europe were much less reserved than in South America. Chad lay on the beach watching several well-oiled shades of tan eye candy. The sun glinted off the ring in Jonathan's navel.

Harry and Pablo, who was fortyish and gorgeous, had flown in from Costa Rica to spend a week with Chad and Jonathan in Barcelona. Pablo's equally handsome younger cousin Carlos, an actor who lived in Barcelona but was on a shoot in Madrid, had driven down to meet them. Carlos brought his rather quiet and awkward Canadian boyfriend (whose name Chad kept forgetting) down for the weekend. Something about the boyfriend, Richard or Ryan maybe, struck Chad as more American than Canadian. Not that it mattered. There were other things on Chad's mind.

Last night Jonathan had said he liked the place so much he was thinking about buying it.

"The hotel?" Chad had asked.

"No, Barcelona."

Pablo seemed to sense Chad's anxiety. "I will join the others," he said in English, peeling off his Speedo (Chad was glad to have sunglasses on just then) and dashing down the beach. Pablo had no tan line.

"We've been together nine years and I'm still not used to the sight of him," Harry said, reading Chad's mind (or following his gaze). When Chad didn't respond right away, Harry asked, "You've been pensive all day. What's on your mind?"

"It doesn't feel over," Chad said. "I know I'm driving Jonathan crazy, but I'm not quite right with all of this."

His cast had been off for three weeks. The bruises had faded. The external ones, that is.

The Venezuelan passports didn't cause any raised eyebrows at any international border he and Jonathan had crossed. They needed visas more often now, but that was a minor complication. It beat an eternity of court dates, assessments, reporters shoving mikes in his face every time he opened the door, and sessions with mental health busybodies. The media uproar in the wake of their disappearance had been intense but brief. Fortunately nobody had thought to look for them in South America yet. With the American and global economies in the toilet, and the world in the usual morass of political turmoil, there was plenty of more entertaining material available to captivate the masses. The national attention span just wasn't long enough to justify more than cursory pursuit. Chad and Jonathan got their few column inches and were promptly consigned to last week's news.

"You're feeling guilty about Martin, aren't you?" Harry asked, gently.

Chad took a deep breath of the salt air, and the sugary coconut-vanilla scent of his sunscreen. Somebody down the beach had brought a boom box; Chad recognized a song by the Belgian group Hooverphonic.

"Not Martin." Chad shook his head. "God, no. I'm much better off with him six feet under. His kids are better off, too. Good riddance. I only wish someone had cut off his head and driven a stake through his heart before burying him, just to be on the safe side. And I'm not grieving over Mona either. It was a miracle she lasted as long as she did. I wouldn't even call this guilt. It's more like . . ."

"You don't deserve a happy ending when so many people around you are dead now?"

"Up to a point. Rose is the one who keeps me up at night." Chad groped for the words. "This shouldn't have happened to her."

"You're right," Harry said. "It shouldn't have. You weren't responsible, though. You do know that, don't you?"

"Knowing it and feeling it aren't the same thing."

Harry nodded. "Well, I have something that may lift your spirits a little. I was going to wait to tell you with Jonathan around to hear it, but we can tell him later.

"One of the nurses at the hospital was just arrested and charged with fifteen counts of second-degree murder, after some kind of hostage stand-off. A young woman, apparently. About your age. When the police were questioning you, they were certainly aware of the other deaths in that hospital. Whatever their suspicions, it was obvious you and Jonathan could not have been involved. So you're off the hook for that one."

"What about the bit about someone matching my description being seen?"

"A bluff," Harry said.

"Christ." Chad watched seagulls for a moment, then shut his eyes. He let his mind drift for a second: the tattoo he'd decided to get on his upper back, before they left Spain—an ornate compass rose that would hurt like hell going on but would look both fierce and elegant afterward; the iMac he and Jonathan had bought for their apartment in Caracas; deeper questions they shared, with regard to staying in Venezuela versus moving to a more stable country.

Jonathan knocked Chad out of his daydreams by flopping down on the towel next to him and engulfing him in a wet sandy sea-lion hug. Harry was blushing, Chad noticed. Funny, the contrast between Harry's fierce professional composure and his propensity to become unglued around delicious young men in the nude.

"Hey, cut it out! You're getting me soaked!" Laughing, Chad gave Jonathan a towel.

Pablo, Carlos, and the blond Canadian boy (Robert?) followed.

"It's getting late," Harry said.

It was hard not to be taken aback by Jonathan's frolicsome nudity. He pulled on a pair of shorts, then wrapped himself around Chad, eyes shut, almost purring.

"If we get going," Harry continued, "we'll have enough time for a drink before dinner."

Nobody objected. They dressed, squeezed into Carlos's Citroën (a big turbocharged CX that looked and rode like a UFO), and zoomed back to Barcelona.

Later, in the shower, Jonathan said to Chad, "You're still doing it. You've gone all quiet. I don't know what to do or what to say." He wrapped his arms around Chad.

"Just say you're not going away," Chad said, squeezing him back.

"Silly goose boy," Jonathan said. "Why would I do something so stupid as that?"

At dinner, a hip new neon-and-aquariums seafood place deep in the Gothic Quarter, Harry's mobile phone rang. He excused himself to take the call. Ten minutes later, he returned with an odd look on his face.

"Chad and Jonathan, may I take you two aside for a moment? I was expecting this call, but didn't want to say anything earlier. You won't want to wait on this news."

All six of them exchanged looks. Chad and Jonathan shrugged like twins and stood to follow Harry down the corridor to the restrooms.

"I won't keep you waiting. That was my associate in Washington, DC. The investigation into Martin's death has been closed."

"You knew it was going to happen while we were here, you scoundrel," Jonathan said. Chad couldn't tell the degrees to which he was impressed, amused, and irritated.

Harry nodded. "Guilty as charged. Yes, the timing was deliberate. I decided not to spoil the trip by letting you two squirm in suspense while we waited."

"So are you going to tell us?" Jonathan asked. "Are we on the FBI's Top Ten list?"

"Number One with a bullet?" Chad added.

Harry shook his head no. "Quite the opposite. The judge said that Jonathan probably saved your life, based on the photographs of your injuries. Overall, Jonathan's case still left a lot more questions unanswered than answered, but where Martin was concerned, it was clear he was trying to protect you. So no murder charges, no manslaughter, nothing."

Jonathan's jaw dropped.

"Which is not to say you should rush back to the States on the next plane," Harry said. "Let me remind you, there are still charges outstanding against both of you. You both failed to appear for your own hearings and are believed to have flown to escape questioning. My associate pointed out that being a minor—well, not anymore—and gay, Jonathan was worried about his own safety, but the judge didn't buy it."

"Are there arrest warrants? Jesus, Harry, what the hell else have you been waiting to drop on us?" Chad asked, appalled.

"Nothing you don't already know. There was no competency hearing for Chad. Cindy followed through on that. The deaths at GW were determined to be suicides. One patient was known to self-injure and the other was deeply psychotic. The IRS and some of Chad's creditors got wind of the suspected flight, and lawsuits have been filed in several jurisdictions."

"Bottom line?" Chad asked.

Harry shrugged. "A lot of bureaucratic messiness, if you want to boil it down to that. Fairly trivial in the grand scheme of things. But there was no warrant out for either of your arrests when you left, and the charges—contempt of court, an assault charge for Jonathan—are all relatively minor. Minor enough that the whole thing will blow over sooner or later. The pictures of Chad's injuries and the details of Rose's murder are enough to keep you guys off *America's Most Wanted.* So you're off the hook."

"But we never really did anything in the first place," Chad said.

"Nothing unwarranted," Jonathan amended.

"Either way, champagne would seem to be in order."

The restaurant had Veuve Clicquot.

"Speaking of *minor,*" Jonathan asked in the middle of the festivities.

"The age of consent in the District of Columbia is sixteen," Harry said. "For both heterosexual and homosexual contact."

They ordered a fourth bottle of the Widow.

Chad sat bolt upright in the middle of the night, a vicious headache chainsawing his cranium in half. He stumbled to the bathroom for analgesics, head spinning. He couldn't tell whether the pain rioting in his skull was because of the idea he'd awakened with or the champagne he'd consumed.

Jonathan shuffled into the bathroom and took a piss while Chad fumbled in the medicine cabinet, then in his toilet kit, for painkillers.

"Earlier today, when you said you weren't going away, did that also mean you'd follow me if I had to do something a little crazy?" Chad asked Jonathan.

He clutched the sides of his head as if his temples were about to burst.

Jonathan nodded. He washed his hands, then knuckled his eyes. Looked five years old. Chad wanted to scoop him up in a gigantic bear hug, but the headache strictly forbade it. His head would fall off and crash to the floor like a Christmas tree ornament.

"Give me two of those after you take yours," he said.

They anesthetized themselves and returned to bed. Jonathan rested his head on Chad's shoulder.

"Where do you need to go?" he asked.

"I need to pay tribute to the dead," Chad replied, knowing he was being a cryptic fuck. But the codeine started to kick in, and before Jonathan could ask for clarification, they were both out cold.

Their visas entailed bribes and a certain amount of bureaucratic wankery, but were approved quickly enough. Two days later, Chad and Jonathan stood overlooking another body of water in a very different country. Harry, Pablo, and the others had agreed to wait for them in Spain while Chad took care of this final detail.

In his arms, he cradled a bouquet of red roses like a fragrant baby, and reflected.

A string of days like pearls on a rope stretched out before him. Before them.

Rose had been a busy girl. She had drained almost a million dollars away from the law firm where she had worked, and had augmented her accounts with a similar sum from second-mortgage lenders on her collection of HUD houses. Not an enormous amount of money but enough to buy him some time. Long enough to answer the question, *Now what?*

Jonathan took his hand and stared out over the waters of the Bosphorus at the Asian side of Istanbul. Ferries chugged back and forth; an immense ship with an Italian name glided east. Behind them were the postcard sights of Istanbul, which they had agreed to explore later. Topkapi Palace, the Haghia Sophia, the mosques and museums of Sultanahmet. They stood at the very southeasternmost point in Europe, a peninsula that looked on the map much like a breast pointing at Asia Minor. If this side of Istanbul was a breast, then they (and the immense statue of Kamil Atatürk directly behind them) were standing on the nipple.

Fitting, Chad thought.

"We should spend more time here," Jonathan said.

"I think so too." Chad took a deep sniff of the roses, then offered half of them to Jonathan. Colors seemed more intense here. Was it from a sense of freedom, or relief? The caffeine buzz from the lethal, syrupy coffee? Or just the fact that everything in Turkey was vividly tiled? "Before we go back to Venezuela?"

Jonathan nodded. "Absolutely. And we have to go to Rio and Buenos Aires."

"There are lots of places we have to go," Chad said.

The time had come.

"To our favorite lying, scheming, conniving dyke bitch," Chad said.

Jonathan nodded solemnly.

"Happily ever after, Rose," Jonathan said, tossing his flowers into the water.

He turned to Chad. "Happily ever after to you, as well."

"Us," Chad said. "To us."

Chad threw his own flowers into the water and watched them drift in the current.

Author's Indulgence

This is the part where I say *Thanks:*
Jason Luciano, PhD, provided much valuable information about the workings of the psych hospital setting, ideas to round out Jonathan's circumstances, advice on the most appropriate medications, and treatment options for my characters. Officer Robert Schoonover of the District of Columbia Metropolitan Police Department read the second draft to catch factual and procedural errors. This book is much stronger because of his involvement. Ellen Cotter, Wil Hawk, and Debbie Langlais read early versions of the manuscript and offered editorial suggestions, observations, and reactions. Early on, Addys Gonzales and Chris Setcos offered useful insights into the Youth of Today. Ian Philips and Mike McGinty read later versions and wrote great comments in the margins . . . and were right there with me during a rather long and tortuous prepublication process. Dav Coleman dragged me out of my apartment for lots of tasty Asian food and art-house movies while I was writing, and was my first Web host. Mistress Vail Rumley designed the original version of my Web site, <www.marshallmoore.net>. Sean Meriwether and Jack Slomovits of <www.blowsquish.com> updated the site and are my new hosts in cyberspace; Jack also did my studly-but-dignified author photo. Jim Gladstone put me up and put up with me in Paris and New York, and offered much advice on marketing and dealing with publishers. Greg Wharton of Suspect Thoughts Press was one of the first editors to show enthusiasm for my work, and has become a good friend as well as a valued colleague. Greg Herren is another editor who along the way has become a great friend; I'm glad he's in my corner. Todd Hedgpeth designed my brilliant book jacket; if you picked up this book in a store, then he deserves a share of the credit. Duane Cramer's photo serves as the basis for Todd's cover design. Can we say "talent to burn," boys and girls? Thanks, eternal gratitude, mad love to you all.

I've been fortunate to have support, encouragement, and advice from a number of fellow writers and editors (some of whose names you have just read): Jill Adams, Noël Alumit, Steve Berman, Poppy Z. Brite, Patrick Califia, Justin Chin, Mitch Cullin, Ghalib Shiraz Dhalla, Neal Drinnan, Warren Dunford, Jim Gladstone, Trebor Healey, Greg Herren, Richard Labonte, Mike Luongo, Durrell Mackey, Travis Mader, Mike McGinty, Sean Meriwether, Ian Philips, Andy Quan, Kirk Read, Michael Rowe, Juliet Sarkessian, Karl Soehnlein, and Greg Wharton. You guys rock. May all your books sell zillions of copies and may your fans not stalk you.

Above all, I want to thank Jay Quinn—editor, friend, and fellow eastern North Carolina expat—for taking a chance on this book. His enthusiasm for my work, his knack for knowing when to leave me alone and when to give me a kick in the ass, and his patience with my raw nerves, repeated questions, and monthly title changes have all made the process of bringing *The Concrete Sky* into print a rich experience.

And this is the part where I say, *But wait, there's more:*

In my nonwriting life, I'm a sign language interpreter. I spent five years in the DC metro area before moving to Northern California. In this novel, I opted to use a number of real settings. Some writers rename real places in their fiction; I find the practice annoying and chose to tinker with the real world instead. George Washington Hospital, for example, exists, but I took liberties: the facility described in this book is a composite of several hospitals where I have worked. There are other examples, but you get the idea. I approach the writing task with more intimate, personal, and specific information than conventional research would provide because, as an interpreter, I've actually been a quasiparticipant in numerous medical and legal situations. I may have incorporated real places with real names, but I have the utmost respect for the people (deaf and hearing) I've worked with, their issues, and their circumstances. I have been careful to steer clear of appropriating anyone's personal information. *The Concrete Sky* is a work of fiction. If you don't know the difference between fact and fiction, real versus make-believe, then the CIA's microwave transmitters have already damaged your brain. I suggest you go live in a cabin in Montana, far away from other people. You'll be safe there. Or start sleeping with a foil-wrapped colander over your head.

For more information about me and my writing, or to send e-mail, please check out my Web site: <www.marshallmoore.com>.

ABOUT THE AUTHOR

Marshall Moore, a native of Greenville, North Carolina, now lives in Seattle, Washington. He was kicked out of the prestigious North Carolina School of Science and Mathematics and went on to earn an undergraduate degree in psychology from East Carolina University. Professionally, he is a sign language interpreter, holding national certification from the Registry of Interpreters for the Deaf. He has worked and studied at Gallaudet University—the world's only four-year liberal arts university for the deaf—in Washington, DC. He drinks too much coffee, buys far too many books, and collects ink in the form of tattoos and passport stamps. His work has appeared or is forthcoming in various journals and anthologies, among them *The Barcelona Review; Of the Flesh: Dangerous New Fiction; Space and Time; Harrington Gay Men's Fiction Quarterly;* and *Velvet Mafia*. This is his first novel. For more information or to contact the author, please visit his Web site: <www.marshallmoore.com>.